THE SEA SHELL GIRL

Seventeen-year-old Merryn Dyer has been helping her mother knit fishermen's jumpers in their little Cornish village for as long as she can remember. Blonde and blue-eyed, she is different to the rest of the villagers and never felt like she fitted in. She takes after her father, her mother says – a seaman who died before she was born. Life's a struggle. So when she is offered a job in a department store in Plymouth, she jumps at the chance, despite her mother's reservations. However, once out of her village she begins to uncover long-buried secrets about her past that threaten to unravel everything that she thought she knew.

THE SEA SHELL GIRL

by

Linda Finlay

Magna Large Print Books
Long Preston, North Yorkshire,
BD23 4ND, England.

British Library Cataloguing in Publication Data.

A catalogue record of this book is
available from the British Library

ISBN   978-0-7505-4442-9

First published in Great Britain by Penguin Books Ltd 2016

Cover illustration © Maria Heyers/Arcangel by arrangement with
Arcangel Images

The moral right of the author has been asserted

Published in Large Print 2017 by arrangement with
Penguin Books Ltd.

Magna Large Print is an imprint of Library Magna Books Ltd.

Printed and bound in Great Britain by
T.J. (International) Ltd., Cornwall, PL28 8RW

With love to Pern, Master Jack and our
sea shell girls Heather, Darcey and Chloe

Chapter 1

'Merryn Dyer, pull your dress down this minute.'

As Grozen's strident voice carried on the stiff breeze, Merry straightened up and climbed out of the pool. She eased her stiff back and then under her grandmother's stern gaze, released her heavy skirts from her bloomers, grimacing as the damp material flapped around her bare legs. She'd been up since dawn prising limpets from the rocks where they clung when the tide receded, and she was cold and hungry.

'Standards need to be maintained at all times, Merry. Showing what you're made of to all and sundry, indeed,' the woman continued, with a sniff. 'How have you done, anyhow?'

'Not too bad, Grozen,' Merry replied, holding up her nearly full basket. 'I'll see what I can sell, then bring the rest back for our meal.'

Her grandmother nodded and gathered up her bundle of sticks. Merry watched as the old woman tottered back up the path towards their cottage, irritation turning to concern when she saw how frail and stooped she had become. The harsh winter followed by the long cold spring had taken its toll on everyone in the little fishing village of Porthsallos. Food was still scarce, with even the pilchards yet to appear.

Guessing her mother would eke out the limpet flesh by making a broth, she added a few strands

7

of glistening seaweed to her basket. Then, ignoring her stinging hands, she eased her frozen feet into her hobbies. Despite the old cloths she'd lined them with she could feel every sharp stone that dug through the worn soles as she squelched her way across the beach. No good moaning, though; it would be some time before she could afford to have them mended.

She made her way round the harbour where the usually bustling shore was eerily quiet, the fishing boats lying idle. Stopping outside the fisherman's shack, she shook her basket, for the contents had settled as the limpets clung to each other and she was desperate to receive the best price for her labours.

'You've been busy this morning, Sea Shell Girl. Come in out of the cold,' Pucky Pint said, giving her the benefit of his toothless grin. Although most people in the village had nicknames, the one they'd given her as a child seemed incongruous now she was a young woman of seventeen, but she was here to do business and didn't dare offend him by mentioning it. As the other men shuffled aside to make room for her, she smiled her thanks. The ramshackle shed, with its familiar smell of old fish and drying nets, was cosy and her fingers tingled as they began to thaw. Without looking inside, Pucky held up her basket and assessed its weight. There was no fooling the old salt, Merry thought.

'Can you use them?' she asked hopefully.

'Aye, they'll make good bait for the long lining if this wind ever eases and we can get the boats out,' he answered, and her heart lifted at the thought of taking a few precious pennies home. 'Trouble is, I'll not be able to pay thee until the pilchards turn up. Soon as I get a catch, though, I'll settle up with thee, you have my word.'

She turned to the other fishermen, who shook their heads.

''Tis the same with us, maid. Ain't been out in a long whilst owin' to they sheep's-head winds. No catch, no money,' Doy Boy shrugged. There was a murmur of agreement from the others. 'Can't remember when I last provided a decent meal for the nippers.'

'Tell thee what, take some of these limpets home to break your fast and I'll still pay you for the full basket when my boat comes in,' Pucky offered. 'Deal?'

'Deal,' Merry agreed, forcing a smile as he emptied three-quarters of the limpets into his pot and handed back her basket. Knowing he couldn't really afford to be so generous, she was about to refuse. Then a picture of her grandmother's pitifully thin body and pinched face flashed into her mind and she hurried away before he could change his mind.

Her mother looked up from her mixing bowl as Merry entered their little cottage.

'Any luck?' she asked hopefully.

'Pucky Pint said he'd buy the limpets but can't pay me until he can get his boat out,' she sighed, placing her basket on the table. 'He said we could have these on account.'

'Well, that's something. I see you brought some weed as well so at least we can have broth.'

'If I have to sup another bowl of salty liquid

with them sea snails floating in it, I'll go as loopy as me stitches, Karenza,' Grozen declared, frowning over her knitting.

Karenza winked at Merry. 'I know, Mother, but we have to eat,' she soothed. 'Poor Merry's been hopping in and out of that icy water since day-break so you make room for her by the fire whilst I prepare our food. There's not enough flour to make bread so I'm mixing dumplings to go in the broth. You know how you like them.'

As her grandmother grunted, then reluctantly moved her chair, Merry smiled gratefully at her mother. Stifling a yawn, she eased off her wet boots and held her blistered feet out in front of the spluttering flames.

Closing her eyes, she listened to the hissing of damp wood. The fire barely gave out any warmth and not for the first time she wished her grand-mother was like the other housewives, who'd had their chimneys walled up and their hearths made smaller so they could burn the newly imported coal. Her grandmother was adamant that things in her home should stay the same as when her husband was alive. Why pay for fuel when you could collect it from the nearby woods, was her philosophy.

'Have you given any more thought to having your hearth changed, Grozen?' she ventured. 'Coal is so much easier to...'

'Not if you have no money to pay for it, Merry,' Grozen snapped. 'That wood might be wet but at least we have a fire, which is more than can be said for some. Besides, you can't bake bread on a coal fire so we'd have to pay to use the bakehouse.'

Knowing what her grandmother said was true, Merry closed her eyes again. The rhythmic clacking of the woman's knitting pins reminded Merry she had a knit frock to finish herself before the agent made his next visit.

'Cors, if Alfred had been lost at sea instead of just dropping dead on the beach, God rest his soul, we'd have been able to claim from the widows' fund.'

Merry sat bolt upright: the widows' fund, of course!

'You could claim, though, couldn't you, Mother?' she asked.

Her mother shook her head and looked quickly away. 'But why not?' Merry persisted. 'Father was a fisherman and you said he drowned.'

'I said your father was a man of the sea and lost to me,' her mother corrected.

'Surely that's the same thing?'

'That's enough, Merry. All your goin' on's giving me one of my heads,' Grozen snapped. 'Why don't you make yourself useful and skein them blinkin' snails instead of talking about things you don't understand.'

'We Dyers have our pride and wouldn't accept charity anyhow,' her mother added, staring at Merry with her clear blue eyes.

Merry shrugged. She knew their situation was dire and had only been trying to help. How she hated this way of life, always waiting and hoping for work and wages. Trying to ignore her rumbling stomach, she closed her eyes again.

'You really should tell the girl,' she heard Grozen mutter.

11

'I know, Mother,' Karenza whispered. 'I wish you wouldn't go on at Merry, though. If it wasn't for her forays on the seashore, we wouldn't have anything to eat at all. She's a good girl and knows the best places to go.'

''Tis no different from other families, and at least we have warmth...'

As the bickering continued, Merry feigned sleep. Three women cooped up in a tiny two-roomed cottage was a recipe for disaster. One day she would have a large house with a roaring coal fire, she vowed. She had no idea how she would achieve this but knew there must be more to life than fishing and knitting.

After their frugal meal, Merry picked up her pins and wool and, glad to escape the tense atmosphere, made her way down to the quay. Knowing their frocks turned out better when knitted outdoors in natural light, and a pleasing finish meant receiving top price, the women would gather in little groups around the harbour. Her mother, being more reserved, preferred to keep herself to herself and could usually be found perched on a stool working by the light from their open front door.

Merry heard the incessant sound of pins clicking before she reached the others. As usual they were sitting in the shelter of the pig house, knitting and nattering. Normally the mood was convivial but today she was greeted by long faces.

'What's up?' she asked, squeezing in beside her friend.

'Word is Agent Sharp's retired and his son's taken over,' Jenna explained without looking up from her knitting.

'What difference does that make?'

'He's only gone and increased our target.'

'What! Why? We can barely make the old one as it is.'

'That's not all,' Jenna wailed. 'It seems we'll have to accept half our wage in goods from the shop he's opening up by Killie Mill.'

'But that's against the law now,' Merry declared.

'I know, but who's got the money or clout to make a stand?' Ailla pointed out.

'Sharp junior's booked a room at Mrs Grace's lodging house so he can put everything in place,' Jenna added.

'What's the new target?' Merry asked.

'Another two knit frocks each, every month.'

'But that's six each! When was this decided?'

'Old Ned brought word back from Logh this morning. Apparently Sharp junior warned if we don't produce the extra, payment will be adjusted or even withheld,' Jenna groaned.

'But we're starving as it is,' Merry pointed out.

Reflecting on their fate, they fell silent. Knowing every stitch counted, they continued working furiously. They'd all been knitting since they were big enough to hold the pins and manage the ribbed trails.

'Will anyone be able to meet this new target?' Ailla asked.

As one they shook their heads.

'It's impossible with everything else there is to do. I've tried but when my pins go faster, I either drop stitches or do a purl when I should be doing a plain,' Jenna sighed. The others nodded. They

13

might know their patterns inside out but numb fingers and worry could make them fumble.

'Don't know how we'll pay the rent if we don't get our full pay.' There was a collective groan.

'We could always resort to damping down,' Kelys pointed out. 'Me old mother used to do it when times was hard. Many's the day she put her work through the mangle to stretch it. Used to make us children socks with the extra wool she amassed an' all.'

'It'd serve him right, the greedy geezer. Ned says he wears expensive suits and smokes fat cigars. And there's us wearing ourselves out trying to earn a living.'

'I'm fed up with being hungry and me shawl's falling to bits,' Maggie moaned.

'Mine too,' Tressa nodded.

'Even the fish are late this year,' Ailla wailed. 'Not that the men could get the boats out in these easterlies.'

'Jem said he doesn't know how we'll manage when the baby comes.' Jenna rubbed her swollen belly and Merry patted her shoulder, wishing she had an answer.

The whole village was dependent on the little income they got from fishing and knitting. Whilst the men were at sea, the women made knit frocks and sold them to the visiting agent. When the pilchards were in the women supplemented this income by salting and packing the fish. These periods of frenzied activity when every available hand was needed were welcomed for nobody minded hard work. Empty bellies were another thing.

'Isn't there anyone else we could sell to?' Merry asked.

'You could take your frocks to old Ma Baker in Logh but you'd have to accept the entire payment in goods and you know that means you won't get anywhere near the true value,' Ailla muttered.

'Or you could deal with the agent in Plymouth. 'Tis a long trek, but you can do the return journey in a day if you know the short cuts over the cliffs,' Kelys said. 'Cors, me old legs would never stand it nowadays.'

'And does this agent pay cash?' Merry asked.

'He does, and I heard he offers a fair price too, especially for the fancies. Bet he'd be interested in yours with that elaborate shell pattern you work into 'em. 'Tis clever, that, and different too,' Kelys answered.

As the others murmured in agreement, Merry shrugged. It was no big thing to her for she just saw these things in her head and tried them out.

'What do you think? Must be worth a try, surely?' she said, turning to Jenna.

'I can hardly make it through the day as it is. Being so near my time I waddle rather than walk,' she laughed. As the sound echoed around the harbour, Merry stared from her friend's bump to the sparkle in her eye and couldn't for the life of her understand how she should be happy tied to a man so young. With a baby to look after as well as her home, she'd have precious little time to herself. Merry shook her head. Although they'd been best friends since their first day at dame school, their outlooks were very different. Merry wanted more out of life before she settled down.

15

'Of course, if you were to marry someone like Nicco, you'd never have to worry about money,' Jenna whispered, as ever picking up on her friend's thoughts. 'He's taken a real shine to you, Merry. What with him being set to take over the fish factory when his father retires, if you were to be nice to him, well...' She winked outrageously and Merry shuddered. Nicco with his oily black hair and staring eyes gave her goose bumps.

'Need to concentrate, Jenna,' she muttered, not wishing to be drawn, for hadn't her mother said much the same, only she'd put it more delicately, of course? The one good thing about the pilchards being late was that she didn't have to encounter him. Knit two, purl six and twist the wool, she silently intoned as she began forming the little shells that had become the mark of her work. With fingers flying and their pins clacking, the little group were hushed as they pondered whether to try to meet the extra target or resort to damping down, as Kelys suggested. They all knew what the penalties were if they were to be caught fiddling.

A jab in her side jolted Merry from her thoughts.

'Look who's coming,' Jenna whispered, jerking her head. As Merry followed her gaze, she saw the ebony-haired Nicco strutting up the hill towards them. Her heart sank. And she'd thought the day couldn't get any worse.

'Must go,' she muttered, jumping to her feet and disappearing into the warren behind.

Chapter 2

Hurrying into their little cottage, Merry wrinkled her nose as the all-too-familiar smell of fish broth greeted her.

'That knit frock doesn't seem to have grown much. Suppose you've spent your time gossiping,' her grandmother grunted, as Merry unclipped the wooden fish, which supported her work, from her skirts and threw her knitting down on the stool.

'We had lots to talk about, Grozen,' she said. 'The agent's son has taken over and he's increased our target.'

'What?' her mother gasped, looking up from the fancy frock she was finishing. Out of all of them Karenza was the most talented and Merry could only marvel at the way the intricate cable pattern flowed naturally from her fingers, although even with her skill, it was a race to meet the deadlines.

'And that's not all. Apparently, we're to receive half our pay in goods from the shop he's setting up at Killie Mill.'

'But he can't resort to that. Trucking's illegal now,' her grandmother sniffed.

'We can barely make ends meet as it is,' Karenza muttered, biting her lip.

'Kelys says we could always resort to damping down to make the target. Apparently, her mother used the extra wool to make socks and...'

'Over my dead body,' her mother's usually calm

voice cut through the room. 'I've brought you up to be honest, our Merry, and won't have you resorting to low tricks like that.'

Trying not to flinch under her mother's direct gaze, which seemed to reach her very soul, Merry nodded quickly. It was true. Her mother prided herself on being truthful and impressed the importance of honesty upon Merry seemingly every day.

'And what if the agent were to do a weigh check?' her grandmother pointed out. 'He'd spread word that we was cheats and our contract would be taken away. Why, I remember when Clara Broad got caught. Old man Muther threatened to cut off her right hand with an axe if she didn't make up the shortage. Never worked again, she didn't.'

Merry shuddered. 'Well, what are we to do? We can't possibly knit another two frocks each every month, can we, Mother?'

'Is that what he's demanding?' Karenza gasped.

Merry nodded.

'May the Lord help us, the rent's due and we have nothing of any worth left to sell,' Grozen moaned, staring around the spartan room.

Karenza idly toyed with her necklace, its blue glass heart catching the light from the fire. 'I'd even sell this if I thought it would fetch anything.' Merry's eyes widened in horror, for that necklace had been a present from her father and her mother hadn't taken it off since the day he died. She said wearing it brought her a small measure of comfort. Things must be dire indeed if she could even consider selling it. 'You can see why I said marrying well would be...'

'Don't worry, I'll think of something,' Merry jumped in quickly, eager to divert her mother from what seemed to have become her pet subject.

The room fell silent as, supper forgotten, her mother and grandmother stared glumly into the fire. The strained faces of the two women she loved tugged at Merry's heart and she knew she couldn't let them risk losing their cottage. Humble it might be, but it was their home.

'Apparently there's an agent in Plymouth who pays a fair price and all of it in cash,' she ventured, remembering what else Kelys had said.

'Plymouth! But that's nigh on a day's round trip. Besides, you've never been out of the village before,' her mother spluttered.

'Then it is high time I did,' Merry declared stoutly, feeling a heady mix of excitement tinged with apprehension at the thought.

'But the town's a big, bustling place, our Merry,' Grozen said, frowning.

'Well, I've got to do something and, who knows, I might even like it,' Merry answered, excitement bubbling at the prospect.

Her mother gave her a level look. 'That's what I'm worried about,' she muttered.

'We're only just managing as it is,' Merry pointed out. 'And with no sign of the pilchards yet, do we have any choice?'

Merry rose early and, careful not to wake her mother and Grozen, dressed suitably in her Sunday best, then crept downstairs. Slipping pattins on her feet to keep her skirts from the mud, she

19

hoisted the parcel of knit frocks onto her back, clipped the wooden fish supporting her current work around her waist and slipped out into the pearly grey of the morning. Fearful of the iron rims on her pattins making a noise as they struck the cobbles, she stole past the stone cottages with their lime-washed walls where her friends were still sleeping. Then, excitement mounting, she quickened her pace as she made her way up the steep hill that led out of the village. Her mother had warned her not speak to any strangers but how was she meant to do business if she couldn't talk to anyone new?

Although she had a long walk ahead of her, she was fizzing with anticipation at the thought of seeing what lay beyond the village. It would have been good to have some company but everyone had a reason why they couldn't come with her. In truth, they weren't willing to risk upsetting the new agent and she couldn't blame them. When word got back to Sharp junior that Merry had taken her work elsewhere, he'd refuse to deal with her in future. Just for a minute she wavered, then hardened her heart. Grozen and her mother worked long days and often well into the night as it was, and there was no way she was having them cheated out of a fair price. The man must be a shark if he thought they could produce more than they did already.

At least she was doing something constructive, she thought, veering right onto the path that would lead to Logh and then on to Plymouth. Here stunted trees rose above the hillside, bowing their heads away from the prevailing winds. Despite the cold spring, the blackthorn was ready to blossom and soon the countryside would be treated to a froth of white. Everywhere was burgeoning with fresh life and Merry couldn't help feeling she was on the cusp of something new herself. To her right waves pounded the cliffs below and she could smell the tang of salt on the wind. Even its sting on her cheeks couldn't detract from her sense of exhilaration.

Busy walking and knitting, she didn't hear the soft fall of hooves behind her until the donkey and cart drew level.

'Morning, Merry. You're looking mighty bonny this morning,' the silky voice purred.

'Nicco! What are you doing here?' she asked, staring at the young man in surprise.

'Just so happens I've got someone to see in Plymouth. Jump in and I'll give you a lift.' He flashed his smarmy grin, teeth gleaming against the olive of his skin.

Her heart sank and the morning lost its brightness. Was it coincidence, him appearing like this? She eyed him suspiciously. As she stood there dithering, the easterly wind freshened, tugging tendrils of hair from beneath her bonnet so they curled around her face in white spirals.

'Come along,' he urged, impatiently. Knowing it would be churlish to refuse, she shrugged off her bundle and threw it into the cart. Deliberately ignoring his proffered hand, she climbed up beside him.

'Who said I'm going to Plymouth?' she asked.

He grinned. 'Well, you're wearing your best clothes and that's where this road leads – unless

21

you were turning off to Logh, of course,' he said, quirking his brow. She frowned but refused to be drawn. 'It's a long trek so you must be pleased I happened along this early into your journey.' He sounded so cocky and sure that she shot him a sharp look, only to receive another grin.

There was no denying it would be quicker by cart. It would do no harm to be polite for the journey and she could lose him as soon as they arrived. She could use the extra time to explore, she thought, her spirits rising again.

As Nicco chattered away, she stared around, taking in the scenery as the track twisted and turned. Here and there splashes of bluebells and golden primroses brightened the hedge-banks, and rock pipits bobbed and swooped low, gathering twigs and moss for their nests. Then the landscape opened up to fields, seemingly spreading forever. It was all very different from the confines of the village.

'So what do you think?' Nicco's voice interrupted her musing.

'Pardon?' she asked, turning to face him. His dark eyes were sparked with irritation. 'Hmm, yes, of course,' she said quickly.

In a flash the grin was back. 'Wonderful, I know just the place.'

'Place?'

'For supper on the way home.' He shook his head. 'You are surprised that I, Nicco Neaple, should invite you to accompany me? Truth to tell I have had my eye on you for some time.'

And don't I know it, Merry thought, suppressing a shudder, but he was in full flow and oblivious.

'Be hard not to notice you, Merry. With your flaxen curls and sea-blue eyes you stand out from the others,' he continued. Merry cussed under her breath. Her colouring contrasted starkly to the dark-haired girls she'd gone to school with, and had long been a puzzle to her. When she'd asked her mother about her white hair, she'd admitted Merry favoured her father, but then she'd clammed up, saying it brought back painful memories.

'We are well on our way now,' Nicco said, patting her hand. 'It is lucky I happened along, eh?'

Merry darted him a searching look but he just gave his smarmy grin, whilst the smouldering look in his dark eyes sent shivers through her. Deciding she'd had enough, Merry yawned.

'Would you think me awfully rude if I snatched a nap?' she asked. 'I had an early start and think it's caught up with me.'

'Yes, you need your beauty sleep,' Nicco grinned.

Not knowing whether to be offended or grateful, she closed her eyes. The next thing she knew she was jolted awake by the rattling and bumping of the cart. Staring around, she saw they were passing over a stone bridge spanning an expanse of rushing water.

'So Sleeping Beauty's awake,' Nicco quipped.

'Have we reached the ferry already?'

He laughed. 'No, this is the River Logh. Over there's the town,' he said, pointing right. 'We have to go up the hill and further along the coast, passing through a hamlet or three before we reach the Tamar.'

'Oh,' she said, trying to quell her impatience. 'Will it take long?'

'Long enough, so settle back in your seat and enjoy the ride. It would have been some walk, though, eh?'

She nodded and he lapsed into silence as the donkey laboured up the steep incline. When they finally gained the top, Nicco pulled onto the verge and jumped down.

He fed the donkey a carrot, then pulled a knapsack from the back of the cart.

'Come on,' he urged, pushing his cheese-cutter cap to the back of his head, then holding out his hand to help her down. 'We'll have a picnic whilst Dozy here has a rest.'

Feeling decidedly hungry, Merry perched on a rock and watched in amazement as Nicco took out two bread rolls, two chunks of cheese and two pasties. It was a long time since she'd seen such a feast and her mouth watered.

'Here you are,' he said, holding out one of each.

'Funny how you've got two of everything,' she commented, looking him straight in the eye.

'Well, if you don't want them...' he shrugged, making to take them back.

Her stomach grumbled as she stared at the golden pastry and floury bread. Unable to resist, she snatched them up and began munching ravenously.

'Anyone would think you hadn't eaten for a month,' he laughed.

'Well, I haven't properly,' she admitted. Only last week she'd had to poke another hole in her inkle tape to keep her fish from falling when she walked. Surely he must know the situation in the village was dire.

'I guess we've been luckier than most,' he commented. 'Perks of Father's position and all that. Of course, they could be yours too if...'

Not liking the direction the conversation was taking or the suggestive look he was giving her, Merry jumped up and shook the crumbs from her skirts.

'I appreciate you sharing your meal, Nicco, but I do need to get to Plymouth in good time,' she said quickly. For a moment she thought he was going to protest but, to her relief, he shrugged nonchalantly.

'We'll talk over supper then,' he said, throwing his bag into the back of the cart then climbing in.

Oh glory, how was she going to get out of that?

The track ahead was narrow and deeply rutted so that Nicco had to concentrate. Relieved, she stared around, taking in an old church with its crooked gravestones facing seaward, the hotch-potch of cottages and never-ending fields, until finally they came to a great expanse of water ahead. Her mother had explained that she'd need to cross the Tamar but she'd never dreamed it would be so wide or this busy. Nicco spoke to the man at the ferry and for the first time since he'd appeared that morning, she was glad of his company.

As he steered the nervous donkey down the ramp and onto the deck, Merry marvelled at the black-and white sailing ships anchored in the turgid water, their masts towering up to the sky. Beyond them, smaller boats with faded brown sails scurried up and down the river, being imperiously hooted at by bustling steam tugs if they dared to cross their path.

She was jerked out of her reverie as clouds of steam and soot belched from a tall chimney. Then with a loud whistle, the chains on the ferry began to clank and they edged slowly away from the jetty towards the huge naval port spread out on the opposite bank.

Once safely back on dry land, she shook her head in amazement. Never had she seen so many people or heard so much noise. Men called out in warning as they loaded their wares onto the boats. Sailors strutted round in their smart blue uniforms, their baggy trousers and white collars distinguishing them from the milling crowds. Everywhere was a frenzy of activity, with smoke billowing out of tall chimneys, the incessant clanging of hammers ringing through the air, and the smell of the sea mingling with unfamiliar noxious odours. Above all, the ever-present gulls screeched as they swooped low, fighting for scraps.

Nicco guided the cart through the throng and Merry wrinkled her nose as she caught whiffs of the stale ale and baccy smoke that filtered out of the open pothouse doors. Then they were on some sort of street with carriages and carts flying past at alarming speed.

'Oh my,' she whispered.

Nicco grinned. 'Hold tight,' he said, urging the donkey faster.

Thank heavens he didn't have a horse, Merry thought, keeping her hands in her lap. She just hoped she'd tied her bonnet securely. Then, just as she'd become accustomed to the traffic hurtling along and the large buildings towering on each side of them, they shuddered to a halt.

'There, I've brought you right to the premises of Mr Fairbright,' Nicco said, gesturing towards the large wooden structure alongside. Her heart sank. Now she wouldn't be able to explore. 'Whilst you go and see him I will attend to my business. Wait here when you're done and I'll collect you.' He handed her down her parcel. 'As I said, I know just the place to stop for supper; then we can really get to know each other,' he added with a suggestive wink.

Fighting down her irritation, Merry smiled her thanks then watched as he boldly steered the cart straight between two carriages. It was only when he'd disappeared that she remembered she'd never told him the name of the agent.

Chapter 3

Merry stared at the building. How should she act? What should she say? Then, she pulled herself together. Her grandmother and mother were relying on her. Smoothing out her skirts, she gripped her parcel tighter, walked up the steps and opened the door.

The room she found herself in was gloomy but clean, with a highly polished counter running its length. Shelves lined every wall, all piled high with knitted garments. She stared round in dismay.

Surely they wouldn't need any more?

'Yes?' a querulous voice demanded.

Merry turned to see a stern-faced woman, dark hair coiled neatly in a bun, frowning at her.

'Good morning, madam. My name is Merryn Dyer and I have some knit frocks I wish to sell,' she said, determined to meet the woman's stare.

'You have an appointment?'

'No, I didn't know I needed one,' she replied, her heart sinking.

'The agent is a busy man and can't see anyone without prior notice. His next appointment is...' the woman sniffed and ran her long bony finger down a list, '...next Thursday at noon,' she stated, looking at Merry triumphantly.

'But I've come all the way from Porthsallos,' Merry protested.

'And that is my fault?' the woman asked, looking Merry up and down, then sniffing at her crumpled skirts and cumbersome pattins. 'Mr Fairbright is a respectable man and deals only with garments of the finest quality.'

'Then this is his lucky day,' Merry exclaimed, placing her parcel on the counter and tugging at the wrapping.

'Really...' the woman began.

'Is there a problem, Miss Brown?' a voice boomed.

'No, sir. I was just explaining to Miss Dyer that you don't see people without an appointment,' the woman called sweetly, glaring at Merry at the same time.

A smartly dressed man, sporting a red spotted kerchief in his top pocket, appeared in the doorway at the back of the room.

'And I was just explaining that I've come all the way from Porthsallos, sir,' Merry said, smiling apologetically. 'I'm sorry but I wasn't aware you saw people only by appointment.'

'Porthsallos, eh?' the man said, raising an eyebrow. 'That is a fair distance,' he agreed, striding over and lifting one of the knit frocks from her parcel. 'Well, well, well,' he remarked, picking up another one and taking it outside.

Merry's heart lurched. Surely he wasn't going to run off with her wares, she thought, hurrying after him.

'This is good, very good, my dear. I've not seen ganseys – or knit frocks, as you call them – of this quality for many a month,' he said, smiling for the first time. 'Come into my office and we'll discuss business.'

Merry's heart leaped as she followed him back inside.

'Please bring us some refreshment, Miss Brown. This young lady has had a long journey.'

The woman's mouth tightened to a red slit. 'Of course, Mr Fairbright, I'll bring you some tea right away.'

'Thank you, and some of your excellent pound cake, if you would be so kind,' he added, hazel eyes twinkling as he gestured for Merry to take a seat. 'Now, my dear, did you make these?'

Merry picked up the knit frocks with the shell pattern on the yoke. 'I knitted these. Grandmother made the plain ones and Mother those,' she said, pointing to the rest.

'It's a long time since I've seen the snake cable,

and never before so expertly executed.'

'Mother's a fine knitter,' Merry admitted.

'Indeed. However, I don't recollect ever having seen a design such as this,' he said, frowning as he took the shell knit from her. Merry's heart flopped. Whatever had possessed her to make up her own pattern?

'I'm sorry. I can make the next ones in the seeds and bars, or the diamonds, if you'd prefer.'

'You misunderstand me, Miss Dyer. You all produce good work, but yours is...' He was interrupted by the door opening and a tray clattering down in front of them.

'Please be careful, Miss Brown. We wouldn't want any tea spoiling these fine garments.'

The woman sniffed and glared at Merry before stomping from the room.

'Oh dear, it would appear I've upset her ladyship's timetable,' he said, raising his eyebrows. 'No, make that I have *definitely* upset it,' he added, staring woefully at the one decent-sized slice of cake alongside which nestled a tiny slither. Merry's mouth watered but when Mr Fairbright proffered the plate she politely made to take the smaller slice. He shook his head. 'That will be for me,' he said, taking it himself.

'Oh, but...' she began.

'You will be doing me a favour,' he assured her, patting his portly paunch. 'Now, what was I saying? Oh, yes, your design is, how shall I put it? Eye-catching ... yes, that's it.'

'You mean you like them?' she asked, her cake halfway to her mouth.

'I do indeed, Miss Dyer. More importantly, I

know I can place them and would like to buy from you. First, though, I need assurance you will be able to provide me with knit frocks of this design and quality on a regular basis.'

She nodded eagerly. 'But what about the others?' she asked.

'I would like to buy those as well and will make you a fair offer. However, it is this shell design that will command a higher price. Now, I just need to speak with someone, so enjoy your refreshment and we'll do business when I return.'

Merry watched as he strode from the room then settled back in her chair. He liked her design and was going to buy from her. She glanced at the cake, deciding she was too excited to manage even one mouthful. The fruit glistened temptingly on the plate and, giving into temptation, she snatched it up and took a bite. It was so delicious that by the time Mr Fairbright returned her plate was empty.

'Just as I thought, we can definitely place these,' he said, smiling at her. As he named a price beyond her wildest hopes, it took all her willpower not to shriek in delight. 'There is one proviso, though.' As he stared at her with those candid hazel eyes, she held her breath. 'I need your solemn promise that you will deliver the same quantity here in exactly one month.'

'Yes, of course,' she assured him, daring to breathe again.

'Good. Then I shall tell Miss Brown to enter your appointment in the diary. It has been a pleasure doing business with you, Miss Dyer, and long may we continue to do so.'

Armed with fresh yarn and a heavy purse, Merry skipped down the steps and onto the street. There was no sign of Nicco and as she stared around her attention was caught by the notes of a hurdy-gurdy. A little white dog sporting a pointed hat was dancing in time to the music and behind him red and white striped awnings flapped in the breeze. Excitement bubbled and she found herself irresistibly drawn towards the attractions.

Merry had never seen anything like it and she darted from stall to stall in delight. One was a treasure trove of gewgaws, ribbons and pearl buttons. Another was piled high with bolts of brightly coloured materials, silks and threads, but it was the jewel-coloured shawls and bonnets edged with taffeta that caught her attention. Oblivious of the crowds milling around, she edged closer. She was just running a finger over the soft kid of a glove and picturing herself dressed in such finery when she felt a jolt in her back and pressure on her pocket.

'Oi, take your hands off me,' she screamed, her hand going to her purse.

'Unhand my girl this minute.' As the authoritative voice rent the air, a shadowy figure hurriedly disappeared into the crowd. Black eyes blazing, Nicco grabbed Merry's hand and pulled her away.

'You fool,' he hissed. 'Anything could have happened to you.'

Merry felt the weight in her pocket and smiled. 'No harm done,' she assured him, holding her purse aloft.

'Put that away at once,' Nicco ordered, marching her towards his cart. 'Have you no sense? This isn't sleepy Porthsallos. The town's a dangerous place, Merry. Why do you think I told you to wait for me? Now climb in and let's get home.' Seeing his angry face, her earlier euphoria drained away.

'I was only looking at the finery,' she explained.

'With a purse stuffed with coins? Really!' he spluttered, slapping the poor donkey's withers.

Feeling stupid, Merry stared down at her boots, the shock of what might have happened sinking in. Supposing her purse had been stolen, what would Grozen and her mother have said? They hadn't been keen for her to make the journey in the first place.

She stole a glance at Nicco. With his back ramrod straight and his face set as a mask, he looked quite overbearing. Not daring to break the silence she watched as he concentrated on avoiding the other carts and travellers. Finally she could stand it no longer.

'Goodness, it's much busier than when we came,' she remarked, eager to break the tension.

'Seeing as you slept most of the way here you are hardly in a position to compare,' he pointed out.

Did he have to be so pompous? She'd only had a tiny nap.

Irked beyond reason, she lapsed into silence and they reached the ferry without further conversation. As they crossed the wide expanse of water, she relaxed and felt her spirits rising. This ferryman, a younger, more handsome man than on the way over earlier, caught her eye and winked. Glad to see a cheerful face, she smiled back, only to have Nicco grab her hand. Angrily, she made to snatch it away but his grip tightened.

'Come on, Merry, surely you've learned your lesson about not trusting strangers,' he hissed. When she didn't answer, he sighed. 'I'm not cross with you any more.'

'Look, Nicco, I admit I shouldn't have wandered off, especially with my purse full, but you are not my keeper.'

'No, not yet,' he answered, staring into her eyes.

'What's that supposed to mean?' she spluttered, but the ferry had reached the bank and for a moment he was too busy gathering up the reins to answer.

'Let's just say I can see why your mother was worried about you going to Plymouth on your own and...' he began.

'What has my mother got to do with anything?' Merry asked, her earlier suspicion returning.

Nicco shrugged, his supercilious expression sending her blood bubbling, but the day had caught up with her and she suddenly felt overwhelmingly tired. She just wanted to get home, she thought, stifling a yawn.

'It's a good job you didn't have to walk,' he said, grinning at last.

'Meeting me on the way was no coincidence, was it?' she asked. As he gave another superior grin something niggled at the back of her mind but try as she might she couldn't think what it was.

The wind rose, buffeting the little cart from side to side and making further talk impossible. Merry shivered, tightening her shawl around her and wishing the journey over. It was growing dark by the time they reached the village and she was pleased to see the welcome flickering of candles coming from the cottages below. As the donkey slowed at the brow of the hill, she quickly gathered up her parcel of yarn and jumped out before Nicco had a chance to remember his invitation to supper.

'Thanks for the lift,' she called. Ignoring his protests, she ran down the hill, darting into the warren that led to their little cottage.

Her mother threw open the door, fussing as if she'd been away a week instead of a day.

'Come in and sit yourself in front of the fire, our Merry,' she urged. 'I'll get your supper.'

'How did you get on?' Grozen asked, getting down to business as usual.

'Very well indeed. Mr Fairbright's a really nice man,' Merry grinned, her good mood returning as she handed over her purse. Her grandmother's relief was evident.

'Why there's enough here to pay the rent and buy food,' she exclaimed. 'I suppose it was your mother's work that commanded such fine payment.'

'Mr Fairbright liked all our work, Grozen, but surprisingly it was my shell-pattern frocks he paid most for.'

'Really,' the old woman said, her eyes widening in surprise. 'You hear that, Karenza?'

'Well done, Merry,' her mother said, handing her a steaming bowl. 'I'll see if I can get us a sheep's head or something tomorrow to celebrate. It'll make a nice change from this limpet broth.'

'Not half,' Grozen replied with feeling. 'Is this the yarn this Fairbright gave you?' As Merry nodded, the woman gathered it up, hurried over to the dresser and placed it carefully on the old scales. 'Well, he's not diddled you,' she proclaimed.

'I told you, he's a nice man, Grozen,' Merry said, pausing mid-sip.

'Doesn't pay to be too trusting of people you don't know,' Grozen grunted, looking meaningfully at Karenza as she settled back into her chair. She looped a hank of the indigo wool over her hands, then leaned closer to her daughter, who automatically began winding it into a ball.

They were acting casually but Merry wasn't fooled, and no sooner had she put down her spoon than they pressed her to tell them about her day. She told them about her deal with the agent and the disagreeable Miss Brown, but omitted to mention the incident in the market. There was no point in worrying them.

'You mean you'll have to make the journey each month?' her mother asked, looking worried.

Merry's heart leaped at the thought and she nodded excitedly. 'I promised I would return with the next order then, and Mr Fairbright even entered my appointment in his diary,' she said, her eyes shining. 'Knowing we'll be paid regularly will make a difference, won't it?'

'Yes, it will mean we can eat,' Grozen said. 'Then when the pilchards come in there'll be the money you'll get for working in the fish store,' she added, giving Karenza a knowing look.

'It can't happen too quickly for we still need to pay the rent. Tell me, Merry, did you meet anyone along the way?' her mother asked, trying to sound casual.

'Yes, lots of people. The man on the ferry was really nice,' she replied.

Her mother frowned but Grozen wasn't to be put off.

'Did you walk all the way, our Merry?'

'Couldn't walk over the water, Grozen, could I?' Merry quipped. She wasn't going to make it easy for them.

'But didn't Nicco give you a lift?' her mother asked.

'Why? Did you expect him to?'

'Well, he did say he had someone to see in Plymouth and...'

'You told him exactly where I was going and when,' Merry cried, remembering how Nicco had taken her straight to the agent's premises. 'Look, Mother, I am seventeen and quite capable of looking out for myself.'

'More like you be the right age to be thinking of getting wed,' Grozen retorted.

'I intend seeing more of life outside Porthsallos before I saddle myself with a husband and family,' Merry retorted, already tired of the conversation.

'But Nicco is...' her mother began.

'Nicco is what?'

'Well, he's fond of you, our Merry.'

'And he would make a good catch,' Grozen added.

'He's not a fish, Grozen.'

'Happen not, but his father owns the fish factory and if you married him...'

'I'd have a comfortable life when his father dies, is that it?'

'Well, it is a consideration, our Merry,' Grozen

37

pointed out, fixing her with a gimlet look.

'And you'd have no need to venture out of the village,' her mother added.

'I'm tired and going to bed,' Merry said, getting to her feet. She had every intention of returning to the town, and next time she would make the journey by herself.

Chapter 4

Despite the disagreement with her mother and grandmother, Merry slept soundly. She knew they meant well but it was her life, and the desire to see more of the world was gnawing away inside her like a mouse in the cheese cupboard. Feeling apprehensive and fearing an argument, she made her way down the little stone steps the next morning. However, her worry was unfounded.

'Morning, Merry,' her mother greeted her brightly. 'I managed to get a nice bit of mutton from butcher Blade so there'll be no forays in the pools for you today. We shall celebrate your success with a decent meal.'

Merry smiled and impulsively kissed the woman's cheek. She should have known her mother wouldn't bear a grudge.

'That'll make a tasty change,' she enthused. 'I was beginning to look like a limpet.'

Her mother laughed. 'Well, here's some porridge for you to start the day. That money you got yesterday will see us nicely through the next couple of weeks, though we'll still have to be careful until the pilchards show.'

Merry smiled as she took the bowl. Breakfast had become a luxury and she tucked in with pleasure.

'You didn't finish telling us about your trip yesterday,' her mother said, not looking up from her chopping board.

'It was lovely to see life outside the village, Mother. There was a fair with all these stalls. You should have seen the brightly coloured materials and trimmings...'

'Think the wind's swung round at last,' Grozen cried, clattering into the room and throwing an armful of sticks down on the hearth. 'The gaffer's offered a reward for the person sighting the first shoal, so get yerself up to the point straight away, our Merry.'

'But I'm in the middle of my breakfast, Grozen,' she protested.

The woman fixed her with a gimlet stare and Merry knew there was little point in arguing. Grabbing her shawl and hitching her work to her belt, she hurried outside. The cliff path was already lined with excited women and the mood was merrier than it had been for many months. Taking up her position she stabbed her ball of wool on a spike of the railings and called a cheerful greeting. Although it was returned, nobody lifted their gaze from the foam-topped waves, for each woman was desperate to be the one to sight the first shoal and collect the reward.

'Keep your peepers peeled for that slick of oil, our Merry.' She jumped as her grandmother's strident tones carried up the hill, sending sea-gulls squawking from the rooftops. Trust Grozen to be watching from their cottage window.

Adjusting the wooden fish supporting the weight of her work, she automatically began knitting as she scoured the waters for any sign of disturbance that would signal the return of the pilchards. While her fingers wound the worsted wool around her pins, her thoughts raced around her head. Of course, she hoped this day would bring the bounty from the sea the village relied on. Yet if it did, she would have to spend the evening packing and salting the fish. The extra money would be welcome but the attention from Nicco wouldn't.

Her mother might think Nicco a good man but Merry knew he had an eye for the girls and she'd already borne witness to his overbearing manner. She could understand her mother wanting her to make a good marriage so that Merry wouldn't have to suffer the privations she and Grozen had. Whilst it might be her dearest wish to see Merry settled down with umpteen offspring tumbling around her feet, it wasn't hers. Unlike her friends, who were happy to marry and bear children, Merry wanted more out of life.

'Just think, if the pilchards are in, you'll be seeing the handsome Nicco tonight,' Jenna called from higher up the path. Merry turned and smiled, wishing not for the first time that her friend wouldn't pick up on her thoughts.

'If I weren't married to my Stanley, I'd be giving you a run for your money, my girl,' Kelys cackled. There was a burst of raucous laughter, for the woman was well into her forties with hair

40

as steel as her knitting pins.

Nicco, Nicco, Nicco, the gulls seemed to mock as they circled overhead. Merry sighed. She knew the others found her reluctance to encourage him strange. They thought him handsome but his penetrating stares and smarmy smiles made her feel uncomfortable, and that was without his declaration on the way to Plymouth.

'Knit two, purl six, and twist the wool,' she muttered, reaching the yoke and beginning her shell pattern. Truth to tell she hadn't done much knitting on the journeys to and from Plymouth and she needed to make up for it now.

Fingers flying and pins clacking, she stared over the water, past Peak Rock to the imposing granite house on the cliff top beyond. How lovely it would be to live in a grand place like that instead of their tiny, cramped fisherman's cottage where you could hear every sound your neighbours made.

A movement caught her eye and she watched as the woman she knew to be Lady Sutherland emerged through the carved wooden door and climbed into a waiting carriage. Wearing a fitted coat over her full-skirted dress, and sporting a hat with three plumes, she cut an elegant figure. Merry grimaced at her own old blouse with its fraying collar and the serviceable apron covering her patched skirt. One day she too would dress and travel like a lady, she vowed. Remembering the finery she'd seen on the stalls in Plymouth, a thrill ran through her.

'Hevva! Hevva!'

She jumped as the excited shout from higher up the hill broke into her thoughts. Knitting forgotten, the eager women crowded closer to the railings, lifting their hands to their foreheads as they scoured the sea for sight of the shoal.

Drat, thought Merry, she'd been daydreaming when she should have been paying attention. She hoped it was a false alarm, thinking of the ticking-off she'd get from Grozen.

Her wish was thwarted as down below the lurker boat was already showing the men in the sean boat the area to be enclosed. Then the nets were shot and silence fell as everyone waited for the signal. They knew the slightest sound could send the fish scattering in all directions.

There was a collective sigh of relief as the master seaner raised his hat and the nets were taken in. Merry watched the mesh encircling the shoal as the ropes tightened. Then, as her gaze took in the thick walls surrounding the harbour, she shuddered, feeling just as hemmed in. Her friends, however, were cheering and clapping Marya on the back. They might be disappointed they hadn't been the ones to spot the shoal but were pleased for this uncomplaining woman, with her crippled husband and seven children to provide for. Besides, tonight would see them busy gutting and salting the fish and nobody minded the extra hard work if it meant full bellies and warm firesides.

'Come along, Merry,' Jenna urged, catching hold of her arm. 'It'll be some time before we're needed to help so let's wait down on the quay and you can tell me about your trip to Plymouth.'

Eager to delay the inevitable ticking-off she'd get from her grandmother when she found out someone else had claimed the reward, Merry nodded.

'Come on then,' she agreed, linking arms with her friend as they followed the others down the winding path.

Those lucky enough to have dried fruit and sugar left in their pantries ran home to make hevva cakes to celebrate the catch of pilchards, whilst the rest of them, ever hopeful their friends would share this traditional fare with them later, made their way to the harbour. No sooner had they taken their seats on the steps than they all turned towards Merry.

'How did you get on in Plymouth?' Ailla asked.

'What was the new agent like?' Kelys said at the same time.

Merry grimaced. 'Plymouth was busy, smelly and so noisy you could hardly hear yourself think. The agent was really nice, though.' She went on to tell them about her discussions with Mr Fairbright and the order he'd placed when he'd seen the knit frocks. The women listened attentively and were pleased for her but it wasn't long before conversation turned to their own problems. Knowing they were unable to meet the new target they'd settled for the damping down of their knitting. As Kelys began telling them the best way to do it without being caught, Merry looked at their earnest faces and couldn't help feeling as if she didn't belong any more. It seemed her life was already taking a different path.

She stared out over the water, where the fishermen were now rowing back to shore. Even from here she could see the enthusiasm in their movements, sense the exhilaration in the air. Then she felt a tugging at her skirts. Remembering her

43

near miss in the market, she went to grab hold of her pocket, only to see a dark-haired girl of about four staring woefully up at her.

'I gone wrong with me knitting, miss. Can you help afore me ma flays me?'

Merry smiled. 'Give it here. Are you making a trail?'

'Trying to,' the girl sighed. 'But me can't get the hang of this rib thing.' She looked so forlorn, Merry's heart went out to her.

'Come and sit by me,' she offered, patting the stone beside her. 'What's your name?' she asked, as she set down her work and began correcting the girl's stitches.

'Primmy. Me sister's Caja. She's seven and does the plain bits. Mother does the fancy seeds and bars. She says me will be able to do that one day but me don't see it,' she said, giving another sigh.

'I'm sure you will; it just takes practice,' Merry said, smiling reassuringly.

The girl looked doubtful. 'You's is pretty. Them looks just like shells,' she said, running a grubby finger over the raised pattern. Hastily Merry moved her work away.

'I used to get my stitches all muddled until Mother showed me an easy way of remembering the rib.'

'There's an easy way?' Primmy asked, curiosity sparking in her dark eyes.

'Let me show you. You knit two, purl two for the rib, right?' Primmy nodded. 'So take your pins and sing: up one, round and through; up two, round and through. Down one, round and through; down two, round and through,' Merry demonstrated. 'Now you sing along with me whilst I do it again.'

'Well, me be blowed!' Primmy exclaimed some moments later. 'It seems easy when you sing like that.'

'And so it is. Now you try it,' Merry urged, handing the girl back her work. She watched, singing along with Primmy, until she got the hang of it.

'I done it, miss,' Primmy shouted, her little face beaming.

'Well done. You'll never forget now, will you?'

'Primmy? Where are you, girl?' As a woman's shrill voice carried on the breeze, Primmy jumped to her feet and ran off.

'You're a natural with children, Merry,' Jenna laughed. 'I can just see you with a brood of your own.'

'A natural honorary auntie's what I'll be,' Merry retorted. 'Look, the boats are in.'

They watched as the men jumped onto the shore and began off-loading their catch. It was a heart-lifting sight after the long barren winter. Then Merry spotted her mother and Grozen making their way towards them to witness the first weigh-in of the season.

'We heard the shout go up,' her mother said.

'And it weren't your voice, our Merry,' Grozen muttered, narrowing her eyes accusingly.

'No, I'm afraid someone spotted the shoal before me,' she admitted.

'Suppose you were daydreaming as usual,' her grandmother grumbled.

'Never mind, at least the fish have finally

45

arrived so there'll be the salting and packing to do later,' her mother said, patting the older woman's shoulder. 'That'll boost the coffers.'

'And Marya can really use the money, Mrs Dyer,' Jenna pointed out. 'I'll see you all later,' she added, wincing as she got to her feet.

'Are you all right?' Merry asked her friend.

'Just a twinge, but I can't tell you how glad I'll be when I can see my feet again.'

Karenza nodded sympathetically. 'Try and get some rest whilst you still can, Jenna.'

'Think I will,' she replied, rubbing her back. 'See you up at the pallace later.'

'Don't think so; there'll be a birth before the sun sets,' Grozen muttered under her breath. 'And I saw three crows on Ma Somers's roof on the way down. She'll be going to meet her maker later, so by my reckoning it will have been the usual one in one out come the morn.'

'You don't know that, Grozen,' Merry exclaimed, wishing her grandmother wouldn't make such pronouncements.

'Yes, I do,' Grozen muttered, turning her attention to the weigh-in. 'Not a great catch, but it is the first of the season so I suppose we must thank the Lord for small mercies.'

Karenza caught Merry's eye and smiled. They both knew the woman's brusque manner was an act and that she was as relieved as everyone that the pilchards had at last shown up.

Just then Merry spotted the black-haired Nicco heading their way and her spirits dropped. Her mother was bound to thank him for giving Merry a lift and would be none too pleased if he spilled the beans about her running off. Luckily, however, her mother's thoughts were on other things.

'By my reckoning that mutton should be cooked so let's go and eat before it's time for work. We'll need some energy, for all that salting and laying-up,' Karenza said, taking her mother's arm and leading her towards the warren.

'And I'll need my energy for the laying-out,' Grozen muttered.

Her grandmother's words were still ringing in Merry's ears as she walked with her mother up to the pallace later that evening. They had to dodge the jubilant fishermen with their bellies full of ale, weaving their way unsteadily towards their homes. The smell of stale beer and pilchards pervaded the air and Merry wrinkled her nose.

'Suppose our hands will stink of fish from now on. Did you never want more than this from life, Mother?' she asked.

Karenza smiled sadly and Merry could have cut out her tongue. What a stupid question. Of course her mother had. It wasn't her fault she'd been widowed when Merry was a baby.

'You have been my life, Merry, and I couldn't have asked for a lovelier daughter,' Karenza replied, patting her on the shoulder. Merry stared at her mother in surprise, for although they'd always got on well, she wasn't one for fancy words.

'What was he like, my father?'

'A fine-looking man, he was, and you have the look of him,' Karenza sighed. Her hand went to the necklace beneath the bib of her apron and she stroked it absent-mindedly as she stared out over the harbour, a faraway look in her eyes. Just when

47

Merry thought she'd forgotten she was there, her mother turned and placed a hand on her shoulder. 'You are young, Merry, and it's understandable that you should want to experience something of life outside the village. Take heed, though, for you'll find the water across the ocean no bluer than it is here.'

Chapter 5

'Come along, you two, or young Nicco will have your guts for inkle belts,' Kelys called.

Karenza and Merry had been so lost in their private moment they hadn't heard the clattering of the village women making their way to the pallace for the evening's work.

'We're coming,' Karenza replied. 'Remember what I said, our Merry. You have the opportunity to make a better life for yourself here if you would but realize it.'

That's all very well, but I want to fly, see things, meet people from different places, Merry wanted to cry. Not wishing to upset her mother, though, she kept quiet as they went to join the others.

Spirits were high as they filed inside the fish store, eager to begin the salting process that would earn them their first real money of the year. Later, as Merry started packing the prepared pilchards against the walls, she realized Jenna was missing and wondered fleetingly if Grozen had been right about her baby coming this evening. She hoped all would be well, but more fish were being passed along to her and, not wishing to interrupt the process, determinedly pushed her thoughts away.

It was hard work building up the bank to the required depth of three feet by six feet high, and before long their backs were aching from the unaccustomed stooping while their hands were red and sore.

'Must have a break,' Marya panted, her face flushed from her exertions. 'Not as fit as I was last season.'

'I'd forgotten how back-breaking this was,' Ailla groaned, easing herself upright.

'You can bet poor Jenna's is aching more, poor love. Happen she'll have a lusty wean mewling for its milk by dawn. Still, that'll give her something else to think about,' Kelys chuckled. 'Well, we'd best get on or nice Nicco won't be so nice, will he, Merry?'

As the others laughed, Merry turned her attention back to the pilchards. How she wished old Mr Neaple still ran the place. His bewhiskered old-fashioned appearance and gentle yet aloof manner never caused any comment. Unlike his son, who thought himself kingpin – or should that be king prawn, she thought, giggling as a picture of dark-eyed Nicco encased in a pink shell flashed into her mind.

'Well done, ladies,' Nicco's silky voice purred from somewhere close behind her. Merry froze as the others began preening and pouting at his praise yet it was her he was staring at.

'That's all for tonight. I'm hoping there'll be more work tomorrow evening, ladies, so I'll see you then.'

'You will be paying us in cash as usual, won't you?' As ever it was the outspoken Kelys who voiced their concerns.

Nicco frowned. 'Of course; why wouldn't I?'

'That new agent for knitting's increased our target and is paying us in kind for the pleasure,' Ailla spluttered. 'We need the money we get here more than ever now.'

'Yes, Father mentioned that. You need not worry, ladies, for Nicco Neaple is a fair man and will ensure payment here continues in the usual manner,' he said.

'Pff, his father owns the place, not him,' Merry snorted, but her protest was lost in the rapturous cheers that bounced off the cellar walls.

'Will we have a party on the last day of St Peter's Fair as usual?' Kelys asked, keen to capitalize on Nicco's good mood.

He smiled. 'How can we not commemorate our patron saint? Keep a note of the 10th of July, ladies. Who knows, we might have cause for a further celebration,' he added enigmatically as he turned and looked pointedly at Merry.

'You lucky duck,' Ailla muttered, nudging Merry in the ribs. As the others chuckled, Merry turned away. How dare he insinuate such a thing in front of her friends?

'Now, ladies, as long as the pilchards show, I will see you all here tomorrow evening,' Nicco added, giving a little bow then making his way towards Merry. Luckily for her, though, the ladies were keen to keep his attention and crowded around him. Taking advantage, she slipped out of the building and sped up the path.

'Where's the fire, our Merry?' her mother called, hurrying after her. 'Honestly, girl, you want your head seeing to, running off like that. Nicco couldn't have made his intentions plainer if he'd proposed there and then.'

'That's the trouble, Mother. It was tantamount to blackmail, him saying what he did in front of everyone.'

'Happen most would give their best knitting pins to be in your place,' her mother pointed out. 'Why, that Wyllow brings him cakes she's baked specially and flutters her eyelids in the way men like.'

'Well, she can marry him then,' Merry retorted. 'I just wish I didn't have to wait a whole month before I can go back to Plymouth.'

A heavy silence descended between them, their companionship of earlier dissipating like early morning mist. With the night air cooling her burning cheeks, Merry felt ashamed for her outburst. How could she expect her mother to understand when she could hardly make head or tail of her feelings herself?

'What is so wrong with life here, Merry?' her mother finally asked.

'I hate being dependent on those smelly fish, for one thing,' Merry moaned as they continued their way home. 'Supposing none appears tomorrow?'

'Then we know we'll have the packing of the hogshead to keep us fed next month,' her mother pointed out.

'But suppose they disappear for ever, what

51

would we do then?'

'Find other gainful employment, of course. Now do come on,' her mother urged.

'I hope Grozen's got the water boiling. I'm parched,' Merry muttered as she opened their front door.

To their surprise the living room was in darkness. As Merry lit a candle her mother hurried over to the grate and fanned the dying embers.

'There, that's better,' Karenza said, swinging the pot over the flames.

'It's not like Grozen to be out after dark,' Merry commented, holding out her hands to warm, then wincing as the numbness was replaced by the inevitable stinging.

'Will you never learn, our Merry?' her mother sighed.

Merry grimaced. That salt found its way into every tiny cut, and blisters were already forming. Of course, the skin would have hardened by the time they'd done another shift or two but, no matter how much she washed, the all-pervading smell of fish would linger.

'Well, she did say she was expecting her services to be required and she's usually right,' her mother pointed out, sinking into her chair and placing her feet on the fender.

Tired after their unaccustomed exertions, they dozed in front of the fire whilst they waited for the water to boil. However, when they'd supped their tea and Grozen still hadn't appeared, Merry began to worry.

'I hope she's all right,' she said, peering at the clock. 'It's after midnight – shall I go and check?'

Karenza shook her head. 'No, happen it will have been a long labour for poor Jenna or perhaps Ma Somers is still holding on. You go on up to bed, I'll wait here till she gets in.'

'I'll stay with you,' Merry said. 'I need to finish my frock anyway,' she added, stifling a yawn as she picked up her work.

As they sat knitting in companionable silence, Merry wondered if she dared to raise the subject of her father again. Her mother hardly ever mentioned him, and although she hadn't really said much earlier, Merry's curiosity had been stirred and she was itching to know more about him. Lost in thought, she jumped when her mother suddenly leaned forward and tossed more wood onto the fire.

'Better keep a nice blaze going. Your grandmother will be cold when she gets in. There's nothing like having your own home and cosy fireplace to return to, you know,' she said, fixing Merry with a meaningful gaze. Merry sighed, knowing only too well what was coming.

'But you left home to go into service when you were younger than me, didn't you?' she said quickly, hoping to pre-empt her mother's lecture.

'I did, but that was only because your late grandfather, God rest his soul, thought I should see a bit of life.'

'And did you, Mother? See a bit of life, I mean?'

'Oh, yes, more than you could imagine,' her mother whispered, staring into the fire, but Merry wasn't about to be sidetracked.

'Then you understand why I...'

The door clattering open interrupted their conversation. As her grandmother staggered into the room, Merry gasped in dismay for the woman was grey with fatigue and looked ready to drop. Merry jumped up and led her over to her chair.

'Mother, whatever's the matter?' Karenza asked, her usually quiet voice rising with concern. The older woman shook her head, staring at them wide-eyed. 'Pour some tea, Merry,' Karenza added, taking her mother's hands and rubbing some warmth into them.

'Here, I've added two sugars,' Merry whispered, passing the cup. It took some coaxing but finally they persuaded the older woman to take a sip of the warm liquid. Wordlessly, she pushed the cup away then and stared into the flames.

'Please speak to us, Mother,' Karenza persisted.

'I got it all wrong. It weren't one in and one out. It were all three out,' she whispered with a shudder.

'You don't mean...?' Merry gasped.

'I'm afraid I do. Baby was breech and by the time I'd managed to turn it, poor Jenna's body couldn't take any more. The little mite was born dead as well, so it was all for nothing. Her poor husband went crazy. Dr James had to come and give him a powder.'

'Oh, no,' Merry gasped in disbelief. Her poor friend, she thought, hot tears streaming down her cheeks. Jenna had been so vibrant and full of life. Merry shuddered to think of the waste of life then, seeing her grandmother's anguished face, struggled to bring her emotions under control.

'Is there anything I can do, Grozen?' she whispered.

Her grandmother shook her head. 'Nothing any of us can do now,' she muttered, poking the fire so hard the sticks collapsed in protest. 'Didn't get it right with Ma Somers either.'

'But she was an old lady,' Karenza pointed out. 'You couldn't have done anything for her.'

'Leave me alone. For God's sake, just leave me alone.' As the woman's pitiful wail rang round their living room, Karenza and Merry exchanged worried glances. 'Go on, the pair of you!'

'Happen she needs time to come to terms with things,' Karenza told Merry as they made their way upstairs. 'You try and get some rest. I'll go back down in a while and see how she is.'

But Merry couldn't sleep. No matter how hard she tried, she couldn't get the tortured look in Grozen's eyes out of her mind. Thoughts of Jenna went round and round in her head. She had been her dearest friend and they'd shared everything from a desk in the school room to pulling faces at the mistress when they'd got told off for talking. The preparations they'd made for her wedding to Jem; then her ecstatic shrieks when she'd found she was expecting. What a terrible waste of life, Merry thought, thumping her straw pillow. Her anguish only increased her determination not to marry Nicco. Finally, exhausted, she fell into a heavy sleep where she dreamed her friend was flying above her bed, looking down at her with sorrowful eyes.

A blanket of sadness fell over their little cottage. Grozen refused to speak to them, wouldn't eat or move from her seat beside the fire. She just sat staring blankly into the flames. Then on the

Sabbath, she refused to go to church. Karenza took hold of her hands.

'Come along, Mother, you've never missed a service yet. The Reverend Mr Mabey will wonder what's happened,' she coaxed.

'He won't want a wicked old woman like me in his church when he hears what I done,' she wailed.

'You did your best. Nothing was your fault. Besides, Ma Somers was an old lady, Grozen.'

'And so am I, Merry,' she whispered, pulling her blanket tighter round her.

'Rubbish, Mother. Ma Somers was seventy if she was a day and you're barely fifty,' Karenza spluttered.

'I'm in my fifty-sixth year, I'll have you know.'

'Please come with us, Grozen,' Merry pleaded, but the woman shook her head and returned her gaze to the fire.

'Don't expect me to come to the funerals either.'

No amount of pleading would change her mind. Boats were drawn up on the beach, shops closed and curtains drawn as the villagers turned out to pay their respects. As the simple coffin with Jenna and her baby was lowered into the ground, Merry bit her lip and vowed she'd never put herself in the same position. Then it was Ma Somers's turn, and whilst everyone was sad for her loss, at the wake afterwards they all agreed that she'd had a good life.

With the pilchards being caught on a regular basis, Merry and Karenza were kept busy. Even though they worried about Grozen, they knew they had to take the work whilst it was there. The rent needed paying and food put on the table, although the older woman refused to eat. She still blamed herself for the deaths and refused to move from her chair. Her knitting pins lay idle and Merry tried not to think of the promise she'd made Mr Fairbright.

'Come on, Grozen, you can't carry on like this. You're wasting before our very eyes. Jenna would be so upset if she could see you,' Merry coaxed a week later when the woman had refused to eat her meal yet again.

'Merry's right, Mother,' Karenza said, patting the woman's shoulder. 'And you always said everyone has their allotted time to come and then to go.'

'Happen I did. But that don't make it right for a girl the same age as our Merry to die, or for that wean not to have a chance. Don't seem any point in doing anything any more.' She gave such a long, drawn-out sigh, Merry and her mother exchanged worried looks. The older woman had been with many people when their time had come but it had never affected her like this before.

'Oh, Merry, I don't know what I'd have done without you these past weeks. Things can't go on like this, though,' Karenza said as they made their way to the pallace that evening. 'I'm at my wits' end trying to make her see sense.'

'Perhaps she'd listen to someone else,' Merry suggested.

'Like who? She's refused to see the vicar.'

'I know. It's so peculiar the way she's blaming herself. I mean, it's tragic about Jenna but so many die in childbirth, and as for Ma Somers, well, she was an old lady. No, Grozen needs someone who can see beyond...'

57

'Merry, you're a genius,' her mother cried, grabbing her arm. 'I know the very person. Can you stay with Grozen tomorrow morning whilst I pay a visit?'

'Of course, but who...'

'Good evening, ladies.' They'd been so engrossed in their conversation, they hadn't heard Nicco approaching.

'Good evening, Nicco,' Karenza said, looking worried. 'I hope we're not late?'

'You are right on time as ever, Mrs Dyer. Why, I can set my pocket watch by you. May I ask how your mother is?' he asked solicitously.

'She's improving, thank you,' Merry said quickly, ignoring the look her mother gave her.

'I'm very pleased to hear it. Does that mean you will be making your trip to Plymouth sometime soon?'

Devil's dewdrops; that man was such an opportunist, Merry thought.

'Merry will indeed be keeping her appointment at the end of the month,' Karenza said. 'Now if you'll excuse us we must get to work or we'll be letting the others down.'

'Of course,' Nicco said, smiling widely as he stood aside so they could enter the pallace.

'Whatever did you have to tell him that for?' Merry hissed as they took their places and began salting the fish.

'What do you mean?' Karenza asked, feigning innocence.

'Don't play games with me, Mother. I am not travelling with him again, got it?'

Her mother smiled but didn't answer.

58

Chapter 6

Although still cross with her mother, the next morning Merry fulfilled her promise and sat with her grandmother. She tried her best to make conversation but the woman stared morosely into the fire. Seeing her pins lying idle in the corner, Merry tried again.

'I need to get on with my knitting. Why don't you do some as well, Grozen? It will take your mind off things and you might find the rhythmic motion soothes your nerves.' The ticking of the clock sounded loud in the ensuing silence. Perhaps she'd try shock tactics whilst her mother was out. 'I don't know what I'm going to say to Mr Fairbright if I don't have the dozen I promised him. Mother and I can't manage any more, especially now we're salting the fish of a night.'

Still there was no answer.

'You don't mind letting me down, then?'

The woman gave a gimlet look, then returned her gaze to the fire. Now it was Merry who sighed for she really was worried about letting the new agent down. She knitted as fast as she dared but knew she'd never be able to fulfil her grandmother's quota as well. Still, if she didn't have the knit frocks, there'd be no need for her to go to Plymouth and no need for her to evade Nicco. She could kill her mother for having told him when her next visit was; she could see by the way his eyes had lit up that he intended accompanying her.

Her musing was interrupted by the murmur of voices as the door was opened.

'Look, Mother, I've brought an old friend to see you.'

Merry stared in amazement as a tiny man with snowy hair and eyes like jade darted across the room and squatted beside her grandmother.

'Rozen, my dear; long time no see.'

'Cador! Well, I'll be,' she cried, holding out her arms in welcome.

'Come along, Merry,' Karenza whispered. 'We'll knit outside and leave them to it.'

They took themselves round to the point and perched on the wall. For the first time that year, the sun had real warmth in it and Merry lifted her face in delight.

'You'll get freckles,' her mother teased, looking happier than she had for some time.

They knitted in amiable silence for a few moments, watching the fishermen in their boats and the gulls squawking hungrily above them.

'Looks like we'll be busy again tonight,' her mother said.

'So who was that funny man?' Merry asked, unable to contain her curiosity a moment longer.

'Cador, you mean? He's a Cornish Charmer, and if anyone can reach your grandmother he will.'

'Oh? How?'

'He has these powers. Some call him a white witch.'

'A witch? But I thought witches were women,' Merry said.

Her mother smiled. 'There are men with the gift too. Cador is special. He can cast charms and heal. He'll spend a while talking to your grandmother and find out what's troubling her.'

'But we already know that,' Merry frowned.

'Do we? All we know is that it has something to do with that dreadful night Jenna and Ma Somers died. We don't know exactly what happened, though, do we?'

Merry put down her pins and thought for a moment. What her mother said was true.

'And if he does find out, then what?' she asked.

'He'll help her heal.'

'How will he do that?'

Karenza shook her head. 'That will be between him and your grandmother. Now let's get knitting or you'll not have enough to take to Mr Fairbright.'

Merry opened her mouth to say how betrayed she felt that she'd told Nicco when she was next going to Plymouth, then saw how much happier her mother was looking and shut it again. There'd be time enough to take her to task when Grozen was well again.

As she resumed her knitting, she saw Lady Sutherland come out of her granite house on the opposite side of the harbour. Today she was dressed in a rose-pink dress with a toning cape draped elegantly around her shoulders. As she stepped daintily into the waiting carriage, Merry thought of the stalls she'd seen in Plymouth with their brightly coloured cloths and trimmings, and her spirits rose. If she saved hard she might have enough for the fabric to make an outfit just like that. Next time she went she would be sure to look at the prices. Oh, there was so much to see, so much to experience; she couldn't wait.

'Come along, Dolly Daydream,' her mother's voice interrupted her musing. 'Let's go and see if Cador has worked his magic on your grandmother.'

'I hope he has, Mother, for I can't bear to see Grozen so unhappy.'

'Me neither, Merry.'

'I've never heard of this Cador before. Is he local?' she asked as they made their way back down the path.

Her mother shrugged. 'He just seems to be around when you need him.'

They arrived back at the cottage just as the man was taking his leave.

'Is everything all right?' Karenza whispered.

'Do stop whispering, Karenza – haven't I told you it's rude?' As Grozen's strident tones rang through the living room, they smiled. It seemed everything was very all right.

'Why, she sounds back to normal,' Merry gasped.

'I don't know what you've said or done, Cador, but once again you have my undying thanks,' her mother said. 'Won't you stay and share our midday meal? You're most welcome.'

'That is kind, my dear, but I have to be in another place. Your daughter has grown into a beautiful young woman,' he said, looking at Merry.

Karenza smiled. 'Yes, you were right, Cador. Although I found it hard to believe all would be well at the time.'

Merry hardly heard her mother's words for this strange man's intense gaze seemed to be burning into her. Then he smiled.

'Your sister in blood wants you to know she is happy and at peace.' Merry stared at him in astonishment. How could he possibly know? But those green eyes were on her again. It was as if he was peering into her very soul. 'I see the yen to travel. You will, however, find your life and love lies here in Porthsallos. Good day.' And with a nod he was gone.

What rubbish, Merry thought, pushing the door firmly shut behind him. Yet how did he know about her and Jenna being blood sisters? They'd been the only ones in the yard when they'd nicked their wrists and swapped blood to tie them together all those years ago. They'd sworn each other to secrecy and Jenna would never have told. Her grandmother's chuckle jolted her back to the present.

'Are you all right, Grozen?'

'Never felt better, young Merry. That Cador's like a tonic. Made me see the error of my ways about Ma Somers, he did.'

'What do you mean?' Merry asked.

Her grandmother sighed. 'I was blaming myself for the way the poor woman took so long to pass. She just wouldn't go. Hung on and hung on even though I could see it was her time. Cador explained that dying can be a difficult process especially if the person persists in fighting it.'

'And that's what Ma Somers did?' Karenza asked.

'Yes, and how. She didn't want to go and clung

on until ... well, that's where Cador put me right about everything. He also said Jenna's wean had a misshapen head and would never have been right had he lived. I was that upset, I never noticed. Didn't think Cador had seen the mite but then you never know with him. He seems to know everything.'

'But how?' Merry asked, but her grandmother shook her head.

'He just does. You'd do well to pay heed to what he told you, our Merry, for Cador is never wrong. Now where's my luncheon?'

Merry looked at her mother and they burst out laughing.

Never had their bread and cheese tasted so good. It was a relief to see her grandmother normal again and for that Merry was thankful. Cador was wrong about her life not lying beyond Porthsallos, though.

'I expect you feel like a snooze after your tiring morning, Mother,' Karenza said as she cleared their plates.

The woman snorted. 'What, after our Merry took me to task about my shirking?' she said, picking up her pins. As the wool flew back and forth between her fingers, Merry let out a sigh of relief. She'd been really worried about not being able to fulfil her promise to Mr Fairbright.

Although they spent the next weeks knitting furiously until their candle guttered, Merry was still one knit frock short when she packed them up ready to take to Plymouth.

'These are really heavy,' her mother commented, helping Merry lift the parcel onto her back.

'Well, no doubt Nicco will just happen to be waiting with his cart at the top of the hill,' she retorted, and saw a blush creep over her mother's cheeks.

'God speed, my love,' was all she said, though, as she kissed Merry goodbye.

There was a fret coming in from the sea and the air was decidedly chill. By the time she'd climbed the hill her hair was curling in damp tendrils and she cursed at having forgotten her hat. She'd slept heavily, the late nights of knitting having caught up with her so that she'd been late rising. Her parcel felt cumbersome, knocking awkwardly against her back as she walked, and it was actually a relief when she turned onto the path for Logh and saw Nicco. Not that she intended showing it, of course.

'Morning, Merry. Your carriage awaits,' he said, jumping down and taking her parcel.

'Nicco, what a surprise, I don't think,' she replied.

He grinned and lifted his hand but instead of helping her into the cart he pointed to her hair. 'You look like a princess with a crown of diamonds on your head.'

Hastily she wiped the beads of moisture from her hair and climbed onto the seat. Chuckling, he took up the reins.

'Talking of diamonds,' he began, and her heart sank.

'Which we weren't,' she replied.

'Well, it's time we did. You know it's my intention to make you mine. I meant what I said about having a special celebration on St Peter's

Day and as it's only a matter of...'

'Look, Nicco, you need to realize this is not how I want things to be,' she said, anxious to get matters straight between them once and for all.

He took hold of her hand. 'No. I can see that.'

Thank heavens he understands, she thought, removing her hand and relaxing back in her seat. The mist was lifting and it promised to be a fine day. She looked around, noticing the trees were now a froth of white blossom, the flowers in the hedge-banks vibrant in their early summer colours.

'We never did stop for that supper last time, did we?' Nicco asked, breaking into her thoughts. She shook her head, relieved he'd taken her rebuttal so well. 'Well, we will this time and then Nicco will propose in the proper manner,' he declared.

'What?' she gasped, sitting bolt upright.

'I can see that you expect things to be done properly and so they shall.' His grin was so cocky, she was shocked into silence. What did she have to say to make him realize she had no intention of having supper with him, let alone marrying him?

'Nicco...' she began, but he put up his hand to silence her.

'No, don't say anything. I will make my formal declaration later and you can accept then.'

She opened her mouth and then shut it again. She was too tired to argue and if it was silence he wanted, silence he'd get, she thought, closing her eyes.

She was woken by the clanking of the chains and saw they were already on the ferry. The breeze tugged at her hair and she tucked the way-ward tendrils behind her ears, drawing her shawl tighter round her.

'I was not kidding when I said I would be marrying Sleeping Beauty, was I?' Nicco quipped, his dark eyes boring into hers. Quickly she turned to look out over the murky waters.

'I didn't mean to sleep for so long. Too many late nights helping Grozen make up her quota for the agent.'

'Ah, yes, your grandmother. I was pleased to hear she has recovered but I've always wondered why you call her Grozen?'

'When I was little I couldn't manage to say "Grandmother Rozen". It came out as Grozen and I suppose it just stuck.'

He frowned. 'Hardly grown up, is it? When we are united in family I shall call her Grandmother Rozen,' he announced grandly.

'Oh, look, we have reached the other side,' Merry said, suppressing a shudder. The thought of their being joined in any way was just too awful to contemplate.

As on their last visit, the place was bustling with activity and the noise was deafening. Merry lapsed into silence as Nicco guided the cart through the mingling crowds and out into the traffic. Relief flooded through her when he finally pulled up outside the agent's building.

'Now I'm guessing your appointment will take the same time as before so I'll make sure I'm back for when you've finished. We don't want a repetition of last month's stupidity, do we?' he said, wagging his finger.

Biting down a rude retort, Merry retrieved her bundle

'Thank you for the lift, Nicco,' she said politely, smiling to herself as she hurried into the building. Confident this appointment with Mr Fairbright wouldn't take as long, she planned to visit the material stall when she'd finished. If she ensured she was back in good time, Nicco would be none the wiser.

The formidable Miss Brown sniffed as she took in Merry's hatless head.

'Name?' she asked.

'Miss Dyer,' Merry answered, trying not to grin as the woman slowly ran her finger down a column in the diary. She stared at the shelves groaning under the weight of ganseys, most in the navy blue but some in fawn, and wondered again where they were all destined.

'I said Mr Fairbright is waiting.' Merry stared at the woman. If the agent was waiting for her what had all that performance of checking the diary been about? 'Follow me,' the woman instructed, walking over and knocking on the office door. 'Miss Dyer, sir,' she announced.

'Come in, my dear,' Mr Fairbright said, smiling as he got to his feet.

'I do hope I haven't kept you waiting,' Merry began.

'Not in the least,' he said, taking out his pocket watch. 'Right on time. I do like punctuality,' he smiled. 'Tidy mind and all that. Some refreshment, if you please, Miss Brown. With two decent-sized pieces of your excellent pound cake,' he added as the woman wrinkled her nose.

'I don't wish to hold you up, sir,' Merry began, although her stomach was growling. It had been a long morning and Nicco hadn't stopped for a picnic this time, no doubt thinking she'd then be starving come supper time.

'Actually, I wish to discuss an aspect of your work,' Mr Fairbright said, unwrapping her parcel. Carefully he spread her frocks over his desk. 'Oh, no,' he groaned, frowning over his glasses.

Chapter 7

'Is there something wrong?' she whispered, staring down at the knits her mother had inspected before she packed them.

'I see there are only eleven here and I commissioned you to bring me twelve. I've already promised them to an important customer as well,' Mr Fairbright frowned.

'I'm sorry, Mr Fairbright. I was about to explain that my grandmother has been ill and although we worked long nights trying to make up her quota, we didn't quite make it.'

'I'm sorry to hear that. She is quite recovered?'

'Yes, thank you,' Merry answered, beginning to worry, for the man was still frowning. 'But there's nothing wrong with our actual knitting?'

'On the contrary, it's the quantity that might pose a problem. Oh well, it can't be helped. I do need your assurance this won't happen again or...' He shrugged and left the sentence hanging in the air.

Merry nodded. 'I promise you will have the full quota next time.'

'Good. As I suspected, your shell design has proved particularly popular. However...' he was interrupted by Miss Brown arriving with their refreshment.

'Just leave the tray there, please,' he instructed, nodding towards the table in the corner. 'Thank you, Miss Brown,' he said pointedly as the woman hovered. There was a sniff and then the door shut loudly behind her. Mr Fairbright didn't seem to notice as he resumed his inspection of Merry's work.

'Exemplary,' he pronounced. 'Though, of course, I can only pay you for the eleven.'

'I wouldn't expect anything else,' Merry said, suppressing a sigh of relief. Mr Fairbright wrote something on a slip of paper, then handed it to her.

'Show that to Miss Brown when you leave. She will make the payment and provide you with sufficient wool for next time,' he said. 'I assume you still have the yarn for the one your grand-mother has yet to make?'

'Yes, of course.'

He nodded. 'Now let's have our elevenses, as my mother insists on calling them,' he said, grinning as he passed her a delicate china plate on which nestled a huge wedge of pound cake. 'Miss Brown seems to have got the message,' he winked. 'It's quite a trek from Porthsallos, isn't it?'

'Oh, I don't mind,' Merry said quickly, fearful

in case he should cancel his order.

He watched her over his glasses as he sipped his drink. 'I have been asked if I can provide good-quality plain knit frocks with pockets for men's watches. Would that be possible?'

'Goodness me, yes,' Merry cried. 'Does that mean you want more of the plain ones then?'

'It does. Eight of them by next month, in fact, plus four with that unique shell design. It's a shame you can't provide more, but keeping the numbers low will create demand. There's nothing like letting people think they can't have something for them to decide they must have it,' he chuckled.

Merry frowned. 'You'll need less of the fancies, then?'

'For the time being. I'll see how things work-out. In the meantime, I shall pay you the same rate for the plain ones with pockets as I do the fancies. Is that acceptable, Miss Dyer?' he asked.

'Yes indeed, Mr Fairbright.'

'Now, if you've finished your refreshment, please ask Miss Brown to make an appointment for the same time next month. I'm trusting you will have the full consignment then. Good day, Miss Dyer,' he said, getting to his feet.

'Good day, Mr Fairbright, and thank you.'

Miss Brown all but snatched the chit from her hand before slapping a parcel of wool on the counter. Then Merry watched as she began counting out the money.

'Miss Brown, I fear you have made a mistake,' Merry said, looking down at the coins on the counter.

'How dare you make such an accusation? I can

assure you I never make mistakes. Take your money and go before I have you up for slander,' Miss Brown ordered shrilly, pointing to the door.

'But you don't understand...' Merry began.

'Ladies, please!' Mr Fairbright protested, appearing beside them. 'What seems to be the problem?'

'This knitter girl here had the audacity to accuse me of short-changing her!' Miss Brown cried, her cheeks as red as the spots on his kerchief. 'As you are well aware, I never make mistakes and...' She stuttered to a halt as the agent held up his hand.

'Miss Dyer, perhaps you can explain?'

'I was trying to, sir. Miss Brown has paid me for twelve frocks and given me enough yarn for twelve more...'

'Which is what your order was for,' the woman spat.

'Did you not look at the chit I issued, Miss Brown?' Mr Fairbright asked.

The woman smiled superciliously. 'As you know I pride myself on knowing what you expect from each of your customers and...'

'And you didn't think it necessary to check my authorization?' Mr Fairbright's voice was low and measured.

'Well, there was no need, was there?'

'Clearly there was, Miss Brown,' he said turning to Merry. 'I think I can see the problem. You were explaining you had only provided me with eleven?'

Merry nodded. 'I couldn't possibly accept payment or replacement yarn for more than I provided.'

'Your honesty is commendable, Miss Dyer, and

I am truly grateful. Miss Brown, please issue payment in accordance with the instructions on my chit and then come to my office. I apologize for the mistake and hope you have a pleasant journey home, Miss Dyer.'

'You'll pay for that,' Miss Brown hissed as the agent's door closed behind him.

'I only want paying what I'm owed, thank you,' Merry replied. The woman glowered then took her time reading the chit. Finally she slapped the correct amount down on the counter and snatched the extra wool from her parcel.

'Thank you, Miss Brown,' Merry said sweetly.

Outside, she leaned against the wall and breathed in deeply. What a nasty woman that Miss Brown was.

Everything had taken longer than she'd anticipated and she hoped she still had time to go to the market. Then she saw Nicco waiting in his cart and cursed. This really wasn't her day.

'You look flustered,' he said, as she climbed up beside him. 'What's wrong?'

She shook her head.

'Well, something's ruffled your pretty feathers.'

'It was just a misunderstanding about payment,' she shrugged, lapsing into silence as he steered the donkey confidently through the busy traffic. Then a carriage swept past them, throwing dirt up in its wake.

'I shall insist Father lends me his pony and trap next time,' Nicco spluttered, but Merry hardly noticed for she'd seen Lady Sutherland, the lady from the granite house, in the carriage that had overtaken them. Her elegant outfit and coiffure

73

only served to remind Merry that her purpose had been thwarted. She stared sadly down at her Sunday best, noting how cheap and unfashionable it looked.

'I said next time we shall travel here by pony and trap,' Nicco repeated.

'Next time?' she asked, her heart sinking. She really would have to think of some way of avoiding him. Perhaps there was another way to get here? She'd ask Kelys. Then she felt a jab in her side.

'Not going to sleep again, I hope. I expect some company in return for the time I invest in these journeys, you know.' Invest? He made it sound as if she was some kind of project or enterprise. As his voice droned on, she sighed inwardly. 'Now what was it you said about being short-changed? I hope you stood your ground.'

Why does everyone jump to the wrong conclusion? Merry wondered.

'I didn't have to, Nicco. Miss Brown tried to pay me for twelve knit frocks and when I pointed out that I'd only delivered eleven...'

'You mean you actually told them they were giving you too much?' he asked, staring at her in amazement.

'Well, yes.'

'Good grief, girl, you should have taken the money and ran,' he spluttered.

'I couldn't have done that. It would have been dishonest,' she protested.

He shook his head. 'Well, it was their mistake. Honestly, Merry, you're as green as seaweed. Nobody else would admit they'd been paid too much.'

'You mean you wouldn't have said anything?' she asked.

He laughed and shook his head. 'I'm not daft.'

'And I'm not dishonest,' she retorted. Glory, this was going to be a long journey home, she thought, sitting back in her seat and trying to memorize the route.

She recognized the approach to the docks but as they boarded the ferry, Nicco began waving furiously.

'Hey, Otto,' he called, throwing Merry the reins as he jumped down from the cart.

She watched as he hurried over to the sandy-haired fellow wearing a brown jerkin, who was leaning against the rail, a battered knapsack at his feet. He looked to be in his mid-twenties – older than Nicco – but by the way they slapped each other on the back and began talking in earnest, Nicco knew him quite well. Grateful for the breathing space, Merry stared out over the water. The chains started clanking but she hardly noticed all the activity as the ferry began moving towards the other side of the Tamar and Cornwall.

What a day it had been. After the upset of the last month, she'd really been looking forward to this day, but her visit to the town hadn't turned out the way she'd hoped. Still, at least Mr Fairbright had been pleased with the work and given her another order... She yawned. It had been a long day and she was ready for her bed. Then, she remembered what Nicco had said about stopping for supper and her heart dropped.

It was only as the ferry bumped to a halt that Nicco headed back towards the cart, followed by the man he'd been chatting to.

'Otto here's coming back to Porthsallos with us, Merry,' he announced.

'If that is agreeable with you, Miss Merry?' the man asked.

'Of course it is, hop up,' Nicco cut in.

However, the man continued staring at Merry with his clear grey eyes as he waited for her to answer. She smiled and nodded.

'Hope you don't mind the intrusion?' he asked, clambering into the back of the cart.

'Oh, I'm much smaller, so let me,' she said, nimbly clambering over the seat and squatting down on her parcel of yarn.

'Are you sure?' Otto asked.

'Oh, Merry doesn't mind,' Nicco answered, urging the donkey off the ferry and onto the bank. Charming, she thought, holding onto the side of the cart as it clattered over the ruts and onto the track.

'You have had a busy day?' Otto asked, turning round and indicating her parcel.

'I have indeed and I secured another order for our knit frocks,' she began.

'Otto doesn't want to hear about domestic matters,' Nicco said dismissively.

'Oh, but I do. My mother made ganseys. Many's the evening I spent hands wide apart whilst she wound her yarn. A dab hand with the lighthouse design, she was. What pattern do you make?'

'Grandmother makes plain frocks whilst Mother does the snake cable and sometimes the seeds and bars when that's required.'

'And what about you?'

'I've devised this shell pattern and...'

'Really, Merry, do you have to bore Otto so?' Nicco snapped.

'Sorry. What do you do, sir?' she asked quickly.

'Otto, please. I'm a cooper, Miss Merry. I make barrels and...' he began.

'And we have important business to discuss, Merry,' Nicco interrupted. 'The pilchards are coming in thick and fast now so how long do you think it will take to make my barrels?'

As the men discussed timescales, Merry closed her eyes. It would have been nice if Nicco had been a gentleman and insisted she keep her seat but at least she was spared listening to any more of his lectures. The voices droned on and her thoughts returned to her most pressing matter. How could she visit Plymouth and the market by herself? Carrying twelve knit frocks on her back as well as walking all that way in her pattins would be no easy feat. If the weather stayed dry, though, she could probably get away with wearing just her hobbies...

She was no nearer solving her problem by the time the cart rattled to a halt at the top of the hill that led down into Porthsallos.

'Otto and I have decided to eat in the tavern, Merry. I know we were going to dine together but, if you don't mind, we'll do so another time.'

'I don't want to intrude, Nicco. I can always meet you later, pal,' Otto said quickly.

'No, that's fine,' Merry said, trying not to grin as relief flooded through her. Hastily she jumped down and picked up her parcel. 'Thanks for the lift, Nicco. Good night, Otto.'

Although it was still light, Merry was surprised to see a group of women gathered outside the building by the mill. Usually they'd be indoors at this time, putting their children to bed or clearing away after their evening meal. Some were looking despondent, others angry, and although they had their knitting with them, the pins lay idle...

'What's up?' Merry asked, drawing alongside them.

'That new agent, that's what,' Ailla muttered. 'He opened his new business today and when we took him our knitting he told us he's had to cut the rate he can pay us.'

'Said there's no demand for our work and he was doing us a favour,' Tressa scoffed.

'But if that were true why would he have increased our target? It's a sham,' Kelys spat. 'Even with the damping down we're out of pocket.'

'He didn't catch on, then?' Merry asked.

'Didn't blinking look at our work long enough,' Marya spluttered, two red spots appearing on her cheeks. 'Just counted the number we handed in, then gave us yarn to make more. Inferior it is too, all the thread's splitting.'

'Like them peas he gave me. They're so split they'll disintegrate as soon as I put them in water.'

'The goods he gave me were stale and barely edible,' Delen spluttered. 'How am I to feed my girls properly? Primmy and Caja might look like sparras but they got appetites like gannets.'

'You just returned from Plymouth, Merry?' Slowly she nodded, not liking the glint in Kelys's eyes. 'How did you get on?' the woman asked, staring pointedly at her parcel.

'Mr Fairbright's given me another order,' she admitted.

'Perhaps he'd take our work too?' Tressa asked.

'I could ask,' Merry offered.

'Well, knitter women, let me tell you something for nothing.' As the steely tones of the new agent cut across their conversation, the little group fell silent. 'Like my father before me, I am a fair man,' he continued fixing them with a gimlet stare.

'And my old man's a bank manager,' Kelys muttered.

'Did you say something?' Mr Sharp asked, pointing to the grey-haired woman.

Kelys shook her head and looked away.

'As I was saying,' he continued. 'I am a fair man and I expect loyalty in return. Anyone not wishing to trade with me, put up your hand now.' The women glanced at each other uneasily but no one moved. 'I will take that as acceptance of my conditions, then. As for you, that maid with the white hair,' he continued, turning the full force of his gaze on Merry. 'What's your name?'

'Merryn Dyer, sir,' she answered, clutching her parcel tighter.

'Well, Merryn Dyer, if I catch you trying to entice my knitters away again, I'll make sure Fairbright hears about it. And if that happens, you can be sure no one will deal with you ever again. Do I make myself clear?'

'But I...' Merry began. But he'd already turned away and she was talking to his back.

Chapter 8

'Of all the cheek!' Merry exclaimed.

'Well, that's our hands tied and he's got your card well and truly marked, my girl, but I don't suppose it matters, does it?' Kelys muttered, giving Merry a final glare before striding off down the hill. As undisputed leader of the knitters, she was clearly put out the new agent had caught them complaining.

'We'd all better get going before stingy Sharp comes back,' Marya sighed. 'I'm pleased you had a better day, dear,' she added to Merry as they began walking towards the harbour.

'My Tomas saw Nicco waiting with his cart this morning,' Delen grinned. 'Did he say anything about that extra celebration he was hinting at the other evening?'

The little group came to a halt and looked at Merry expectantly.

She shook her head. 'He brought a cooper back in the cart and the talk was all business,' she replied. That part at least was the truth.

'What's this cooper like?' Wyllow asked, her eyes sparking interest as she patted her dark curls.

'Knowing you, you'll soon make it your business to find out,' Tressa laughed. 'Perhaps the handsome Nicco will have to vie for your attention and that double-ended pasty you were making this afternoon. Oh sprats; I'm sorry, Merry.'

'You needn't be. Nicco doesn't get any encouragement from me, I can assure you.'

'What's his name, is he good-looking and how old is he?' Wyllow asked, grinning wickedly.

'He's called Otto and very pleasant. That first lot of pilchards will be ready for packing and so you're bound to meet him then.'

'And Nicco will pay us cash for that,' Marya said, brightening.

Merry smiled, marvelling, not for the first time, at how resilient these women were. Nothing kept them down for long.

They reached the harbour to find Kelys leaning against the wall.

'So what was this new order for then?' she asked Merry.

'A dozen knit frocks.'

'And you got paid all in cash for the last lot?' Merry patted her pocket and nodded. 'Well, haven't you got it made,' Kelys snarled. 'Not content to have the boss's son running round after you, you use your charms on that agent to get a better rate.'

'But it was you who suggested...' Merry began, but once again she was talking to herself for the woman was stalking towards her cottage. The others glanced awkwardly at each other, then, with apologetic looks at Merry, followed after her.

Kelys didn't waste a moment. No sooner had they gathered around than she began holding court. Merry sighed, once again feeling an outsider in her own village. How she wished Jenna was still with her. Her friend would have stood up for her, making the others see sense and laughing until Kelys's good humour was restored.

She stood gazing forlornly over the harbour where the boats were tied up for the night, their gaff jaws creaking against their masts, and the water slapping against the clinker hulls. Fishermen leaned against their huts, enjoying a last smoke of the evening, the tips of their home rollies glowing red against the lengthening shadows. Village life was going on as normal around her, yet Merry felt curiously detached, as if she no longer belonged. Perhaps it was time she gave serious thought to how she was going to turn her dream of a new life beyond this little fishing port into reality. Her gaze automatically went to the granite house on the opposite cliff.

A slither of silver moon glimmered in the darkening sky as it rose behind the chimneys. It was surrounded by a scattering of stars that glittered like diamonds on a brooch. With a jolt she was reminded of Nicco and his proposition that morning. Not for the first time she thanked her own lucky stars for his fortuitous meeting with Otto. At least she'd been spared having to stop for supper. Thinking of food made her realize she was hungry, and with a last wistful look at the little group of knitters who were still listening to Kelys, she wended her way through the warren to home.

The next few weeks passed in a frenzy of activity. By day Merry knitted furiously, determined to fulfil her order for Mr Fairbright. When she'd joined the little army of women in their usual place, Kelys had made it plain her company wasn't welcome so she'd taken her pins up to the point. Alone with her thoughts, her brain worked as quickly as her hands as she pondered her predicament.

Far out at sea she could see the little boats bobbing on the swell as Pucky Pint and his fishermen worked tirelessly hauling in the pilchards. True to his word, he'd sent the money he owed for the limpets and, as was her way, Grozen had stashed it in the tea caddy to help see them through the winter when there would be no fish to supplement their knitting.

On the quay below, Otto was whistling cheerfully as he fashioned the strong barrels that would hold their precious catch, before it was preserved and transported to distant shores. Merry noticed he'd discarded his jerkin in the heat and his arms were as brown as the wood he was fashioning. She couldn't help smiling, when at noon each day Wyllow sauntered casually over to offer him a pasty or floury bap. He would smile and take them politely before immediately resuming his work. From her vantage point, Merry could almost reach out and touch the girl's frustration.

Come early evening, with her work growing satisfyingly heavy, Merry would return to the cottage to share a bite to eat with her mother and grandmother. She was pleased to see they were happier and healthier now they had sufficient to eat and money to pay the rent. Yet as her mother and Grozen chatted over their meal, Merry couldn't help brooding on the future.

The abundance of work at the pallace meant everyone's spirits were high, and slowly Kelys began to thaw. One evening the two women were standing side by side, pressing down fish in the hogsheads with heavy weights, when they saw Nicco hurry past.

'Not paying you much attention these days, is he?' Kelys commented.

'Thank heavens for small mercies,' Merry said with feeling.

'Well, I can't begin to understand you, girl. As I've said before, I wouldn't say no to a handsome man like that, especially with his prospects. Still, happen you've always thought yourself above the likes of us.'

'What's that meant to mean?' Merry asked, turning to face the woman.

'Well, you've made it plain we're not good enough. You want to meet new people and...'

'There's nothing wrong with Merry wanting to make a better life for herself, Kelys,' Karenza interrupted, linking arms with her daughter.

'Ah, but as you know, the moon doesn't always shine brighter elsewhere, does it?' the woman retorted.

Karenza shrugged. 'Well you can't blame a person for wanting to find out, can you? How's that damping down going, by the way?' The woman bristled with indignation and Merry thought Kelys was about to explode but then she seemed to shrivel before their eyes.

'I ain't doing it out of choice,' she sighed. ''Tis the only way to pay the bills.'

'Is it?' Karenza asked, staring at the woman until she looked down at the ground.

'It's all right for you; you've got your Merry to sell your frocks. My family's too busy with their own affairs to worry about their old mother.' The woman's eyes clouded and she looked so sad, Merry's heart went out to her.

'Perhaps I could speak to Mr Fairbright...' Merry began.

'Not if she's cheating on the agent you won't,' Karenza cut in. 'Come along, Merry, Grozen will be waiting with a warm drink.'

As her mother pulled her away, Merry frowned. 'But I might be able to help, Mother.'

Karenza shook her head. 'We don't want to be associated with any dodgy dealing, Merry. Mud sticks and that woman changes her mind more often than she casts on her stitches. Come on, I want a word with you before we get home.'

'There's nothing wrong with Grozen, is there?' Merry asked.

'Funnily enough, she asked me the same about you earlier. Said you'd taken to knitting up at the point by yourself. She thinks you've been fretting over something. It's not that Nicco, is it? I know he's not been very attentive but it is his busiest time and...'

'I'm enjoying the break from his suggestions, Mother, believe you me,' Merry said with feeling.

'What's wrong then? You should be happy now you're going to Plymouth every month.'

'I've only been twice, Mother, and each time Nicco's watched me like a sparrowhawk.'

'He's just looking out for you. Not that he has recently, I admit, since he's taken to going to the tavern with that Otto each evening.'

'For which I'm truly grateful,' Merry said with feeling.

'Come along, let's sit here a while and we can

talk properly,' her mother said, pulling her down beside her on the stone steps. 'So if it's not Nicco troubling you, what is?'

Merry thought for a moment, wondering how best to tell her mother that visiting Plymouth once a month wasn't enough.

'You were in service near Plymouth, weren't you?'

'You know that, our Merry, although I stayed on the Cornwall side of the Tamar. Work at that big house was busy in the extreme, rising before dawn and not getting to bed till the last bit of tidying-up was finished.'

'It sounds more exciting than here, though,' Merry whispered.

Her mother gave a harsh laugh. 'We didn't get paid as much as we do at the pallace, although, granted, it was regular work.'

'But you met different people and...'

'Oh, don't you go listening to that woman. Kelys might have had a hard life but then so have most round here. There's a lot to be said for family, and if she'd been nicer to hers they might want to visit her now.' Her mother turned to face her. 'I can see there's more, so spit it out, our Merry.'

'I'm fed up with smelling of fish and I want to do something different.' As the words came bursting out, her mother looked thoughtful.

'I heard Mrs Grace is looking for help in her travellers' lodging house. It's only at the top of the village so you would be able to come home each evening.' Merry's heart sank. That was where Sharp junior was staying and there was no way she could work there. Besides it wouldn't get her away from here, would it? Catching sight of the outline of the imposing granite house opposite, her resolve hardened.

'Come along, Grozen will wonder where we've got to,' her mother urged, getting to her feet.

'I think I'll take a walk and clear my head,' Merry replied, hurrying down to the beach before her mother could dissuade her.

As her feet crunched over the pebbles, she lifted her face to the cool breeze wafting in from the sea. Picking up a handful of stones she threw them as hard as she could then stood listening to the plopping sounds as they landed in the water. Gradually, the rhythmic shooshing of the waves being sucked in and out of the shingle soothed her spirits. She stared out at the horizon, which now, at nearly midsummer, was navy rather than black, and she couldn't help wondering what lay beyond.

Lost in her reverie, it was some moments before she heard the crunch of footsteps on the stones behind her. Turning quickly, she saw Otto making his way towards her.

'Evening, Merry,' he called, lifting his cloth cap in greeting. 'I was leaving the tavern when I saw you flinging those stones like fury and thought I'd better see if I could save the poor things.'

'But I was only...' she began, then, seeing he was teasing, giggled.

'That's better. Why don't we take a pew and you can tell me what's troubling you?' he said, gesturing to a nearby groyne.

Sitting side by side with him in the near darkness, with the waves lapping at their feet, Merry suddenly felt self-conscious. She didn't really know this man, after all.

'Mother always said if you share a trouble then someone else can worry about it as well,' Otto said.

'Are you close to her?' she asked. She heard him sigh into the darkness.

'I was before she was taken last winter.'

'Oh, Otto, I'm sorry and here's me...' Her voice tailed off.

'And here's you what? Come on, tell Father Confessor.'

She smiled but there was something compelling about his gaze and, under the cover of the evening skies, she found herself telling him of her hopes and desires.

'So you see, Otto, the other knitters resent me for getting paid a fair price. Grozen and Mother want me to marry Nicco and stay in the village but I want to see what life lies beyond before it's too late. I'm already seventeen, after all.'

'A great old age indeed,' he agreed, so solemnly she had to laugh.

'Now you're mocking me.'

'Not really. Nobody can make you settle down with Nicco – or anyone else, if it comes to that. It's your life, your choice.'

'But Nicco won't take no for an answer,' she cried. 'Although since you've been here I've hardly seen him.'

'I have my uses then,' Otto laughed. 'Nicco's a good man, just a tad headstrong. He naturally assumes everyone wants the same as he.' They lapsed into silence as she digested what he'd said.

'I suppose you think I'm selfish and stupid,' she

said eventually.

'No, I don't, Merry. In some ways I understand only too well for I couldn't wait to leave the village of my home either. It seems to me there are two points here, though. The agent these other women deal with has treated them badly and they are taking it out on you. Then there's your desire to have a different life from the one your family want for you.'

'Well, yes, but it's far more complicated than that,' she protested.

'Is it? Or is it your conscience getting the better of you?'

'My conscience?' she asked, not understanding.

He nodded. 'Maybe you're feeling guilty for getting a good price for your work, even though you've put yourself out to seek it. I mean, that Mr Fairbright never came knocking on your door, did he?'

Merry giggled at the thought of the dapper man standing outside their humble cottage.

'That's better. You can only help people if they're willing to accept it. Although if you're intending to leave here who would carry on that fancy pattern of yours?'

'I hadn't thought of that,' she admitted.

They sat in silence, watching as the moon rose higher in the sky, casting silver shadows like rungs of a ladder over the sea.

'My mother used to say, if you take one step at a time you can usually see the way ahead. Not that I took any notice of her when I was your age, of course, any more than you will of yours. 'Tis the way of life that we have to find out what life's about for ourselves. 'Cos if we don't we end up feeling resentful.' He leaned forward and chucked her under the chin.

'Oi, what you doing with my girl?' As Nicco's angry voice carried on the night air, they sprang apart.

Chapter 9

'What the hell do you think you're doing, Otto?' Nicco demanded. 'I told you, Merry's my girl.'

'Keep your hair on, pal. We were just having a chat,' Otto replied in such a reasonable voice Merry almost wanted him to declare he'd been courting her himself. Then she saw the set of Nicco's chin, the glint in his eyes.

'If Merry has anything to discuss she will speak to me,' Nicco spat. 'Come along, girl, I'll walk you home. You shouldn't be out at this time of night,' he said, proffering his hand.

Ignoring it, she jumped to her feet. 'I can see myself home, thank you, Nicco. Good night, Otto, and thank you for listening.' As she crunched her way back up the beach, she heard Nicco's angry voice followed by Otto's calm tones.

Thankfully her mother and grandmother were asleep as she tiptoed past their beds and threw herself down on her mattress. How dare Nicco refer to her as his? He made it sound as if she was a toy, something to be possessed. She'd make sure she stayed out of his way the next evening.

Fate was against her, though. She was in the pallace, checking the specially made drains that collected the oil and salt were clear, when a shadow fell over her.

'Good evening, Merry,' Nicco said, grinning as if their disagreement of the previous night had never happened. She forced a smile but remained silent. 'I fear I have been negligent in my duties this past month.'

'Surely not,' she said, staring around at the barrels of fish that lined the walls, the pots of 'train oil' waiting to be sold for use in the preparation of leather and as nightlights. 'It looks as if it's been a very productive time, Nicco.'

'I wasn't referring to my work, Merry. Nobody is more industrious or conscientious than Nicco Neaple. No, I meant in paying attention to my betrothed.' As he flashed another grin, she felt herself grow hot.

'We are not betrothed, Nicco,' she reminded him, trying to keep her voice level so as not to attract the attention of the others.

'Nicco.' At the sound of his father's voice, Nicco sprang away from her.

'Father, how good of you to pay us a visit,' he replied, resuming his professional manner. 'See how productive I have been,' he said, gesturing around the storeroom as though he had filled it single-handedly. 'As you can see, the business is in good hands now, and...'

'I have merely been ill, Nicco, and I would remind you that this is still my business,' Mr Neaple said curtly. 'Now that I have recovered, you may show me exactly how many barrels are ready to be transported.'

As Nicco hurried to do his father's bidding, Merry breathed a sigh of relief. Thank heavens for old Mr Neaple, she thought. Then saw the others nudging each other.

'You won't forget to remind Nicco about our St Peter's Fair celebrations, will you?' Tressa asked.

'Yes, it's getting close now,' Marya added.

'That's if she can be bothered to remember her friends when she's being wined and dined,' Kelys sniffed.

'Merry knows how to treat her friends,' her mother said, appearing beside them. 'Come along, Merry, I'll be glad to get home and put my feet up. It seems to have been a long day and I've still got that last frock to finish before you see Mr Fairbright.'

Making their way outside, they could hear Mr Neaple having a heated discussion with his son.

'He was no good, Father, so I sent him packing.' Nicco's voice rose as the old man frowned, running his hand over a newly finished barrel.

'This looks like good craftsmanship to me, son.'

'Trust me, Father, he was more trouble than he was worth. Glad to see the back of him, to be honest.'

Mr Neaple didn't look convinced.

'You have been overseeing the work and I would have expected more barrels packed by now.'

'Come along, Merry,' her mother said, giving her a nudge. They called good night to some of the workers who had clustered in a group just outside the entrance.

'You mean he's gone?' Wyllow wailed.

92

'Not yet. I heard him arranging a lift with the carter for two days' time,' Delen said. 'You'd best hurry if you want him to notice you, girl. Not that you've had any luck so far.'

The others chortled and their good-natured banter followed after Merry and her mother as they made their way home. Merry hardly heard, though, for her thoughts were racing. Her appointment with Mr Fairbright was in two days' time.

'So I was wondering if I could travel with you as well,' Merry asked, staring up at the kindly carter.

'Well, there ain't much room but...'

'I can squeeze up, sir, and I've provisions enough for three in my knapsack,' Otto assured him, shifting from one precariously balanced piece of wood to another.

'Oh, go on then,' the carter muttered.

'I truly appreciate it,' Merry said, handing her parcel to Otto, then clambering up beside him.

With a jolt they began to move and Merry looked furtively over her shoulder. It was much earlier than when she usually left home and she was hoping Nicco would still be in bed.

'You seem edgy,' Otto said.

'I'll be pleased when we're out of the village,' she muttered.

'Ah,' Otto said, looking at her knowingly. She peered round again, then realized they were passing the fork where the lane veered off to Plymouth.

'Are you not turning off here?' she asked the carter.

'Never get this lot along that narrow track,' he

said. 'I'll be taking the high road. 'Tis further but will be quicker in the long run.'

Merry let out a sigh of relief.

'I take it Nicco uses the other route?' Otto said.

She nodded. 'Not that he makes any arrangements. He just waits on the track with his cart.'

'He's definitely a man on a mission,' Otto said grimly, and Merry remembered their last meeting on the beach.

'What happened between you two? Nicco said your work wasn't up to scratch but old Mr Neaple wasn't having any of it.'

Otto grimaced, his hand automatically going to his eye and in the growing light, she saw the livid bruise. 'He didn't do that?' she gasped.

'Don't concern yourself. It was merely a lads' tussle.'

'Is that why he sacked you, because of me?' she asked, suspicion rising.

He shrugged, then grabbed hold of the side of the cart as it lurched to the right.

'Hang on,' the carter called. ''Tis a sharp bend coming up.' They laughed at his belated warning.

'Don't you worry about me, Merry. I'm used to looking after myself. Like as not I'll get work in Devonport. They're always looking for good coopers there.'

'But Nicco said...' she began, remembering the discussion between him and old Mr Neaple.

'I can imagine,' Otto smiled wryly. 'But I know my trade and am good at what I do. Nicco sure is possessive about you, though, Merry.'

'Tell me about it,' she sighed, automatically casting a glance behind them.

94

'What are your plans? I know you're going to see that agent today but how will you get home again?'

'I can walk. It's these frocks that are bulky,' she said, patting her parcel. 'Once Mr Fairbright has purchased them, I'll just have the wool to carry and besides I shall have time to look around the market,' she added, brightening at the thought. Picking up her pins, she began to knit.

'That looks interesting. Is that the pattern you were telling me about?' Otto asked, peering at her work.

Merry nodded. 'I got bored doing the same every day and just sort of saw it in my head.'

'My mother used to vary her work too. That's quite effective, though, I must say. Have you shown the others how it's done yet?'

'They're more interested in the St Peter's Fair celebrations,' she sighed, turning her work.

As the sun climbed higher in the sky, they lapsed into companionable silence and Merry couldn't help comparing Otto's easy way with Nicco's haughty manner and interminable questions. She stared around at the unfamiliar scenery. Here the road was bordered by fences with stiles interspersed along the route. Cows and sheep grazed the pastures and in the distance she could see what looked like mauve hills rising, seemingly to the sky.

'Goodness,' she exclaimed.

'They be the heather clad moors,' Otto said, smiling at her expression. 'Hope you've been good or the Boggy Beast will be after you.'

'What?' she gasped, then saw he was teasing.

'You've never seen the moors?'

She shook her head. 'I've only been out of Porthsallos twice before,' she admitted.

''Tis a bit different the village, isn't it?' he asked, lifting his cap politely as another cart passed. 'Mind you, Porthsallos is a nice village.' She gave a snort and he laughed. 'Sometimes you have to experience other things to appreciate what you have,' he said then lapsed into silence as if his words had reminded him of something.

The cart rattled precariously as it turned down the hill leading to the water and Merry and Otto giggled as they clung to the sides. When they finally reached the ferry, Otto scrabbled in his knapsack, sharing out the bread and cheese he'd brought with him. As the vessel clanked its way across the river, Merry ate ravenously, enjoying the simple meal far more than Nicco's proposed extravagant feast.

'I was intending getting off when the ferry docks but could always travel on to Plymouth with you,' he offered, but Merry knew the best offers of work came first thing and she shook her head.

'That's kind of you, Otto, but I really do want time to visit the market in Plymouth. I'm sure you'd be bored stiff wandering around stalls laden with materials, ribbons and lace.'

'Happen you're right,' he said, gathering up his things as the ferry bumped to a halt. 'Take care of yourself, Merry.'

'You too, Otto,' she said.

Otto hesitated then turned to face her. 'Look, Merry, Nicco is a nice man but he can be hot-headed. I guess what I'm trying to say is, nobody can make you marry if you don't choose to.'

'I understand,' she replied, knowing what he was trying to say. 'What about you, Otto? Do you have anyone special in your life?'

He shook his head. 'Like a rolling stone, me,' he laughed. 'I ain't the marrying kind.'

'I'm sure there's someone who would love to receive your attentions,' she said, thinking of Wyllow.

He patted her hand. 'Like I said, marriage ain't for the likes of me. Now I'll bid thee farewell, Merry. Carter, stop here, if you please.'

The cart shuddered to a halt and Merry watched as Otto bent and whispered something to the kindly man before handing him some coins. What a nice man Otto was, she thought. He'd confirmed her suspicions about Nicco, though.

To her surprise, the carter followed the same route from the ferry as Nicco had. She'd become used to the noise and the bustle but was surprised when the cart came to a halt outside the premises of Mr Fairbright.

'Here you are, miss,' the carter said, grinning broadly.

'But how did you know where I was headed?' she asked.

'The gent insisted I deliver you to the door,' he said. 'Paid me handsomely too.'

'Oh,' she said, drawing out her purse. The carter shook his head.

'No need for that, miss. Hope you have a good day,' he called.

Smiling her thanks, Merry took her parcel and walked up the steps.

'Yes?' the formidable Miss Brown asked, as she

stood by the counter.

'I have come for my appointment with Mr Fairbright,' Merry said, forcing her lips into a smile.

'Name?'

'Miss Dyer,' she replied. Really, she could do without these games, she thought, watching as the woman slowly ran her finger down the list of appointments.

'You are very early, Miss Dyer.'

Merry stared at the clock on the wall and shook her head. 'I think you will find I am on time, for it is almost eleven o'clock.'

The woman gave a supercilious sneer. 'Ah, but your appointment is not until tomorrow.'

'No, it's definitely today,' Merry began, but the woman was already looking past her.

'Good morning, Mr Didcot,' she gushed as a smartly suited gentleman walked through the door, the tapping of his silver-topped cane echoing on the stone floor. 'I'll let Mr Fairbright know you're here.'

'Thank you, Miss Brown,' he said. 'It was good of you to fit me in at the last moment.'

'But...' Merry began.

'Is something wrong?' the gentleman asked, turning to Merry.

'Yes, you see my appointment is...'

'Please do not trouble Mr Didcot; he is a very busy man. I'll announce your arrival, sir,' the woman effused, patting her bun and hurrying over to knock on Mr Fairbright's door.

'Mr Didcot is here to see you,' she announced importantly. With a puzzled look at Merry, the man followed her.

'Miss Brown, it is such a long journey from Porthsallos that I would hardly mistake the date of my appointment with Mr Fairbright. It was definitely for eleven o'clock today and...' Merry began.

'As I said, you got it wrong,' Miss Brown hissed. 'Now some of us have work to do, so kindly go away and come back on the right day.'

Chapter 10

Merry stared at the woman in disbelief but could see by her dismissive attitude that further argument would be futile. Picking up her parcel, she turned to go.

'Could we have some refreshments, please, Miss Brown?' Mr Fairbright said, appearing at his door. Catching sight of Merry, his eyes widened. 'Miss Dyer? What are you doing here? I was given to understand you had to change your appointment?' he said frowning.

'Change my appointment? I would never do that,' she replied.

'It would appear she got the day wrong,' Miss Brown said, raising her eyebrows.

'I most certainly did not. I meticulously noted it down,' Merry said, scrabbling in the pocket of her skirt and pulling out her little notebook. 'I would never get such an important thing wrong.'

'Clearly you have,' Miss Brown sniffed. 'So if you'd like to come back tomorrow, Mr Fairbright will see you then. Now, sir, I'll get your tea,' she said, disappearing through a door behind the counter.

'There seems to have been some misunderstanding, Miss Dyer,' the agent said, frowning again.

'I guess it can't be helped, Mr Fairbright,' she answered politely, her heart sinking. She couldn't possibly travel all this way again tomorrow.

The agent was staring at her thoughtfully. 'Look, Miss Dyer, my business with Mr Didcot will take about an hour. I usually take a break at noon, but if you wouldn't mind waiting I could see you then?'

Her heart lifted. 'That would be most kind, Mr Fairbright,' she said, gathering up her parcel once more.

'You are welcome to wait here. Perhaps you'd like to sit by the window – you can at least watch life go by?' he added.

'Ah, Miss Brown,' he said, turning as the woman bustled through the door carrying a tray of tea and cake. 'I'll take that.'

'But Mr Didcot's waiting and I...' the woman began. Ignoring her, the agent took the tray from her hands.

'Miss Dyer has graciously agreed to wait until noon so perhaps you could make her some tea and show her where she can refresh herself after her long journey?'

'But you take luncheon then, and Mr Didcot...' she began, glaring at Merry.

'Mr Didcot will be gone by then and I will require an explanation as to how this unfortunate mix-up with appointments has occurred, Miss

Brown.' He gave the woman such a searching look, her cheeks flushed and she looked down at the counter. 'Please make yourself comfortable, Miss Dyer,' he said, turning back to Merry. 'I will try not to keep you waiting longer than necessary.'

As Mr Fairbright disappeared back into his office, Miss Brown looked up and glowered at Merry.

'I don't know what you said to him but if you made him any promises...'

'Promises? I'm sure I don't know what you're insinuating, Miss Brown. Now I believe Mr Fairbright said you would make me some tea,' she said, smiling sweetly. The woman's eyes widened and Merry was sure she heard her utter a curse as she disappeared.

Merry shook out her skirts, then settled herself in the chair. Taking up her pins, she continued with her knit frock. Clearly someone had muddled her appointment and it didn't take a genius to work out who. The question was: why? She hadn't intentionally upset the formidable Miss Brown, although she supposed Mr Fairbright would have taken her to task about the overpayment. Still, that wasn't Merry's fault and she couldn't have pocketed the extra money, could she?

She jumped as a cup of tea was slammed down on the table in front of her, the hot liquid spilling into the saucer.

'You needn't think I made that out of the goodness of my heart,' she spat.

'Why, Miss Brown, I didn't know you had one,' Merry quipped. The woman might be Mr Fairbright's assistant but Merry had no intention of putting up with rudeness. She turned her attention back to her knitting, leaving the woman no choice but to return to her stool behind the counter.

Her fingers automatically settling into the rhythm of the pattern, she glanced out of the window. People were bustling about their business and, further down the street, she could see the brightly coloured booths, their stripy coverings flapping in the breeze. Excitement bubbled up inside her. With no Nicco waiting for her, after concluding her business she'd be free to browse the materials and trimmings. She was so busy planning what she might buy that she only noticed Mr Didcot had emerged from the office when the tap tap of his cane on the floor came to a stop by her side.

'Miss Dyer?'

She looked up quickly. 'Yes, sir?'

'I understand you have been inconvenienced this morning and I wish to convey my apologies.'

Merry stared at the dapper businessman in surprise. 'It's no trouble, sir,' she answered, putting down her pins and smiling up at him.

'You are right, Fairbright. Miss Dyer is charming in the extreme. She has also put the time she had to wait to good use,' he said, turning to the agent, who was hovering behind them. 'Good day, my dear. I've a feeling our paths will cross again very soon.' Before Merry could ask him what he meant, he gave a little bow, put on his topper and tapped his way smartly from the premises.

'Come along, Miss Dyer,' Mr Fairbright said. 'I can only apologize again for the misunderstanding. You can be assured, however, that I will be getting to the bottom of it.' He frowned at her untouched cup with its tea-filled saucer. 'Miss Brown, please bring us some refreshment and do try to keep a steady hand, if that is not too much trouble.' Merry could feel the woman's glare on her back as Mr Fairbright showed her into his office. She might be able to afford fancy leather for her feet but Merry wouldn't like to be in her shoes later.

She waited patiently whilst the agent spread her knit frocks over his desk, then inspected them. His room smelled of beeswax polish and tobacco, and she relaxed back in her chair, content to read the titles on the bound volumes in his bookcase while she resumed her knitting. He was still checking the tension of stitches and regularity of the pattern when Miss Brown slunk into the room and put the tea tray on the table. She stood there awaiting acknowledgement but Mr Fairbright ignored her and with a sniff she flounced from the room.

'Those pockets for the watches have been worked impeccably and I am pleased to say I have received more orders for your shell-patterned ones. I see you have produced the required dozen frocks this time,' he said, pushing them to one side. Taking up his pad he scribbled, then tore off a chit, but instead of passing it to her as usual, he sat back in his chair and eyed her candidly. 'Tell me, Miss Dyer, are you happy in your work?'

The question took her by surprise. What should she say? If she told him she was bored with knitting day in and day out he would certainly cancel the order. Yet she'd been brought up to be honest.

'Well, it is certainly satisfying to finish a garment,' she began. 'And I'm grateful that you pay a fair price.' She was about to add, 'unlike the stingy Sharp' but thought better of it. Mr Fairbright smiled and passed her cup to her.

'You must be thirsty after your travels for it is some distance from Porthsallos. How did you get here, by the way?'

'I caught a lift with the carter.'

'Hmm,' he said, steepling his fingers. 'I dare say the journey there and back must take the best part of a day?'

'Yes, it does, and that is why I would never make a mistake about the date,' she said.

He took a sip of his tea and seemed to be pondering his next words. 'Now young ladies are beginning to travel more, there is a demand for suitable attire, waterproof clothing being a prime example.'

'And you think because I travel from Porthsallos I require such things?'

To her surprise Mr Fairbright rocked with mirth.

'You are such a tonic, my dear. No, I'm talking about ladies who travel the globe. Those with money... Look, Miss Dyer, I have been most impressed with the way you conduct yourself and think you would be perfect. Why, I was saying the very same thing to Mr Didcot earlier and he seemed most interested in you.'

'Interested in me?' she frowned. 'Why?'

'Have you ever thought of procuring work in the town?' Her heart skipped a beat. Had she? Then she saw the serious look on the agent's face and her heart flopped. Was he going to cease trading with her?

'My dear, forgive me; as ever, I am ahead of myself. Mr Didcot and I are jointly investing in a draper's shop in the town.'

'So you won't be requiring my knit frocks any more?' she gasped, staring at him in dismay.

'While there is still a demand for those, one must move with the times. Young ladies in particular no longer wish to spend time visiting their dressmakers for numerous fittings. They want nice quality clothes, customized to their personal requirements, that they can take away from the shop and wear that same evening if they choose. There is an increasing demand for a more up-to-date service and this is where I think you would be ideal.'

'Me, Mr Fairbright? I'm sorry but I don't see how.'

'That's easy, Miss Dyer. You could become a sales assistant in our new store. Of course, you would have to pass an interview and an elementary mathematical test, but I'm sure that would be a mere formality.'

'A sales assistant? But I have no skills in that kind of work.'

'You have already shown yourself to be honest, pleasant to people under challenging circumstances and are obviously a hard worker. These are the attributes we require, Miss Dyer, so what do you say? Would you be happy to be interviewed for such a position?'

'Well, I don't know. I mean, I have already travelled here this morning and...' Her words tailed off as butterflies of excitement skittered in her stomach. Wasn't this what she'd been dreaming of? Yet what would her mother and Grozen say?

'Mr Didcot is aware of your situation and would be happy to meet us at one o'clock,' he urged. Seeing him take out his pocket watch and frown, Merry forced herself back to the present. 'We've just time to get there, if we hurry. Come along,' he insisted.

Realizing she had nothing to lose, Merry followed him out of his office where he was already handing the chit to Miss Brown.

'Please make payment and reimbursement of wool for Miss Dyer, the correct amount this time, Miss Brown,' he said. 'I believe I am now free, unless you have seen fit to rearrange my appointments again?' He quirked an eyebrow but the woman was frantically pulling down hanks of wool. 'No hurry, Miss Brown. Miss Dyer will collect everything upon her return,' he said, snatching his hat from the stand in the corner.

As the agent strode along the busy street, Merry endeavoured to keep up. Her mind was spinning like a merry-go-round at the fair as she tried to take in what he'd said. She didn't have time to ponder for long, for already he was disappearing down a side road that led through to the main thoroughfare. Finally he came to a halt outside a large double-fronted shop with a door at each side. Before she'd had time to take note of the items in the window, the door on the left was thrown open and a regal-looking woman dressed in black was greeting the agent effusively.

'Good afternoon, Mr Fairbright. Mr Didcot is waiting in the office for you.'

'Thank you, Mrs Smale. This is Miss Dyer,' he said, barely pausing as he marched inside.

The woman frowned down her glasses and shook her head as she took in Merry's appearance. Hastily smoothing her skirts, Merry followed after the agent. She just had time to take in the glass-fronted counters flanked by rows of wooden drawers before she was ushered up three short flights of stairs to the first floor and into a spacious office.

Mr Didcot welcomed them and bid Merry take a seat in front of his highly polished desk. As the two men began explaining about the new business, she automatically picked up her pins, only to receive a frown from Mr Fairbright.

'It would be advisable to pay attention, Miss Dyer, for we have much to cover.'

'Sorry, sir,' she said meekly.

Mr Didcot nodded and continued talking about their venture, then asked Merry what she had done in Porthsallos. She'd only just finished explaining how she fitted in her knitting around the fish packing when he began firing mathematical questions at her. Just when she thought her brain was going to burst, he sat back in his chair.

'Well, Fairbright, I don't know what you think, but I've made up my mind,' Mr Didcot said, his grey eyes twinkling.

Mr Fairbright nodded. 'I think Miss Dyer has shown herself adept in numeracy and conversational skills.'

'Really?' Merry said, her eyes widening.

'Indeed, Miss Dyer. Such industriousness does you credit and is to be applauded, so I am happy to offer you a trial position here in our new store.'

'Thank you,' she gasped, staring from one to the other.

'Well, would you be happy to faithfully serve and keep the secrets of Didcot and Fairbright?'

'Yes, I think so, sir, but where would I stay? I couldn't possibly travel from Porthsallos each day,' she said, knowing her mother and Grozen would be sure to object.

The two gentlemen chuckled.

'The terms of your indenture determine you live on the premises. You will share rooms above the store with the other trainee sales ladies.'

'My indenture?' Merry asked.

'The terms of your agreement, Miss Dyer,' Mr Didcot replied. 'Now we will need your father's signature on the paper, along with yours.'

'I don't have a father, sir. He died before I was born.'

The two men exchanged looks.

'I didn't realize, Miss Dyer,' Mr Fairbright frowned.

'I live with my mother and grandmother. Does that make any difference?'

'No, of course not,' Mr Fairbright said quickly. 'Leave it with me, Didcot. I'll see to things.'

'All being well, I shall see you on Monday then, Miss Dyer,' Mr Didcot smiled, then began shuffling his papers together.

'So soon?' Merry gasped.

'We begin the training of all new personnel on Monday of next week,' Mr Fairbright explained, ushering her out of the office. 'Ah, Mrs Smale,' he smiled as the woman hurried towards them, 'Miss Dyer will be joining us for staff training on Monday.'

'Indeed? Then I hope she will be more suitably attired, Miss Dyer,' she said, frowning down at Merry's hobnail boots.

Mr Fairbright cleared his throat. 'That will all be taken care of, Mrs Smale.'

'Will I wear a posh black frock like that?' Merry asked, fascinated by the little lace collar and tiny glass buttons running from neck to waist of Mrs Smale's dress.

The woman raised her eyebrows until they met with her parting.

'Certainly not. You will be dressed in the customary grey befitting to your humble shop-floor status.'

Chapter 11

Mr Fairbright insisted on giving Merry a lift home, saying he had business to attend to in the village.

'I'll leave you to tell your family your exciting news, then call upon you in the morning to introduce myself and get your mother's signature on the indenture. Naturally she should feel free to ask me any questions she may have, although I am certain she will approve,' he smiled.

'Thank you, Mr Fairbright,' Merry replied, as

she climbed down from his carriage. 'Oh, you don't know my address.'

'But I do, for you gave me the details for your papers of employment,' he reminded her, his eyes twinkling.

Honestly, what must he think of her, Merry mused as she all but ran down the hill. She couldn't wait to tell her mother and Grozen about her new position and for once hardly noticed the sea and the boats in the harbour.

However, far from being pleased the two women were outraged.

'Live in Plymouth?' her mother gasped. 'Oh, no, Merry, I don't think so.'

'But it is the opportunity I've always dreamed of, Mother. I thought you'd be pleased for me – proud of me, even.'

Her mother shook her head. 'I am proud of you, daughter. Always have been, for you are a skilled and conscientious worker, but...'

'Surely you won't stand in my way?' Merry cried. 'You understand, Grozen, don't you?' Merry pleaded, turning to her grandmother.

The old woman sighed. 'I do, Merry, more than you realize,' she said, staring meaningfully at Karenza.

'Well, you obviously don't think I'm capable of succeeding at this job. Or perhaps you don't like the idea of me bettering myself,' Merry muttered, glancing around their tiny living room. True, it was homely and she'd been happy here, but she wanted to experience more than could be found at home.

'Oh, Merry, don't sound so bitter. Of course we

want you to get on. Heaven knows, you've talked of nothing else since you were a nipper.' Her mother let out a long sigh. 'It's just that you'll be meeting new people and...'

'You mean I can go?' Merry asked, hope fluttering in her breast.

'We'll see what your Mr Fairbright has to say in the morning for we'd not want to stand in your way, would we, Karenza?' Grozen asked, frowning at her daughter.

Slowly Karenza shook her head. 'No, of course not,' she muttered, taking hold of Merry's hand. 'We'll miss you if you do go, though.' Merry swallowed hard, knowing this was an opportunity she just couldn't turn down.

'I'll come back and visit often. Just think, I'll be able to tell you what goes on in the outside world,' she joked. To her consternation, her mother's eyes clouded.

'That's what I'm afraid of. Look, Merry, if you are determined to go then there's something you should know...'

'Yes?' she asked, frowning as her mother faltered to a halt.

'Oh, go and get some rest. We'll talk in the morning,' Karenza muttered.

Seeing her mother's pursed lips, Merry knew there was no use arguing but as she made her way upstairs she heard her grandmother's voice.

'I know it's difficult but you have to let her go, Karenza. Afore she does, though, you really need to tell her...'

Merry paused, straining to hear more, but her grandmother had lowered her voice. Oh well, no doubt she'd find out in the morning, she thought.

However, when she entered the living room the next morning she found her mother and Grozen engaged in a frenzy of activity.

'What are you doing?' she asked, staring from the chairs that were upturned on the table to the polishing cloths and broom they were wielding.

'Making the place respectable for that Mr Fairbright,' her mother muttered, impatiently tugging a stray tendril of hair back into its knot.

'He's coming to see you, Mother, not inspect the cottage,' Merry laughed.

'We have standards here, our Merryn,' her mother admonished. 'Now put the pot to boil whilst I make myself look presentable.'

'There's really no need...' Merry began, but her mother had disappeared up the stairs. She shrugged and stared at her grandmother. 'Mr Fairbright is really a nice man.'

'I'm sure he is, but your mother wants to do you proud so put out the best cups before he arrives.'

Seeing the set look on her grandmother's face, Merry did as she was told and had just finished when there was a knock on the door.

'Do I look all right?' her mother asked, hurrying into the room dressed in her Sunday best.

'You look fine,' Merry whispered, hurrying to let her employer in. 'Do come in, Mr Fairbright,' she said, then made the introductions.

At first, her mother and Grozen seemed in awe of the smartly dressed man but by the time he was settled at the table with a cup of tea, they began to relax.

112

'I have a paper here that explains the terms and conditions of Miss Dyer's employment. As you can see, she will be trained to the highest standard, have all meals and her uniform provided.'

'What about her living-in arrangements? I understand there will be male employees on the premises as well?' Karenza asked.

Merry frowned. 'Really, Mother.'

'Don't worry, Mrs Dyer,' Mr Fairbright smiled. 'Your daughter will be sharing a room with two female trainee assistants. The accommodation for the males will be on the other side of the building.'

'But what if she gets in with the wrong type of man?' Karenza whispered. 'I mean, she's not used to the smooth tongues of town gentlemen.'

Merry grinned wryly, thinking of Nicco, but before she could say anything, Mr Fairbright smiled.

'I'm sure you have taught your daughter right from wrong and can trust her to be sensible.'

'Yes, we've brought up our Merry to be a good girl, haven't we, Karenza?' her grandmother replied.

Mr Fairbright smiled. 'Miss Dyer will be under the auspices of Mrs Smale, the manageress. She is a woman of the world, used to dealing with female requirements.'

'What about time off? I mean, will we get to see her? Merry hasn't been away from home before and...'

'Mother,' Merry gasped, but again Mr Fairbright smiled gently.

'We will be recommending our staff maintain contact with their families. With your daughter

113

having only the Sabbath off, the distance between here and Plymouth might pose a problem for her to make regular journeys home but I can promise you will be kept informed of her progress, perhaps by letter?'

'It would be good to know how she is doing,' Karenza admitted.

'I do understand your concerns,' Mr Fairbright assured her, 'but I'm sure you want to encourage your daughter to spread her wings and fulfil her potential.' He paused and Merry thought what a clever man he was.

Slowly her mother nodded. 'We wouldn't want to hold her back,' she sighed. 'And I'm sure Nicco could bring her home in his cart on occasions.' Merry frowned, then realizing her mother was weakening, squeezed her hand.

'As my food and room will be paid for, I'll be able to bring money home.' Her mother smiled although Merry noticed it didn't reach her eyes.

'But will it be enough to cover the money we'll lose from her knitting? After all, she does get more for her fancies.' Grozen fixed the agent with her gimlet stare.

'That is very true. Which is why I propose you let Miss Dyer show you how to work the shell pattern so that you can knit those fancies too.'

'Why, you got something up your sleeve, then?' Grozen asked, quirking a brow.

'Grozen,' Merry gasped.

Mr Fairbright smiled and got to his feet. 'You are a shrewd woman, Mrs Dyer, and hopefully when I return I will be able to reveal my plan. In the meantime, Miss Dyer can spend the rest of the morning showing you the pattern whilst I conclude my business in the village. I'm sure you will wish to read the terms of your daughter's employment,' he said, turning to Karenza. 'If you could give consideration to signing the indenture form, I would be most grateful. Now if you'll excuse me, I shall be back at noon. Hopefully Miss Dyer will have your blessing to return to the store with me then.'

As soon as the door closed behind him, Grozen turned to Merry.

'Seems a nice gentleman but I'm not sure about learning this new fancy stitch of yours.'

'You could at least try, Grozen. If it means you earning more money then...' Knowing Grozen would never turn down such an opportunity, Merry left her words hanging in the air.

By the time Mr Fairbright returned both women had perfected the shell stitch and Merry, having convinced her mother to sign her indenture, was ready and waiting. He took the signed paper, then inspected the samples Grozen and her mother had knitted.

'Impeccable work, ladies,' he enthused. They smiled delightedly. 'Now, you might be interested to know that Sharp junior has decided he no longer wishes to trade in Porthsallos.'

'What?' Karenza gasped. 'But everyone here relies on him.'

'Shark that he is,' Grozen grumbled.

'His departure has left vacant premises, which I have this very morning leased,' Mr Fairbright said. 'I have taken the liberty of speaking with those ladies who traded with him and have come

115

to an agreement. In future they will deal with me and I will pay them a fair rate, in cash, of course. Although I have made it plain that should I find any evidence of unscrupulous practices having been undertaken, trading will cease forthwith.'

Merry smiled to herself. Now she understood why he'd questioned her about the activities of Mr Sharp on their journey to Porthsallos.

'Good, we don't want our reputation brought into disrepute by a few local women,' Karenza said.

'Although it has to be said they were under extreme pressure to provide for their families,' Grozen pointed out.

'Well, I hope the new arrangement will be more suitable for everyone. I shall return each month to collect the work and make payment, so I will see you ladies then.'

Excitement fizzed Merry's insides as she smoothed down the skirts of her grey bombazine dress and checked her appearance in the shiny glass mirror on the door of the closet. It wasn't fly-spotted like the one at home, and she'd been told by the formidable Mrs Smale that she must be impeccably turned out at all times. Apparently, they were to be inspected first thing each morning and then again in the afternoon. Her new, highly polished, black laced shoes squeaked as she nervously paced the floorboards waiting for the two trainee shop girls who would be sharing her room to arrive. It was strange not having a frock on the go, but Mr Fairbright had been adamant her new position would keep her too busy for knitting. She peered out of the little skylight and could just make out the sloping roofs of the shops opposite. It was like being on top of the world and very different from her home in Porthsallos.

Merry was still smiling at the surprising turn events had taken, when the door opened and a red-haired, green-eyed girl burst into the room.

'Fancy having to get up at this time of the morning; it's hardly light. Hey, this is all right, isn't it?' she cried, staring around. 'I'm Frankie Brice, by the way; Freckles to my friends. Bet you can't guess why. That your bed?' She jerked her head to the one alongside the far wall beneath the skylight on which Merry had laid out her night things.

'Hello, I'm Merryn Dyer, though most people call me Merry. You can have this bed if you prefer,' she replied.

'No, you're all right,' Freckles said, hefting her bundle onto the one nearest Merry's. 'You speak different – where are you from?'

'Porthsallos, the other side of Logh.'

'You're from Cornwall? Well, I never. Plymouth born and bred, me. Da works on the docks. Blimey, these dresses are stiff,' she grimaced, easing her fingers between the starched collar and her neck. 'As for these squeaking shoes, Da says he hopes they're bought and paid for. Hey, get the view,' she said, standing on tiptoe to peer out of the skylight. 'Wonder if we can climb onto the roof. Might be a good ruse if we want to break curfew,' she chuckled.

Merry grinned at the whirlwind that had blown into the room. Sharing with this lively girl looked like being fun.

The door opened again and a sandy-haired girl of similar age, a cloak over her grey dress, stared warily at them.

'Well, come on in, girl, and introduce yourself,' Frankie urged. 'I'm Frankie Brice but you can call me Freckles, and this is Merry Dyer.'

The girl smiled tentatively. 'Prunella Prim.'

'Well, Pru, come on in and dump your bag.'

'I prefer to be called Prunella, if you don't mind.'

Freckles raised her eyebrows. 'Well, posh Prunella, have you travelled far?' she asked, eyeing the girl's smart valise.

'From Higher Framington.'

'Figures,' Freckles grinned. 'How did you get here?'

'Father put his coach at my disposal,' she said, taking off her cape and looking round for somewhere to hang it.

'It seems we have to share this closet,' Merry smiled, pointing to the corner. 'It's got a lovely mirror on it.'

'Which is to be hoped you will put to good use,' a brusque voice said. They looked up to see a woman of middle years, the dark grey of her dress relieved by a white lace collar, standing in the doorway. 'I am Mrs Rose, your supervisor. Please check your appearance and follow me ready for inspection. You'd better look sharp, Mrs Smale hates to be kept waiting,' the woman added before bustling away.

'Aye aye, Captain,' Freckles whispered, giving a salute and marching after her. 'Wonder how many of us trainees there'll be,' she whispered as

118

they descended the three flights of narrow stairs to the first floor.

'There will be the three of you trainee sales assistants for the ladieswear side of the store, and three young,' Mrs Rose coughed discreetly, 'males to assist Jenkins in menswear. Not that you will have much to do with them after your induction this afternoon.'

'Want to bet?' Freckles giggled.

'I am not a betting person, Miss Brice, and I sincerely hope you are not either.' Mrs Rose coughed, then continued her way down the stairs.

'Blimey, she's got ears in her bottom,' Freckles whispered. Merry smiled but Prunella frowned.

'I do think you should be quiet,' she whispered.

'Oh glory, a Goody Two-Shoes,' Freckles muttered, raising her brows.

The bottom of the third flight opened into a bright corridor and they followed the woman into a small, comfortably furnished room. As Freckles went to sit in one of the comfy chairs, the supervisor coughed again and frowned.

'Remain on your feet, please, Miss Brice. Now stand tall, hands at your sides, whilst I inspect you before Mrs Smale arrives.'

Fighting down the urge to giggle, they did as they were told and the woman walked slowly round peering up and down.

'Hands out.' As Merry complied, the woman clicked her tongue. 'Your skin is rather rough and red, Miss Dyer. If you are to handle the delicate materials in the store, you must rub them with lanolin each night to soften them.'

'Yes, Mrs Rose,' Merry answered, and was

about to ask where she could obtain some but the woman had moved on.

'Yours could be cleaner, Miss Brice.'

'Yes, Mrs Rose,' Freckles murmured.

'But yours, Miss Prim, are beautifully manicured. Perhaps you could show the others how to keep their nails shaped and shiny.'

Prunella gave a self-satisfied smile.

'Now stand ready to be presented to your manageress,' Mrs Rose announced.

As the unsmiling Mrs Smale marched into the room and gave each of them a searching look, Merry's heart sunk. Had she made a mistake coming here?

Chapter 12

'Good morning, ladies. I will begin by outlining the rules and regulations of Didcot and Fairbright. You have already been made aware that your position here is under constant review and that for the first six months you are on probation. It goes without saying therefore that to disobey the rules would be foolhardy in the extreme.' She paused and stared at each of them in turn. 'You will rise at six o'clock each morning to clean the store and set out the stock. During this time you will wear the white smocks provided to cover your dresses. Once your duties have been carried out satisfactorily you will be permitted to have breakfast. You will then return to your room, remove your smocks and make yourselves ready for inspection. Provided you pass, you will follow Mrs Rose onto the shop floor and be assigned your duties for that day. Any questions?'

'Will we take it in turns in serving the punters, Mrs Rose?' Freckles asked, turning to the supervisor.

The girls watched in fascination as the woman's cheeks turned from pink to red and her mouth opened and closed like a fish's. It was Mrs Smale who answered, her words coming out staccato as if they'd be fired from a pistol.

'You will not serve at all, Miss Brice. You will shadow.'

'What?'

'It is your duty to follow Mrs Rose, observe what she does and the way in which she performs her tasks. You will not speak unless she asks you a question and we do not have *punters*. We have clients.'

'Oh clients,' Freckles said, in such a perfect imitation of the woman that Merry had to bite her tongue to stop herself laughing out loud.

'The store is open from eight a.m. until ten p.m. Monday to Saturday with half-day closing on Wednesday,' the woman continued, oblivious.

'Oh, goody, so we have the rest of Wednesday off then,' Freckles said, turning to Merry.

'No, Miss Brice, you do not.' As the woman took a step towards them, the smell of stale cabbage wafted their way and Merry had to fight the urge to turn aside. 'Sunday will be your day off. You will, of course, be expected to attend church, after which the rest of the day will be free. Whilst the store will be closed to clients on Wednesday afternoons it will remain open for carriage trade, when their servants can call to collect their employers' purchases. Naturally they will use the trade entrance at the back of the store, as will you. The staff door is locked at ten thirty p.m. prompt, and anyone not in their room by that time will be severely reprimanded, if not dismissed. Now, if there are no more questions we will go through to the shop floor and appraise the stock.'

As the woman marched from the room, Mrs Rose following in her wake, Freckles turned to Merry.

'Blimey oh rimey,' she whistled.

'I do think we should hurry,' Prunella urged. 'We don't want to get into trouble on our first day, do we?'

'No, girl, that would never do,' Freckles muttered. 'Is she for real?' she whispered to Merry.

As Merry didn't know if she was referring to Mrs Smale or Prunella, she just shrugged.

The rest of the morning passed in a whirl as seemingly drawer after drawer was opened, and numerous paper packages unwrapped to reveal their contents. There were shiny ribbons, intricate lace, braiding, threads, embroidery silks, buttons, gloves and scarves. Each drew a lengthy explanation from their manageress as to its quality and why it had been included in the stock. This was followed by examination of the materials. There were flannels, calico, linen, sheeting and any number of dress materials from muslins to bombazines, silks and satins in jewel colours. Instinctively, Merry reached out to stroke the glossy material, only to receive a frown from Mrs Smale.

'You do not touch the merchandise, Miss Dyer, unless Mrs Rose or myself ask you to pass something to us. Now you have seen the wonderful array of stock that Didcot and Fairbright have and it will be up to us to ensure our clients are offered choice.'

'You mean we've got to show them everything?' Freckles gasped.

The manageress clicked her tongue. 'Not everything, Miss Brice, but enough to meet requirements and preferably surpass them.'

'By offering excellent service, you mean?' Prunella asked.

'That goes without saying, Miss Prim, for the client is paramount. What I actually meant was, if for example a client asks to see a hat, we will show them what we have, advise on suitability. When they have made their choice, we then offer matching accessories.'

'You mean we encourage them to spend more than they intended?' Freckles laughed.

'I meant that it is our duty to show them what might complete their outfit,' Mrs Smale sniffed.

Freckles nudged Merry. 'Just like I said,' she whispered. 'We get them to spend as much as possible.'

Merry had to smile at her new colleague's knack of hitting the nail on the head.

'Is this amusing you, Miss Dyer?'

'Actually, I'm finding it all fascinating,' Merry replied.

'I'm pleased to hear it. Now everything will be

customized as necessary to meet the client's requirement. However, you will find out more about that when the store opens. We shall also be providing a prompt service for mourning requirements, and, of course, the family of the deceased will be treated with the utmost respect. Right, ladies, you may now take a fifteen-minute break for luncheon. The housekeeper, Mrs Jolly, will have a hot meal waiting in the staff-room, which is situated adjacent to the kitchen on the lower ground floor. Any questions?' Mrs Smale asked.

But mention of food made them realize they were hungry, and Merry and Freckles quickly shook their heads.

'I have one, Mrs Smale,' Prunella ventured.

'Yes, Miss Prim?'

'You've shown us everything apart from what's in that cupboard over there.'

'Ah,' the woman said while Mrs Rose coughed. 'That is where we store the ready-made undergarments.'

'A drawers drawer, you mean,' chortled Freckles.

There was a sharp intake of breath.

'Before the male trainees join us this afternoon, I think a lesson in diplomacy and manners is required. We will therefore reconvene at twenty minutes after noon,' Mrs Smale told them. 'Come along, Mrs Rose.' With a glare at Freckles and Merry, the women marched from the room.

'Blimey oh rimey,' Freckles muttered, raising her eyebrows at Merry as they took their places at the table.

'Why the glum faces, dearies?' a rosy-cheeked woman asked, bustling in with bowls of mutton stew on a tray.

'We think we may have upset our new manageress,' Merry replied, her mouth watering in spite of her worries.

'I'm sure I didn't,' Prunella said, looking self-righteous.

'Oh, you don't want to worry about Mrs Smale. Her new position has gone to her head. She'll settle down in a few days. I'm Mrs Jolly, the cook-cum-housekeeper employed by Mr Didcot to look after you all. You girls can call me Joanie, though. It's nice to meet you all. I'll be in the scullery behind, if you want anything else. Now get that meal down you while it's hot, then things won't look so bad.'

'My name's Prunella Prim and I'd like a soup spoon, if you please?'

'Well, the silver canteen is in Mr Didcot's drawing room and...'

'For heaven's sake, girl, use the one you've got,' Freckles cried.

'But it's a dessert spoon and it...'

'...will be fine for soup,' Freckles finished, raising her eyebrows at Merry again. While the two of them tucked in ravenously, Prunella sighed, then began delicately sipping.

Between spoonfuls of the delicious food, Merry looked out of the window. There was a neatly kept kitchen garden, stocked with herbs, and a crazy-paved path bordered with pansies leading onto a large yard with outhouses and stabling beyond. She returned her attention to the room, which was comfortably furnished, a fan of ornamental flowers arranged in the fireplace and pictures of woollen mills adorning the walls. It was all airy and spacious, and with a jolt Merry realized the whole of their cottage back home in Porthsallos would have fitted comfortably inside it.

'That was lovely,' Freckles said, pushing her empty bowl away. 'If this is what we'll be eating every day, I won't have no complaints.'

'Me neither,' Merry agreed.

'Personally, I feel a touch more seasoning would have...' The rest of Prunella's sentence was lost as Merry and Freckles groaned.

'Finished, dearies?' Joanie asked, bustling back into the room. 'I'd have done a nice spotted dick for afters but Mrs Smale was adamant you were to stay alert for your training this afternoon.'

'Mrs Smale was right, of course,' Prunella agreed.

'I would have liked some, especially if it's as good as that soup,' Freckles said.

Merry nodded, passing over her now empty dish. 'Thank you, that was delicious. You're a good cook, Joanie.'

The woman beamed, dimples appearing in her plump cheeks. 'In that case I'll steam one ready for your supper. Is there anything else you need?'

Merry held up her hands. 'Do you have any lanolin, only Mrs Rose said my hands need looking after if I'm to touch the fine material?'

'Don't know about lanolin but I'm sure I can let you have some dripping. That might help.'

'Thank you, Joanie,' she replied, trying not to shudder.

'Now if there's nothing else, I'll show you where the privy and pump are,' she said, bustling from the room and leaving them to follow.

'Going to be freezing out here in the winter,' Freckles muttered as they stood washing their hands. 'Mind you, your hands will be nice and warm coated in gloopy dripping,' she hooted.

'Don't,' Merry groaned.

'What I'm worried about is having to come all this way in the middle of the night,' Prunella said, glancing up at the attic room where they were to sleep.

'Didn't you see the guzzie under your bed?' Freckles asked.

'The what?' Prunella frowned.

'The pot you can use if you're caught short in the middle of the night. Blimey, girl, even you must have had one at home.'

Prunella shook her head. 'Actually, our facilities are indoors.'

'Blimey, you must be seriously rich,' Freckles whistled.

Seeing Prunella's discomfort at being reminded of her circumstances, Merry changed the subject.

'This is a huge yard, isn't it?' she said, staring around.

'Indeed it is, Miss Dyer, and soon it will be bustling with activity,' Mrs Rose said, appearing by their side. 'Can't you just visualize the carts rolling in with deliveries, carriages calling to collect client's purchases?' She clapped her hands in delight.

'And guess who'll be doing all the work,' Freckles muttered.

127

'I beg your pardon, Miss Brice?' the woman frowned.

'I said, it's a good job they'll have all this room to park, Mrs Rose.'

'Indeed it is. Now come back inside. We mustn't keep Mrs Smale waiting.'

Once they'd assembled in the same room as earlier, Mrs Rose carried out her inspection then gave a discreet cough. As if it were some prior signal, Mrs Smale appeared.

As she walked past them, Merry detected that smell of stale cabbage again. She turned to Freckles, who pinched her nose and grimaced.

'Is something wrong, Miss Brice?' the manageress enquired, with a quirk of her brow.

'Just had an itch, Mrs Smale.' The woman frowned.

'Now before the male trainees join us, there are a few things we need to discuss,' the manageress began. 'Firstly, ladies, under-things are never referred to within clients' hearing. In fact, should you have reason to refer to them at all it will be in hushed tones.'

'But we all wear drawers, Mrs Smale.'

'Whilst we are aware of that, Miss Brice, it is not ladylike to talk about such things and certainly never in the manner in which you refer to them. Should a client request any item of lingerie, they will be taken through to the dressing room and the article brought to them either by Mrs Rose or myself.'

'And you wouldn't expect us to shadow then,' Prunella said.

'Quite, Miss Prim, that would indeed be improper. Whomever of you is assisting at the time will wait outside the dressing room in case the client requires another size. Then you will fetch the same and pass it discreetly through the curtain without showing your face. Client privacy is paramount.'

Merry smothered a smile. Back home, with them all sharing the one small room, privacy was something that was in short supply. In winter, when the windows were rimmed with ice inside, the main focus had been getting dressed as quickly as possible, if indeed they'd undressed in the first place.

'Now we come to the etiquette of our establishment,' the woman continued, her eyes narrowing as she stared intently at each of them in turn.

'The what?' Freckles whispered to Merry.

'Miss Brice, you will please address me if you have any questions,' Mrs Smale said. 'Now, can either of you enlighten your colleague?' she asked, turning to first Merry and then Prunella.

'I believe you are referring to protocol, Mrs Smale,' Prunella replied.

The manageress beamed. 'Indeed I am, Miss Prim. On the shop floor it is I who oversees everything, Mrs Rose is my number two, and although you may ask her any questions, it is to me she defers. We will attend the clients and you will stand ready and waiting to assist when requested. There is to be no talking whilst on duty, unless you need to ask a pertinent question about a client's requirement. If you accede to these simple rules then the shop floor will run smoothly.'

She was interrupted by two sharp raps on the

door. 'Do come in, Jenkins,' she called.

A man of middle years, wearing a black suit and white-collared shirt, marched stiffly into the room. He was followed closely by a slightly younger man in dark grey and three nervous-looking youths dressed in jackets and trousers of the same lighter grey as the girls wore. Clearly this was to denote their status, Merry thought, jumping as Freckles jabbed her side.

'Hey, things are looking up. That one with the sandy hair looks all right.'

As Merry looked at the young men, two of them grinned whilst the third bespectacled one stared down at the ground.

'This is Mr Jenkins and he is in charge of menswear, assisted ably by Mr Perkins,' Mrs Smale said graciously as she stood aside.

'Thank you, Mrs Smale.' Mr Jenkins's lips curved into a smile although his eyes remained serious. Then he turned to face them. 'These young gentlemen are here to serve Didcot and Fairbright in the same capacity as yourselves, only in the menswear side, of course. Although the store is one, for propriety reasons it is separated from ladieswear by a corridor. Whilst it is hoped all members of staff will work well together, there are certain house rules. I am sure it goes without saying that males and females are never to venture into the upstairs rooms of the opposite sex.'

There was a guffaw from the boys, which was quickly stifled at a glare from Mr Jenkins.

'This could be fun,' Freckles whispered, grinning at the sandy-haired one.

'Wish they'd hurry up and finish this drilling,

though,' Merry whispered back.

'Now where was I?' the man continued. 'Ah, yes. The store will close for one hour at noon. Mrs Smale's staff will take the first sitting at luncheon. Then in order to engender good feeling you will all partake of supper together.'

At this the boys locked eyes with them and Freckles gave a quiet cheer. Mrs Smale frowned and Mr Jenkins held up his hand.

'It seems appropriate here, to remind you that you are all on six months' probation. Any member of staff found flouting the rules will be severely reprimanded, if not dismissed on the spot. However, I am sure you are only too aware that you have been offered a wonderful opportunity and would not wish to jeopardize your futures by inappropriate behaviour.' He gave a nod to Mr Perkins, who led the boys from the room.

Mrs Smale turned to face the three girls.

'Right, ladies, Mr Jenkins and myself have the final arrangements for the Store's opening to discuss so Mrs Rose will take you through to the store and show you how the purchases are to be wrapped.'

The rest of the afternoon was spent in a flurry of brown paper and string as they mastered the perfectly packaged parcel. It was second nature to Merry, who was used to packing knit frocks, but Prunella's efforts were cumbersome and she couldn't get the hang of the required slip knots. Freckles giggled when yet another of her parcels was rejected by Mrs Rose.

'I'm just used to the servants carrying out such tasks,' she sighed.

'You have servants? Blimey oh rimey. What are you doing here then?' Freckles asked, her green eyes wide.

'Father's business suffered a setback and we had to let them go,' Prunella said, looking so upset Merry's heart went out to her.

'That must have been difficult for you. Here, let me show you the best way to hold the package whilst you tie it up,' she offered. It took a few attempts but finally Prunella managed to satisfy the supervisor. 'Don't worry, it'll get easier,' Merry whispered.

'So where do we put the money we take?' Freckles asked Mrs Rose.

The woman's eyes widened in horror and she clutched the counter so tightly, Merry thought she was about to fall into a faint.

Chapter 13

'This is not a market stall, Miss Brice,' Mrs Smale cried, appearing behind them. 'Here at Didcot and Fairbright we do not mention the word "money",' she went on, whispering the last word. 'Purchases will be on approbation, with accounts being sent to the clients' homes every six months.'

'You mean they walk away without paying? Blimey oh rimey, what happens if they do a runner?'

Merry was thinking the self-same thing, but before she could say anything, Prunella said,

132

'That is the difference in our classes. My father would always settle his invoices promptly. It is a matter of honour.'

'Indeed it is, Miss Prim. I'm pleased you at least understand. I've a feeling you will go far.'

'And we won't,' Freckles muttered, turning to Merry.

'Want to bet?' she answered, for she was determined to do well in her job. 'Mrs Smale,' she began, but the woman was looking at the longcase clock that was situated behind the counter.

'Right, ladies, it is the store's policy to dress the window each morning and clear it after the store has closed. Today, we set out an array of our accessories in order to attract clients' attention ready for our opening tomorrow. Now, everything needs to be put away and the windows thoroughly cleaned before the shutters are pulled down.'

When everything was put away to the woman's satisfaction, and the counters covered with dust sheets, the trainees were dismissed.

'Tomorrow is a big day, ladies, with the store opening to the public. I will see you here promptly at six fifteen, smartly dressed, with your white smocks covering your dresses. Miss Dyer, do try to do something with those red hands, and all of you, make sure your hair is suitably groomed. Good evening, ladies.'

'Makes us sound like blooming horses,' Freckles muttered as they made their way to the staff-room.

Merry grimaced at her reddened hands. How was she to get them smooth-looking by the morning?

'I have some hand cream in my night valise,'

Prunella said. 'If you put some on before bed and then again in the morning it will help.'

'Thank you, Prunella, that's really kind,' Merry said, looking at her in surprise.

'It's the least I can do when you were so good as to show me how to wrap the packages neatly. I just hope I can remember,' she sighed.

'You will,' Merry reassured her. 'It's exciting to think we will be attending to clients tomorrow, isn't it?' she beamed.

'I'm used to being attended to,' Prunella said sadly. 'Still, I suppose I'll get used to it. Needs must, and all that.'

'Welcome to the real world, girl,' Freckles said.

They'd no sooner taken their places at the dining table than they were joined by the boys.

'Hello there, ladies, I'm Chester Hall,' the sandy-haired lad with the cheeky grin announced. 'This here is Edward Bear, known as Teddy.' The one with dark hair groaned.

Merry smiled at him, immediately taken by his unassuming manner.

'And this is Nicholas Smith.'

The young man flushed and fiddled with his spectacles.

'Well, I'm Frankie, known as Freckles, although I can't think why,' she laughed. 'And this is Merry, and Pru, who prefers to be called Prunella.' As Freckles raised her eyebrows Nicholas turned to Pru.

'I like to be called by my full name too.'

'Well, you two will get on like a house on fire, then,' Freckles laughed.

'You're a right dolly dazzler with that mane of

white hair, aren't you?' Chester said, staring at Merry admiringly. She tucked the escaping tendrils back in her braid but was saved from answering by the appearance of Joanie.

'Here we are, dearies,' she said, balancing a tray piled high with plates of buttered bread as she pushed open the door. Merry jumped up to help but Ted beat her to it.

'Thanks, dearie, this lot's heavy and no mistake, but I reckoned you'd be hungry after your first day. How did it go?' she asked, staring round the table at them.

They gave a collective groan.

'We're to flit around like shadows and never mention the word "drawers", begging your pardon, gentlemen,' Freckles hooted.

'I think Mrs Smale was merely pointing out that we should behave with decorum,' Prunella said.

'You'll soon settle in, dearies,' Joanie assured them.

'Something smelled delicious when we passed by the scullery, Joanie,' Freckles said.

The woman winked. 'Get that bread and butter down you and I'll see if the spotted dick is cooked yet.'

They didn't need telling twice and tucked in hungrily. Merry looked around her fellow trainee assistants and felt excitement bubbling. It was akin to having brothers and sisters, just like when she used to share supper with Jenna and her family. As ever, thoughts of her friend sent a pang through her, hardening her resolve never to marry and have a child. Knowing her sister in blood was at peace gave her comfort and she would have been pleased that Merry had fulfilled her ambition to leave Porthsallos and make a new life for herself.

The next morning, Merry stood behind the counter alongside Freckles and Prunella, her insides fizzing with anticipation. They'd spent the hours since breakfast ensuring everything was ready for the opening and, having passed a rigorous inspection, were now awaiting the arrival of Messrs Didcot and Fairbright.

'Remember, ladies, smile sweetly, say nothing,' Mrs Smale reminded them for the third time just as the men walked into the store.

'Good morning, ladies,' they said in unison.

'Is everything ready, Mrs Smale?' Mr Didcot asked.

'Indeed it is, sir,' she assured him.

'This is a momentous occasion, is it not, Fairbright?'

'Indeed it is, Didcot, and as Mrs Smale obviously has everything under control here, I think we should go through to menswear and check all is well with Jenkins before we open the doors to the public.'

'Of course, sir,' Mrs Smale beamed, stepping forward.

Mr Fairbright held up his hand. 'Please do not trouble yourself, Mrs Smale. I am sure you have enough to do,' and with that the men began to walk away leaving the manageress gaping like a guppy.

Freckles nudged Merry. 'That told her,' she whispered.

'All seems to be in order, Mrs Smale,' Mr Didcot said. He consulted his pocket watch and nodded to Mrs Smale. 'If you are ready, I think we may open for business.'

As he crossed the floor and threw open the doors with a flourish, Mrs Smale turned to face them.

'Remember, ladies, you are to shadow, smile but never speak unless addressed,' she reminded them yet again. Freckles raised her eyebrows in such a comical manner Merry had to bite her tongue to stop herself from giggling.

If they were expecting a surge of people they were disappointed. It was some two hours before the first client entered the premises, closely followed by her servant. She was a young woman in a sprigged cotton dress, glossy auburn hair just peeking beneath her summer bonnet. Merry watched in awe as her gaze swept over them to the drawers beyond.

'May I help you, modam,' Mrs Smale enquired, hurrying towards her.

'Blimey oh rimey, what's happened to her voice?' Freckles whispered.

'Perhaps if modam would care to say what it is she is looking for, I may assist?' Mrs Smale simpered.

'I am seeking leather gloves in an exact match,' the woman said, holding up her reticule.

Mrs Smale nodded. 'Of course, modam. If you would care to be seated, modam,' she replied, indicating the chair placed before the counter. 'Mrs Rose, pass me the required item.'

Mrs Rose nodded and opened a drawer.

As she'd been instructed, Merry moved obediently to one side of the supervisor, then watched in growing consternation as the woman's fingers hovered over first one pair and then another.

'Quickly, Mrs Rose. We do not wish to keep modam waiting,' Mrs Smale hissed. Still the woman dithered between the tan and the ox blood. With a glance at the client's bag, Merry handed the tan ones to the supervisor, who snatched them up and passed them over.

The woman tried them on, nodded acceptance and Merry was ordered to wrap the purchase. Then she gave the parcel to Mrs Rose, who passed it to Mrs Smale, who handed it to the client with a flourish. What a performance, Merry thought. How would they cope with a shop full of clients?

'Miss Brice and Miss Dyer, please go to the stockroom and bring back another pair of gloves to replenish the stock,' the manageress ordered.

'What was all that about with Mrs Rose?' Freckles whispered.

'Probably nerves,' Merry replied.

'Well, modam was not amused,' Freckles said, impersonating the woman's posh voice.

Merry began searching through a shelf piled high with gloves and nearly sent them toppling when the other girl let out a loud whistle.

'Look at all this stuff. Imagine wearing this down the dance hall of a Saturday night,' she said, winding a length of sable material around her shoulders and parading up and down. 'That Chester would think me a right dolly dazzle, an' all.'

'Like him, do you?' Merry asked.

'Well, I wouldn't say no,' she grinned, hugging the soft material closer.

'Better put that back before you get caught,'

Merry urged, not wishing to be dismissed on their first day. 'Ah, found them,' she said, locating the correct size. 'Come on, let's get back.'

'I'll shadow you, Miss Dyer,' the irrepressible Freckles chortled, following after her.

They returned to find another client seated in front of the counter. Mrs Smale was passing muslin to Prunella for packaging while Mrs Rose measured a length of ribbon along the rule affixed to the counter. As Merry replaced the gloves, she couldn't resist running her fingers over the supple skin. One day she would wear a pair like these, she vowed. Already her hands were looking better. The cream Prunella had loaned her was like a balm it was so rich, and the smell was divine. How lovely to own such luxurious things, she mused, but Mrs Rose was clicking her tongue and she emerged from her daydream and hurried over to assist.

After their luncheon, they assembled in the closed store ready for their next lesson.

'Here at Didcot and Fairbright we pride our-selves on customizing everything to requirement,' Mrs Smale enthused. As the smell of her cabbagy breath wafted towards them, Merry and Freckles turned their heads.

'Do you think we should say something?' Merry whispered. 'I mean, it could be very un-pleasant for the clients.'

'Miss Dyer, if I have to reprimand you one more time for talking, you will find yourself in serious trouble,' the manageress hissed.

'There's your answer, girl,' Freckles whispered. 'It is up to us to show clients the full range of our stock, advising what to put with what, although, of course, it will be me who will be actually attending, unless I am busy, in which case that honour falls to Mrs Rose. You will observe closely and learn. Perhaps, Mrs Rose, you will demonstrate what colour ribbon would best adorn this bonnet,' she said, indicating a straw example on the nearby block.

'Um, well...' the woman dithered as her hand ran over the reels.

'Really, Mrs Rose, we don't have all day. In fact, we have precisely fifteen minutes before the store is due to reopen,' Mrs Smale said, consulting the clock.

'Miss Prim, perhaps you could give us the benefit of your opinion.'

Prunella smiled, plumping for the yellow. Mrs Smale smiled too. 'Perfect, Miss Prim.' Merry frowned. 'You do not agree, Miss Dyer?'

'Well, it is the safe option but it reminds me of an Easter bonnet. Surely with the sun being higher in the sky now, a stronger colour would be more exciting.'

'Exciting, Miss Dyer?' Mrs Smale enunciated, shaking her head. 'May I remind you we are here to advise the ladies of the environs, not the ... the...'

'Is everything all right, Mrs Smale?' Mr Fairbright asked, appearing by their side.

Immediately the woman broke into a smile. 'Yes, thank you, sir. I'm just giving our trainees their first lesson in advising our clients on their purchases.'

'Excellent. Let us hope the store will be busier

140

this afternoon.'

'I'm sure it will be when word gets round,' Mrs Smale assured him.

'But surely...' Merry began, only to receive a glare from the manageress.

'You were saying, Miss Dyer?' Mr Fairbright asked.

'I'm sure you are too busy to worry about the thoughts of an inexperienced trainee,' Mrs Smale jumped in.

'Indeed I am not,' the man said. 'If we are to succeed then input from everyone is invaluable, especially in these early days. Miss Dyer?'

The genuine interest in his eyes gave Merry the confidence to continue.

'It was just that you said about us being busy when word got round – well, shouldn't our opening have already been broadcast?'

'That's right,' Freckles cried. 'Me da says you couldn't even sell the Queen's jewels if nobody knows you got them.'

'Really, Miss Brice, that's quite enough,' the manageress cut in.

'You have hit the proverbial nail on the head, Miss Dyer. We have been so busy preparing our store for the opening we have quite neglected to advertise the fact. Well done, girls. I can see Didcot and Fairbright are going to benefit from having bright young things like you in our employ. Now please excuse me.'

He strode away, leaving Mrs Smale gaping in her guppy-like way after him.

Chapter 14

As the manageress turned to face them, Merry saw her cheeks were bright red but Freckles was shaking her head in disbelief.

'Blimey oh rimey, fancy him listening to us,' she muttered.

'If you hadn't interrupted our conversation in such a rude manner, you would have realized I was about to draw our esteemed employer's attention to the fact we needed to publicize our existence,' Mrs Smale snapped. 'It is now almost two o'clock and time for the store to reopen. As you have wasted valuable training time you will remain behind this evening for an extra thirty minutes.'

'But that will make us late for supper,' Freckles wailed.

'You should have thought of that, Miss Brice. It is my duty to instil politeness and decorum into my staff and that I fully intend to do, however long it may take.'

'But we were responding to Mr Fairbright's question,' Merry protested.

'You seem to be getting ideas above your station, Miss Dyer,' Mrs Smale hissed, her eyes glittering. 'You may care to remember it is my commendation you require if you wish to pass your probation and so far you do not have it.'

'But I...' Merry began. The manageress held up

her hand.

'I have heard quite enough. In the process of trying to impress our employer, you forgot the first rule of your training. Your duty is to shadow, not speak. Should you have anything of worth to communicate, it is to be relayed through myself. Do I make myself clear?'

Seeing further protest was useless, Merry swallowed down her retort and nodded.

'Blimey oh rimey, girl, she's got it in for you good and proper,' Freckles murmured as they hurried to the staff-room that evening. It had certainly been a long afternoon, for nothing Merry had done had met with Mrs Smale's approval.

'Well, hello there, girls,' Chester said, looking up from his supper as they entered the staff-room. 'You're mighty late.'

'We were kept in. Took me back to me school days, I can tell you,' Freckles sighed as she sank onto a chair.

'Sorry we didn't wait, girls,' Teddy added. 'But we were starving after spending the afternoon pounding the streets.'

'You what?' Freckles asked, helping herself to bread and butter.

'Mr Jenkins had us walking all round town wearing placards advertising the store,' Chester said, frowning at Merry. 'You look even paler than usual; you all right?'

'Well...' she began.

'Old Smelly had a right go at her.'

'Like the name,' Teddy grinned at Freckles.

'Well, her breath reeks of old cabbage. Anyway, she really went for Merry just 'cos Fairbright

143

liked her idea of advertising the store's opening.'

'Ah, so we've you to thank for our poor aching feet?' Chester moaned, grimacing at Merry.

'I just said to Mr Fairbright that I thought we needed to let people know we were open.'

'Forget it for now, girl, and get some hot tea down you. That'll make you feel better,' Freckles said, picking up the large brown pot.

As the others bantered and compared notes of their day, Merry sipped the scalding liquid. Why had the manageress taken against her? She'd only been trying to help, and she'd carried out every task she'd been assigned to the best of her ability.

'What do you think, Merry?' She came to with a start to find five faces staring at her expectantly.

'We were planning what to do on our first Sunday off,' Chester explained. Merry stared at her new friends, wondering if she should go home. But it was so far, and she'd only have been away a week. Also, she really didn't want to risk bumping into Nicco.

'After we've been to church, of course,' Prunella added.

'Oh, yes,' Nicholas agreed.

'Or not, as the case may be,' Teddy winked. 'We thought if we chatted nicely to Joanie, she might pack us a picnic.'

'Oh, you did, did you, Master Bear?' the house-keeper said, bustling into the room to clear their plates.

'Your food is the best ever, Joanie,' Chester wheedled, rubbing his stomach appreciatively.

The woman grinned. 'Pleased to hear it, young man, and I'll be pleased to pack a picnic ready

144

for you to collect after morning service,' she said, wagging her finger at him.

'You're a hard task mistress,' he protested.

'But a proper one, young man,' she retorted. 'Now who'd like some bread and butter pudding?'

The rest of the week passed in a whirl. The boys had been sent out again with their placards and, as word spread, the store became busier. Determined not to get on the wrong side of Mrs Smale again, Merry meticulously carried out her duties but she could feel the woman watching her every move. It was a relief to cover the counters and clear the window on Saturday evening.

The sun was hot on their skin, their mood jubilant as the trainees made their way back from church the next morning. Merry inhaled deeply, revelling in the fresh air after having been cooped up indoors all week.

Chester smiled at her. 'Mind all the dust these carriages are stirring up,' he said, gesturing to the Sunday worshippers passing by. 'It's the perfect weather for eating al fresco, though, is it not?'

'Thought we were having a picnic in the park,' Freckles giggled, nudging his arm.

'Al fresco means an informal meal prepared for eating in the open air,' Prunella informed them.

'You are clever, Prunella,' Nicholas said, gazing at her in wonder before looking quickly away.

'We'll go on and collect the food,' Chester said. With whoops of delight, the boys ran ahead, leaving the girls watching after them.

'I think you've got an admirer there, our Pru,'

Freckles commented. 'All Nicholas needs is a bit of encouragement.'

'I don't think so,' Prunella said seriously, not bothering for once to reprimand Freckles for shortening her name. 'My time here is purely a temporary measure while Mother seeks a suitable marriage prospect. She wishes me to marry a duke or, at the very least, a lord in order for me to have a title.'

'Blimey oh rimey,' Freckles muttered, raising her eyebrows at Merry as they approached the store. She hadn't realized before now just how imposing the building was. It was set in a row of large brick houses, most of which now had sizeable shop windows fronting the street. They were about to turn down the path that led to the back yard, when a figure stepped out of the shop doorway.

'Cop a load of that,' Freckles whistled.

As the man came closer Merry's heart flopped.

'Hello, Merry,' Nicco said, his smarmy grin encompassing Freckles and Prunella.

'Nicco, what are you doing here?' she stuttered.

'I've come to see you, of course. A seagull told me it was your day off so I thought we could spend it together. Been waiting ages,' he grumbled.

'Well, we'll leave you to it,' Freckles said. 'Don't want to be goose-gogs, do we, Pru?'

'Oh, don't go...' Merry began, but Nicco took hold of her arm.

'Nice to meet you, ladies, but I'm sure you'll understand I wish to spend time alone with my betrothed.' He pulled Merry towards the donkey and cart, leaving them staring after him in amazement.

'I am not your betrothed,' Merry hissed, pulling her arm away.

'Oh, come on, we told everyone we'd be making it formal at the fair next month. Of course, I hadn't known then that you intended running off to Plymouth. Still, it's obviously something you had to get out of your system. I told Father I'd let you do it then you'd be ready to settle down and be a good wife.'

'Settle down? Be a good wife? Nicco Neaple, you are the most conceited man I've ever had the misfortune to meet.' She was so incensed she didn't notice the little group of Sunday worshippers gathered close by, watching in amazement.

'Come along, you're creating a scene,' he said, taking her arm again.

Angrily, she shook him off. 'Look, Nicco, let's get one thing straight...' she began.

'Stop making an exhibition of yourself. Get into the cart and we'll go somewhere more private,' he insisted. 'Then we'll talk.'

She narrowed her eyes and stared at him. 'Only if you promise to listen to what I have to say.'

'Yes, yes, but do hurry up,' he said, already gathering up the reins.

Knowing she needed to sort things out once and for all, Merry reluctantly climbed up beside him. He urged the donkey on and guided them through the bustling crowds until they came to a quieter street with tall houses on one side, an imposing pillared stone theatre and open parkland on the other.

As her body settled into the rocking rhythm, she found herself beginning to calm down. She'd never been to this part of the town before and watched in awe as they passed by a busy railway station and goods yard, with smoke and steam belching from sooty black trains, which shunted back and forth, clanging and hissing as they went.

Climbing higher up the cliff road, she stared down at the harbour where dozens of masts swayed in the breeze and men scurried around unloading crates and barrels onto the quays. Even from here she could see these boats were larger than the luggers that ferried goods into Porthsallos. Then the cart turned a corner and she could see the open sea shimmering in the distance. Her spirits lifted and she inhaled the salty air greedily. Noticing, Nicco smiled and patted her arm.

'You might have moved away from the sea but it's still inside you,' he declared. Although what he said was true, she wasn't about to admit it. She'd enjoy the ride, but when he stopped she needed to explain once and for all that she had no intention of marrying anyone, ever.

Then she realized he'd pulled up at a green beside a tea room with tables and chairs overlooking the Hoe and the sea beyond. Jumping down, he tethered the donkey through the railings, then immediately put out his hand.

'Come on,' he said. Not wishing to make a fuss, Merry allowed him to help her down from the cart.

She noticed the people already seated were smartly dressed, and was glad she was wearing her Sunday best although she had to admit it was looking slightly the worse for wear now. Soon she'd be able to buy some material and run up a new dress, she thought, her spirits rising.

'It's a bit early for supper,' Nicco said. 'There-fore I intend making my declaration over lunch-eon.'

Merry's eyes widened in horror and, as if the sun had fallen from the sky, she shivered.

'Please don't, Nicco,' she whispered. 'I really need to talk to you...' She stuttered to a halt as a shadow fell over them.

'You wish to order, sir?' the waiter asked.

'Just a lemonade for me, please,' Merry said quickly.

'Ah, yes, you are playing hard to get,' Nicco grinned at her. 'That's fine. I will bide my time. Two glasses of lemonade, please, waiter.'

They sat looking out over the water until their drinks were placed before them.

'Here's to us,' Nicco said, raising his glass to hers.

'Look, Nicco...'

'I couldn't believe it when I called to collect you from Fairbright's, only to learn you'd travelled back to Porthsallos with him.'

Merry stared at him in surprise. 'You went to Mr Fairbright's?'

'Indeed I did. I had intended taking you to Ply-mouth as usual but Father had things he wished to discuss at the pallace and kept me later than I'd anticipated. Heard you'd travelled by carter with that Otto,' he muttered, scowling into his glass.

She was about to say he was a good man then thought better of it. It wouldn't do to rile Nicco.

'I had to keep my appointment, Nicco. Mother and Grozen rely on me.'

'I'm glad you realize that. They both send you their regards and hope you'll pay them a visit soon.'

'You make it sound as if I've been away ages,' she sighed, picking up her drink.

'It feels that way to me,' he replied, giving her a sombre look. Quickly, she stared out over the sea. She refused to be blackmailed. 'Anyway, I took the pony and trap and rode like the wind in order to bring you back from Plymouth. You'd already left, though, and that Brown woman told me you'd used your charms to secure this job...'

'What!' Merry spluttered, banging her glass down on the table so that the people seated at the next table turned to look. 'Look, Nicco, I got the job fair and square,' she hissed. 'I had to attend an interview, answer mathematical questions and then, and only then, was I offered the job.'

He shrugged. 'It is of no consequence, Merry.'

She stared at him in disbelief. 'Clearly you have no idea how I feel, Nicco. But then it's always been about you and what you want, hasn't it? This is the best opportunity I've ever been offered and I intend to make the most of it,' she retorted, jumping to her feet.

Dashing away her angry tears, she hurried off. Really he was the most arrogant man, and who did that Miss Brown think she was? Using her charms, indeed! Why didn't anyone credit her with any intelligence? Hearing footsteps behind, she quickened her pace but it wasn't long before Nicco caught up with her.

'That's what I love about you, Merry,' he chuckled, falling into step beside her.

'What, my wish for independence?' she asked, hope rising that perhaps he did understand after all. When he didn't answer she turned to face him. He was staring out over the water.

'See all those sparkles?' he said, his voice low. 'They're just like the diamonds I want to give you.'

'Oh, Nicco,' she groaned. 'Look, I really do like you but I don't want to marry you – or anyone, come to that.'

He sighed and was quiet. 'It's this job, isn't it?' he asked finally.

'That's part of it, yes,' she admitted. 'I need to prove to myself that I can do it, Nicco, and I really want you to understand.' He nodded and her heart lifted.

'Well, Nicco is nothing if not fair. You may stay in this little job. I shall bide my time until you've got it out of your system. Then we shall marry.'

'No!' she gasped. 'That's not what I meant at all. You must understand...'

'I will tell everyone back home we have decided on a year's betrothal and that we'll marry come the fair next year,' he butted in.

Merry opened her mouth to protest then closed it again. He would never listen so what was the point?

'I'd better be getting back; the others will wonder where I've got to,' she said quickly.

'Don't think I'll forget this conversation, Merry. I will make my formal declaration in one year from now.'

Merry relaxed back into her seat as they made the journey back to the store in silence. A year was an age and anything could happen during that time.

'I'll come and see you next Sunday,' he said, pulling on the reins as they drew up outside the store.

'No, don't do that. Everything's new here and I need to spend time with the other assistants,' she said, quickly climbing down. 'Give my love to Mother and Grozen and tell them I'll make the journey home to see them before long.' He opened his mouth to reply but, not wishing to hear any more, she turned, ran down the path to the yard and fled inside.

Closing the heavy door with a sense of relief, she leaned against it and breathed in deeply. Would Nicco never get the message? While she intended going home in the near future, he needn't know that, need he?

Chapter 15

'Surely you haven't been out by yourself, Miss Dyer?' Merry looked up to see the manageress frowning at her.

Although it was their day off, the woman was still attired in her black dress and was looking as officious as she did on the shop floor.

'A friend from Porthsallos came to visit, Mrs Smale,' she answered.

'A gentleman, perhaps?'

Merry flushed, uneasy at the gleam that sparked

in the woman's eyes. It reminded her of something, but she couldn't for the life of her remember what.

'Let me remind you that the terms of your employment require permission be granted before you may have a follower.'

'Nicco is not my follower, Mrs Smale. Like I said, he is a friend...'

But the manageress wasn't listening. 'You can be sure this misdemeanour will be marked on your records, Miss Dyer.'

'But I haven't done anything wrong, Mrs Smale,' Merry insisted, but the woman was already marching away.

'Oh rats,' Merry cried, fighting back hot tears as she hurried up the stairs. Sinking onto her bed, she kicked off her shiny shoes then lay back against the pillow and stared up at the skylight. A breeze must have got up; white clouds were scudding across the sky like puffs of cotton wool. What a day, she thought. At least she had a year's grace from Nicco's persistent pestering.

In the meantime, she would concentrate on her job. She loved the smell of the materials, the soft feel of the kid-skin gloves, the glossy sheen of the colourful ribbons. Why, she'd even spotted drawers of worsted wool and would be able to advise the clients on its durability and suitability. If only their manageress hadn't taken against her, she would have been quite happy.

She couldn't help comparing the shrewish woman with her gentle mother, and was seized with a sudden urge to return to Porthsallos and see her. How comforting it would be to feel her mother's arms around her. Even the sharp edge of Grozen's tongue seemed mild next to Mrs Smale's bitter barbs. Merry sighed, knowing she would have to leave it a few weeks so Nicco wouldn't be expecting her. Honestly, where was her courage? She'd spent the past few months dreaming of getting away from the village and here she was, at the first hint of trouble, planning her return.

'Blimey oh rimey, you're a dark horse,' Freckles cried, bursting into the room. 'Or perhaps, with your cloud of white hair, I should say light horse,' she spluttered. 'Fancy you being betrothed and to such a good-looker too. Not that you ain't good-looking yourself, of course. Poor old Chester's gutted so I'll just have to console him...'

'But he's not,' Merry said, raising herself up on her elbow.

'He is, old thing,' Prunella agreed.

'No, I mean Nicco is not my betrothed.' Freckles and Prunella exchanged perplexed glances. 'He might want us to marry but I don't,' Merry explained.

'Is he not eligible material?' Prunella asked.

Despite herself, Merry grinned. 'Nicco is set to inherit the pilchard factory when his father passes on, so in that respect he is very eligible.'

'You mean he's got money as well as looks?' Freckles whistled. 'Blimey, girl, what's your problem?'

'I don't want to get married,' she said.

'You mean never?' Prunella gasped. 'But Mother says that is why we women have been put on this earth, to have...'

'Yes, yes,' Freckles interrupted. 'Here, guess

what: you know Chester said he'd made a bloomer on his first day? Well, he finally got round to telling us what it was. Oh, this will make you laugh. He was shadowing Perkins up in the tailor's room when the client was asked which side he dressed. Anyway, Chester, bless him, said he couldn't understand why it should make a difference which side of the room he stood,' she shrieked. 'What a wheeze, eh?'

'Sorry, I'm not sure I understand,' Merry said.

'No, I didn't. And it's really quite shocking,' Prunella gasped.

'Oh, for heaven's sake, I reckon you two have only just crawled out from under your gooseberry bushes. It means which side a man has his equipment in his trousers.'

'Equipment?' Merry frowned.

'Blimey oh rimey have you never seen a naked man?'

'No, of course not,' Merry stuttered, shocked at the notion.

'Well, I shared bath night with me brothers and...' She was interrupted by the clang of the supper gong. 'I'll explain later. Let's go down; I'm famished,' Freckles cried. 'You missed a good picnic. Joanie packed enough for an army but all that fresh air's made me hungry again.'

'I think I'll give supper a miss,' Merry said, unable to face the inevitable questions about her day.

'Do you have a bad head, Merry?' Prunella asked. 'Only I have some smelling salts in my valise.'

Merry smiled. 'That's kind but really I'm not

hungry. I am very tired, though,' she said, yawning as she lay back on her pillow and closed her eyes. Luckily they took the hint and Merry heard the latch click behind them.

The next morning, after they'd dressed the window and removed the dust covers from the counters, Mrs Smale gave them each an appraising look. Mindful of their altercation the previous day, Merry held her breath but the woman nodded.

'Already you are looking more like trainee assistants. It is good to see you have been paying attention to what I've been telling you. Now, before I give you today's lesson, which will be in the art of selecting fabric, our esteemed employer Mr Didcot wishes to have a few words, so please stand to attention,' she commanded.

'Good morning, ladies,' Mr Didcot greeted them, his cane tapping on the stone floor as he crossed the room. 'I have some exciting news I wish to impart. However, before I do, I would like to thank you for all your hard work in helping to get our store up and running. Mr Fairbright and myself are of the firm belief that our enterprise will only be as good as its employees.' As he paused and beamed at them, Mrs Smale began to clap.

'A round of applause for Mr Didcot, ladies.' They duly put their hands together only for him to shake his head.

'Thank you, but that is hardly necessary. Now the reason I am here is to welcome our new dressmaker who is joining us today. You may already know that we have a tailor working above menswear and now we are to be graced with our own lady tailoress. Life is moving on apace and women are now travelling further than they have before. This means they will require suitable attire but have less time to attend dress and hat fittings. As you will already have seen, we have purchased in bonnets and hats in various shapes and sizes, which just need customizing. We have also been fortunate in acquiring beautiful materials, and also dresses that have already been part made.' He paused as they gasped and looked at each other in surprise. Then, smiling knowingly, he continued, 'The idea being, the client will need only one fitting, which can be done on the premises. The item will then be finished and packaged ready for carriage collection.'

'That sounds a brilliant idea, Mr Didcot, but will the nobs wear that, so to speak?' Freckles asked.

Mrs Smale frowned. 'I'm sure Mr Didcot has better things to do than answer your ridiculous questions, Miss Brice.'

'That is quite all right, Mrs Smale, and, as it happens, a very good point, Miss Brice. This is indeed a new venture and we have yet to see if it will become popular. As such, I would request you mention this service to our clients whenever appropriate. Now, I know you have a busy day ahead so I will leave you to it.' As he tapped his way towards the stairs, Mrs Smale turned to address them.

'Right, ladies, you have heard what Mr Didcot has to say about our new service. Now I want you to pay close attention for you are about to receive your first lesson in the art of showing clients the wonderful fabrics and dress lengths we have for sale.' Opening the glass doors of the floor-to-ceiling cupboard, she gestured to the bolts and bales of materials that lined the shelves. They were arranged in their various colours and as she stared at the wonderful array, Merry felt a pang of excitement. At last she was going to learn the secrets of good dressing.

'Mrs Rose, perhaps you would pass me that wonderful sea-green cotton.'

'Oh, um, yes of course, Mrs Smale.' To their surprise the woman stood there, her hand hovering over the various green materials.

'Quickly, Mrs Rose. I really do need to conduct this lesson before the store opens,' the manageress tutted, going over and pulling out the required bolt herself. Freckles nudged Merry's side.

'You'd think she was colour-blind,' she hissed.

'Perhaps she's just nervous,' Merry whispered, seeing how shaken the supervisor looked.

'Now, in order to show the client this wonderful fabric to best effect, rather than spread it along the counter, display it against your body so that she can see how it could look on her,' Mrs Smale continued, holding it against her black dress.

'That is beautiful,' Prunella gasped. 'Imagine having a gown made up in that.'

'And that is precisely the wonderful service the store will offer. Now, in this other cabinet here we have the part-made items Mr Didcot mentioned. It will be our duty to sell the client what they request, whether it be a length of material or one of the unfinished garments, and then escort them upstairs to the dressmaker. As Didcot and Fair-bright is the first store to be offering such a comprehensive service in the town, we have the most marvellous opportunity to make our store a success, which is splendid, is it not?'

'So we sell the client the material or dress length, then take them upstairs to the dress-maker,' Freckles said.

'No, Miss Brice, you do not. Mrs Rose and myself have been trained to carry out these roles. Your duty will be to shadow us, for of course there will be silks to match to the material, buttons to offer for selection and any manner of accessory the client may wish to add. Here at Didcot and Fairbright it is our aim to provide customization.'

'Customization for the customer, that's good,' Freckles laughed.

'Thank you, Miss Brice. Now come over here, all of you, and I'll talk you through all the labels of these wonderful materials. It will sound more professional if you can refer to them by their name.'

'Here, madam, let me show you our Peter and this is our Paul,' Freckles gushed. Merry couldn't help giggling but luckily the manageress was so enthralled by her task, she didn't hear.

As word of the new service spread, the store be-came busy and Merry marvelled at the well-dressed ladies who came in requesting to be shown the merchandise. Now, as instructed, they were lined up behind the counter waiting to be called on to help.

'That's what we're like,' Freckles muttered,

jerking her head to a servant hovering patiently behind her mistress. 'Shadows be blowed; servants more like.'

'Do I have to wait all day for assistance, Miss Brice?' Mrs Smale called, sending a withering glance their way.

'Coming, Mrs Smale,' Freckles cried. 'Immediately, Mrs Smale, at your beck and call, Mrs Smale,' she added in such a low voice only Merry heard.

Merry stared around as she waited to be summoned. There was a buzz of excitement about the place that morning as women marvelled at the hats displayed on their blocks, felt the lengths of materials swathed around the dummies, then pointed to the reticules artistically displayed along the shelves behind the counters.

'If their quality is up to scratch it will save me from having to make the tiresome trip to the capital each season,' one woman declared, as she stopped and held up her lorgnette to inspect the bales of materials displayed behind the counter.

'It will indeed be a blessing,' her companion agreed. 'Although whether they will stock the latest mode, remains to be seen.'

'Well, I've heard they have a dressmaker on the premises...' Their voices became inaudible as they moved further down the store. Then Merry noticed a familiar figure enter the store. It was Lady Sutherland, the lady from the granite house in Porthsallos. She was immaculately dressed as ever, and Merry watched in fascination as she seemed to glide across the floor. How lovely to be so elegant, so poised, she thought as the lady approached the counter.

'Excuse me, my dear,' she said, stopping in front of Merry.

'How may I help you, madam?' Merry asked politely, trying to quell her nerves.

'I just wondered if there was something wrong. Has my hat pin dislodged or has perchance a smut from the dusty road outside landed upon my face?'

Merry's eyes widened in horror. 'Oh, no, madam, please forgive me for staring. It's just that I have seen you in Porthsallos.'

The woman peered closer. 'Ah, yes, the girl with the beautiful white hair – I, too, have seen you.'

'May I be of assistance, modam?' Mrs Smale asked, frowning at Merry as she hurried across the room. 'Please forgive Miss Dyer for not showing you any of our merchandise. She is but a trainee assistant and...'

'She is looking after me perfectly well, thank you. As I was saying, Miss Dyer, the weather will be changing soon and I am seeking material for my dressmaker to run up a more suitable outfit for the autumn. Perhaps you could advise something appropriate?'

'Please allow me, modam,' Mrs Smale simpered. 'I am Mrs Smale, the manageress here.'

'Really?' Lady Sutherland replied, her lips twitching in amusement. 'Then perhaps you could give me the benefit of your expert opinion.'

'Of course, modam. I feel the sea green would be perfect. Miss Dyer, please hand me the sea-green wool crepe.'

161

Merry looked at the woman and frowned. Surely with those hazel eyes and dark hair that colour would be too cool against her skin.

'But...' she began.

'Now, Miss Dyer, I'm sure our esteemed client doesn't have all day.'

'Indeed I do not, which is why it will be such a help having the benefit of your expert advice,' the woman said.

'Thank you, modam. Now, Miss Dyer, perhaps you could display the material as I demonstrated.'

Merry held the material up against her dress and turned this way and that so the woman could get the full effect.

'It is indeed a wonderful colour but would you think it right for me, my dear?'

As Lady Sutherland turned the full force of her amused glance on Merry, she felt obliged to shake her head.

Chapter 16

'Then perhaps you would be so kind as to show me what you consider would be suitable, my dear?' Feeling the manageress bristle, Merry turned towards her.

'Do as the client requests, Miss Dyer,' she ordered in a tight voice.

Merry nodded and, turning back to the materials, selected a heavier fabric in a darker pine green. As she held it up against her, Lady Sutherland nodded.

'That would indeed make a beautiful skirt. And can you recommend material for a blouse to go with it?' Ignoring the manageress's sharp intake of breath, Merry turned and selected a bolt of cream silk then displayed it against herself. 'Perfect. Now, buttons, I think.'

'Whilst Miss Dyer is selecting some in pearl, may I take this opportunity to advise you that we have our own dressmaker on the premises. I would be happy to take you upstairs to meet her and discuss your requirements,' Mrs Smale gushed.

'Surely you weren't about to suggest pearl buttons, Miss Dyer?' Lady Sutherland asked, putting her hand to her mouth in horror.

Merry had to stifle a giggle for the woman was clearly enjoying herself. 'Well, actually no, I wasn't,' she replied.

'Thank heavens, for I cannot abide them; they remind me of my grandmother's blouses. I will leave the choice to you, Miss Dyer; you obviously have good taste.' Lady Sutherland smiled at Merry before turning to Mrs Smale. 'One cannot beat the enthusiasm of youth. They see things with such a fresh eye, don't they?'

'Indeed, modam,' Mrs Smale said stiffly. 'Although personally speaking I feel experience counts for more. Now I was telling you about our new dressmaker and you will be delighted to hear about our new service. We are proud to be the first store in the area to offer part-made items of clothing. They require only one fitting, which I'm sure you will agree will prove invaluable in the saving of your time.'

Lady Sutherland glanced at the clock then shook her head. 'Talking of time, I'm afraid I am running late for my next appointment. However, I will call in another day and ask Miss Dyer to show me what you have to offer. In the meantime, if you could have everything packaged, I will send my driver round to collect them. Thank you for your advice, my dear. You have a very good eye for colour. Good morning to you both.'

The woman had hardly left the store before Mrs Smale rounded on Merry.

'Miss Dyer, may I remind you that I am the manageress of ladieswear and you, as a lowly trainee assistant, are here to do my bidding. In future you will wait until I ask you to assist with a client.'

'But you were serving someone else and...'

'It is not your place to argue with me, Miss Dyer. I would also point out that you failed in your duty to mention our new part-made service. That is a serious omission after Mr Didcot's instruction, and one that will be noted on your records. Now get those items packaged ready for collection,' she ordered.

Merry swallowed hard as the woman strode away across the store. She'd only been trying to help.

'Blimey, she's really got it in for you, girl,' Freckles whispered as she passed by on her way to the stockroom. 'I'd keep my head down if I were you.'

Merry spread out brown paper on the counter, then forcefully cut a length of string, knowing what she'd really like to tie it round. Why shouldn't she help a client if she was asked? And that Lady Sutherland had seemed really nice. Still, Freckles was right: she'd better not give the manageress any further cause for complaint.

'But I expressly asked for crimson ribbon and this is scarlet.'

Merry was brought back to the present by the indignant voice of a client. Mrs Rose was standing beside her looking mortified.

'I do apologize, madam,' the supervisor simpered. Then, seeing Merry watching, she gestured her over. 'Please bring the client the roll of crimson ribbon, Miss Dyer,' she instructed.

'Of course, Mrs Rose,' Merry said, turning and selecting the correct red. This wasn't the first time the woman had picked out something in the wrong colour and Merry couldn't understand how anybody could make such an elementary mistake.

'Yes, that's the one,' the client nodded as Merry held out the roll for her to inspect. 'I would like a yard, please.' As she carefully measured the ribbon against the rule, the client scanned the rolls of ribbon before turning back to Mrs Rose. 'I will also take a yard of the emerald, I think.' Mrs Rose gaped at the various rolls of green. 'Today, if you please. I don't have time to waste,' the client snapped, making the supervisor jump so that the roll she'd just selected clattered to the floor.

'Oh, no,' the supervisor gasped, putting her hand to her mouth.

'That was the wrong green anyway,' the client rebuked, clicking her tongue.

Swiftly Merry selected the emerald and handed it to Mrs Rose. She was about to retrieve the roll when Mrs Smale appeared at her side.

'It is unforgivable to drop the merchandise on the floor, Miss Dyer. You will remain behind when the store closes for luncheon and explain yourself. Now get this tidied up immediately. I do apologize, modam,' she said, turning to the client, who was shaking her head.

'Yes, that was most careless of you, Miss Dyer, get this tidied up immediately,' Mrs Rose echoed. Merry stared at the woman in disbelief until she flushed a dull red and turned away. With great difficulty Merry fought down a retort, then bent and retrieved the ribbon. If that was how she wanted to play it, so be it. Merry wouldn't be helping her again.

'Blimey, that weren't fair. It's just not your day, is it?' Freckles said, crouching down beside her.

'I know,' Merry sighed.

'Miss Brice, return to your station at once,' Mrs Smale snapped.

'I'm only helping Merry to roll up the ribbon,' Freckles began but the manageress's eyes narrowed. 'Since you are so keen to help your friend, you may remain behind with her at noon. Miss Prim,' she called to the girl, who was returning from the stockroom. 'Please assist Mrs Rose by wrapping her client's purchases.'

Merry duly tidied away the ribbon, then noticed an elderly lady hovering by the drawers containing hanks of wool. She glanced around but Prunella was still assisting Mrs Rose, and of Mrs Smale there was no sign.

'Can I help you, madam?' she asked, hurrying over.

'I do hope so, dear. Mother asked me to buy her some wool. She doesn't get out much and knitting keeps her occupied.'

'What is it she wants to make?' Merry asked politely, taking in the woman's stooped figure and speculating how old her mother must be.

'She wishes to make a scarf,' the woman explained. Merry glanced at the woman, who despite the warm day, was dressed in elegant cashmere, and frowned.

'I can show you the wool we have, but I'm not sure any will really be suitable,' she began, placing a drawer on the counter.

'Oh, I think this will be perfect,' the woman enthused, picking up a hank of the navy blue.

Merry frowned down at the rough yarn. 'This is worsted wool. It has quite a rough texture due to the tight twist.'

'She makes scarves and mittens for the Missions to Seamen,' the woman said with a smile.

'Then this will be perfect...' Merry began.

'Good morning, modam, may I be of assistance?' Mrs Smale interrupted, appearing by their side.

'No, thank you. This young lady has already been of great help. I will take six hanks of this yarn you recommend,' she said, turning back to Merry.

'Of, course, madam,' Merry answered as she began counting them out.

'I will issue your receipt, modam,' Mrs Smale simpered.

The woman wrinkled her nose and turned back

to Merry. 'I'm sure this young lady is perfectly capable.' As the manageress stood gaping in her guppy-like manner, Merry had to fight down the urge to laugh.

'Remember you are to see me at noon,' Mrs Smale hissed, before marching over to Mrs Rose.

As soon as the shop bell sounded Mrs Smale turned to Prunella.

'Miss Prim, you have done a good morning's work and may take yourself to the staff-room for some well-deserved luncheon. As for you two–' she glared at Merry and Freckles – 'well, I've never seen such an outrageous performance in all my years.'

'And that's some long time,' Freckles muttered.

'I beg your pardon, Miss Brice,' the manageress gasped.

'I said you are still in your prime, Mrs Smale,' she smiled.

'Hmm,' the woman murmured, eyeing Freckles suspiciously.

'Let's be fair about this, Mrs Smale, it wasn't Merry's fault that ribbon fell on the floor.'

'Oh? Then whose fault was it, pray?'

The girls turned to face the supervisor, who was hovering behind the opposite counter.

'Mrs Rose, can you shed some light on this?' the manageress asked.

'No, I most certainly can not,' she answered piously. 'If you don't need me for anything else, Mrs Smale, I too shall go for my meal.'

'Very well, Mrs Rose,' the manageress sighed. As the woman hurried out of the room, Merry and Freckles exchanged looks of disbelief.

'So you lie as well as drop the store's goods on the floor, Miss Dyer,' the manageress continued, eyes glinting like a cat's.

'I am certainly not a liar, Mrs Smale...'

'Please do not compound the issue, Miss Dyer. You will spend the rest of the break tidying up the drawers of wool. The state you left them in earlier was quite unacceptable.'

Merry opened her mouth to protest but Mrs Smale was already addressing Freckles.

'As for you, Miss Brice, in future you will obey orders and remain at your station until you are called upon to assist. Now I will escort you to the staff-room before we are accused of keeping the assistants from menswear waiting for their meal.'

'Oh, I'm not hungry. I'll stay and help Merry...' Freckles began.

'You most certainly will not, Miss Brice. Come with me.'

Merry watched as the manageress ushered Freckles through the shop, then walked over to the drawers that held the hanks of wool. It was so unfair for she'd been in the middle of tidying them when Mrs Smale had insisted she stop and wrap a client's purchase. As for Mrs Rose, why had she lied like that? Her pulse raced with the unfairness of it all. However, as she began sorting the hanks into their various dye lots, the familiar feel of the yarn was soothing to the touch, and before long her low mood lifted.

'Whatever are you doing, Miss Dyer?' Merry looked up to find Mr Didcot staring at her from the doorway.

'Just tidying the wool away after attending to a

169

client, sir.'

'And did this client purchase any?' he asked politely.

'Six hanks, sir.'

'That's very good. No doubt your knitting expertise helped. I have already heard agreeable things about your service to our clients, young lady. Ah, Mrs Smale,' he said, looking up as the woman bustled into the room, 'I was just commending this young lady on her sales this morning. Her dedication to her job is admirable. However, I do not feel we should impose upon staff during their luncheon break. In future please see that all your assistants repair to the staff-room for their meal. Miss Dyer, you must be hungry so please go down and get yourself something to eat.'

'But I...' Mrs Smale began.

'Thank you, Mrs Smale, that will be all,' he cut in. 'Good afternoon, ladies.' He nodded, then walked smartly on down the corridor, his cane tapping on the flags in his wake.

'I see you have been currying favour yet again, Miss Dyer. Well, don't think it will do you any good for I shall be making a full report of this morning's poor performance on your records,' Mrs Smale spat, her eyes glittering. 'You have ten minutes to eat your meal and then be ready for your briefing. When you return to the shop floor, your behaviour had better be impeccable for you can be sure I shall be watching your every move.'

'Blimey oh rimey, don't tell me you talked old Smelly round?' Freckles remarked as Merry joined her at the table

'No, Mr Didcot insisted I come and have something to eat. Smelly looked about to explode when he told her that she was to ensure we all had our luncheon break.'

'He's a good sausage, is Mr Didcot,' Joanie said, bustling in with a plate of coddled eggs and bread. 'Here, get that down you, dearie; you look as white as my tablecloth.'

'Thank you, Joanie, but I'm not sure I can eat a thing. It seems I've blotted my record good and proper this morning. I don't know what I've done to upset Mrs Smale but she's really got it in for me.'

'Doesn't take a genius to work out why, dearie,' Joanie said. Merry looked at her in surprise. 'She had your job lined up for her niece.'

'Her niece?' Freckles said.

'Yes, Miss Brown, she's called. Works for Mr Fairbright in his wool place. Thought she'd have a better future here and asked her aunt to put in a good word for her. Mrs Smale was hopping mad when Mr Fairbright told her they'd offered the position to you.'

Chapter 17

'Well, hello there, you're late today,' said Chester, coming into the room closely followed by Teddy and Nicholas.

'Old Smelly kept us behind,' Freckles groaned. 'She's really got it in for Merry. Do you know...' Her voice trailed off as Prunella peered around the door.

'Hurry up, Mrs Rose is waiting to inspect us and give us a lesson in how we should address clients.'

'I'd like to give her a lesson in addressing the truth,' Merry said getting to her feet.

'And give Smelly one in nepo ... nepa ... oh, what's it called when you try and use your influence to curry favour for one of your own family?'

'Nepotism,' Nicholas said. 'You must tell us all about it at supper. Meantime, we chaps will try and come up with something,' he added, winking at Teddy.

'Why are you smiling?' Freckles asked as they hurried along the corridor. 'I thought you'd be hopping mad about old Smelly and her niece.'

'I am, but what you said about currying favour has given me an idea,' she whispered as Mrs Rose stood in the doorway glaring at them.

'Hands out,' she ordered as soon as they'd lined up inside the room. 'I trust you have washed those, Miss Brice?'

'Of course, Mrs Rose,' she said. 'First thing this morning,' she added under her breath.

'Yours are as beautiful as ever, Miss Prim,' Mrs Rose said, smiling at Prunella. 'Whilst yours, Miss Dyer, are a great improvement,' she grudgingly admitted. 'Now, we need to address the way in which you are speaking to our clients. From now on, you are to say, "Good morning, madam. My name is Miss Prim, Brice or Dyer–" obviously you will use whichever is appropriate – "how may I be of service?"'

'Blimey oh rimey, that's a mouthful and no

mistake. The client will probably be back outside before we get that lot out,' Freckles giggled.

'Your job is to entice them to stay and buy,' the supervisor sniffed. 'And one must remember the client is always right.'

'What, even if she asks for something that doesn't suit her?' Merry asked.

'Well, one should be diplomatic, of course. A little white lie can hide a multitude of sins, Miss Dyer.'

'Or even a green lie,' Freckles said pointedly.

'I hardly think the colour relevant, Miss Brice,' Mrs Rose said, missing the point. 'It is the principle of the matter. To spare someone's feelings...'

'What, like your lie this morning, Mrs Rose?' Merry couldn't help asking.

The woman turned red. 'I'm sure I don't know what you mean, Miss Dyer,' she spluttered.

'I think you do,' Merry replied. As the woman turned puce, Freckles jumped in.

'You know, Mrs Rose, there are so many different colours in the ribbon and accessory cupboards I've never seen before. In order to provide this good customer service, don't you think you should teach us all their names?'

Mrs Rose waved her hand as though swatting away a troublesome fly. 'We have more important things to address, like acting with decorum. The store should be an oasis of calm for our clients to browse. Now it is time you were back at your stations,' the supervisor said quickly.

When they returned to the shop floor, however, it was anything but calm for Mrs Smale was standing on a chair waving her arms in the air.

'Get that thing out of here, get it away from me,' she screamed. They stared at the usually dignified manageress in amazement.

'Are you all right, Mrs Smale?' Prunella ventured.

'No I am not, you silly girl. Do you think I'm up here for the good of my health? There's a dangerous green thing hopping around all over the place. For goodness' sake, get one of the male assistants to capture it.'

As if on cue, Chester popped his head around the door.

'I heard a scream, is everything all right in here, Mrs Smale?' he asked solicitously, before turning and winking at Merry and Freckles.

'Get rid of that thing immediately,' the woman gasped.

'What thing would that be?' Chester asked.

'The green thing that's been following me all round the room,' she gasped.

'What, you mean that shiny green, helpless little frog?' Chester asked, kneeling down on the floor. Merry and Freckles exchanged a look. A frog?

'Yes, boy, get it out of here.'

'I'll do my best, Mrs Smell, I mean Smale,' he said, but the woman was so agitated she didn't notice his intentional play on her name.

'Come along, little frog,' he cooed. 'Oh dear, look it's gone and jumped over there.' They all looked where Chester was pointing but couldn't see anything. 'Stay still, little man, and let Chester take you outside where all good little frogs belong.'

'Must you speak in that silly voice?' the

manageress snapped.

'Indeed, it's the only way to catch them quickly,' he assured her. 'Now, froggy-woggy, come here. Can't you see you're upsetting the lady?' As Chester crawled around the room on his hands and knees, Merry and Freckles shook with laughter. It was obvious he was tormenting the manageress by taking his time. It was only when Mr Jenkins appeared that he finally pounced and scooped the frog up.

'There, all safe now,' Chester said, holding his hands up to Mrs Smale, who recoiled so quickly she nearly toppled from the chair.

'Please get that thing out of here at once,' she gasped.

'I'll just take this little fellow out to the yard, Mr Jenkins, then I'll be back on the shop floor,' he announced.

'Be quick about it, Hall. Allow me to help you, Mrs Smale,' Mr Jenkins said, holding out his hand.

'Thank you, Mr Jenkins,' she said, clambering down, just as the first customer of the afternoon pushed her way through the door. 'To your stations, ladies,' she ordered, patting her hair and smoothing down the skirts of her dress. 'I am in dire need of my smelling salts so please take over, Mrs Rose.'

'Wonder where it came from?' Merry said.

'How it got in here, more like,' Freckles grinned.

'Poor Mrs Smale,' Prunella commented. 'She looks quite shaken.'

'I wouldn't waste your sympathy on that old crone,' Freckles commented. 'After the way she treated Merry this morning, she deserves all she gets.'

Mrs Smale didn't return to the floor and in her absence Mrs Rose seemed to flounder, but luckily there were only a handful of clients that afternoon.

By early evening the store was quiet, and the trainees had just begun tidying away when a woman of middle years entered the store. She looked around for a moment before making a beeline for Mrs Rose. The supervisor seemed to freeze and when she didn't say anything, Merry stepped forward.

'Good evening, madam,' she said. 'My name is Miss Dyer. How may I be of service?'

'Goodness me, do you have to say all that to everyone who comes in?' the woman exclaimed.

'It's what our manageress has decreed,' Mrs Rose said, finding her voice at last.

'Hmm. Well, as you asked so nicely, please can you show me your ready-made undergarments?' the woman said, addressing Merry.

'Yes of course, madam,' Merry replied, looking to Mrs Rose for direction, but the woman had turned scarlet and was looking down at the floor. 'Please follow me, madam,' she said, leading the client over to the cupboard in the far corner.

'I will attend to madam,' Mrs Rose squeaked, finally finding her voice. 'You will shadow me, Miss Dyer.'

The client raised her brows, then shrugged. 'I am staying with my aunt and find myself short of bloomers,' she said. 'She, of course, still wears those dreadful pull and tie corsets that suck the life out of you but I prefer something more comfortable.'

'I'll show you what we have in stock,' the supervisor whispered.

'You'll have to speak up, woman. I was struck down with a dreadful infection last winter. Confounded nuisance, it was, and it's left me partially deaf. Now I can only hear clear voices, like that young lady behind you has, so it would be better if she attends to me.'

'As you wish, madam,' Mrs Rose said. 'Miss Dyer, please will you show madam the bloomers we have in stock? Discreetly, of course,' she added, lowering her voice and staring around in case they were being watched. Merry nodded and pulled open the heavy door to the cupboard. Quickly she assessed the woman for likely sizing, then unwrapped various packets and placed a few pairs on the counter for her to inspect.

'Please direct madam to the dressing room, Miss Dyer. You simply cannot display them here for all to see,' Mrs Rose spluttered.

Merry looked around the empty store.

'What is she saying?' the client asked.

'Mrs Rose thinks it would be more discreet to go to the dressing room.'

'Piffle,' the woman scoffed. 'Please tell her we are now in the eighteen eighties, a time of greater enlightenment. Really, I can't be doing with a draper's store assistant being so prudish. Now let me have a look at these.' The woman sorted through the underclothes then held a pair to the light to inspect them further. Behind her Mrs Rose give a strangled gasp and Merry had to turn back to the cupboard to hide her smile. She'd never seen some of the garments before and was just trying to make out what some of them could be for when the client spoke.

'I think these will suit perfectly, thank you.' Merry spun round to find the woman consulting the labels. 'I've heard that this Harracks brand is very good so I'll take two pairs please.'

'Certainly, madam. I'll wrap them for you straight away,' Merry said.

'I expect you would like them on approbation, madam?' Mrs Rose enquired.

'No, I would like them on my posterior,' the woman hooted.

Merry felt her lips twitching. How lovely to serve a woman with a sense of humour.

'Quite. I'll leave you with Miss Dyer,' Mrs Rose squeaked, before scuttling to the other side of the room.

The woman watched then shook her head. 'You wouldn't think we all wear these, would you, my dear?'

Merry smiled politely as she gently smoothed out the silky garments. If only she had the chance to wear such finery, she thought.

'Here you are, madam. I hope you find them comfortable. May I wish you a good evening and hope we will see you in our store again soon,' she said, handing the woman her parcel.

'Thank you, my dear,' she smiled at Merry. 'I am sure you will.'

'Blimey oh rimey, what a day,' Freckles muttered as they took their seats in the staff-room that evening. 'You should have seen old Rose's face when you thanked that woman for her custom and said you hoped she'd find her purchases comfortable. She scuttled over and shut that cupboard as if she was afraid all the undergarments would jump out and do a jig around the shop.'

'I know. It's ridiculous the way she talks about under-things in hushed tones. The client thought her quite old-fashioned,' Merry agreed.

'Mother always says such things should never be discussed in public,' Prunella said. Freckles raised her brows at Merry, then smiled as the boys clattered into the room. 'And certainly never in front of a male,' Prunella added.

'Well, hello there,' Chester greeted them. 'How was your afternoon? Did Smelly recover from her shock?'

'I really don't think you should refer to Mrs Smale like that. She is our manageress, after all,' Prunella said.

'I agree; a little respect goes a long way,' Nicholas agreed, smiling at her over the table.

'Well, she was hopping mad earlier, wasn't she?' Chester hooted.

'I wonder where that frog came from,' Freckles said, staring straight at him.

'I wonder,' he said, tapping the side of his nose. 'Especially one that hopped all round her like that.'

'Did you release it out in the yard?' Merry asked.

'Let's just say it's back where it belongs,' he chuckled.

'Let's hope it stays there,' Prunella said, shuddering.

'Oh, it will,' Joanie said, coming into the room with a pot of tea. 'Unless Mr Jenkins decides to check your work clothes, Master Hall.'

'I'm sure I don't know what you mean, Joanie,' he said, pretending to look hurt.

'Well, that green head poking out of your back pocket is a bit of a giveaway,' she chuckled. 'I'll go and get your supper.'

'You'd better come clean, Chester,' Freckles demanded.

Grinning, he put his hand in his pocket and drew out a toy frog. 'Thought my little friend here might come in useful one day.'

'But that's a tin model and Mrs Smale said it was jumping all round the room,' Merry pointed out.

'Oh, I get it, you were just pretending to chase after it, weren't you?' Freckles cried. 'And that soppy voice you were using. "Here froggy-woggy" – oh, that was priceless.'

'Well, the old bat needed teaching a lesson for picking on Merry like that,' he said, staring intently at her.

'Wish you'd stick up for me like that,' Freckles sighed.

'You can look after yourself well enough,' he scoffed. 'Whilst others bring out my protective side.' He gazed at Merry across the table, his meaning clear.

Chapter 18

Just then Joanie clattered through the door with a loaded tray, and as Chester jumped up to help her, Merry breathed a sigh of relief.

'Lucky duck,' Freckles whispered, digging Merry in the ribs.

'Don't be silly,' she replied. After Nicco, the last thing she wanted was any involvement, especially with someone at work.

'That smells wonderful, Joanie,' Chester enthused.

The woman beamed. 'It's my special rabbit casserole and there's jam roly-poly to follow.'

'Yum, yum,' Teddy said, rubbing his stomach in appreciation.

Eagerly they tucked in and the room fell silent apart from the scrape of cutlery on china.

'My, that Joanie can cook,' Chester said, putting down his knife and fork. 'The girl I marry will have to produce meals just like that.'

'Oh,' Freckles said, looking crestfallen. 'Me da says he'd rather eat in the alehouse than suffer one of my attempts. I suppose you can cook?' she asked Merry.

'Yes, Mother and I take it in turns. At least, we did when I was at home.'

'We had a cook,' Prunella sighed. 'Mother would never dirty her hands in the kitchen.'

'Horses for courses, dear,' Joanie said, as she

reappeared and began collecting up their plates.

'Oh, we never had horse, Joanie,' Prunella said with a shudder.

The others raised their brows but Joanie smiled. 'I'm sure you never did, dearie. I'll get your pudding.'

'What did you eat, then?' Nicholas asked.

'Father had a fondness for game,' she said.

'And woodcock perhaps?' Chester enquired.

'Probably; why?' Prunella frowned.

'Well, I've heard they're a delicacy, especially when cooked with their innards intact.'

'Oh...' she shuddered again.

'What was that you were saying earlier about nepotism?' Teddy asked quickly.

'I'd forgotten about that,' Freckles said. 'We couldn't figure out why Smelly had it in for Merry, like that. Anyway, it seems Merry got the job she wanted for Miss Brown, her niece. Isn't that right, Joanie?' she asked, as the housekeeper set their dishes of pudding before them.

'It certainly is. She had a right go at Mr Fairbright. Tried to get him to change his mind but he said Merry was more suitable for the position and his decision stood. I think Mr Didcot only agreed to employ Mrs Rose to keep her sweet. The women share a bedsitter, you see,' she winked. 'Well, I'll leave you to it.'

'Blimey oh rimey, the mind boggles,' Freckles whistled.

'I suppose it makes sense for them to share if they work together,' Prunella said. 'After all, they're both called "Mrs" so they're probably widows.'

Freckles raised her brows and shook her head.

'It's half-day closing tomorrow,' Chester said, endeavouring to keep a straight face. 'We've had more clients this week so it will be interesting to see how much carriage trade there'll be after luncheon.'

'I do hope I don't have to attend to one of Mother's friends' servants. That would be simply dreadful,' Prunella gasped.

'It'll make a change from having to suck up to the snobs,' Freckles pointed out.

'And it'll break up the week,' Teddy added.

'Shall we make plans for after church on Sunday?' Chester suggested 'What do you say to us all taking a ride on the horse tram?' He included them all in the invitation, but it was Merry his gaze rested on.

'We can pretend we're toffs on a sightseeing trip,' Freckles jumped in, oblivious. 'What do you think, Merry? Fancy a ride around the town?'

Merry's heart flipped. Would she?

Dressed in their best clothes, they waited excitedly by the Clock Tower for the tram. Prunella was looking so smart in her new season's attire that Merry felt quite the poor relation. Staring down at the old dress that barely fitted, she knew she'd have to purchase material and make a new one. She wondered if she might even use one of the new patterns the store sold. All thought of clothes disappeared when they heard the clip-clopping of horses rounding the corner.

'We girls can sit at the front, then I can point out the sights to you two country bumpkins.'

Freckles laughed. Chester looked momentarily deflated then smiled.

Merry gazed around at the tall brick warehouses, then the shops with their ornate frontages and striped blinds, which lined both sides of the wide street. She was staring down on the people bustling past at street level when Freckles gave her a nudge.

'Now we know how one feels driving along in one's carriage, staring down at the *hoi polloi*,' she said in a fair imitation of Prunella. They hooted with laughter and even Prunella smiled.

'What's that?' Merry gasped, staring at the grey structure they seemed to be approaching at eye level.

'Blimey oh rimey, haven't you ever seen a train?' asked Freckles.

'Not this high up.' Now they were crossing over a wide bridge with the sea on one side and a large lake on the other. As she felt the cool breeze on her face and breathed in the familiar salty tang, her pulses began to race. How she'd missed the briny ocean.

'That was Halfpenny Bridge, and this has all been built for the dockyard,' announced Freckles importantly, but the others took no notice as the tram was pulling to a halt.

As they headed towards the river Chester endeavoured to walk beside Merry but Freckles, not wishing to be left out, linked arms with him. They passed through terraces of old brick houses, which had broken windows hung with scraps of dirty curtains. This was obviously a poorer area of the town and Merry shivered when she saw the skinny cats scavenging for scraps around the bare-footed urchins playing in the gutter. To think she'd thought her cottage in Porthsallos was tiny and run down. Compared to this, it was a palace, and whilst the families were poor they went out of their way to ensure their children had boots on their feet, however worn and handed down they might be. Feelings of guilt curdled in her stomach. No matter how little food they'd had, her mother had always ensured Merry had eaten, whilst Grozen's foraging for wood meant the fire, provided at least some vestige of warmth. How ungrateful they must think her. She mustn't let many weeks go by before she paid them a visit, she vowed.

By tacit consent, they walked quickly on but as they got closer to the huge dockyard, with its wide expanse of water beyond, they noticed a small group of dirty, ragged children following them.

'Whatever do they want?' asked Prunella, nervously pushing her hands further into her pockets.

'Probably never seen anyone like you before,' declared Freckles. 'With that fancy hat and mantle they probably think you're a toff and are hoping you'll throw them a few farthings.' As Prunella visibly shrank, Nicholas smiled reassuringly and moved closer to her.

'Don't worry about them,' said Freckles. 'It's the sailors falling out of the pub on the next corner you need to keep a weather eye out for. This is their entertainment area and they'll think any lady all dolled up like you is fair game.'

'What kind of game?' Prunella squeaked.

185

'Blimey oh rimey; game for a good time, of course.'

'I suddenly feel quite faint,' gasped Prunella.

'Don't worry, old thing, I'll look after you,' Nicholas declared.

'Thank you, Nicholas, but I think I'd like to return to the tram before we are set upon.'

'Suppose we'd better be getting back anyway,' agreed Freckles. 'It's always a bit rowdy down here of a Sunday.'

Merry sighed with relief. There was no way she'd be returning to this Devonport place again.

The weeks sped by. It was one morning towards the end of summer and the girls had cleaned the shop and were setting out the stock ready to dress the bay window as usual.

'Will we be displaying garments for the new season soon?' Merry asked, as she surveyed the straw bonnet, swathe of muslin and white lace gloves on the dummy.

'Hardly, Miss Dyer. Why, it is still summer,' Mrs Smale sniffed.

'Yes, but winter drawers on, as me grandma used to say,' Freckles giggled.

'That's quite enough, Miss Brice,' the woman frowned.

'But surely the clients will want some idea of what we will be stocking for when the weather gets cooler?' Merry persisted.

'May I remind you that you are still a trainee, Miss Dyer?'

'And a very competent one, if I may say.' They spun round to find Mr Fairbright behind them.

'Do forgive me for startling you. You were so en-grossed in your work you didn't hear me approach,' he said.

'Good morning, Mr Fairbright,' Mrs Smale simpered. 'As you can see, I am instructing our trainees in the dressing of the store's models.'

'Indeed, and I am sure you will be giving thought to the new season's stock, which has already been unloaded into the stockrooms. In the meantime, I would like to address you all before the store opens.'

'Please line up in front of Mr Fairbright,' Mrs Smale ordered. 'He wishes to address you.'

As Mrs Rose hurriedly took her place beside the manageress, Mr Fairbright shook his head.

'I think it would be more appropriate to have this meeting in my office, so if you would care to follow me...?' he said, leading the way down the corridor and up the stairs.

'Blimey oh rimey, I hope we're not in trouble,' Freckles whispered as Mr Fairbright took his seat behind the desk, then gestured for them to be seated.

'Right, ladies, it is now some eight weeks since the store opened and whilst Mr Didcot and myself feel things are generally going well, there are some matters we feel need attention. Mr Didcot is, at this very moment, addressing the male employees in the same vein. Right now, first of all, are you all happy in your work?'

The question took them by surprise and there was stunned silence.

'Well, of course we are, Mr Fairbright. I think I can speak for the entire department when I say we are all extremely grateful for the wonderful opportunity you have bestowed upon us. Although I must say, speaking as manageress, some are doing better than others,' Mrs Smale said, narrowing her eyes at Merry.

'Watch out, claws at dawn,' Freckles whispered.

'I entirely agree, Mrs Smale, and that is partly the reason for our meeting. In order to get a fair idea of how everything has been progressing, Mr Didcot and myself have sent friends and family into the store unannounced – incognito, as it were. They all either bought or made enquiries about various items for sale, then, as instructed, made a note of who attended them and the manner in which they had been served. Their findings have been most interesting, to say the least.' Mr Fairbright glanced down at a sheet of paper in front of him. 'Most of you are doing extremely well but I regret to say it is felt one of you will never make the grade and will be leaving us.' There was a collective gasp as they all looked from one to the other. Mrs Smale and Mrs Rose exchanged smug smiles.

'Looks like they know who's going,' Freckles whispered.

'I will be speaking to that member of staff later on,' Mr Fairbright continued.

'If you would rather I did, Mr Fairbright...' Mrs Smale began.

'Thank you but no, Mrs Smale. As I said, most of you are doing well and your progress has duly been noted on your record cards. These will, of course, be a contributory factor on whether you are asked to remain in service at the end of your probationary period. Now, before you return downstairs, I have here some caps, which Mr Didcot and I feel will enhance your appearance on the shop floor. Obviously they are black or grey to match your current uniform and I would appreciate it if you would put them on before the store opens for business this morning.'

'You mean Mrs Rose and I will have to wear these caps as well?' the manageress spluttered.

'All members of staff will be required to have their hair covered, Mrs Smale,' he said, taking out his pocket watch and frowning. 'Now if you have no further questions, it is almost time for the store to open.' As they filed out of the room, Mr Fairbright looked directly at Merry.

'I'd be obliged if you would remain behind please, Miss Dyer.'

Chapter 19

Merry felt sick. To be asked to remain behind could only mean one thing. She sneaked a peek at Freckles and saw the same dismay on her friend's face. Mrs Smale smiled smugly as she hovered in the doorway.

'Please close the door behind you, Mrs Smale,' Mr Fairbright said firmly. 'Now, Miss Dyer, I have a note here for you.' As he rustled through the papers on his desk, Merry thought her heart would stop beating. Whatever could she have done to be dismissed?

'Ah, here it is,' the man said, passing her a folded piece of paper.

'But why me?' Merry squeaked. 'I've worked really hard.'

Mr Fairbright frowned. 'Well, it's from your mother so naturally it's for you.'

'My mother?'

'Indeed. When I was in Porthsallos seeing how the ladies were progressing with their knitting, I made a point of telling your mother how well you were doing here. I understand you haven't returned home yet?' He paused and stared at her over his glasses.

Merry swallowed, feeling guilty that despite her intentions she had yet to return.

'I keep meaning to only it's been so busy here during the week. Don't get me wrong, sir, I don't mind hard work, but we only get Sunday off and by the time I've been to church there's not much of the morning left to make the long walk to Porthsallos. I'd only get a few hours at home before I have to turn round and come back...' Her voice tailed off as a picture of her mother and Grozen surfaced.

Mr Fairbright smiled gently. 'I do understand, Miss Dyer, and your hard work has not gone unnoticed. However, family is important, is it not?'

'Yes, sir,' she murmured.

'Now, you will be pleased to know the ladies have produced some excellent frocks with not a hint of damping down to any of them,' he said, his voice lighter now. 'I think our arrangement is going to work well. Everyone seems happy and your mother has agreed to teach some of them

190

the shell design, which has proved so popular. Naturally, they all wanted the opportunity to earn the enhanced rate but I left it to your mother to decide who would be best suited.'

'My mother is sorting that out?' Merry gasped, thinking how she disliked mingling with the others.

'Hmm, quite the businesswoman, she is. I can see where you get your capabilities from, Miss Dyer.'

'Me?' She looked at the man, fearful he was jesting. He stared candidly back.

'I have heard good things about you, Miss Dyer. Apparently you are,' he glanced down at his sheet of paper, 'polite, helpful and not afraid to step in where others fear to tread.'

'Pardon, Mr Fairbright?'

To her surprise the man grinned. 'That formidable cupboard in the corner of ladieswear, which I believe Mrs Rose finds distasteful? I have to confess that was my sister setting the cat among the pigeons,' he grinned.

Merry stared at him in amazement. Surely that loud woman was never his sister?

'She is somewhat of an actress,' he added, as if reading her thoughts.

'I did notice she was friendly compared to some of the clients. I mean, most of them just ask for what they want and barely acknowledge us as people.'

'Such is our lot, Miss Dyer, for we live in a class-based society.'

'But you're one of them, sir, what with this large business and everything,' she commented,

191

then put her hand to her mouth. Hadn't Grozen always told her to think before she spoke?

'And it is because of this business that I am regarded as trade. Now, tell me, Miss Dyer, in your opinion does Mrs Rose contribute to the good running of ladieswear?'

Merry thought of the woman's mistakes with colours, the lies she had told and her general prissy demeanour, but she could hardly mention these to her employer, could she? As she cast around for something to say, he raised his brows.

'Well, I, erm, I mean...' she stuttered to a halt.

'Thank you, Miss Dyer. Although your loyalty is commendable, you have answered my question. Now it's high time you were on the shop floor or Mrs Smale will be wanting me to add another black mark to your record card,' he said, giving Merry such a complicit look she wondered just how much he knew.

'Yes, Mr Fairbright,' she said. He nodded and looked back down at his papers. Knowing she'd been dismissed, she took her leave, but just as she got to the door he gave a little cough.

'Just one more thing, Miss Dyer, I understand your grandmother has a special birthday coming up. I know she would appreciate your paying her a visit and I believe transport may already have been arranged so...' He let his sentence tail off and Merry nodded.

'Oh, yes, I wouldn't miss her birthday, Mr Fairbright,' she assured him, clutching her note tighter. Out in the corridor she let out a sigh of relief, then smiled. Her grandmother deemed all her birthdays special. Suddenly Merry couldn't wait to return and see both her and her mother again. The St Peter's Fair celebrations would be well out of the way and she'd feel comfortable returning to Porthsallos. Putting the note in her pocket to read later, she hurried down the corridor.

As she entered the shop, Freckles came hurrying over, her grey cap slipping on auburn curls.

'Blinking thing. I'll have to find some clips to keep it in place. Are you all right? What happened?' she asked, anxiety showing in her eyes.

'Have you come to collect something, Miss Dyer?' Mrs Smale asked, a grin curling her lips.

'Indeed I have, Mrs Smale.'

'Well, do be quick about it; we have a business to run here.'

'I know, so if you'd kindly hand me my cap I'll put it on ready to serve,' Merry said, giving the woman her brightest smile.

'You mean you are staying?' she spluttered.

'Of course. I have a job to do,' Merry replied, trying not to laugh as the woman gaped at her in amazement.

'You mean Mr Fairbright didn't...? Then who...? Oh, here,' she said, all but throwing the grey cap at Merry.

Luckily the store began to fill up and there was no time for further questioning. Hastily affixing the cap over her coiled braid, Merry smiled at the woman who was waiting to be served.

'How may I be of assistance, modam?' Mrs Smale asked, adopting the hoity-toity voice she reserved for clients.

'I hear you have lengths of material that can be

made into dresses here in the store?'

'We do indeed, modam. What had you in mind?'

'Well, I have noticed the evenings are becoming chilly already so something in a warm fabric, I think.'

'Perhaps you will show modam something suitable, Miss Dyer?' the manageress said, her eyes glittering as she turned to Merry.

'Of course, Mrs Smale,' she answered, trying not to laugh as she opened the cupboard containing the pre-cut materials. 'Would this be suitable, madam?' she asked, displaying a length of dimity against her body as she'd been shown. 'The woven texture gives it a warmer feel without being too heavy.' She heard the manageress's sharp intake of breath but, seeing the client's interest was piqued, she couldn't help adding, 'The stripe adds a certain elegance, don't you think?'

'You know, it does,' the woman nodded. 'And how do I go about getting this made up into a dress?'

'Thank you, Miss Dyer. I will attend to modam now. Our dressmaker is upstairs,' Mrs Smale said, ushering the woman towards the corridor.

'But you'll need the matching thread as well,' Merry began, but she was talking to thin air.

'Do you think I should go after them?' she asked Mrs Rose, who was hovering nearby.

'Certainly not. How many times do we have to tell you that your job is to shadow? Besides, Mrs Smale will soon notice that you have been negligent,' the woman sniffed.

'What?' Merry spluttered, but the woman was already attending to another client and had signalled Prunella to assist.

'Do you think she sucks lemons in her spare time?' Freckles asked, as she returned from the stockroom with a handful of lace-edged handkerchiefs. 'Here, can you imagine blowing your nose on one of these dinky things?'

Merry smiled. It was hard to stay cross with her friend's cheery banter.

'I think they're for show really.'

'You should see the new stock they've just unloaded. There are more of those lengths of fur, and some of the gloves are edged with it as well. Wouldn't mind a pair of them to keep me pinkies warm in the winter. Blimey, look at old Pru sucking up to Mrs Rose.'

Merry glanced over and saw that Prunella was smiling up at the woman and hanging on to her every word.

'She's probably trying to ensure her position is safe,' Merry replied. Then, realizing what she'd said, she put her hand to her mouth.

'So if hers is safe and yours is; that means it's yours truly for the chop,' Freckles sighed.

'I hope not,' Merry said, putting her hand on the girl's arm.

'Why did Fairbright ask you to stay behind...'

'Miss Dyer, come here this instant.' As the manageress's voice cut across the room, Merry sighed.

'Here we go. I'll tell you at luncheon.'

'Blimey oh rimey, am I glad to get this thing off,' Freckles said, as she sank onto her chair in the staff-room. 'Makes me feel like I've got nits,' she

195

added, scratching her head.

'Not over my tablecloth, please, young lady,' Joanie reprimanded as she hurried into the room with bowls of broth.

'Sorry, Joanie,' Freckles said, looking anything but. 'That smells good.'

'You got carrot and potato in that from me old man's allotment. Proud as punch, he is, of his veggies. Cors, Mr Didcot pays a fair price. Where's young Pru?' she asked, looking at the empty chair.

'I don't know,' Merry replied, exchanging a look with Freckles.

'I'd better keep this warm then,' the housekeeper sighed, bustling out of the room with the remaining bowl. Just then Prunella hurried into the room, shaking her head.

'Mrs Rose has been summoned upstairs to Mr Fairbright's office and Mrs Smale went marching up after her. In a right old state, they were. Oh, thank you, Joanie,' she said, as the housekeeper placed her bowl on the table.

'Seems to be a bit of a hoo-ha going on upstairs,' she informed them. 'Neither of them wanted their luncheon so if you girls want seconds let me know.'

'You seemed mighty pally with old Rose earlier,' Freckles said, turning to Prunella. 'What was all that about?'

To their surprise the girl flushed and began sipping her broth with great concentration.

'Secrets, eh?' Freckles persisted. The girl shook her head, then carefully set down her spoon.

'If you must know, she said I was doing extremely well and that if I shadowed her all day, pointing out the colours of the ribbons and cloth, she would ensure it was noted on my records.'

'So she does have a problem,' Freckles muttered.

Merry ran her fingers over her letter. She was dying to read it but realized this wasn't the time. Sighing, she put it back in her pocket.

'Come on, it's time we went out to the yard. Heaven forbid Mrs Rose should find us with sticky fingers at inspection.'

It was Mrs Smale who was waiting for them. Her face was pinched, her lips a tight line.

'I have to inform you that Mrs Rose has left us,' she said. 'Until a replacement is appointed, it will fall to me to inspect you.'

'Why...' Freckles began.

'It is not your place to ask questions, Miss Brice. Although you can be sure I have made my feelings clear to Mr Fairbright. It is time to return to the shop floor,' she added.

'Blimey oh rimey, she must be in a state: she never even checked our hands!' Freckles exclaimed.

With only four of them to attend to the clients, the afternoon passed in a whirl of serving and wrapping. It was only when Merry was undressing for bed and heard the crackle of paper in her pocket that she remembered the note from her mother. Taking it closer to the candle, she squinted at the familiar writing.

Dearest Merry,

I hope this letter finds you well. Mr Fairbright says you

have the makings of a good assistant, which pleases us greatly. We are well here and have mastered that shell pattern of yours. Don't know how you came up with that, but you always did have an eye for these things. Please know, daughter, we are very proud of you.

As you know, it is Grozen's birthday next week and she would so like you to be with her – as would I, of course. Nicco has kindly offered to collect you next Sunday and bring you back to Porthsallos for the day. Mr Fairbright says that will be in order. We miss you and very much look forward to seeing you.

Forever your loving mother,
Karenza

Carefully she blew out the candle and climbed into bed. Staring up at the darkening sky through the little skylight, she couldn't help letting out a heavy sigh. She'd been happy until she read the bit about Nicco collecting her. While it meant she would get to see her mother and Grozen again, would she never be free of him?

'You all right old thing?' Freckles whispered.

'Yes,' she whispered back.

'Don't know why we're whispering,' Freckles laughed, propping herself up on her elbow. 'You can hear old Pru's snores from the yard. Honestly, anything less ladylike I've yet to hear.'

Merry laughed back. Her friend was better than Grozen's tonic tincture.

'So why the sigh?' Freckles persisted. 'I thought you said your mother was inviting you to your grandmother's party. Sounds fun to me.'

'I thought so too until I read that Nicco is

198

collecting me.'

'What, that dark-haired hunk of a man? Coo, I wouldn't say no. Mind you, Chester will be upset; he's got his eye on you. Honestly, some gals have all the luck.' This time it was Freckles who sighed.

Merry lay back on her pillow. Did it really matter if Nicco collected her? She could spend time with her grandmother and mother and then return here to the job she had come to love.

'What a day,' Freckles said, yawning loudly. 'Still, old Rosey had to goesy; now all we have to do is sort out Smelly Smale. Here's to new beginnings, eh, gal?'

'Yes, to new beginnings,' Merry replied.

Chapter 20

Despite her misgivings, Merry was pleased to see Nicco waiting outside the store on the following Sunday. She'd been so excited at the thought of returning home, she hadn't slept a wink. Joanie had insisted she take some of her baking home with her, and Mr Fairbright had allowed her to purchase a gift for Grozen at a very reasonable rate. Carefully she handed her basket to Nicco before climbing up beside him.

'Your transportation awaits, my lady,' Nicco said, giving her his widest grin.

'Thank you, Nicco. It's good of you to come all this way to collect me, and in your best cart too.'

'As I've said before, I'm looking after my future interests. Anyway, I persuaded Father to lend me it along with the fastest horse. Said we wouldn't have time to get there and back otherwise,' he grinned. 'You're looking well, Merry,' he added, looking her up and down appraisingly, then frowning. 'Where's all your beautiful hair gone?'

'I've clipped it back into a chignon. It's all here under my bonnet,' she laughed, patting the knot on the nape of her neck.

'Well, I prefer it when you wear it flowing down your back, and I don't like seeing you in that grey cap thing either,' he grunted, carefully negotiating his way through the Sunday traffic. She was about to mention she had to tie it back under her uniform cap, then thought better of it. He would only moan.

Instead she settled back in her seat and looked around. Already they were passing the theatre, going in the same direction as when they'd ridden out to the Green. However, this time, rather than turning towards the sea, he carried straight on and crossed in front of the railway station, then on behind the wet basin full of boats, which were today quietly moored against the quays. On the other side of the street, set well back, there was a formidable grey stone building in its own grounds.

'That's one of the hospitals,' said Nicco.

'How many do they need?' asked Merry, staring at the huge building in amazement.

'There is a main one further inland, but that one's reserved for the navy.'

Already they had moved on, though, and were now coming up to a junction. As Nicco turned

200

right, Merry could see an inlet to the sea, with a tall-masted black-hulled ship anchored in the Sound, and a grey hulk abandoned on the beach nearby. They came to another junction and this time turned left.

'This is Halfpenny Bridge and that is Devonport,' announced Merry excitedly, ready to tell him about her trip on the tram.

'Yes, I know that,' said Nicco, waving his hand dismissively. 'More importantly we're nearly at the ferry.'

As he clearly wasn't interested in how Merry had come to know the names of the landmarks, she sat back in her seat. If he wanted to be Mr Know-All then so be it.

They made their way onto the ferry in silence but as the chains rattled and it began its journey across the water, Merry felt her excitement mounting. *Home, home, home,* they seemed to clank. It was wonderful to feel the breeze on her face after being cooped up indoors. So much had happened in the past few weeks she felt like a different person from the one who'd left Porthsallos.

'Farthing for them?' Nicco offered.

She shook her head. 'I was just wondering where the past weeks have gone. It seems ages since I left.'

'It is, and you missed the St Peter's Fair,' he grunted. 'The girls were right peeved not to have our betrothal to add to the celebrations. Just wait until next year, I promised them,' he added, looking at her meaningfully.

'Nicco...' she began, but the ferryman appeared beside the cart asking for their fare and he turned away. Just get through the day, she told herself.

As Nicco had the larger cart, they took the higher road to Porthsallos. Staring at the vast expanse of moors gleaming like gold in the distance Merry was reminded of her earlier journey with Otto. His quiet reassurance had given her confidence and she wondered how he was doing. Sighing, she stared at the rows of trees they were passing, hardly able to believe the leaves were already turning russet and orange.

'Your mother's been cleaning and cooking like crazy,' Nicco said, breaking into her thoughts. 'Anyone would think you were coming home to stay.' He turned and gave her one of his intense looks.

'Well, I'm not,' she replied.

'Yet,' he added.

She clenched her hands to stop herself from rising to the bait.

'How are things at the pallace?' she asked, changing the subject.

'Well, of course we're still very busy with the pilchards. I've suggested some new ideas to speed up the operation but Father's seen fit to resist them. Still, he'll retire soon and then I can run it as I wish. Life's moving on and we'll be in danger of falling behind if we don't take some short cuts.'

Merry frowned, not liking the sound of that.

'Are all the girls well?' she asked, her heart lifting at the thought of seeing her friends again.

He nodded. 'They've plenty of work to keep them busy and put money in their pockets. That Fairbright man's paying them a fair rate for their knitting as well so, all in all, everyone's content.

Well, apart from Kelys, who's got her stitches knotted 'cos he's put your mother in charge.' Merry remembered Mr Fairbright remarking on her mother's capabilities. Her gentle mother taking charge of the knitting ladies seemed as likely to Merry as she herself being made manageress of Didcot and Fairbright. She opened her mouth to say as much but Nicco was still carrying on with his tale.

'As for them do-good teetotallers, they only want to turn our inns into temperance establishments. You can imagine what the fishermen think of that. I mean, if a man can't have a pint of ale after he's been grafting at sea then what's the world coming to?'

Not being in the least bit interested in ale, Merry was happy to let him witter on, and as the landscape became familiar, her excitement mounted. Then, almost before she knew it, they were at the turning for Porthsallos and beginning their descent. Already she could see the loom over the harbour, smell the familiar tang of tar and fish, hear the screech of the gulls.

'If you wait while I see to the horse, I'll walk to your cottage with you,' Nicco offered, drawing to a halt by the mill.

'Sorry, Nicco, I'm too impatient to wait. Besides, I want to see my folks first,' she said, jumping down. 'Thanks for the lift. No doubt you will be popping in to give Grozen your birthday wishes and have a piece of cake?'

'I will that, so make sure you save me some,' he said, handing down her basket.

Merry all but flew down the almost deserted

lane. This being the Sabbath, the women were indoors preparing their luncheon. She hoped she'd see them later when they gathered in their usual spot to knit and chat.

'Look what the wind's blown in.'

Merry turned to see Kelys glaring at her from her front doorstep.

'Good morning, Kelys,' she replied, ignoring the woman's hostile manner. 'How are you?'

'I was fine until your mother got ideas above her station. 'Twill be where you get it from.'

'But...' Merry began, but Kelys had stamped indoors, slamming the door behind her.

Remembering Kelys's sharp tongue, Merry ignored the woman's outburst. Turning, she stared around the harbour where the fishing boats were all tied up for the day, for no self-respecting fisherman would risk incurring the wrath of God by putting out to sea on the Sabbath. No doubt they would all be in one of the alehouses supping their pints while they waited for their midday meal. Automatically, she glanced up at the house on the cliff and smiled. It was hard to believe she'd actually spoken to the elegant Lady Sutherland, whom she'd long admired. Turning into the warren, she heard a squeal of delight and her heart skipped when she saw her mother waiting in the doorway.

'Here she is, Mother,' Karenza cried, throwing her arms around Merry and hugging her tightly. Enveloped in her mother's warmth, Merry had to blink back the tears that sprang to her eyes.

'Well, aren't I allowed in?' she asked finally.

'Of course,' her mother laughed, reluctantly

letting her go.

'Well, look what the tide's brought in,' Grozen called from her chair.

'Oh, it's so good to see you,' Merry cried, flying across the room and kissing the woman's papery cheek. 'Birthdays greetings for tomorrow, Grozen,' she added.

'No need to remind me I'll be a year older, I'm sure,' her grandmother grumbled, but the warmth in her eyes belied her blunt words.

Merry sniffed the savoury aroma that was filling the little room appreciatively. 'Something smells good. That reminds me, Joanie, the house-keeper, sent some of her baking for you both,' she said, lifting the cloth from her basket and drawing out an iced fruitcake on a plate, and ginger biscuits wrapped in greased paper.

'My, my,' Grozen gasped. 'No wonder you've filled out, our Merryn, if you've been eating rich food like that.' Merry stared down at her Sunday dress, which was straining at the seams, and grimaced.

'Don't tease the girl,' her mother chided, her little blue necklace swinging back and forth as she shook her finger at the older woman. 'It's good to see you looking so well, dear. Now take off your bonnet and make yourself comfortable while I make a brew to keep us going till luncheon. The kettle's on the boil.'

Merry smiled: when wasn't it?

'Is Nicco not with you?' Karenza asked, staring over Merry's shoulder as if expecting him to materialize.

'He'll be down later to wish you happy birthday,

Grozen. I promised him a piece of your cake.'

'I should hope so, after him making that journey to collect you,' Grozen muttered. 'He's a good boy, popping in like he has with news of your progress.'

'I've only seen him once since I began work, Grozen,' Merry pointed out. She was so busy looking around the familiar room that she didn't notice her mother and grandmother exchanging knowing looks.

'Don't do to keep him waiting for too long. There's plenty keen to jump in your shoes,' Grozen sniffed.

Not wanting to argue with her grandmother, Merry changed the subject.

'Tell me how things are here. Mr Fairbright said he was pleased with the knitting you are producing and the way you have mastered the shell pattern.'

'Fancy stitches. Don't know what was wrong with the pattern you always knitted before,' Grozen muttered.

Karenza smiled. 'Don't go on, Mother; our Merry's always been creative. Don't forget it was her initiative to go and see Mr Fairbright in the first place that turned our fortunes round.'

'I haven't seen no riches,' the woman muttered.

Karenza smiled at Merry. 'Don't take any notice, Merry. She's as happy as the rest of us to be getting a fair price for her work. The regular money's meant we've been able to eat well and I don't think you're the only one who has plumped out a bit.' Karenza leaned forward and patted her mother's shoulder. 'See, more meat than bone.'

The older woman narrowed her eyes, making them laugh.

'About time we heard about life in the big town, isn't it?'

'You're right, Mother,' Karenza nodded. 'Mr Fairbright said he's pleased with your progress but are you happy in your job? Are the others nice? Do you get time to rest?'

'Steady on, Mother,' Merry cried. 'I'm enjoying my new work very much, though with the store being open from eight o'clock in the morning until ten at night, by the time we've eaten our supper we're ready to fall into bed. The manageress is a bit of a tartar, though, and her breath smells like old cabbage.'

'She should munch parsley then,' Grozen muttered.

'That's a good idea,' Merry agreed. 'Anyway, the other trainees are really nice and, as you can tell, Joanie, the housekeeper, is a great cook. Not as good as you, of course, Mother,' she added, sniffing the air.

'Your mother got Ma Rooster to kill one of her chickens in your honour. Up at dawn plucking the thing, she was,' Grozen said. 'I said to her, it's only our Merryn coming home, not royalty visiting.'

'It's in honour of your birthday, Mother. You know we are celebrating today whilst Merry is with us. Of course, if you'd prefer your normal pilchards...'

'Didn't say that, Karenza. If I eat any more of them I'll look like a ruddy pilchard,' the woman groaned. Merry and her mother laughed for, come the winter and the inevitable return to surviving on limpets, the woman would be lamenting the passing of the tasty silver fish.

'Well, it should be about ready,' her mother said, getting up and spreading her best embroidered cloth over the table. Merry set out the cutlery and by the time they sat down to enjoy their meal, it felt as if she'd never been away. The chicken was cooked to perfection, with the skin crispy, just how she liked it, and the potatoes, baked in the ashes, soft and fluffy inside their jackets. Her mother chattered about life in the village and seemed happier than Merry had ever seen her.

'That Mr Fairbright put your mother in charge of the knitting,' Grozen grinned. 'Kelys got in a right strop. Still, the others were relieved not to have to deal with her funny moods, and they were only too happy to learn that fancy stitch of yours.'

Merry smiled at her mother. 'Well done, Mother. And talking of Mr Fairbright, that reminds me...' she said, jumping up and pulling a wrapped package from her basket. 'This is for you, Grozen, with happy birthday wishes.'

'You shouldn't go spending your money on gifts for...' The woman stuttered to a halt as she held up the soft pink socks. 'My, oh my,' she said, shaking her head.

'They're bed-socks, Grozen. You know how cold your feet get in the winter.'

'Oh, Merry, they're quite beautiful, aren't they, Mother?' Karenza said, reaching out and stroking them. 'They must have cost you a fortune.'

Merry smiled. 'Mr Fairbright let me have staff discount,' she said proudly.

'I shall wear them this very night,' Grozen declared.

'But it's not winter yet,' Merry pointed out.

'Well, I'm getting on, you know. Why after tomorrow I shall be in my fifty-seventh year,' the woman declared. They were still laughing when there was a knock at the door.

'May I come in?' Nicco called.

'Get a move on, young man,' Grozen called. 'I'm waiting for a slice of my cake and you can't hang around at my time of life, you know.'

The rest of the afternoon passed quickly and it seemed like only minutes later that Nicco looked up at the clock on the shelf.

'We'd best be making tracks,' he said.

Reluctantly, Merry gathered up her things, then kissed Grozen and her mother goodbye.

'Come back soon,' Karenza whispered, pulling her tight.

'I will, Mother,' she promised.

Chapter 21

It was only when Merry was lying in bed mulling over the events of the day that she realized she hadn't had time to speak to her friends in the village. Nicco had rushed her back up the hill to where his horse was tethered, saying they needed to hurry if he was to get her back on time. Then, despite her asking him to take her round to the back of the store, he'd insisted on stopping outside the front door, shaking his head in disgust when she scuttled round to the trade entrance.

'When we marry, you will enter that building through the front door,' he had called after her.

He was so bossy, she mused, sighing up at the inky sky. Then a thought struck her. How had he known she wore a grey cap at work? She knew she'd never mentioned it, and what was it Grozen had said about him reporting back to them on her progress? Surely he hadn't been spying on her?

Merry was still thinking of Nicco's words when she entered the shop the next morning. However, she was brought sharply back to the present when she saw Mr Didcot waiting, a strange woman by his side.

'Ladies, I'd like to introduce you to Mrs Winter, your new supervisor,' he announced. 'I am sure you will make her welcome and show her the way things are done here.' They nodded, then smiled politely at the tall, dark-haired woman who stared back, her eyes as grey as the sea on a stormy day.

'Blimey oh rimey,' Freckles muttered. 'She looks a right tartar.'

The woman gave a sharp cough.

'Did you say something, Miss Brice?' Mrs Smale asked, narrowing her eyes at Freckles.

'I asked if Mrs Winter would like a drink of water,' Freckles replied.

'If I require anything, I will let you know, thank you,' the woman replied in a well-modulated voice.

'Well, it's good to see you making your new supervisor welcome. One point I wish to raise is that from today, the gaslights will be lit at dusk. It wouldn't do for our clients not to be able to see what they are purchasing, although doubtless most will be wending their way home earlier now that the evenings are drawing in,' Mr Didcot said, pointing to the globes on the wall, which Merry had hardly noticed before. 'Now, if you'll excuse me...' He gave a little bow and turned to leave.

Mrs Smale waited until the sound of his cane tapping on the floor had receded, then clapped her hands.

'Whilst I show Mrs Winter the contents of our display cabinets, you will clean and tidy the store ready for opening.' Merry and Freckles exchanged looks, for having cleaned and tidied the store the night before, unless boggarts had been at play, there had been no one in the store to mess it up again. Surely their time could be better spent sorting through the stock? It was only when Mrs Smale frowned in their direction that they realized she was still talking.

'Then, when you have dressed the window and partaken of breakfast, reassemble here for your daily instruction.'

'We don't have daily instruction, so what was all that about?' Merry asked, as they duly began sweeping the already clean floor.

'We do now, old love. Mrs Smale's asserting her authority in front of the new supervisor. You know, establishing the pecking order,' Freckles added when Merry looked askance.

'Hierarchy,' Prunella agreed, nodding. 'It's what our housekeeper always did when a new maid started.'

'You have finished your task already, ladies?'

211

Mrs Smale enquired, her voice dripping sarcasm.

'Better jump to it,' Freckles whispered. 'I've a feeling this is going to be a long day.'

After a hurried bowl of porridge, they duly filed onto the shop floor and lined up in front of the manageress. Mrs Winter, however, continued inspecting a mannequin.

'Mrs Winter, if you would like to come over here, I am ready to issue today's directive,' Mrs Smale ordered. The new supervisor narrowed her eyes and pointed to the dummy.

'Wouldn't the time be better spent redressing that ... that effort?' she replied.

'I dressed the mannequin myself only last evening, thank you, Mrs Winter. Now if...'

'It's a bit summery for this time of year, though, don't you think?' the supervisor persisted.

'No, actually I don't,' the manageress said. 'I'm sure you mean to be helpful, Mrs Winter, especially as it's your first day, but you must rely upon my experience. I know what our clients require.'

'Really?' she asked, quirking a brow, then shaking her head at the mannequin.

'Yes, really. Now, Miss Prim, you will shadow myself today; Miss Dyer will shadow you, Mrs Winter, although, of course, you are free to ask me for any assistance you may require. Whilst the trainees are progressing well, they still require direction. Miss Brice will replenish the stocks and generally keep the place tidy.'

'So what else is new?' Freckles muttered.

'Did you say something, Miss Brice?' Mrs Smale frowned.

'I said it must feel strange for Mrs Winter, being new,' Freckles replied, smiling innocently.

'I have worked in far grander places so this is...' the supervisor shrugged. Fortunately, the ringing of the bell prevented further discussion.

'Opening time, ladies. Assume your positions, please,' Mrs Smale ordered.

From the minute the doors were unlocked, they were rushed off their feet. Word about the store's new part-ready clothing with finishing-off dress-making service had spread over the summer, and by now they were regularly inundated with requests to see materials, buttons and silks.

This was the favourite part of her job, Merry decided, as she held up a swathe of silvery silk, followed by blue, then emerald. The woman she was serving nodded.

'I do believe I shall take all three. It is better to have more dresses than not enough, I always think,' she announced.

How lovely to be able to buy just what you wanted without having to count the cost, Merry thought, thinking of her one presentable dress, which was now fitting more snugly than was decent.

'I understand you have a dressmaker on the premises. The party season is fast approaching and as I shall need my new attire by the end of the week, perhaps you could point me in the right direction?'

'I will take you upstairs and introduce you,' Mrs Winter offered.

'No need to trouble yourself, Mrs Winter,' Mrs Smale said, appearing at their side. 'I will attend to modam.'

'I am quite capable of seeing to *my* client,' Mrs Winter assured her.

'You will remain on the shop floor, Mrs Winter, and don't forget to enter the purchases in the ledger,' Mrs Smale hissed. Then with a bright smile she turned back to the client. 'Do please follow me, modam.' The woman stood there looking from one to the other of them. 'I am the manageress, you see,' Mrs Smale gushed, as with a triumphant smirk, she ushered the client out of the shop and towards the stairs.

'Not for long,' Merry heard the supervisor mutter. 'Get this counter tidied at once, Miss Dyer,' she snapped.

The rest of the day passed in the same manner with the two women determined to outdo each other. Finally, after Mrs Smale had leaned across the counter and berated her for some minor detail, the supervisor turned to her.

'Mrs Smale, I feel it my duty to point out that your breath smells less than fragrant.'

'What did you say?' the manageress gasped.

'I said your breath reeks and in the interest of our clients I feel you should know,' Mrs Winter smirked.

'I'll have you know my breath smells as fresh as sweet peas,' Mrs Smale snapped.

'More like marrowfat peas,' Freckles whispered, nudging Merry in the ribs.

'Kindly tidy the button drawer, Miss Brice,' Mrs Smale ordered, glaring at Freckles.

But as the woman turned back to the mannequin and began straightening the bonnet,

214

Merry saw the hurt look in her eyes. Suddenly Merry felt sorry for the woman and going over to her, whispered, 'My grandmother said that chewing parsley sweetens the breath and...'

'When I need the advice of a country bumpkin I will ask for it, thank you, Miss Dyer. Now if you've nothing better to do than stand gossiping, you can polish the glass on the mirror in the dressing room.'

The highlight of the day was the lighting of the gaslamps. Merry had never witnessed anything like it and found the rosy glow that lit up the store and the sound of the soft hissing strangely comforting. It was in stark contrast to the icy atmosphere between manageress and supervisor, and it was a relief when they'd finally cleared away for the day and the trainees could make their way to the staff-room.

'What a day,' Freckles muttered, sinking into her chair.

'Mrs Smale and Mrs Winter are never going to get on, are they?' Merry said, remembering the way they'd glared across the floor at each other, like two cats sizing each other up.

'Mrs Winter does speak nicely, though,' Prunella pointed out.

'Hello there, is that your new supervisor you're talking about?' Chester asked, coming into the room closely followed by Teddy and Nicholas.

'Afraid so,' Merry sighed.

'I don't reckon she's got any feelings. Cold as ice, she is,' Freckles said, pretending to shiver. 'She even told Mrs Smale straight to her face that her breath smelled. So now we've got

215

Smelly and Frosty.'

'And we've got Jerky and Perky,' Teddy chortled.

'Why Jerky and Perky?' Prunella asked, looking at Nicholas, who looked embarrassed.

'Old Jenkins' hands shook so much when he was attempting to measure a client's inside leg by the light from the gas globe, we renamed him,' Teddy said.

'And then we shortened Perkins to Perky to match,' Chester added.

'The supervisor's first name is Jacqueline,' Prunella told Nicholas. 'I heard her telling Mr Didcot that she always has to spell it out for people. I think that's such a pretty name.'

Freckles burst out laughing. 'So we've got our very own Jackie Frosty,' she hooted.

'I'm surprised to see you all in such good spirits,' Joanie said, appearing with their supper. 'After all that moaning you girls were doing at luncheon I thought you'd never take to the woman.'

'She's all white, Joanie,' Chester grinned.

As they all dissolved into peals of laughter Joanie shook her head. 'Mad as hatters, the lot of you. I'll go and get the teapot.'

'Frosty will never fit in,' Freckles commented, helping herself to a slice of bread. 'She's too snooty and Smelly will never put up with her. Why, it's already become the battle of the tongues.'

Over the next couple of days, much to the amusement of the girls, the manageress and supervisor continued vying for supremacy although it was Mrs Smale who retained responsibility for the ledgers. When the store closed on

Wednesday for the carriage trade, Mrs Smale turned to the supervisor.

'Mrs Winter, as I have to carry out an important stock-take, I shall have to delegate you the onerous task of dealing with the servants,' the manageress announced, a triumphant gleam lighting her eyes. If she expected the supervisor to demur, she was disappointed.

'It will be a pleasure, Mrs Smale. I am honoured you deem me competent to the task after such a short time,' she replied.

Merry hid a smile for although the woman had answered politely enough, her lips had tightened into a determined line.

She didn't have time to dwell on it, though, for the bell indicating the arrival of the first carriage was ringing out. Immediately, Mrs Winter set to, sorting the wrapped packages into orderly piles. She then instructed each of them to stand behind one so that instead of having to form a queue, the servants could be handed their mistresses' purchases on arrival.

'Hey, this is a turn-up and no mistake,' one maid announced with glee. 'Why, I'll have time to have a browse round the market stalls.'

'Keep your voice down, Nan,' another servant muttered as Mrs Winter frowned in their direction. ''Tis a good idea, though. I'll get Andy to wait by the pie stall.'

'If we carry on like this we'll be finished early so perhaps we can get away too,' Freckles said, turning to Merry.

'It would be nice to get some fresh air,' she agreed, looking at the rapidly diminishing pile.

'We'd better ask Mrs Winter's permission first, though,' Prunella said.

Freckles raised her eyebrows. 'Reckon your name should be Goody Two-Shoes,' she muttered, then straightened up quickly as Mr Fairbright appeared.

'Good afternoon, ladies. You seem to be dealing with everything in an orderly fashion, I must say. I couldn't believe how speedily the carriages were coming and going when I looked out of my office window.'

'Good afternoon, Mr Fairbright,' Mrs Winter replied, hurrying over. 'I'm so pleased you approve of my new system. It's all about being organized, don't you think?'

'I do indeed, Mrs Winter. I commend your initiative,' he said, raising his hat as he made his way outside. As the supervisor stood beaming after him, Merry and Freckles exchanged looks.

'Who's currying favour now?' Merry whispered.

'As there are only a couple of packages left awaiting collection, you may remain here, Miss Prim. Miss Dyer and Miss Brice, please see that the floor is swept. Goodness only knows what those girls have brought in on their boots,' Mrs Winter sniffed, looking at the floor as if expecting to see it alive with insects or worse.

Stifling the giggle that rose in her throat, Merry turned to collect the broom only to bump into Mrs Smale, who was hurrying through the door.

'For heaven's sake, girl, do look where you're going.'

Before Merry could say anything, the manageress was addressing Mrs Winter. 'Was that Mr

218

Fairbright I saw leaving? Did he require me for anything?'

'Don't worry, Mrs Smale, Mr Fairbright didn't even notice your absence. But then he was busy complimenting me on my new efficient system,' the supervisor smirked.

'What new system?' Mrs Smale asked, her voice ominously low. 'I didn't implement any new system.'

'No, you didn't, did you?' the supervisor began, then noticed Merry and Freckles watching. 'I thought I told you girls to get this floor swept.'

As they scuttled away, they could hear the shrill voice of their manageress berating the supervisor for exceeding her position. Merry could hardly believe how their assumed posh voices turned to common bawling when they thought they were out of earshot.

'Blimey oh rimey, they're like a couple of fish-wives,' Freckles muttered.

'I can assure you the wives of fishermen never resort to such language,' Merry retorted, realizing for the first time how proud she was of her background. Poor they might be, but they always looked out for each other.

Chapter 22

Over the next few weeks, the rivalry between manageress and supervisor became more heated, each vying to serve the most clients. Merry was kept busy shadowing Mrs Winter and had to admit the woman had soon got to grips with all the items they stocked, serving everyone quickly and efficiently. If there hadn't been the constant undercurrent, she would have enjoyed her work for she had already learned more than she ever had when Mrs Rose had been supervisor.

One afternoon Merry was busy tidying away the materials she had just shown to a client when she felt she was being watched. Looking up, she saw Mrs Winter giving her a strange look. She glanced quickly down at the counter in case she had made a mess, but everything looked neat and orderly.

'I wonder if you might assist me?' a soft voice said.

Merry looked up again, then blinked. 'Oh! Sorry, I mean how may I help?' she stuttered, staring at the fair-haired woman in surprise.

'Goodness me, Saphira, this shop girl looks the very spit of you, darling, apart from that quaint accent and service uniform,' the woman's willowy, red-haired companion sneered.

'Alexandria, really,' the woman protested.

'Allow me to assist you, ladies,' the supervisor

said quickly.

'That's all right, Mrs Winter, I will attend,' Mrs Smale said, hurrying across the room and placing herself firmly in front of her subordinate.

'We do indeed appear quite similar, don't we?' the elegant young lady continued, looking past Mrs Smale to Merry.

Merry nodded, taking in the similar white hair and blue eyes.

'It is quite uncanny, is it not?' Alexandria commented, tossing her head so that the glossy artificial cherries on her hat clacked together.

'It is, and she will certainly be the right person to advise me on my purchases.'

'Alas, Miss Dyer is not yet fully trained so it is I who shall advise, modam,' Mrs Smale said, smiling as she leaning across the counter.

Immediately the women recoiled. 'Indeed you will not,' the fair-haired woman declared, wrinkling her nose. 'I wish for Miss Dyer to attend to me.'

'I can permit Miss Dyer to shadow,' Mrs Smale condescended. 'However, as manageress, I must insist you look to me for advice.'

'Where is your etiquette, madam? If, as you say, you are the manageress then surely you must know the client is always right?'

As Mrs Smale opened her mouth to protest, Mr Fairbright hurriedly crossed the room to see what the fuss was about. It was only then that Merry noticed the other shoppers had stopped browsing and were watching the exchange with great interest.

'Good afternoon, Miss Meredith. How kind of

you to grace our modest store with your presence. I hope nothing is wrong?' Mr Fairbright enquired.

'Good afternoon to you, Mr Fairbright. I have heard good things about your emporium and as my friend and I were in the vicinity, we thought we'd call in and have a look. Allow me to introduce my friend, Miss Alexandria Courtland.'

'Miss Courtland,' Mr Fairbright smiled and gave a little bow. 'Welcome, both of you. How may we be of assistance?'

'I require some new clothes for a forthcoming vacation and have been informed you are stocking part-made garments that only require one fitting. If this is true, you will be the answer to my prayers, for as usual I have left it much too late for my customary seamstress. She is quite brilliant, you understand, but requires me to try things on numerous times,' she trilled.

Mr Fairbright smiled indulgently. 'I am honoured, my dear, and what you hear is indeed true. I am proud to say we stock only the finest materials, both in the usual bales and already pre-cut so that they merely require making-up to your pattern. I am sure we can find something that will suit each of you.'

'Tell me, Mr Fairbright,' Miss Meredith began, her blue eyes twinkling mischief, 'do you hold the belief that the client is always right?'

'Indeed I do, Miss Meredith. The client's wish is paramount,' he assured her.

'I am pleased to hear it, for you see I requested this young lady here assist me,' she explained, smiling graciously as she gestured towards Merry. 'A reasonable request, don't you think, bearing in mind we appear to be of similar age and colouring?' Mr Fairbright nodded and glanced at Merry, but Miss Meredith hadn't finished speaking. 'However, this manageress of yours insists I should be attended to by her. Perhaps you would be kind enough to relay to her that I have no desire to be served by an older woman whose breath smells of stale cabbage.'

'Well, of all...' Mrs Smale began, but Mr Fairbright held up his hand.

'Do not concern yourself, my dear. I am sure Mrs Smale has misunderstood your request. Miss Dyer, perhaps you will be kind enough to assist Miss Meredith and her companion,' he said, turning to Merry.

Then he frowned and turned back to the client, his eyes widening. 'Goodness,' he muttered. 'The similarity between you is extraordinary.'

'It is rather, isn't it?' Miss Meredith agreed. 'As such, Miss Dyer will be the perfect person to assist me.'

'As you wish, modam. However, in my capacity as manageress I must insist I advise,' Mrs Smale said, having recovered her composure.

'Mr Fairbright, will you please tell this annoying woman that it is Miss Dyer and Miss Dyer only to whom I will look for advice?' Miss Meredith requested, waving Mrs Smale away as if she were a bothersome fly. 'I feel we are going to get on tremendously,' she added, smiling warmly at Merry.

As Mrs Smale stood glaring at them, Mr Fairbright coughed discreetly.

'Miss Dyer, perhaps you would take these ladies up to my office where you can discuss their requirements in private?' he suggested.

'Oh, goodness me, is that the time?' Miss Court-land said, peering at the clock in the corner. 'Saphira, darling, you will have to excuse me or I shall be late for my engagement. Now you have the services of this shop girl you really won't be re-quiring my assistance. Good afternoon.' With a swift nod that set the cherries clattering once more, the willowy redhead disappeared from the store.

'If you would care for some refreshment, Miss Meredith, I shall have some sent up,' Mr Fair-bright suggested.

'That would be most welcome. The smell of all those horses on the street makes one quite thirsty, I find.'

'Indeed. Right, Miss Dyer, you know the way, don't you?'

'Of course, sir,' Merry replied.

Ignoring the withering look of Mrs Smale and the stunned looks of Mrs Winter, Freckles and Prunella, she led the way to Mr Fairbright's office.

'I say, this is so exciting,' Miss Meredith said as she followed Merry up the stairs.

'Please take a seat, Miss Meredith,' Merry said, showing her into the office. Then she looked around the room. What was the protocol? Should she sit in Mr Fairbright's chair opposite the client or pull one up alongside? However, the solution was provided when the woman perched daintily on a chair in front of the desk.

'Isn't it fascinating how similar we are in looks?'

'It is, Miss Meredith,' Merry agreed, taking the seat behind Mr Fairbright's desk.

The woman gave a tinkling laugh. 'That formality makes me sound as old and stuffy as that woman downstairs. My name's Saphira so you may call me that. What's yours?'

'Merryn, but my friends call me Merry,' she replied. 'But I can hardly address you so informally,' she began as Joanie came bustling in with a tray of refreshment. If the housekeeper was surprised to see Merry sitting in Mr Fairbright's place she didn't show it.

Silence descended as Joanie poured their drinks and passed them a plate of her home-baked biscuits. As the fragrant spices mingled with the smell of beeswax polish, Merry twisted her hands in her lap. How should she act? What should she say? Idly she picked up Mr Fairbright's pen.

'Ah, you are going to make a list, good idea. I say, these are absolutely delicious,' Saphira commented, nibbling daintily at the edge of a biscuit. 'Now, as I was saying earlier, I celebrated my eighteenth earlier this year and received a modest inheritance. I intend to use some of it to visit a dear friend and thus am requiring garments for travelling. Do you have materials that don't crease? There's nothing worse than arriving somewhere and finding one's skirts have rumpled and crumpled, don't you find?'

'Indeed,' Merry replied, smiling politely and hoping the dress of her uniform still looked pristine.

'Tell me, Merry, have you journeyed much?'

'Oh, yes,' she replied. 'I have travelled all the way from Cornwall.' Although Saphira nodded politely, Merry was certain she detected a hint of amusement in her eyes. Quickly looking down, she made a note to check for materials that would travel well.

'I shall also require something in a waterproof material in case the weather should turn inclement. Although I really cannot abide the terrible smell or funny feel of mackintosh,' Saphira said, wrinkling her nose.

'Then you will be interested to know that Didcot and Fairbright have brought in a waterproof that has no smell and is comfortable to wear,' Merry replied, recalling what Mr Fairbright had told her that day in his office.

'Really!' Saphira exclaimed, her eyes lighting up.

'I believe previously that it was the coal tar used to dissolve India rubber that made textiles waterproof. Unfortunately, it also gave them that nasty smell. I am led to believe the new material has no odour and is pleasant to the touch,' Merry added, trying to remember all she'd been taught.

'Well, in that case, I shall have to have something made up in this waterproof textile you mention,' Saphira declared.

'Certainly,' Merry replied, adding 'waterproof' to the list, then carefully pressing it with the blotter.

'If you have finished your refreshments, perhaps you would like to come back down to the store. I can show you some materials I think will be suitable and, when you are happy we have met your requirements, introduce you to our dressmaker.'

As they re-entered the store, Mrs Smale, who'd obviously been hovering, came bustling over.

'Is everything all right, Miss Meredith? Only, if

you feel you need advice from a more experienced...'

'Miss Dyer, please tell this wretched woman that if she doesn't leave us alone I will be making a complaint to Mr Fairbright,' Saphira requested.

As the manageress opened and closed her mouth in surprise, Merry swallowed. She could hardly tell her boss to disappear, could she? She saw Freckles grinning and giving her the thumbs up from behind the counter. Mrs Winter was smirking from behind the mannequin whilst Prunella was gazing at Saphira's elegant coat with something akin to envy. For a moment it was as if time stood still.

'Ah, Miss Meredith, I trust Miss Dyer is looking after you?' Mr Fairbright asked, striding over to them.

'Indeed she is, thank you. With her help, we now have a list of the items I require to buy and I must say her knowledge of your materials is admirable. Why, whoever knew there was now a waterproof that not only has no smell but is pleasant to wear?'

'That will be her training, which I myself...' Mrs Smale began.

Saphira let out an exasperated sigh. 'Mr Fairbright, might I please have a moment of your time?' she asked.

'Of course, Miss Meredith. Would you care to step this way?'

As soon as their backs were turned, Mrs Smale rounded on Merry.

'Come and see me the moment the store closes, Miss Dyer,' she hissed before turning to where their employer was now in earnest discussion with Miss Meredith. For once Merry didn't mind about the manageress's sniping.

'Do I have to wait all afternoon for assistance?' a client demanded. As her strident voice carried round the store, Mrs Winter stepped forward to help.

'Right, that's sorted at last,' Saphira said, returning to Merry. 'It is agreed that you and only you are to bring a selection of materials and trimmings to the dressing room. If that is all right with you, of course?' she asked.

Merry could only nod that this well-dressed young lady should seek her approval.

With her head buzzing with all she needed to collect together, she was only vaguely aware of Mr Fairbright taking Mrs Smale aside for a discussion and the woman striding back to the counter, her face like thunder.

After that, Merry was left alone as she scuttled back and forth with lengths of dress materials, trimmings and accessories she thought might be suitable. As instructed, she waited respectfully outside the dressing room until her opinion was sought. Once when she was tilting a hat to the right angle on Saphira's head, she caught sight of their reflections in the mirror. With their bright blue eyes and sleek white tresses, Merry couldn't help but marvel once more at their similarity, and if she were dressed in similar...

'You have such a good eye for colour, Merry,' Saphira sighed, interrupting her thoughts. 'Now let's see what else you have selected.' Merry duly held up a length of material for her to see the effect. 'I would never have chosen this rose pink but it is so complimentary, it makes my face come alive somehow, don't you think?'

'It does indeed. You look truly beautiful,' Merry agreed.

'Thank you. I shall take two lengths. You should purchase some in this colour too,' Saphira suggested.

Merry smiled politely, knowing she could never afford such riches on her meagre wage.

'I have been pondering our likeness in appearance, Merry, and feel I must ask. Are you by any chance related to the Merediths of Merrivale, here in Devonshire?'

'Why no, I come from Porthsallos and am Cornish through and through,' Merry assured her.

'Perhaps the stork collected us from the same angel, then deposited us under different gooseberry bushes,' Saphira replied. As her tinkling laugh echoed around the dressing room, Merry couldn't help smiling too. 'Oh, well, back to the task in hand. It's quite trying ensuring one has enough changes of outfit to cover every occasion, don't you find?'

Merry nodded politely as she turned back to her list. Choosing new materials and accessories a chore? And to think all she desired was enough material to make a single new dress.

Chapter 23

When Saphira finally decided she had all the material, trimmings and accessories she needed, Merry showed her upstairs.

'This is Mrs Stitches,' she said, introducing Saphira to the dressmaker.

As her tinkling laugh rang out once more, the woman grinned.

'Dreadful name, isn't it? It wasn't till after my Arthur proposed that I realized what I'd let myself in for. Still, could be worse, I suppose. I mean, imagine if it were Darning?' she chuckled. 'Now please take a seat and tell me how you want your outfits finished.'

As Saphira sat down in front of the woman's treadle, Merry excused herself. She was about to make her way back downstairs when Mr Fairbright beckoned her from his office.

'Is everything all right, Miss Dyer?' he enquired.

'I think so, sir. Miss Meredith seems happy with her all purchases.'

'Yes, I saw the mountain of materials you carried up with you. The store's takings will increase handsomely,' he said, rubbing his hands with glee. 'No doubt Mrs Smale is, at this very moment, totting up all the sales in the ledger.'

'Yes, sir. I did wonder, though...' She tailed off, not wishing to appear rude.

'Do go on, Miss Dyer.'

'Well, sir, you know the store's policy is to allow clients to have their purchases on approbation? Will that apply to the part-made garments as well?'

Mr Fairbright frowned. 'Is there any reason they should be any different?'

'When clients purchase materials they are presumably given on approval before their own dressmaker makes them up. I mean, you could hardly accept material back if it had been turned into a dress to someone's measurements, and if Mrs Stitches makes up the part-made garments whilst the goods are on approbation...'

'And the client decided she didn't approve of the fabric later on, she might refuse to pay, you mean?' Mr Fairbright supplied.

Merry nodded. 'Not that I wish to imply Miss Meredith would...' She realized she was in danger of insulting the woman she'd spent most of the afternoon advising. And after she'd treated Merry so well too, not like that condescending companion of hers. Whatever had made her ask such a stupid question? Of course, Mr Fairbright would have already thought of everything. Grozen had been right when she'd told Merry she should think before speaking out.

'You know, Miss Dyer, that is indeed a very good question and I have to confess one that neither Mr Didcot nor myself has given any consideration to. I shall make a note to discuss the matter at our next meeting and you can be sure I will have an answer for you then. Now you'd better get back to the shop floor before Mrs Smale comes looking for you.'

'Yes, sir. Thank you, sir,' Merry said, but as she turned to go Mr Fairbright called her back.

'Miss Dyer, I almost forgot. There is something delicate I wish to ask you.' He sat there looking so uncomfortable that Merry wondered what on earth she could have done. The tick of the clock on the mantel sounded loud in the ensuing silence. She could hear the sound of hooves on the cobbles below and remembered how Mr Fairbright had said he could see out over the yard from this office. He hadn't witnessed her committing some minor misdemeanour, had he?

'Miss Dyer,' Mr Fairbright cleared his throat before continuing. 'Please tell me in the strictest confidence, of course, is Mrs Smale's breath less than fragrant? I have never detected anything myself but, suffering from asthma as I do, my sense of smell is not particularly good.'

'Well, Mr Fairbright, in the interest of your clients I do feel you should know it has been commented that her breath smells of old cabbages.'

Her employer smiled. 'That's the thing I like about you, Miss Dyer. I can rely upon you to be direct. I shall get Mrs Winter to mention it to her, sort of woman to woman; perhaps suggest she chew some parsley after her meals,' he added.

Merry tried not to grin as she took her leave and made her way back down to the shop floor. How she hoped she'd be there to witness the fireworks that would certainly ensue. However, all such thoughts were quickly dispelled the moment Mrs Smale caught sight of her.

'How magnanimous of you to join us, Miss

Dyer,' she hissed, the shadows cast by the gas globes making her look more fiendish than ever. 'Did it really take that long for you to introduce Miss Meredith to the dressmaker?'

'No it did not, Mrs Smale. Mr Fairbright called me into his office.'

The woman's eyes narrowed. 'And pray what did our esteemed employer wish to discuss with one of his lowly trainee assistants?'

'He said how pleased he was with the number of purchases Miss Meredith made,' Merry replied, thinking it prudent not to mention her bad breath. The woman let out such a hiss it could have been mistaken for the gas globes and Merry wished she'd remained quiet.

'And naturally, I have already entered them in the ledger. However, Mr Fairbright wouldn't be so pleased if he were to see the abominable state you've left the dressing room in. Go and tidy the stock away immediately then give the room a thorough cleaning. I shall inspect everything before supper.'

'Yes, Mrs Smale,' she replied, knowing it was quicker just to agree. Seeing the worried looks Freckles and Prunella were giving her, she smiled in assurance to them as she passed.

Whilst the dressing room did need tidying, she'd been careful to keep the materials stacked in their colour ways so it took her only a few minutes to put them neatly back in their places in the cupboard. Seeing the rose-pink silk, she remembered Saphira's words and couldn't resist holding the material up to herself. Immediately her face looked energized, as if she'd been for a walk along the beach. If only, she thought, sighing as she carefully folded the material away and closed the door.

Determined to make the changing area look spotless, she smoothed the velvet covers on the chair straight and shook out the chiffon scarves clients were encouraged to place around their necks when trying things on. Then, as she was giving the mirror a polish, her attention was caught by something sparkling on the floor. It was a gold chain with some kind of stone attached. Picking it up, she ran her fingers over the blue heart and couldn't help thinking how similar it was to the trinket her mother always wore, although that was dull and lustreless by comparison. It must have come adrift when Saphira had been trying on a garment, she thought. She was just wondering whether the woman was still upstairs with the dressmaker, when Mrs Smale came bustling into the room.

'Have you not finished, Miss Dyer?' she snapped, then caught sight of what Merry was holding. 'Stealing from a client is grounds for instant dismissal,' she added, a gleam sparking in her eyes.

'Stealing?' Merry gasped, shaking her head. 'You misunderstand, Mrs Smale. I found this on the floor when I was tidying up...' she said, holding out the necklace, but the woman snatched it from her hands.

'Come with me,' she ordered, striding towards the stairs.

'Hello there, is everything all right, Merry?' Chester asked, leaping aside as Mrs Smale almost barged through him.

'I don't think so,' Merry whispered, her heart beating faster than the tall-case clock in the corner.

'Miss Dyer,' the manageress cried, and with a helpless look at Chester, Merry scuttled up the stairs.

'Come,' Mr Fairbright ordered as Mrs Smale rapped briskly on his office door.

'Mr Fairbright, this girl here is a thief. She has been caught stealing a client's necklace and...'

'Now then, steady on, Mrs Smale. That is a dangerous accusation. I am sure there has been some misunderstanding. Perhaps you would start from the beginning,' Mr Fairbright ordered, his voice measured.

Bewildered, Merry stared at him and then around the little office where only a short time ago she had been commended for her service, hardly able to believe she was being accused of theft.

'...And so you see, Mr Fairbright, in my capacity as manageress, I have to recommend you dispense with Miss Dyer's services immediately,' Mrs Smale concluded.

Mr Fairbright stared from the necklace the woman had placed in front of him to Merry, his brows furrowing.

'I don't think Miss Dyer...' he began.

'Oh, you may think butter wouldn't melt in her charming little mouth, but you haven't seen her behaviour on the shop floor. Miss Dyer criticizes the way I dress the mannequins, suggesting I might be behind the seasons, if you please. She rushes forward to attend to clients when, as you

235

know, we observe a strict code of practice with senior staff...' Her voice tailed off as Mr Fairbright held up his hand.

'That's quite enough, Mrs Smale. As manageress it is your duty to encourage trainees to fulfil their potential. We all have our strengths and weaker areas, do we not?' He paused, looking pointedly at her. 'The enthusiasm and opinion of all members of staff is vital to the good running of the store and...'

'But you have no idea...' she butted in.

'I think I am beginning to see for myself, thank you. The store is still open, Mrs Smale, so I'd be obliged if you would return to the shop floor.'

As the woman stood there gaping like a guppy, Mr Fairbright turned to Merry. 'Perhaps you would care to explain how you happened to have this in your possession?' he asked.

'I told you, Mr Fairbright...' Mrs Smale began, then, seeing the look on her employer's face, flounced from the room.

Mr Fairbright took his red spotted kerchief from his pocket and dabbed his forehead but Merry could wait no longer.

'Mr Fairbright, I found this on the dressing-room floor when I went to tidy up. It is my belief that it came adrift whilst Miss Meredith was trying on a part-made garment.'

'That would make sense,' he agreed, picking up the necklace and running the chain through his fingers.

'I intended to find out if Miss Meredith was still on the premises and return it, but Mrs Smale came into the dressing room and, well, she accused me of taking it. I would never do anything like that, I assure you,' she cried.

To her surprise, Mr Fairbright smiled. 'I never for one moment thought you would, Miss Dyer. After all, I do recall you pointing out to Miss Brown that she had overpaid you. No, your integrity is not in question.'

'You mean you aren't going to dismiss me?' she asked, hoping flaring in her breast.

'I most certainly am not. Mr Didcot and I have high hopes for your future here, Miss Dyer. However, as Miss Meredith will obviously have left by now, my immediate concern is to see this is returned to her at once. She will doubtless be anxious when she notices a necklace of such worth is missing.'

'Yes, I expect it's of sentimental value to her,' Merry said, thinking how devastated her mother would be if she found her own trinket missing.

'I think you misunderstand, Miss Dyer. Unless I am mistaken, this is a sapphire of some monetary value,' he said, taking out his pocket watch and frowning. 'It is nearly time for the store to close so it would probably be prudent for you to go directly to the staff-room.'

'But Mrs Smale...' she began.

'You may also leave the matter of Mrs Smale with me. It appears she needs to be put right on this and a number of other things,' he said. 'Good evening, Miss Dyer.'

'Good evening, sir,' she replied, taking her leave and hurrying down the stairs. It was only when she reached the staff-room and sank onto her chair that she realized she was trembling.

'Well, hello there,' Chester said, coming into the room a few moments later. 'Hey, are you all right, old thing?'

'I think I am now, thank you, but it's certainly been a day and a half.'

'Freckles filled me in,' Chester said. 'What a rat bag old Smelly is. Can't have her upsetting my favourite girl, now can I? I'll have to think of something more appropriate than a frog, though.'

Before she could answer, Freckles and Prunella rushed into the room, anxious to hear how she'd fared with Mr Fairbright. Merry stared around the table, thankful to have the support of these wonderful people who had become her friends.

Filing onto the shop floor the next morning, the young women were surprised when they were greeted by their supervisor and not the manageress.

'Mrs Smale is with Mr Fairbright so it is up to me to see that everything is ready for when the store opens,' Mrs Winter announced in her clipped tones.

'Hope she's getting her comeuppance,' Freckles whispered.

'Miss Brice?' the supervisor asked with a quirk of her immaculate brow.

'I said it's amazing how much stuff you can buy for tuppence,' Freckles smiled, gesturing to their trimmings drawer.

'It is indeed remarkable what the store sells for such a modest sum, Miss Brice. Now I think it is high time we arranged the window to reflect the changing seasons. Perhaps you would collect some fur fabric from the stock cupboard along with some warm gloves and mufflers.'

'Blimey, while the cat's away,' Freckles giggled to Merry as she hurried across the shop floor.

'Miss Prim, perhaps you would change the display of buttons and silks to go with the heavier fabrics that we shall be using. I notice you have an artistic eye.' Prunella beamed and eagerly turned her attention to the task. As Merry wondered what she would be assigned to do, Mrs Winter pointed towards the mannequins that were positioned on either side of the window. 'Miss Dyer, you will assist me in re-dressing these.'

The next hour passed in a flurry of activity as they did as they'd been asked. By the time they were dismissed for their breakfast, the store had been transformed.

'Blimey oh rimey, old Smelly will have a fit when she sees what Frosty's done,' Freckles chortled, waving her spoon in the air.

'Well, you have to admit it does look more suitable for the colder weather,' Merry said.

'I think Mrs Winter is quite nice really,' Prunella said. 'At least she let us all help.'

'She's only trying to get one up on Smelly, Pru. Surely you realize that. Come on, eat up or we'll be late for inspection.'

However, Mrs Winter merely glanced at their appearance when they filed into the store. Instead she proudly announced that as Mrs Smale was still with Mr Fairbright, she would take charge of the running of the department.

'Of course, that means we shall all have to work harder but I know I can rely upon your assistance,' she said, her lips curling into a grin as she looked at them. 'Now it's time for the store to open,' she added.

'It's like she's turned into a human being,' Freckles muttered as they took their places behind the counter.

Trade was brisk, with clients drawn into the store by the new window display. They were kept so busy with requests to see the warmer fabrics and accessories that they hardly noticed when Mrs Smale finally appeared. As she stood in the doorway taking in the changed displays and the re-dressed mannequins her cheeks flushed bright red. Narrowing her eyes, she marched over to Merry.

'You are wanted in Mr Fairbright's office right away.'

Chapter 24

'Come,' Mr Fairbright called, and Merry swallowed hard as yet again she found herself entering his office.

'Ah, Miss Dyer, this is Lieutenant Meredith, Miss Meredith's brother. I sent word that you had found his sister's necklace and he has come to collect it on her behalf. Whilst he is here, he wishes to thank you personally for handing it in.'

Merry turned and saw the tall, fair-haired man standing beside the window. Smiling, he crossed the room and held out his hand. Merry glanced uncertainly at Mr Fairbright, who nodded encouragingly. As the man clasped her hand firmly in his, a tingle shivered up her arm and she stared at him in surprise. Eyes, a paler blue than his sister's, gazed intently into hers.

'My sister told me of your similarity in looks and I have to admit the likeness is remarkable. We are both deeply grateful for your honesty in handing in her necklace. Saphira was quite distressed when she returned home and found it missing. Then she received word from Mr Fairbright that it had been found in the store and I was immediately dispatched to collect it. It belonged to our grandmother and is irreplaceable so we would be happy if you would accept this small reward as a token of our appreciation.' He took a package from his inside pocket and held it out.

'Oh, no, please. I was only doing my duty,' Merry protested.

The lieutenant gave her a searching look and Merry felt her breath catch in her throat.

As he continued to hold out the package, Mr Fairbright chuckled. 'Miss Dyer is a woman of principles so I think you are going to have to admit defeat, Lieutenant Meredith.'

'A Meredith never admits defeat, Mr Fairbright. However, he is prepared to compromise. In order that I may express the gratitude of both my sister and myself, would you do me the honour of dining with me, Miss Dyer? I believe Sunday is your day off, so perhaps luncheon?'

'Oh,' she said, surprised that this fine gentleman should want her company. 'But I...' she cast around the room, wondering how to reply.

'How thoughtless of me: a charming lady such as yourself will already be booked up for months ahead,' he said, looking so serious that she burst out laughing.

'No such luck, I'm afraid.'

Mr Fairbright coughed discreetly. 'I told you Miss Dyer was nothing if not candid, lieutenant.'

'Indeed you did, Mr Fairbright, and I have to say such frankness is quite refreshing. Most young ladies would demur and then pretend to consider. Personally, I find such games tiresome. Dare I hope you will permit me to call upon you at noon on Sunday, Miss Dyer?'

'Yes, why not?' she said recklessly, then wondered why both men chuckled.

Mr Fairbright coughed again. 'As Miss Dyer's employer, might I enquire where you will be taking her?'

'The Madison, I think, the food there is always good. I promise behaviour beyond reproach and her safe return by five o'clock,' he replied formally, although Merry was certain she saw his lips twitch.

'Blimey oh rimey, you mean that toff asked you out?' Freckles gasped, as Merry updated them over their midday meal.

'Yes, but only to show his appreciation for me handing in Miss Meredith's necklace.'

'That's his excuse,' Freckles chortled. 'Old Smelly will have a fit. Where's he taking you?'

'Somewhere called the Madison,' Merry replied.

As Freckles whistled, Prunella turned to Merry. 'You do realize that is the best hotel in town?'

'Is it?' Merry gulped. Whatever had she been thinking of, accepting such an invitation?

'Oh, yes. Father used to meet his business associates there. It is incredibly smart. Apparently the *maître d'hôtel* was trained at the finest hotel in France.'

'The *maître* what?' Merry asked, giving up all pretence of eating her broth.

'*Maître d'hôtel* – he oversees the dining room, ensures the table has been laid with the correct cutlery, the right wine is served with each course and...'

'Each course?' Merry squeaked. 'How many will there be?'

Prunella shrugged. 'Five, maybe six, although at luncheon you might get away with only four.'

As Merry looked aghast, Freckles sighed. 'Blimey oh rimey, girl, whatever have you got yourself into? One knife, fork and spoon is enough for me.'

'What do you mean?' asked Merry.

'One set of cutlery for each course,' replied Freckles, laughing at Merry's obvious disbelief.

'There's nothing to it,' Prunella assured her. 'You just work from the outside in.'

'So what will you wear? You can hardly go to a swanky place in your Sunday threads, can you?' Freckles pointed out. Merry shook her head and stared around the room as if seeking inspiration.

'You may borrow my new bonnet and mantle,' Prunella offered.

'And I can put your hair up in that new style. I know, let's have a dress rehearsal on Saturday night after work,' Freckles said excitedly.

Merry smiled gratefully at her friends. What had she been thinking by accepting Lieutenant Meredith's invitation?

For the rest of the week as Merry went about her work, her emotions fluctuated from the giddy desire to see him again to nerves at how she should conduct herself. Would she be permitted to keep Prunella's mantle on during the meal? Even if she'd had the money to purchase new fabric, there was no time to make a replacement for her best dress. And what would she talk about? A lieutenant such as he would hardly be interested in hearing about the daily routine of the store. Round and round the questions rolled in her head until she thought it would burst.

When the store finally closed its doors on Saturday night, Freckles led her excitedly upstairs to their room.

'Well, how do I look?' she asked some fifteen minutes later as she twirled in front of the candle.

'She looks a dolly dazzler in your bonnet and mantle, doesn't she, Prunella?' Freckles declared.

Prunella looked unsure but as she opened her mouth to say something, there was a sharp rap on the door and Mrs Stitches bustled into the room.

'I've managed to get this finished,' she puffed, holding out something in rose-pink material. 'Mind you, it was touch and go whether I'd get it done in time. That Miss Meredith sent me a commu ... communi ... a note asking me to turn one of the lengths of silk into a blouse for you, Miss Dyer. Said as it suited her so well she knew it would be perfect for you and she wanted to thank you for finding her necklace.'

Merry stared at the woman in surprise. 'This is for me?' she asked.

'That's what I said, dear. Worked all day to get it finished, I have, not that she said anything about you needing it for tomorrow, but I guessed you'd want to look your best.'

'But how did you know my size?' Merry frowned.

'That Miss Meredith said to make it up the same as hers. Well, I'd best be off or the old man will be back from the alehouse and wondering where his supper is.'

As the door closed behind her, Merry continued staring at the blouse in bemusement.

'That must have cost a bit,' Freckles whistled. 'Well, hurry up and pop it over your dress, then you can put the mantle on top.' Merry did as they suggested, then stood back for them to see.

'That's much better. The pink blouse makes all the difference, doesn't it, Pru?' Freckles pronounced.

'Yes, you look all soft and womanly now,' Prunella agreed.

'And it hides those straining seams,' Freckles chortled. 'Now, you'd better get some beauty sleep or you'll have bags like saucers under your eyes by the time his nibs arrives.'

Promptly at noon Lieutenant Meredith's brougham pulled up outside the store. As Merry approached, the driver opened the door and let down the step for her. If only her mother could see her being treated in such style, she thought.

'How lovely it is to see you again, Miss Dyer.'

'And you, Lieutenant Meredith,' she replied,

settling herself on the leather squab.

'Please call me Carey. We can hardly dine together whilst being so formal. May I be so bold as to call you Merryn?'

She nodded. 'My friends call me Merry.'

'Delightful, and it rather captures your sunny nature. However, Merryn is a pretty name and you're a pretty girl so I shall call you that,' he replied. As his aquamarine eyes gazed at her admiringly, she felt the heat of a blush creep over her cheeks. Flustered, she looked out of the window and was pleased when he called to the driver to drive on.

The atmosphere inside the carriage was so highly charged she barely noticed the passing scenery. It was only when Carey began pointing out various landmarks that she relaxed enough to look at him again. Now he was gesturing towards a large ship with smoking funnels and tall masts that towered over the buildings in the distance.

'That's the transatlantic Royal Mailboat anchored offshore.'

'Why does it have to wait out there?'

'It is simply too big to enter the inner harbour,' he said.

They rounded a corner, and an imposing limestone building with towering chimneys and a turret at one corner appeared in view. 'Our destination,' he proudly announced.

She blinked in amazement. Were they really going in there?

No sooner had the driver pulled to a halt than a uniformed porter hurried over to greet them. He led them up three steps and through the revolving doors, where another uniformed man stepped forward to greet them.

'May I take your mantle to the cloakroom for you, madam?'

'Oh, yes, thank you,' she said, fumbling for the clasp. Smiling, Carey leaned forward to help and she caught a whiff of his spicy cologne, felt the warmth of his touch through the thin material of her blouse. Quickly she smoothed down the folds of her dress, glimpsing her clumpy black shoes in the process. Hopefully nobody would notice, she thought as a well-dressed woman wearing elegant jewel-encrusted slippers passed by.

'Allow me to show you through to the lounge,' the man said, leading the way along a burgundy-carpeted corridor.

'May I get you some drinks, sir?' he asked as they took their seats in the comfortable lounge over-looking the water. 'As we are celebrating I think we will have a bottle of elderflower champagne at the table, if that's all right with you, Merryn?' Carey asked, looking to her for confirmation. Champagne? Goodness, she thought, accepting the embossed leather-covered menu the waiter handed her. She almost gasped in dismay when she saw the numerous dishes listed.

'I can recommend the venison pâté with melba toast, followed by the turbot,' Carey suggested. 'And I'm told the roast sirloin is particularly good here, unless you would prefer to select from the à la carte menu, of course?'

She shook her head in disbelief that there was even more choice.

'Whatever you suggest will be fine,' she replied,

thinking that no matter how delicious it was, she'd never manage half of it anyway. Although the blouse covered the upper part of her dress, she was still mindful of the straining seams across her hips. The man finished noting down their order and moved away.

'What a delightful view,' she said, looking out over the harbour to Plymouth Sound and the Breakwater beyond.

'I see we share a love of the sea,' he said. 'My sister did let slip that you hail from Porthsallos, which is a fishing village, I believe,' he enquired, looking at her as if her answer really mattered.

'Yes, it is, and the pilchards have been plentiful this year providing plenty of work.'

'Your father is a fisherman?'

'My father died before I was born,' she said quietly.

'I am sorry; that was clumsy of me,' he replied, looking upset.

'You weren't to know. I lived with my mother, Karenza, and Grozen before coming to Plymouth.' He quirked a brow and she told him how she'd come to call her grandmother by that name.

'She can be a bit formidable but is as soft as silk underneath. Mother's easy-going – as long as you tell the truth, that is. She has a right thing about honesty.'

'Good for her,' he applauded. 'The world would be a better place if more were like her.'

Their conversation was halted by the arrival of a smart black-suited gentleman with a white bow tie.

'Your table is ready, sir,' he announced, giving a little bow.

They followed him into a bright, airy room, where a silver-haired man in a white jacket was playing a piano softly in the corner, and were shown to a table for two in the bay of the window. Merry couldn't believe it when her chair was pulled out for her and a snowy white napkin was placed on her lap. She watched in fascination as the man took a bottle from a cooler beside the table, gently eased the cork from the bottle, then poured the fizzing liquid into their glasses. Only then did she notice the array of shiny cutlery and other crystal glasses set in front of her.

'I would like to propose a toast,' Carey said, breaking into her thoughts as he raised his glass. 'Here's to your honesty, Merryn, and to a lovely lunch in elegant company.' He chinked his glass against hers.

'I do believe that is two toasts,' she replied, to cover her awkwardness.

'Then we shall have to chink again,' he grinned. 'And partake of another glass of bubbly, I think.'

'Oh, no, this will be enough for me,' she replied, quickly covering the glass with her hand.

Their hors d'oeuvres arrived and as he carefully spread the pâté, she watched and followed suit.

'This is delicious,' she said, trying not to shower crumbs on the snowy cloth.

'So tell me, if you were happy at home what made you leave?' he enquired.

She hesitated, but the way he had of looking at her as though what she had to say mattered, encouraged her to open up.

'I've always had this desire to forge my own way in life, see something outside Porthsallos. Don't get me wrong, it's a lovely place, but all my friends think the be-all and end-all to life is marrying and having children.'

'And you don't want that?' he enquired.

'Not for years, if ever. It seems like a life sentence of drudgery to me,' she said with feeling. 'I have been given this opportunity to fulfil my dream and I intend to work hard and make the most of it.'

'Goodness, you sound like Queen Victoria. She believes women should have the chance to fulfil themselves,' he quipped, his lips curling into a smile.

'Then it's up to us to make sure we do.' Her reply came out more sharply than she'd intended for it was important he understood.

Chapter 25

There was silence for a moment and Merry wondered if she'd overstepped the mark, but then their fish course arrived and Carey turned his attention to eating. Again she watched which cutlery he selected, then followed suit. Prunella had been right when she said to work from the outside in, she thought.

As they ate their way steadily through the meal, Carey turned the conversation to lighter subjects, which enabled Merry to relax and enjoy the delicious food. She ate far more than she would ever have imagined possible and hoped the seams on her skirt would hold.

'Shall we have our coffee in the lounge?' he suggested, placing his napkin on the table.

He waited until she'd settled herself once more in the comfy chair and then asked about her job in the store.

'I'm sure a man like you wouldn't be the slightest bit interested in the day-to-day running of a high-street draper's,' she exclaimed.

'A man like me?' he asked, quirking his brow in the way she'd come to recognize.

'Yes, a lieutenant in the navy. You must be a very clever man to have a job like that.'

To her surprise, he threw back his head and laughed.

'It's not as glamorous as you imagine, I'm afraid,' he said, waving his hand dismissively. 'Actually, Merryn, we have quite a lot in common, if you think about it.'

'We do?' she frowned. 'I don't see how.'

'We both have to wear uniform, obey instructions, deal with the day-to-day minutiae of the running of things, albeit you in a store and me on a ship,' he explained, looking so earnest it was her turn to laugh.

'But I'm only a trainee assistant. I don't run the store.'

'Nor I my ship. So you see, Miss Dyer, we do have quite a lot of things in common. And talking of obeying orders,' he said, taking out his pocket watch and grimacing, 'I promised Mr Fairbright to have you back at the store by five o'clock so we'd better be making tracks.' He signalled to the *maître d'hôtel*.

Outside, the carriage was pulled up alongside the steps and once again, as he helped her inside, Merry's skin tingled from his touch. To cover her confusion, she stared out of the window. It was already beginning to grow dark and candles and gaslamps shone out from windows as they passed. Suddenly she became aware of his gaze upon her.

'I still can't get over the likeness between you and Saphira. Although, if I may be so bold, I feel bound to say you are far prettier,' he murmured.

'Oh, hardly,' she demurred, certain he must be mocking.

'I mean it, Merryn. Fond as I am of Saphira, she can be something of a minx and I find your company more stimulating.'

'Oh?' she asked, staring at him for any sign he was teasing. 'You will miss her when she embarks on her travels, I am sure.'

'I shall indeed. However, it would be more than my life's worth to let her know that,' he grinned.

'It must be nice to have a sister,' she said, as they made their way ever closer to the store.

'Yes, but Saphira can be quite a handful.' She was about to ask him about his parents and if he had any other siblings when the carriage drew to a halt.

'Goodness, we're back at the store already,' she said, staring out of the window in surprise.

'I have enjoyed this afternoon enormously, Merryn, and do hope we may meet again,' he said.

'I'd like that,' she replied, her heart flipping. 'Thank you so much for the delicious meal.'

'My pleasure.' He helped her down from the carriage. It didn't move away, though, and as she made her way round to the staff entrance she could feel his eyes burning into her back.

Her heart still fizzing, she opened the door and made for the stairs. All she wanted was to steal up to her room and reflect on the wonderful time she'd had.

'So there you are,' Mrs Smale called from the hallway.

It was as if she'd been lying in wait, Merry thought, her heart flopping. However, she pinned a smile on her face.

'Yes, here I am, Mrs Smale,' she called brightly. 'Lieutenant Meredith ensured he got me back on time.'

'Pah, I don't know why you're looking like so pleased with yourself. He merely used getting his precious family necklace back as an excuse, an opening, if you like. Men like that only take the likes of you shop girls out for one reason,' she spat. Then her eyes narrowed. 'You look extremely flushed, Miss Dyer. Have you been imbibing alcohol?'

'I had only one small glass of elderflower champagne,' Merry replied.

'And that is one glass too many. It is strictly against the rules of your indenture, Miss Dyer.'

'Whatever are you doing here on a Sunday afternoon, Mrs Smale?' Mr Fairbright said, peering over the banister.

'I had things to attend to, Mr Fairbright,' she replied. 'Have you seen that shop display?'

'Indeed I have. A great improvement, if I might

be so bold as to say, and the window is looking much more in keeping with the changing season. It is already feeling much colder, don't you think?'

'Oh...' the manageress stuttered. 'Well, I'm pleased you like it. Of course, I do pride myself on my displays,' she gushed. As she stood there preening like a puffed-up peacock, Merry wanted to point out that it was Mrs Winter who was responsible for the change; then she saw the twinkle in Mr Fairbright's eye and realized he knew all along.

'Did you have a nice afternoon, my dear?' he asked.

'Yes, thank you, Mr Fairbright,' she answered.

Mrs Smale opened her mouth to speak but Mr Fairbright beat her to it.

'Good. I see Meredith kept his word and brought you back on the dot of five o'clock. It is most conscientious of you to see your staff return safely home, Mrs Smale,' he added.

'Oh, yes, well, of course that is another thing I pride myself on,' the manageress gushed.

'Good, good. Well, you get off home now for I am sure Mrs Rose will be waiting for you. How is she getting on in her new position?' he enquired.

'She is much happier as companion to Mrs Crawford, thank you, and most grateful for your recommendation.'

Mr Fairbright beamed. 'Well, it seems everything worked out then. I did feel Mrs Rose's caring nature would be more suited there. Now I really must insist you go home, Mrs Smale, and I'm sure Miss Dyer has things to attend to before the store reopens tomorrow. Good evening, ladies.'

As the manageress stood gaping after him, Merry stifled a grin and took the opportunity to run up the back stairs to the little room in the attic. For once she was relieved the others were out, for she wanted to think back over her wonderful afternoon with Carey. Despite the early hour, she undressed quickly, clambered into bed and closed her eyes.

Immediately she saw his aquamarine eyes staring into hers and, recalling the heat of his touch as he'd helped her on with her mantle, she sighed contentedly. The way he'd gazed at her as if she was the only woman in the room, listened attentively to all she said, responding with his dry sense of humour and self-deprecation – why, he'd made her feel as if she was someone important. She couldn't help comparing that to Nicco's high-handed manner and the way he dismissed her opinions as being of little worth. There was no doubt about it: Carey Meredith, with his quiet intelligence and easy good manners, had drawn her in. Then she remembered what Mrs Smale had said and her heart plummeted. He probably had just been kind, taking her out as a reward for finding the necklace, and it was hardly likely she'd hear from him again.

She must have fallen asleep for the next thing she knew, Freckles was tugging at her bedclothes.

'Come on, Merry, it's time to get up. We are dying to hear all about your assignation with the dashing lieutenant.'

'Hmm,' she murmured, the thought of him immediately conjuring up his easy smile...

'Merry Dyer, stop smirking and get out of bed

this instant,' Freckles ordered.

'You are mean,' she moaned, pulling the covers back over her head.

'And you'll be late if you don't get a move on. Why, you didn't even come down for supper. Chester was right put out. He wanted to tell you about the new plan he's hatched. By the way, Joanie has been told to put a sprig of parsley on all our plates and two on Smelly's,' she hooted.

Obviously Mr Fairbright had seen fit to take action, Merry thought, remembering their recent conversation.

'Do hurry,' Freckles urged as Merry stretched lazily. 'Look at you. Anyone would think you were Lady Muck.'

'All right, all right,' she muttered, quickly stepping into her uniform, then covering it with the voluminous apron.

'Did you have a good time?' Prunella asked, as they hurried down the stairs.

'Yes, I did and thank you again for lending me your bonnet and mantle. It made such... What was that?' she asked.

'It sounded like old Smelly,' Freckles said, quickening her step.

'Oh, the smell, it's revolting,' the manageress screamed. She was standing in the entrance to ladieswear, an expression of sheer disgust on her face.

'What's the matter, Mrs Smale?' Freckles asked.

'Look,' the woman wailed, pointing to something brown just inside the door. 'Oh, heavens above, there's more over there and there and...'

'What is it?' Prunella asked.

'Looks like dog muck,' Freckles said.

'Oh, the smell is getting stronger. It's quite overpowering. Get that mess cleaned up at once,' the manageress ordered, covering her nose with her hand.

'Something wrong, Mrs Smell? I mean, Mrs Smale?' Chester asked, appearing behind them.

'A dog,' the manageress spluttered.

'There is a dog in the store?' Chester asked, shaking his head in disbelief.

'I sincerely hope not,' she replied. 'But look at all that mess. It's everywhere and the smell is indescribable.'

Chester sniffed and then sniffed again. 'Cripes, it is quite vile,' he agreed.

'I can't smell anything,' Freckles muttered to Merry. Chester turned and winked, then went over to the manageress.

'Stand back, Mrs Smale. I will check if there's a dog in the room and then clean up the mess,' he said, but the trainees could see he was trying to keep a straight face.

'Thank you, Mr Hall,' the manageress said, putting her hand to her heart.

'Here doggy-woggy,' Chester called. 'Come to Chessy Wessy.'

As he made a great show of searching behind the counter, Merry turned to Freckles. 'He's behind this, isn't he?' she whispered.

'Probably,' Freckles shrugged. 'I told you he'd come up with another ruse. Look at old Smelly's face: if she puts her nose any higher she'll be able to wipe the ceiling with it.'

'Can't see any sign of a dog, Mrs Smale,'

257

Chester was saying, 'but I've cleaned up all the mess.'

'Thank you, young man,' she gasped, quite oblivious to the fact he had no brush or cloth in his hands. 'I can still smell it, though, so I think you'd better open the windows whilst you're here. Ladies, go and have your breakfast. You can prepare the shop later when the air has refreshed.'

They were making their way back along the corridor when Chester, Teddy and Nicholas caught up with them.

'Mrs Smale has ordered both the shop floors be scrubbed so we've been told to join you in the staff-room,' Teddy said, grinning at Chester.

'I suppose you boys were behind that prank,' Freckles giggled as she took her seat. 'What a performance. Can't say I smelled anything, though.'

'Well, you wouldn't have because these don't smell,' Chester said, carefully taking half a dozen brown shapes from his pocket. 'Thought old Smelly needed taking down a peg or two after the way she's treated Merry.' As he sat beaming at her proudly across the table, Merry couldn't help thinking that he suddenly seemed very immature. She was saved from answering by Joanie coming through the door, carefully balancing a tray.

'I hear you've been up to your tricks again, Master Hall,' she said.

'A good wheeze, don't you think, Joanie?' he chortled, taking his dish of porridge from her.

'You'll cop it one of these days, young man, you mark my words,' she warned.

A hush descended as they tucked into their breakfast. Merry, still full from the previous day, stared across the table at Freckles and Chester pretending to hold their noses as they ate. Teddy was grinning at them whilst Nicholas and Prunella were quietly eating their meal.

It suddenly struck her how ladylike Prunella was, from the erect manner in which she sat to the way she delicately held her spoon and took tiny mouthfuls. Merry decided that was how she would behave in the future. In the meantime, she was going to look through the patterns and materials in the store and see if there was something simple yet stylish she could make. Whilst she was good at knitting, her sewing skills left much to be desired.

The next couple of days were busy in the store and the assistants only just had time to snatch a hurried luncheon before the carriages began arriving for the Wednesday afternoon trade collection. As before, Mrs Smale had taken herself off to the stockroom, leaving Mrs Winter to take charge.

'Wonder if we'll manage to get away early this week. I'd so like to visit the market,' Freckles whispered as they waited behind their allotted piles. 'I was thinking that if you're seeing that toff, I might try me luck with Chester. Mind you, I'll need something to make him notice me.'

'I think he's already done that, Freckles,' Merry replied.

'I don't think we'll be getting away early,' Prunella said, pointing to Chester and Nicholas, who were adding more packages to their piles. Trade had been brisk that week and sales more numerous than ever before. Mrs Smale had been quite gleeful when she'd totted up the ledger earlier.

Merry sighed for she too had been hoping Mrs Winter's system for speedy collection would mean they could finish early. She was becoming increasingly self-conscious of her shabby clothes and having already seen material that would make a perfect skirt, she was keen to look through the patterns whilst the store was closed. Then she let out a long sigh. Even with her staff discount, she knew she would have to wait until pay day before she could purchase anything.

Chapter 26

Just then the servants began filing in through the back door, jolting Merry from her reverie. As she took in their plain dress and heavy boots, she couldn't help reflecting on the difference in the fortunes of the various classes of society. It was something that had been on her mind since the previous day when she'd heard a client lamenting the fact that her husband was mean with her allowance. Apparently he'd given her only enough to purchase material for one silk dress, a few muslins and some trimmings. Added to this, she had to make do with one new summer and winter bonnet each year. Merry had stared at the well-turned-out woman in astonishment. Obviously, she had no idea how lucky she was.

As the girls lined up, she turned her attention to the pile of packages waiting for distribution. The time flashed by with ever more servants arriving to collect their employers' purchases. Mrs Winter, who insisted on checking out each purchase, was busy ticking items from her list when a woman entered and stood looking around uncertainly. Spotting Merry, her eyes widened and she hurried over, announcing she'd come to collect the purchases for Miss Meredith. At the sound of the familiar name Merry's heart gave a flip but she smiled and began collecting together the parcels labelled for Carey's friendly sister.

'Master Hall,' Mrs Winter said, looking up and snapping her fingers. 'Assistance is required here, please.'

As Chester hurried over, the girl leaned forward and placed something in Merry's hand.

'A communication for you from Miss Meredith,' she whispered. Seeing Mrs Winter frowning in their direction, Merry hurriedly placed the note in her pocket.

For the rest of the afternoon, every time Merry moved the note crackled in the pocket of her dress, reminding her it was waiting to be read. Why would Saphira write to her? She was dying to find out. However, the carriage trade continued into the evening and by the time the trainees had tidied and cleaned everywhere, it was supper time.

'So much for getting away early,' Freckles sighed, wiping a hand across her brow. 'Come along, you two, my belly thinks my throat's been slit.' Linking arms with Merry and Prunella, she pulled them towards the staff-room. However, Merry was curious to know what was in the letter and pulled away.

'I need to get something from upstairs, so I'll see you in a few moments,' she said, hurrying down the passage before her friend could ask any questions.

Up in the attic room, Merry quickly lit the candle, took the note from her pocket and carefully broke the seal.

My dear Merry,

You have my heartfelt gratitude for finding my necklace. I can't tell you how distraught I was when I arrived home and discovered it was missing.

I did so enjoy our afternoon selecting materials and trimmings and am indebted for your invaluable advice. However, as your Mrs Stitches pointed out, I purchased far too much for my immediate requirement (my enthusiasm does so run away with me at times), and that I would need to return to discuss further orders. As you know, I am shortly leaving on vacation so alas this will not be possible. I would be most grateful therefore if you would also accept the surplus fabric as a small gesture of my appreciation for your honesty. I know the colours will suit for I am still in absolute shock at the likeness between us.

I have penned a letter of instruction to this effect to Mr Fairbright so there can be absolutely no misunderstanding by any member of the staff! I do hope that repugnant woman is now chewing parsley as per my recommendation.

Yours affectionately,
Saphira Meredith

PS. Carey has been looking really happy since his luncheon with you!

Ah, so that was where the parsley on their plates had come from. That Saphira had suggested Merry should have the surplus fabric and trimmings was exciting news in itself, but it was the postscript that made her heart jump. Dare she hope Carey Meredith might contact her again? No, that was a silly notion: he'd merely been polite, rewarding her for her honesty. Still, as soon as she could, she'd collect the material from Mrs Stitches and make a start on something new to wear.

Merry threw herself into her work during the week then, much to her friends' chagrin, spent her Sunday off sewing a new skirt.

'That toff's turned your head, if you ask me. Fancy spending the day indoors when you could come on the tram with us,' Freckles scoffed.

Merry smiled as she picked up her sewing.

The sage-green material Saphira had given her was finer than anything she'd ever dreamed of owning and she was anxious not to make a mess of the skirt. Mrs Stitches had loaned her a pattern and even showed her how to pin it to the cloth before cutting it out. However, it took longer to make up than she'd envisaged and although she spent the rest of the day sewing, it was only when the shadows were lengthening that she placed the final stitch. Hurriedly, she tried it on and then slipped into the blouse Saphira had given her. As she'd thought, the green of the skirt complemented the pink beautifully. Sighing she took them off and hung them carefully in the closet, wondering how long it would be before she would be able to wear them.

The next morning was busy and nothing any of them did seemed to please Mrs Smale. One client got so impatient at having to wait, Merry even ventured to ask if she could attend to the woman herself.

'Indeed you may not, Miss Dyer. Please remember you are still a trainee and as such it is your duty to shadow.'

'I merely wish to purchase buttons,' the woman persisted.

'If modam would care to wait just one moment, I will attend her personally,' Mrs Smale insisted.

'No, modam does not care to wait a moment longer,' the woman said, picking up her reticule and marching from the store.

'If you didn't take so long wrapping purchases, that would never have happened,' the manageress snapped at Merry.

'Perhaps Miss Dyer could be permitted to assist clients with trimmings and accessories,' Mrs Winter ventured, only to receive a withering look from Mrs Smale.

'I feel it pertinent to remind you that I am in charge here, Mrs Winter.'

'I was merely pointing out that it won't do the store's reputation any good if clients walk out because they have not the time nor inclination to wait until you can serve them personally,' the supervisor replied.

'When I require the opinion of my deputy I will ask for it,' Mrs Smale snapped.

'Is everything all right, ladies?' They'd all been so engrossed in the battle between manageress and supervisor that nobody had heard Mr Didcot's cane tip-tapping across the floor.

'Yes, thank you, Mr Didcot,' Mrs Smale simpered.

'Not really, sir,' Mrs Winter replied at the same time. Just then the bell sounded for the store to close for luncheon and Mr Didcot turned towards them.

'You take yourself off for your meal, girls,' he said. 'Mrs Smale and Mrs Winter, perhaps you would remain behind a moment.'

'Do you think they'll be reprimanded?' Prunella asked Merry as they followed Freckles along the corridor.

'I don't know but we can't have the clients walking out like that,' Merry replied.

'I hope they both get what for,' Freckles grumbled, pushing open the door to the staff-room. 'Ooh, look,' she squealed, pointing to the table on which lay a small bouquet of flowers, wrapped in a lace doily and tied with satin.

'I wonder who they are for,' Merry gasped.

'Well, they've been put in your place, you numkin,' her friend giggled, nudging her arm. 'Coo, they smell lovely. They must have cost a fortune.'

'But who...?' Merry began, her heart thumping madly.

'Why don't you read the card?' Prunella suggested. Hurriedly Merry tore open the little envelope that was pinned to the ribbon.

My dearest Merryn,

Please accept these flowers as a token of my affection and appreciation for the pleasure of your delightful company. I wonder if you will do me the honour of joining me again this forthcoming Sunday? I shall wait in the yard as before, but if you do not feel able to join me, I will quite understand.

Fondly yours,
Carey Meredith

'Oh,' she gasped, her heart racing. Slowly she returned the card to its envelope, then saw Freckles and Prunella staring at her expectantly.

'Come on, tell us,' Freckles demanded impatiently. 'Is it from him?' As Merry nodded, Freckles gave a sniff. 'I'd have expected something more luxurious than a bunch of mixed blooms.'

'Well, it's the finest tussie-mussie I've seen in a long time, and it was delivered, too,' Joanie said, placing their bowls of broth garnished with sprigs of parsley on the table.

'Floriography is such a marvellous conveyance of one's feelings,' Prunella said.

'Flori what?' Freckles asked.

'Floriography. It's a way of communicating a message through flowers. Each one symbolizes a different emotion.'

Merry gazed at Prunella in wonderment. Was there no end to her knowledge?

'So what do these pink things mean?' Freckles persisted, pausing mid-mouthful.

'Pink camellias mean longing, the white mean

adoration, gardenias mean you're lovely, forget-me-nots, wonderful memories, and the forsythia anticipation. Oh, Merry, that's how he thinks of you,' Prunella sighed.

'Blimey oh rimey, give me red roses any time,' Freckles muttered. 'You know where you stand with them.'

'And I suppose you've received many such bouquets, have you?' Joanie asked. Freckles pouted and the housekeeper grinned. 'It seems your Lieutenant Meredith is more subtle, Merry. A gentleman like him knows how to court a woman properly. Would you like me to put these in water till supper time?'

'Oh, no,' Merry cried. 'I've never received flowers before and I want to keep them beside me so that I can look at them.'

'Is that wise?' Prunella asked, looking worried as they made their way back onto the shop floor.

To their surprise Mr Didcot was still talking to Mrs Smale and Mrs Winter.

'Ah, Miss Dyer, those will brighten our counter nicely,' Mrs Smale said, smirking as she took the flowers from Merry.

'But I...' Merry protested.

'I'm sure Miss Dyer will be pleased to share her beautiful flowers with our clients until she finishes for the evening,' Mr Didcot said, smiling at Merry. 'Now, ladies, you have been here for nearly four months and I feel it is time to put your training into practice. From now on you will attend to our clients yourselves.'

Freckles winked at Merry. 'No more shadowing old Smelly,' she whispered.

As Mrs Smale glared in their direction, Mr Didcot added, 'You will, of course, still be guided by Mrs Smale and Mrs Winter.' There was a sharp intake of breath and Mr Didcot turned to the manageress. 'Naturally, I will still be looking to you to continue your meticulous recording of our sales in the ledger, Mrs Smale.'

'Of course, Mr Didcot,' the woman simpered, and Merry thought again how adept he was at making everyone feel they had an important role to play.

Sunday dawned at last and, knowing she'd be seeing Carey in half an hour, Merry could hardly contain her excitement as she and Prunella made their way back to the store after church. The others, having decided to investigate another part of the town, had already hopped onto a waiting tram.

'You can borrow my mantle again, if you wish,' Prunella offered.

'Are you sure you won't need it?' Merry asked.

The girl shook her head. 'Father has something important to discuss so is sending his carriage to collect me. I can wear my second-best one home and bring another back with me.' Merry's eyes widened. She knew her friend's parents were of good standing but even so, to be able to leave wearing one mantle and return in another was beyond her comprehension.

'I know you want to look good when Lieutenant Meredith calls for you. Hey, isn't that your friend Nicco?' Prunella asked, pointing to a figure in a donkey cart that was pulled up outside the front entrance. Merry's heart plummeted. Whatever was he doing here? She barely had enough time to refresh herself before Carey arrived as it was. Quickly she ran over to him.

'Such eagerness to see me is heartening,' Nicco grinned.

'You never told me you were coming,' Merry cried.

'And good day to you too,' he replied. 'Nothing to say I have to book an appointment to see my girl, is there?'

'I am not your girl, Nicco. How many times must I tell you that?'

'I love the way your cheeks go red when you're excited,' he grinned. 'However, Nicco, being a man of the world, knows it is all part of the playing-hard-to-get game you girls like to engage in.' Merry fought down the urge to scream. She didn't have time for this.

'Well, I'm sorry but you've had a wasted journey for I have made prior arrangements,' she replied, anxiously looking around for any sign of Carey's arrival.

'Oh?' he asked, his dark eyes narrowing. 'And what could be more important than going out with me?'

'I've already told you, I spend my day off with my new friends,' she said.

'Is that all?' he shrugged dismissively. 'Come on, climb up and we'll go for a ride.'

Merry felt like screaming at his high-handed manner.

'Are you coming, Merry?' Prunella called. 'Father's carriage will be arriving soon and we mustn't keep him waiting.'

Nicco stared at Prunella then back to Merry. 'You're going out in a fancy carriage? No wonder you don't want to be seen in a mere donkey cart,' he muttered, his lips tightening into a line. 'Far be it from me to keep you from your posh friend. I have other things to do anyway.' With a final glare, he picked up the reins and shouted to the donkey to get going.

Sighing with relief, Merry watched him trundle away. She was sorry if he'd had a wasted journey but she hadn't asked him to come, had she?

'Come along, Merry,' Prunella urged, breaking into her thoughts.

'Thank you so much, Prunella,' she said. 'I don't know how I would have got rid of Nicco had you not inferred I was travelling with you.' Her friend smiled and together they made their way down the side path.

They'd only just pushed the door shut when they heard hooves clattering on the cobbles in the yard. Peering through the glass, Merry gasped in dismay.

'He's early.'

'Don't panic,' Prunella said, shrugging off her mantle and handing it to Merry. 'Here, slip this on.' Smiling gratefully, Merry threw off her old cloak but as she shrugged on the mantle, her hands were shaking so badly, she could hardly fasten the clasp. Prunella stepped in to help, then took off her bonnet. 'Come on, this goes better with the mantle.'

'I feel sick,' Merry said, swaying back against the banister. 'I can't meet him feeling like this.'

270

Chapter 27

'Here, this will settle you,' Prunella said, taking a small bottle from her reticule and holding it under Merry's nose.

'Crikey, whatever's that?' Merry spluttered.

'Smelling salts, and they've worked a treat. You've got beautiful pink cheeks now, so off you go.'

'Are you sure I look all right?' Merry asked, smoothing down her new skirt.

'You look lovely. Now remember, a lady never panics nor hurries. Take a deep breath and glide serenely out of the door. A man's first glimpse of you should make his heart beat faster as he is enchanted by your sweet countenance. Well, that's what Mother always says, anyhow,' Prunella confessed.

Merry didn't know about Carey's heart beating faster; hers was pounding like crazy as she went outside and walked as elegantly as she could towards the carriage. His eyes lit up as he saw her approach and he reached out to help her inside.

'I'm so pleased you could join me,' he greeted her. 'The food at the Madison takes some beating therefore I've reserved a table there again. I hope that is all right with you?' As his aquamarine eyes searched hers for approval, she couldn't help thinking how different he was from Nicco, with his arrogant presumption that she would quietly go along with whatever he suggested.

'That will be lovely,' she replied, settling herself onto the leather squab. Then she felt his gaze upon her and her pulses began racing again. 'Thank you for the beautiful flowers.'

'You got the message?' he asked, and she knew by the way he was staring at her that he meant their significance rather than the blooms them-selves.

'Yes, I did and I was immensely flattered,' she smiled, hoping she hadn't been too forward.

'May I say how delightful you look,' he said.

'I expect it's this new skirt,' she replied, running her hand down soft folds of the material.

'You ladies and your attire,' he laughed. 'To be honest, I hadn't even noticed what you were wearing. Very remiss of me, I know, but it was your confidence to which I referred. You seem more at ease with yourself somehow. Goodness, here we are already,' he said, peering out of the window as they pulled to a halt.

He waited until they had ordered their meal before pursuing their conversation.

'I mentioned earlier how much more self-assured you seem, so what have you been up to since we last met?'

As his gaze held hers, she again felt that strange fluttering in her chest. How could she explain that it was wearing respectable clothes that made her feel more poised in his presence? He was always immaculately turned out and she didn't wish to show him up. She could hardly say that, though, for someone like him would take good clothes for granted.

'We have been permitted to attend to clients ourselves rather than shadowing the manageress and supervisor,' she replied, hoping this answer would suffice.

'That's marvellous. Saphira said you had immediately grasped what she wanted, which is in itself a miracle, for she changes her mind as often as her brooches. You must tell me more about it during our meal,' he said getting to his feet as the *maître d'hôtel* arrived to show them to their table.

Merry enjoyed herself so much that the time sped by and almost before she knew it, they were on their way back, then pulling up in the yard. Again she appreciated the way he didn't question her use of the staff entrance.

Then she froze, certain she could feel someone watching her. Turning to look out of the window she thought she saw a shadow lurking in the corner of the stables. She pressed her head to the glass but all she could see was the hay piled up against the wall. Then, with a jolt, she realized Carey was speaking.

'Thank you for a splendid afternoon, Merryn,' he said, leaning forward and patting her hand. 'Saphira told me you will be celebrating your birthday mid-month.'

'Why, yes! So much has happened recently, I'd almost forgotten,' she laughed.

'As my ship is being deployed in two days' time, regrettably I shall be away. I hope therefore you will accept this small gift and allow me to take you out by way of a late celebration when my ship returns?' he asked, holding out a small package.

'Thank you,' she said, staring at the beribboned parcel in surprise.

'I trust it will be to your liking. If not, you may blame Saphira for she helped me to choose. Now no peeking until the day itself,' he said, jumping down from the carriage and holding out his hand to help her down. At the touch of his fingers, she felt that funny tingle travel up her arm. 'Many happy returns, my dearest Merryn. I shall be thinking of you.' He leaned forward and took her hand. As he slowly raised it to his lips, a delicious feeling of warmth spread through her body. With a rueful grin he jumped back into his carriage.

'And I you,' she whispered, hugging her present closer as the carriage pulled away.

'Blimey oh rimey, girl, you're all lit up like a gas globe,' Freckles said, joining her as she made her way inside. 'No need to ask if you had a good time. Mind you, we did too. Come on, let's get inside, it's freezing,' she cried, stamping her feet.

A gust of wind howled through the passage by the privy, shaking the last of the leaves from the trees and Merry noticed for the first time that it had got very cold.

'Went all the way to the ferry port, this tram did, then Chester and I shared a poke of chips to warm us up. Where did you go?' Freckles continued as they made their way up the stairs.

'The Madison,' Merry replied.

'You got a decent spread then. Either that Carey ain't got the imagination to think of somewhere different or he's trying to impress you by taking you to the best hotel again. Blimey, gifts as well?' Freckles asked, pointing to her package.

'It's a birthday present,' she said without thinking.

'When's the big day then?' Freckles asked, her green eyes sparking curiosity.

'Not till next weekend, but Carey's ship is being deployed so I won't be seeing him,' Merry sighed.

'Never mind, girl, we'll have a celebration here, eh?' Merry smiled, knowing her friend was trying to cheer her up. 'Aren't you going to open it then?' Freckles asked, lighting the candle, then staring at Merry expectantly.

'Carey said not to until the day itself.'

'Oh, go on, he won't know, will he?' her friend urged, but then the door creaked open and Prunella came staggering into the room, half hidden behind a huge box.

'Coo, what you got there, girl?' Freckles asked.

'Mother and Father are moving residence so I took the opportunity to bring back a few extra clothes,' she said, collapsing onto the bed and taking off a bonnet and mantle they hadn't seen before.

'Are you all right, Prunella?' Merry asked, noticing her friend's pallor.

'Father's allowance doesn't run to tipping the driver so he refused to help me carry them up. I haven't missed supper, have I?'

'No, you're all right. Didn't they roast the fatted calf then?'

Prunella sighed. 'Mother's had to let the cook go and she just about managed to serve up cheese and biscuits.'

'Poor old thing, you should have come with us;

we had chips. Mind you, I'm starving now. By the way, Merry, we saw that Nicco of yours lurking around here earlier. Looking livid, he was.'

Remembering the shadow in the stables, Merry's heart thudded. Surely he hadn't been watching her? Then a low boom sounded, breaking into her thoughts.

'Oh, good, there's the gong. Are you coming, Merry?' Freckles asked.

'Sorry, I couldn't eat another thing,' she admitted, relishing the prospect of time to herself to reflect on her afternoon with Carey. He was just wonderful, she thought, running her fingers over the crisp wrapping paper and wondering what her present could be.

With the weather taking a turn for the worst, few clients ventured out and the store was quieter than usual. Even the manageress and supervisor, with no cause to compete, were quiet, and the trainees were tasked with tidying out all the drawers and cabinets. By Saturday, everywhere was so tidy Merry wondered how they would pass the day.

'I think we will take ourselves off to the stockroom and run a check on the linen, Mrs Winter,' Mrs Smale said.

'What are we to do, then?' Freckles asked.

'Look after things in here, of course, Miss Brice,' the manageress replied, hurrying from the room.

'Not sure we'll be able to cope with so many clients,' Freckles said, staring around the empty store. Merry laughed, then noticed Prunella frowning out of the window at the snow-lined paths.

'You all right?' she asked for the umpteenth time that week. Prunella nodded quickly and turned her attention to the already tidy display. Merry sighed. Whatever was on the girl's mind she was keeping it to herself. She'd certainly been preoccupied since she'd returned from her visit home. Home! If she'd been at home her mother would have been busy making her a birthday cake and Grozen would be grumbling at her extravagant use of the butter and eggs. Merry wondered how they were and if it was snowing back in Porthsallos.

Then the door burst open and two women swathed in fur coats were blown in on a gust of wind. They were chatting like magpies and hardly paused for breath as they stamped their booted feet on the bristle mat.

'Stiff in his bed, he was. Always was an awkward man. Of course, he couldn't have been considerate and died in the summer when the weather was warmer. Oh, no, he had to wait until we had a snow storm, didn't he? Typical of him,' the larger woman sniffed. 'He probably hopes I'll catch my death at his graveside.'

'There, there, dear, don't go upsetting yourself,' her companion answered.

'Good afternoon, how may I be of assistance?' Merry asked. She'd long since shortened the greeting to what she considered was polite but not long-winded.

'My friend's husband has just died,' the smaller woman said, in hushed tones.

'I am so sorry,' Merry said. 'You will be requiring some suitable attire for the funeral?'

'I'll be taking a yard of black ribbon,' the larger woman sniffed. 'I haven't got money to waste on things I won't be wearing again.' Merry stared at the well-dressed woman in surprise. 'One yard of black ribbon and not an inch more, and do be quick about it, girl, before we freeze to the floor.'

'Yes, of course, madam,' Merry said, carefully unrolling the band along the measure stick on the counter.

'Blimey, they look like a couple of hooded crows,' Freckles said. The trainees watched the women, heads bent close as they continued chatting, leave the store and climb into a phaeton that was pulled up outside. 'Bet the old fella died just to get a bit of peace. Poor thing probably worked all his life to provide them riches, an' all. Just think, if you marry that lieutenant of yours, you could spend your days riding around in something like that.'

Merry stared at her friend in horror.

'Miss Brice, you are not paid to gossip,' Mrs Smale snapped, as she came back into the room.

Merry turned back to her tidying. What a notion for Freckles to suggest! Having finally achieved her independence the last thing she wanted was to give it up. Yet she couldn't deny that she liked Carey. As ever, though, when she thought of Carey, she found herself wondering how he was and now she wondered where his ship was being deployed. It was a shame he'd be away on her birthday but he had taken the trouble to buy her a present and she couldn't wait to open it.

'Miss Dyer, a word if you please.' She looked up to see Mr Fairbright beckoning her from the corridor. What had she done now, she wondered.

'I have just returned from Porthsallos, Miss Dyer. An arduous journey it was too, for I hardly need tell you what the roads are like when it snows. Anyhow, I understand it is your birthday tomorrow and your mother and grandmother send their best wishes along with these gifts. They weren't sure if you intended visiting, and though they would love to see you they wouldn't want you risking an accident in this weather.'

Merry felt a pang of guilt for she'd been so caught up in her new life, she hadn't considered going home for the day.

'Thank you, Mr Fairbright,' she said, taking the proffered parcels.

'You will be pleased to hear they are still attaining their knitting targets and being paid accordingly. Something, I understand, they will be relying upon more now that the pilchards have disappeared.'

'Yes, sir, that is true.' Again she felt guilty for she hadn't thought about that either.

'Now the weather has grown colder, we have decided to sell a selection of their garments in our menswear department, which we hope will boost sales and sustain that source of income.'

'That is wonderful news,' agreed Merry gratefully.

'Anyway, they enquired as to your progress and if they were likely to see you at Christmas. I told them you showed great promise and that if you maintain the high standard of customer service you have so far shown, then I anticipate you making good progress, perhaps even to management one day.'

'Goodness, thank you, sir,' she gasped. She was doing well, she showed promise. Her heart sang with joy in the knowledge she was at last making her dreams come true. Then she realized Mr Fairbright was still speaking.

'As the store will be closed for Christmas and Boxing Days, I also took the liberty of telling them I felt certain you would be paying them a visit then.'

'I will, sir. It is good to know they are both doing well.'

'I am sure you will wish to write and thank them for their presents and let them know when they can expect you. I will be happy to convey your letter to them on my next visit. Now, allow me to wish you many happy returns for tomorrow and I trust you will enjoy your celebrations.'

'Thank you, sir,' Merry said, hurrying back to her position and placing her parcels behind the counter. What celebrations? Still, he wasn't to know Carey was away at sea, was he? And despite Nicco's prolific promises, he had never actually produced anything. Of course, in previous years, her mother and Grozen had always made a point of spoiling her with her favourite meal but life moved on, didn't it, she thought, staring around the store.

Chapter 28

After another hour, with no more clients show-ing, Mr Didcot decided to close the doors.

'I'm starving,' Prunella announced as they made their way to the staff-room for an early supper. Freckles had gone on ahead and they could hear the sound of merriment as they pushed open the door.

'Here she is, the birthday girl,' Teddy cried. Merry stared in surprise at her friends, who were gathered around the table, which was spread with sandwiches, sausages rolls and all manner of tasty-looking titbits. Then she saw another tussie-mussie placed carefully in the centre. This one comprised carnations, white clover and fern, bound with a red satin ribbon. In the middle was one perfectly striped carnation.

'Oh,' she cried, delightedly snatching it up and inhaling the heady fragrance.

'Looks a bit sparse compared to the last one,' Freckles declared.

'No, this message is...' Prunella began, but Chester, eager to begin the festivities, held up a bottle of cider.

'Mr Didcot gave us this so that we could drink a toast to you, Merry,' he said, passing round tumblers of the amber liquid. 'Happy birthday, girl,' he cried. As they all noisily toasted her, Merry couldn't help thinking of Carey and the

281

tender way he'd gazed at her over the top of his crystal glass.

'We didn't know what to get you so we clubbed together and bought this,' Freckles said, breaking into Merry's thoughts as she handed her a package wrapped in the store's paper.

'And I made you this,' Joanie said, coming into the room bearing a large chocolate cake.

'Oh, thank you,' Merry cried, quite overcome by their kindness.

'Come on, open your present, whilst Joanie hands round the cake,' Freckles suggested. Merry eagerly tore at the wrapping and gasped in delight at the length of fur trimming.

'We thought you could use it to edge your mantle for when you next go out with the lieutenant. We know you like to dress all posh-like for him,' Freckles cried. The others dissolved into hysterics as Freckles wiggled and giggled her way across the room.

'I've got another one upstairs you might like to borrow,' Prunella whispered. Merry smiled at her friend.

'This is delicious cake,' Teddy declared, far more interested in his stomach as usual. As the celebrations continued, the talk turned to how they would spend their free time the next day.

'How about going on the train?' Teddy asked, turning to Merry. 'You've never been on one before have you?'

Remembering the sooty, noisy things they'd seen hurtling over the bridge, Merry shuddered.

'Perhaps you would prefer another tram trip or we could wander down to see the sights on the

Hoe?' Chester suggested.

'The Hoe would be lovely,' Merry agreed, remembering her last visit with Nicco, when she hadn't been allowed time to stop and stare.

'A new pier has just opened and there's an old lighthouse you can climb up.'

'How exciting,' Merry cried.

'That's decided then: tomorrow after church, we'll go exploring and treat our Merry to a poke of chips, agreed?' They all cheered and Merry smiled.

'Thank you for spoiling me, everyone,' she cried, carefully collecting up her presents and the tussie-mussie. 'I think I'll go upstairs now,' she said. She was itching to be by herself so that she could read Carey's note, for she knew the flowers could only be from him. To her dismay, Freckles caught hold of Prunella's hand.

'Come along, old thing, we need you to tell us what those flowers mean.'

Up in their little room, Freckles lit the candle, then sank down on the bed beside Merry and Prunella. 'Well?' she asked, impatiently.

'Carnations mean fascination; white clover, think of me; fern, secret love; and that striped carnation in the centre means thinking of you and wishing I could be with you.'

Merry's heart skipped a beat. What lovely senti-ments, she thought, inhaling the heady fragrance once more.

'Must have cost a fortune at this time of year,' Freckles said. 'Blimey oh rimey, girl, if I had a toff like that sending me all them flowers I'd want to know what he wanted in return,' Freckles giggled, tossing her auburn curls.

'I'm sure the lieutenant's intentions are honourable,' Prunella declared, frowning at Freckles.

'Ah, what a shame,' Freckles pouted. 'Anyway, what does lover boy have to say in his card?'

'Perhaps Merry would prefer to read it by herself?' Prunella ventured, and Merry shot her a grateful look.

'Don't be daft. He might be intending to whisk her away and we'll need to know where she's going, won't we?' Freckles reasoned.

Seeing she was beaten, Merry slid the card from its envelope and quickly scanned the contents.

Happy 18th birthday, dearest Merryn. I'm sorry I can't be with you in person but please be assured my thoughts are. I shall be counting the days until we can next be together.

Ever yours, Carey xx

'Oh,' she gasped, flushing with pleasure, then quickly placing the card in her pocket.

'Spoilsport,' Freckles muttered. 'So what else did he give you?'

But Merry was too busy unwrapping the present from her mother to answer. Smiling, she held up the blue shawl knitted in warm worsted wool.

'That'll be ideal this weather,' Prunella said.

Merry nodded. Her grandmother's gift revealed matching gloves. Knowing how long they would have taken her grandmother and mother to make, she sent her thanks winging through the air to Porthsallos. When she next got paid, she'd choose them something really nice from the store to take home for Christmas.

'Come on, then,' Freckles urged, bouncing on the bed impatiently as Merry picked up the be-ribboned parcel from Carey.

Carefully she peeled back the paper. 'Oh,' she gasped, shaking out folds of lacy cashmere that shimmered in a sea of greens and blues.

'Blimey oh rimey, there's no comparison between them, is there?' hooted Freckles, holding up the blue shawl. Feeling a pang, Merry snatched it back. Whilst the home-made shawl and gloves were not of the same quality, her mother and grandmother would have scrimped and saved to buy the wool and then knitted long into the night. She would write a letter to thank them and ask Mr Fairbright if he could take it with him when he next went to Porthsallos.

'That blue suits you a treat, Merry, and the shawl and gloves will keep you lovely and warm this weather, especially if we take the tram to-morrow,' Prunella pointed out. 'And the other will look beautiful over your blouse and skirt when you next dine with Lieutenant Meredith.' Again Merry smiled gratefully at her friend.

'No present from that Nicco, then?' Freckles asked.

Merry shook her head and laughed. 'He doesn't go in for that sort of thing. Says words mean more.'

Freckles snorted. 'Except he didn't turn up to say anything, did he? Well, I'm for me bed. I think Chester is beginning to notice me at last, so mind you two stay out of the way tomorrow.'

However, when they woke the next day, it was obvious nobody was going anywhere.

'Blimey oh rimey, it's so bright me eyes are hurting,' Freckles said, glaring at the light streaming in through the skylight. 'I never drank that much cider, surely?'

'It's so quiet,' Merry said, peering out through the glass. 'Oh my, everywhere is white and my feet are freezing.'

Dressing quickly in their warmest clothes, they hurried downstairs to find the boys already tucking into bowls of porridge. As Joanie poured their tea, Merry wrapped her icy hands gratefully around the mug.

'What'll we do today then?' Freckles asked, looking at Chester.

'Perky told us we had to clear the yard,' Teddy moaned. 'Apparently Mrs Smale nearly slipped on her way to the privy yesterday. He said she could have had a nasty accident.'

'She would have if she didn't make it in time,' Freckles hooted. 'She'd have been a right old smelly then.' Merry saw Prunella and Nicholas exchange exasperated looks and wished their friend wouldn't be quite so crude. 'We can have a snowball fight with the snow you pile up.'

'Great idea,' Chester said brightening. 'Come along, you lot,' he said, jumping to his feet.

As the others followed him out of the room, Prunella turned to Merry. 'I think I'll go upstairs and sort out the things I brought back with me.'

'Want some help?' Merry offered.

Prunella smiled. 'You don't fancy a snowball

fight either, then?'

While Prunella emptied the contents of her box onto the bed, Merry tidied her birthday things away into her drawer of the closet. She was already wearing her new shawl and the gloves would certainly be useful this cold weather too. As she neatly folded the cashmere stole, she thought again of Carey and wondered how long it would be before she saw him. Catching sight of her flowers she thought again of their message. Was he thinking of her now? Did he really find her fascinating? She couldn't think why. As for secret love, the very thought sent shivers tingling all up and down her spine.

A sob broke into her thoughts and she saw Prunella gazing at her bed, tears rolling down her cheeks.

'Prunella, whatever's wrong?' she asked, hurrying over and putting her arm around the girl's shoulder.

'It was seeing these clothes,' she sobbed. 'It reminded me how much my life's changed. Mother and Father have removed to that ghastly house and...'

'You'll still be able to visit them, though, won't you?'

Prunella stifled another sob with her lace kerchief. 'Not if I marry the man they've found for me.'

'They've found a man for you?' Merry gasped. Of course she knew such things went on, especially among the upper classes, but this was the eighteen eighties after all. 'Is he nice?'

'According to Father, he will make a marvellous match. I've yet to meet him, though, for he lives miles away in Gloucestershire.'

'Surely that's not so far by carriage?'

'But he's sixty-one and bed-ridden,' Prunella sobbed.

'Then why...?'Merry began, then the penny dropped. 'He has money?'

'And a title,' she squeaked. 'Just when Nicholas and I...' She stared down at the bed.

So her suspicions had been correct, Merry thought.

'Look, let me help you put your things away and we can talk whilst we work,' she said, remembering Grozen telling her how it was easier to open up about things that were worrying you when your hands were busy.

'I shan't go,' Prunella declared. 'That's why I brought all these things with me.'

'You do have some lovely clothes,' Merry whispered. 'Come on, let's get them hung up or you'll have to borrow Joanie's smoothing iron.'

'But I don't know how to use one,' Prunella wailed. 'My maid always ensured my attire was laid out ready for me to step into.'

Merry blinked at her in surprise. 'Oh, I see,' she replied, and began shaking out the creases.

'If Nicholas and I...' Prunella began. 'Well, if we... I suspect I'll have to learn how to do all these things, won't I?'

'And if I am lucky enough to go out with Lieutenant Meredith again, I shall need to learn how to conduct myself correctly, so we can help each other, can't we?' Merry replied.

The two girls looked at each other and smiled. And even if she was being presumptuous about Carey, Merry decided, it would do no harm to learn how to act more like a lady, would it?

Although the weather remained cold there was no more snow, and people began venturing into the store again. Merry was pleased to be occupied for, truth to tell, she was spending far too much time thinking about Carey. She hadn't heard anything from him since her birthday but guessed that, he being in the navy, that was something she'd have to get used to. If he wanted to see her again, that was. His flower message had implied that he did.

'Miss Dyer, if it's not too much trouble perhaps you would assist Mrs Winter,' Mrs Smale's strident tones cut into her thoughts.

'Yes, of course, Mrs Smale,' Merry replied, hurrying over to the supervisor, who was leading a rather rotund woman towards the dressing room. 'How may I help, Mrs Winter?'

'Madam requires some new undergarments but is not sure of her size,' the supervisor whispered. 'Please be on hand to fetch and carry. This may take some time.'

Merry spent the next hour traipsing from the dressing room to the corset closet – as Freckles had named it – and back again.

'This is testing even Harracks's ingenuity, not to mention my patience,' Mrs Winter whispered, as Merry handed her yet another size.

'This is the largest we stock,' Merry murmured, handing over the garment, then resuming her place a discreet distance from the dressing room. Even from here she could hear the frustrated sighs and groans as the woman endeavoured to squeeze her body into the corset. Finally the client admitted defeat and emerged red-faced.

'These are just not made correctly,' she announced, tossing the garment at Merry. As Mrs Winter followed after the woman, Merry heard a titter. Looking up she saw Saphira Meredith's friend, the formidable Alexandria, watching, a sneer curling her lips. Merry smiled politely but the woman ignored her and turned to her friends.

'I can't imagine anything worse than having to purchase ready-made undergarments – other than having to sell them, of course.' As high-pitched laughter rang around the floor, Merry noticed Mrs Smale frowning in her direction.

'May I help you, Miss Courtland?' she asked, thankful she'd remembered the woman's name.

'I hardly think so. Imagine purchasing anything from a place such as this,' Alexandria grimaced to her friends, who let out derisive sniggers. 'When a man takes me out I always take great pains to dress properly.' She paused and gave a theatrical sigh. 'It means couture, of course, but then a man such as Carey expects nothing less.' At the mention of his name, Merry's heart jumped. 'Come along, darlings, let's leave this little shop girl to her tidying up. After that sensational party at the weekend I have a feeling I shall be requiring something very feminine indeed.' She gave an affected titter, then, with a final sneer at Merry, turned and marched from the store, closely followed by her entourage.

'What an absolute cow,' Freckles hissed, appearing at Merry's side. 'Don't you take no...'

'Am I to wait all day for that stock, Miss Brice?' Mrs Smale's imperious voice demanded. 'Miss Dyer, will you please see those undergarments are tidied away from view,' she added, lowering her voice.

With heavy heart, Merry did as she'd been told. Had Carey taken that Alexandria out as she'd implied? If he had, then he couldn't be away like he'd said, could he? She didn't have him down for a liar but the woman wouldn't have announced such a thing if it wasn't true, would she? Come on, Merry, get a grip, she urged herself. Worse things happen at sea, as Grozen always said. The irony hit her in the stomach and she bit her lip. All she had to do was ask him when he next got in touch. That was always supposing he did contact her again.

Chapter 29

Despite her intentions to put Carey to the back of her mind, Merry found thoughts of him popping up at all hours of the day or during the long hours of darkness. To keep her attention focused elsewhere, she threw herself into her job and disciplined herself to act more the lady, like Prunella.

At the beginning of December, to encourage more clients into the store, Mr Fairbright arranged for a small fir tree, decorated with ribbons and candles, to be placed in each of the two bay windows.

'If it was good enough for Prince Albert then it is certainly good enough for the dear people of Plymouth,' he beamed at them. Then he became serious. 'Due to the inclement weather, the store's takings were very low last month. I am depending upon you to encourage our clients to increase their purchases. Mr Didcot is at this very moment addressing the men in the same vein. Remember, it is one month until the end of your probationary period. Good luck and good morning, ladies.'

As he made his way across the floor, Freckles turned to Merry. 'Blimey oh rimey, blackmail or what?' she whispered.

'Would you care to share your pearls of wisdom with us, Miss Brice?' Mrs Smale asked.

'I said we would encourage the punters in if the store was a bit more hot,' she said, pretending to shiver.

'Whilst your grammar leaves a lot to be desired, young lady, your reasoning is sound,' the man-ageress admitted. 'Mrs Winter, perhaps you could hurry after Mr Fairbright and make that sugges-tion.'

Freckles and Merry exchanged glances. 'Why doesn't she do it herself?' Merry whispered.

'Probably thinks he'll give her what for,' Freckles replied.

However, when the supervisor returned some moments later, her smile was brighter than the candlelit window.

'I wonder what she suggested?' Freckles snorted, nudging Merry in the ribs.

Just then the bell sounded for the store to open and they hurried to their places behind the counter. Clients swarmed in, enticed by the tree-lit window, and the assistants were rushed off their feet. Then, to their surprise, Joanie appeared. Wearing her best apron and bearing a silver tray, she began circulating among the shoppers offering them small glasses of spiced wine. As the aroma of cinnamon and cloves wafted around the store, the atmosphere became convivial, inviting the eager clients to linger and purchase.

Word spread and the store became ever busier by the day. Mrs Winter's smile grew wider while Mrs Smale, knowing she'd been bested by her deputy, prowled around scowling and picking on anything and everyone.

'Crafty as a coot, that one,' Freckles declared, staring at the supervisor admiringly as they passed her on the way to the staff-room. 'Still it worked, didn't it? We must have taken squillions this week.'

'I can hardly feel my feet,' Prunella whispered.

'Thank goodness it's Saturday. I just want to go to bed and sleep,' Merry groaned. However, all such thoughts vanished in a flash when she saw the pretty plant, swathed in red ribbon, that was waiting for her on the table. She knew immediately who it was from and despite her intentions, her heart leaped. It had been so long since she'd heard from Carey she'd worried he'd forgotten her or, worse, been entertained by other distractions.

'Come on, clever clogs, what does the flori ... ori ... thing mean for this effort?' Freckles asked, pointing in disgust to the plant.

'Nutmeg geranium means to expect a meeting,'

293

Prunella explained.

Merry's heart flipped.

'And soon, I should think,' Joanie said, coming into the room. 'I heard the lieutenant's ship docked this morning.'

'Oh,' Merry cried. So he *had* been away, after all, she thought, impatiently snatching up the card.

My Dearest Merryn,

The past few weeks have been the longest of my life. To think of you yet be unable to see you has been almost more than I could bear.

I shall be waiting at the usual time in the usual place and it is my dearest wish that you will be free and agree to spend the afternoon with me.

Ever yours,
Carey xx

Carefully, she replaced the card and then hugged herself. Did she wish to spend the afternoon with him? Of course she did. She would be careful to act casually, though, ask him about his trip and see what he had to say.

Next day she waited until the others had left for church before rising. She knew her mother and Grozen would be horrified if they discovered she'd missed Sunday service but she wasn't going to risk bumping into Nicco. Now that the weather had improved he was just as likely to be lying in wait for her. She spent the morning washing and brushing her hair until she was satisfied it was as shiny as it could be. Then she dressed in her pink blouse and green skirt and threw the shimmering stole around her shoulders. On the dot of noon, she ran down the stairs, then remembering Prunella's advice, forced herself to walk sedately out to the waiting carriage. Although she'd told herself she would act with restraint, as soon as she saw him smiling at her through the open door, her heart double flipped.

'My dear Merryn, how happy I am to see you,' he said, reaching out and helping her inside. As their hands touched, she felt that delicious tingling travel right up her arm. He must have felt something too, for his eyes darkened and he held on to her for longer than usual. Then, as if remembering his manners, he reluctantly let her go. 'If you only knew how often I dreamed of this moment,' he whispered.

And I too, she wanted to reply but, determined to act the lady, she just smiled.

As Merry settled herself on the squab opposite, she could feel Carey's eyes following her every move.

'You are looking even more delightful than I remember,' he murmured.

'It's probably due to this beautiful stole you gave me for my birthday. I can't thank you enough,' she replied, pulling it closer around her shoulders and caressing the soft fabric.

'I'm pleased you like it. Though embellishment, however lovely, can only enhance the natural beauty that is there in the first place,' he smiled. 'I thought we'd have a change from the Madison this time. The lads from the ship have decided to dine there and, being thoroughly selfish, I would like you to myself. You don't mind, do you?'

'No, of course not,' she replied, her cheeks flushing from the warmth of his gaze. Quickly she turned and looked out of the window. 'I see we are travelling in a different direction.'

'I thought we'd have a picnic overlooking the river.'

'A picnic?' she gasped, looking uncertainly at the snow that was still piled in drifts at the side of the road. 'You mean dine al fresco?' she added, as Prunella's definition popped into her head.

He gave a hearty laugh that almost sent the carriage rocking. 'Sorry, that was rude of me, but you should have seen your expression. There is a log cabin at the bottom of our garden. It overlooks the river and my housekeeper has prepared a hamper of food. I thought it would give us an opportunity to catch up on all our news and perhaps find out a little more about each other. Hotel restaurants have their places but are hardly conducive to personal exchange,' he said, gazing at her meaningfully.

Not sure how to answer, she looked back out of the window. Already they had left behind the tall buildings with their smoking chimneys and in the distance she could see the dark green and purple of the moors. They were capped with snow and reminded her of icing on a cake.

Then they veered left, and through the stark outline of trees she saw the shimmer of water.

'Is that the Tamar?' she asked excitedly.

'It is indeed, though of course we are still on the Devon side,' he grinned mischievously, but she wasn't about to be drawn.

They'd just passed by the huge railway bridge over the river when her attention was caught by a row of glassed buildings gleaming in the weak winter sun.

'What are those?' she asked.

'Have you never seen hothouses before? The temperate climate here is perfect for growing flowers and fruit,' Carey explained. 'Uncle Fergus, or Fingers, as Saphira insists on calling him, is a dab hand at growing anything and everything.'

'Freckles likes giving everyone nicknames as well,' Merry laughed. 'She calls Mrs Winter, Jacky Frost – her first name is Jacqueline, you see – and...' Her voice tailed off. It wouldn't be seemly to mention their name for Mrs Smale. But by now the horses had turned into a gravelled driveway and he didn't notice her hesitation.

'That is where we live,' he said, pointing to the house ahead.

Merry stared up at the square three-storey limestone building, with its large slate roof, over-hanging eaves and tall windows either side of a large black painted front door.

Before she could say anything, the carriage continued along the path to the side of the house, coming to a halt beside a log building over-looking the water. Some cabin, she thought. Why, their living room back home would have fitted inside it.

'Come along, Merryn, you must be famished. I'm dying to see what Mrs Simmons has left for us,' Carey said, jumping out and helping her down from the carriage. A gust of wind tugged at her skirts, making her shiver, and she pulled her stole tighter round her. 'Let's get inside. Dawson, you can take yourself up to the kitchen for a spot of luncheon and return in a couple of hours,' Carey called to the driver. 'That should give us time for a leisurely meal,' he said, turning back to Merry and grinning.

It was cosy inside the cabin and the views over the river, as it wended its way out to sea, were spectacular. As ever when she was close to the water, Merry felt her spirits soar. She hadn't realized before how much she'd missed the movement and brightness, tucked away as she was in the heart of the bustling town.

'Take a seat,' Carey invited, pointing to the chairs set beside a table. He hurried over to the hamper set on the shelf and eagerly undid the flaps. Drawing out a cloth, he began spreading it over the table. Automatically Merry leaned forward to help, and as his fingers brushed hers that familiar tingle shot up her arm. Their glances met and held for a long moment, then his face relaxed into a smile.

'You must be hungry,' he said, his voice husky. Unable to trust her own voice, she nodded. Turning quickly he delved into the wicker basket, drawing out crusty rolls with curls of golden butter, ham, tomatoes and a small bunch of glossy green grapes.

Merry's stomach rumbled at the sight but Carey was busy drawing the cork from a bottle and didn't notice. As he poured generous quantities of wine into their glasses, she frowned and he grinned roguishly at her expression.

'My intentions are honourable, I can assure you,' he teased.

'Oh, I didn't mean...' She stuttered to a halt and he laughed.

'Let me propose a toast. To us,' he said, clinking his glass against hers. 'And to many more such occasions,' he added.

'That's two toasts, Carey, and you know it,' she said, taking a sip then grimacing.

'Don't you like it?' he asked.

'Not really. It tastes sort of sour, somehow.'

'Really?' he chuckled. 'Just wait until I tell the wine merchant the Chablis he recommended has been called into question. I'd forgotten how direct you are, Merry. Most women would have said it was delicious. Would you care for something else instead?' When she nodded, he delved into the hamper once more and drew out another bottle. 'There's only lemonade, I'm afraid.'

'Lemonade would be lovely.' She watched as he poured it, then eagerly took a sip. 'That's much better, thank you.'

They ate in companionable silence, looking out over the wide expanse of water. It was busy with boats plying their trade but then she caught sight of a ship further out.

'Did you have a good trip?' she asked.

'Same as usual really,' he replied, shrugging and taking a sip of his wine.

'Do you get invited to many parties?' she persisted, remembering Alexandria's comments when she'd visited the store.

'Parties? On board, hardly,' he laughed. She was about to ask him about parties at home but he began regaling her with antics of his crew and she could only shake her head at his tales.

'Well that's quite enough about me,' he said. 'I'm afraid I don't need much encouragement to unburden when back on dry land, and you are a captive audience, so to speak. It's your turn now. How is life at the glamorous store? Have you had any interesting clients calling in?' he asked.

She looked at him sharply. Had Alexandria told him about her visit? But his gaze was clear as he waited patiently for her to answer. Not wishing to spoil their time together, she forced thoughts of the odious Alexandria to the back of her mind and began recounting some of the pranks Freckles and Chester had played.

'It would appear your assistants are as mischievous as some of the crew,' he smiled. 'Saphira mentioned seeing some characters on her visit.'

'Is she still on vacation?' Merry asked.

'Indeed. She is spending a couple of months with relatives in Scotland. Not my choice of venue this time of year but she's had this yen to go back ever since we visited many moons ago. She loves to paint and thought the scenery stunning. I have to confess I found the place too cold and wet for my liking,' he said, taking a sip of his wine.

That would explain the waterproofs, Merry thought.

'She'll be away for Christmas then?'

'Alas, yes. She deserves a break, though, for it fell to her to nurse Mother through her final illness last year.' His eyes clouded and he took another sip of his wine.

'I'm sorry,' Merry murmured. 'That must have

300

been a difficult time for you.'

'It was. That's why I encouraged Saphira to use some of her inheritance to follow her dream of returning to Scotland. She has Mother's necklace, of course, but still wasn't sure about spending money on a vacation, especially as it necessitated her buying fabrics and all that other paraphernalia. I understand she went a bit mad,' he smiled.

Merry stared guiltily at her pink blouse and green skirt. She'd assumed Saphira was used to buying new clothes and hadn't realized the girl had been sharing her inheritance. Suddenly aware Carey was talking again, she jerked back to the present.

'She said she couldn't resist all those bright colours after wearing sober clothes for so long. Mind you, since her birthday she seems to have developed a love of parties so at least I'll be spared those.'

'Parties?' she asked. 'Do you have many?'

'Saphira and her friend Alexandria always seem to be planning something or another,' he shrugged.

'You see a lot of Alexandria then?' she asked, trying to keep her voice light.

'Well, of course, she's a family friend.' Although he also kept his voice light, Merry couldn't help noticing he looked uncomfortable.

Chapter 30

As silence fell over the little cabin, Merry stared out over the water. Whatever had possessed her to ask about Alexandria? Hadn't her grandmother always told her she should only pose a question if she really wanted to hear the answer?

'I must apologize for burdening you with my troubles,' Carey said. 'We were so fond of Mother and her death left a gaping hole in our lives. I don't normally talk about it but you have such a sympathetic ear. Forgive me?' he asked, staring at her so intensely that, despite herself, she felt her pulses quicken and all thought of Alexandria disappeared. 'I'd much rather hear more about you. Do you have any plans for Christmas?'

'I shall be going home to Porthsallos,' she replied.

'Then we must have our own celebration beforehand,' he said. 'That's always supposing you can bear to spend more time with me?'

'I'll think about it,' she teased, eager to return to the banter that normally existed between them.

'Well, in that case...' he began, but just then the brougham drew up outside.

'Goodness, don't tell me two hours have passed already? We'd better get you back before Mr Fairbright sends out a search party,' Carey said, rising to his feet.

Quickly she helped him pack the remaining

food back into the hamper, then they hurried outside. The winter sun was already setting, casting pink and orange shadows across the horizon.

'It's such a pretty sight,' she sighed.

'Indeed it is,' he replied, staring at her until she felt her cheeks flushing the colour of the sky. Quickly she looked back over the water. 'Your eyes blaze like cornflowers while your hair has the shimmer of snowdrops,' he whispered.

She smiled, wondering at his words. He made her feel quite special. Then the devil appeared on her shoulder.

'What about Alexandria. What flower is she?' she asked.

'Alexandria?' he asked, looking surprised. 'Well, she'd be a hothouse bloom, I guess.' Typical, Merry thought. She reminded Carey of the common flowers that grew in hedgerows and woods whilst the stunning red-haired Alexandria was some exotic blossom.

He put out his hand to help her but she pretended not to notice and climbed into the carriage unaided. If he noticed her reticence on the return journey, he chose to ignore it, pointing out the ships and landmarks they were passing. It was only when they drew up in the yard outside the store that he leaned forward.

'About that pre-Christmas celebration we mentioned earlier. May I take you out for luncheon next Sunday? I'll treat you to the finest food in town.' She shook her head and he frowned. 'You mean I have bored you with my ramblings so that you cannot bear to spend more time with me?' he asked, looking so affronted, she couldn't

303

help but laugh.

'No, you chump. I meant I couldn't imagine there being any food finer than you have already treated me to.'

'That's all right then. Honestly, Merry, we do need to spend more time together for we seemed to have jumped to some strange conclusions today, don't we? Now I think you'd better go in for I can see we are being watched,' he said, pointing to the attic window.

'That Freckles,' she sighed. 'Until next Sunday then.' She allowed him to help her down from the carriage. Then, to her surprise, he leaned forward and grazed her cheek with his lips. As the carriage drove away, she put her finger to her tingling cheek.

'Suppose you had to suffer the Madison again,' Freckles sighed as Merry entered their room. 'My heart bleeds for you, girl, it really does.'

'Actually we had a picnic in a log cabin down by the river,' Merry replied.

'What, just you and the lieutenant? Ay, ay, nudge, nudge, wink, wink and I saw him kiss her too,' Freckles chortled, digging Prunella in the ribs. 'Well, Chester and me, we... Oh, there's the gong. You lot coming?'

'No, I'm not hungry,' Merry replied.

'Nor me. Nicholas and I had a rather splendid luncheon together,' Prunella flushed.

'Blimey, you wait till I tell Chester he's short-changed me. A poke of chips, indeed,' Freckles muttered, hurrying from the room.

'You had a good day then?' Merry asked Prunella.

304

'Oh, I did,' she enthused. 'Teddy went to see the boys in the ironmongers and Nicholas asked if I'd like to step out for a bite to eat. He is so different when the others aren't there. He sort of comes into his own and is so...' She stuttered to a halt, her hazel eyes gleaming with emotion. 'How about you – did you manage to act the lady?'

Merry carefully hung up her cashmere wrap, then perched on the bed. 'Most of the time, though I fear I let my feelings show more than they should at times,' she replied, but Prunella had already climbed into bed and her eyes were closed.

Clambering out of her clothes, Merry smoothed down the folds of her skirt and the silk of her blouse and sighed. How kind Saphira had been letting her have the surplus material, especially as Merry now knew she had been spending her inheritance. She'd certainly jumped to conclusions thinking Saphira was used to buying new things. As soon as she returned, she'd make sure she knew how grateful she was. Perhaps she'd jumped to conclusions about Alexandria, too, although the thought of Carey comparing the woman to a hothouse bloom whilst alluding to herself as a wayside flower still rankled. Did that reflect his opinion of her? She took a pride in her job but the fact remained she was an assistant in a store, and a trainee one at that.

All this analysing was making her head hurt and, unable to think any more, she jumped into bed and closed her eyes.

'I forgot to tell you that Nicco was waiting for you again yesterday,' Freckles told Merry over breakfast the next morning. 'He was right mad when I told him you'd gone out. Asked all sorts of questions, he did. Kept going on about loyalty and you being his intended. Chester didn't like the way he was looking and just said we'd tell you he'd called. Nicco said to be sure to tell you he'd promised your mother he'd take you home for Christmas and would be waiting outside the store at first light to collect you.'

'Oh,' Merry said, her spirits sinking even lower. She wasn't sure she could put up with Nicco's overbearing manner these days. So much had happened since she'd last seen him, she felt like a different person. 'Well, we'd better get a move on. It'll soon be time for the store to open.'

Mr Fairbright was leaving the shop floor as they filed in.

'Good morning, ladies. I have an important meeting upstairs and have just been discussing strategy with Mrs Smale. She will brief you before the opening bell.' With a brief nod, he hurried up the stairs and the trainees turned to their manageress expectantly.

'Right, ladies, my first job is to tell you to look out for fingersmiths. Apparently there have been reports of thefts from other stores, so keep alert, and if you spot anyone loitering suspiciously you are to notify myself or, if I am busy, Mrs Winter.'

'Are these people dangerous?' Prunella whispered, glancing anxiously around the empty store.

'No, I don't think so, Miss Prim. More like opportunists. However, Mr Jenkins will be keeping a weather eye on us in ladieswear.'

'Oh, that's a relief, I don't think. He couldn't

wrestle a rat,' Freckles whispered. Privately Merry agreed but the manageress, full of her importance, was in full flood.

'With the store being so busy it would be easy for someone to pocket an accessory or some small item. That is why Mr Fairbright has taken the precaution of having our displays moved to higher shelves.' She gestured to the display stands, which had indeed been raised. 'Clients can still see them but will require assistance should they wish to examine anything. However, we will need to be vigilant.'

'Don't worry, Mrs Smale, I'll keep me peepers peeled,' Freckles declared.

'Thank you, Miss Brice. Just one other thing before you go to your stations. As these next two weeks are predicted to be our busiest time of year, from today until Christmas Eve the store will be remaining open during the luncheon period. You will therefore stagger your meal break with each taking no more than twenty minutes.'

'Blimey oh rimey, that's slave labour,' Freckles muttered.

'Miss Brice?' Mrs Smale sighed.

'I said I suppose it will be a favour,' Freckles said innocently.

Mrs Smale gave her a sharp look. 'If by favour you mean you are prepared to give your time freely, then I'll inform Mr Fairbright of your kindness, Miss Brice. He did assure me your efforts would be reflected in your Christmas box but...' She left her words hanging.

'Then it would be rude to refuse his generous offer,' Freckles grinned.

The day passed in a hectic whirl as, despite the cold weather, clients descended upon the store, intent on fulfilling their Christmas lists. The shop was so busy that even the manageress and supervisor temporarily buried their differences as they endeavoured to deal with everyone. Merry had never wrapped so many purchases in a day, and ensuring the counters were tidy and the stocks replenished took all her attention. She was just attaching another reel of ribbon when a familiar voice made her stomach sink.

'I say, girl, do you think you can assist?'

Fighting down the desire to wipe the sneer from the haughty Alexandria's face, and ignoring the titters of her friends, Merry forced a smile.

'How may I help you, Miss Courtland?'

'I am in need of Christmas gifts for my staff. I have no idea what to buy them and thought with you being a shop girl you would,' she said with an affected sigh.

'May I interest you in a cup of cheer?' Joanie asked, appearing at the woman's side with her tray of mulled wine.

Alexandria sniffed and shook her head. 'At this time of day, I don't think so, do you?' she replied, turning to her friends, who shook their heads too. Looking put out, Joanie moved on to another group of clients.

'Shame, it'd warm you up, you old trout,' Freckles muttered.

'I beg your pardon,' Alexandria exclaimed.

'I said there's a lot of cold air about,' Freckles responded with a polite smile.

'Who exactly are you buying for?' Merry asked

308

quickly as she saw Mrs Winter making her way towards them.

'Well, the cook, the housekeeper and I suppose I'd better get that maid of all things something as well. Tea towels or dusters would fit the bill, I suppose.'

As the woman waved her gloved hand in an off-hand manner, Merry felt her temper rising. 'A bit boring, though, don't you think?' she ventured, ignoring the woman's raised brow. 'I understand that these days it is the done thing to give a gift of a personal nature to show one's gratitude. Or do you not feel that would be appropriate?'

'As I thought, this is more your sort of thing, so what would you suggest?'

'With the weather being as it is, something to keep them warm would be appreciated, I'm sure,' Merry replied, staring at the fox fur stole and matching hat Alexandria was wearing. 'How about a nice warm shawl each, or a hat or some gloves?' As the woman's brow arched even higher, Merry fought down the urge to laugh. 'We have some lovely ones in the finest wool. But they are rather expensive so perhaps that is more than you wanted to spend?'

Aware that her friends were waiting for her answer, Alexandria nodded and waved her hand. 'Money is not an issue, Miss Dyer. I really don't have time to spend in idle speculation. Select whatever you judge suitable and add it to my account.'

'Of course, Miss Courtland,' Merry demurred. 'Be sure I shall arrange to have three of our finest shawls with matching hats and gloves gift-wrapped and set aside for collection as per your instructions.' She watched as the woman swallowed hard.

'Getting ideas above your station, shop girl? Well, you can be sure I shall not forget this,' the woman hissed before turning and marching from the store, followed by her friends.

'Goodness, well done, Miss Dyer,' Mrs Winter cried. 'I came over to assist only to find you selling some of our finest knitwear.'

'Well, I'm sure her staff deserve to receive good-quality presents for their services,' Merry replied. 'Especially having to deal with that haughty madam every day,' she added under her breath.

'Blimey oh rimey, girl,' Freckles muttered. 'Imagine if we was on commission, you'd be getting a jolly good Christmas present of your own. Mind you, I didn't care for the way she glared at you as she left. Now I know what they mean when they say "if looks could kill".'

Merry shrugged, thinking it wouldn't do the woman any harm to treat her staff, for once, especially if she spoke to them in the same condescending manner.

It was a long day and by the time the store closed all Merry wanted to do was eat her supper and fall into bed. However, as she made her way to the staff-room Mr Fairbright beckoned her from the stairs. Her heart sank. Don't say Miss Courtland had complained about her. To her relief, though, her employer smiled.

'Ah, Miss Dyer, I just wondered if you had that letter for your mother? The recent cold snap has left our stocks of knit frocks sadly depleted and I am journeying to Porthsallos tomorrow to collect more.'

Merry's heart sank. Although she'd started it, having spent her precious time off sewing and going out with Carey she hadn't got round to finishing it.

'Well, actually, I did start it...' Really, she had no excuse.

Seeing her flustered look, Mr Fairweather shook his head. 'I know you have been busy, Miss Dyer, but it would only take you a minute to finish it, surely? I suggest you do so this evening, then leave it on the hall table. I will collect it first thing before I leave.'

'Thank you, sir,' she muttered.

'I know you intend going home for Christmas but a letter confirming that would mean a lot to your mother.'

'Yes, Mr Fairbright,' she replied, and although he'd spoken mildly she felt as if she'd received a telling-off from the schoolmaster.

'Come on, Merry, we'll walk with you to the staff-room,' Chester said, catching up with her as she made her way down the hallway. 'We had such an exciting afternoon, didn't we, Nicholas? Teddy saw a chap pocketing one of those new...'

'Sorry, Chester, I'll not be eating with you tonight. I have something I must do,' she interrupted, hurrying towards the back stairs.

'What's up with her?' Teddy asked.

'That lieutenant's giving her ideas above her station, if you ask me,' she heard Chester reply.

Chapter 31

Ideas above her station indeed, Merry thought as she lit the candle in her room and took up her sheet of paper. Although she was fond of the other assistants, there was no denying the lack of privacy got on her nerves at times. At least at home her mother and Grozen would sense when she needed to think and leave her alone – well, most of the time, anyway. Quickly she read what she'd already written.

Dear Mother and Grozen,

I hope this letter finds you well. I was pleased to receive yours and thank you most sincerely for my lovely shawl and gloves. The colour is perfect and...

Taking up her pencil, she thought for a moment then began to write.

they are ideal for the snow and cold weather we have been having. I wonder if you have had much snow in Porthsallos. Hope you are keeping warm and the fire well stoked, Grozen. We have been very busy here. Would you believe Mr Fairbright arranged for a fir tree lit with candles to be placed in both of the bay windows? It all looks very festive and brings lots of people into the store.

She paused, wondering if she should mention Carey. But knowing they still expected her to marry Nicco, she decided against it.

I miss you both very much and am very much looking forward to seeing you when I come home for Christmas.

Ever your loving
Merryn

Placing her letter on the side to take downstairs first thing, she turned her attention to what she should wear for going out with Carey on Sunday. It might still be a few days away, but if the activity in the store today was anything to go by, she'd be hard-pressed to find any free time later in the week.

Knowing she shouldn't miss another service, and trusting it was too near Christmas for Nicco to be visiting Plymouth, Merry joined the others for church on Sunday morning.

'Are you coming out with us today?' Chester asked as they walked out through the lychgate.

'Merry's got a date with the dashing lieutenant, so you'll just have to treat yours truly to another poke of chips,' Freckles teased, linking her arm through his.

'We're coming with you, though,' Prunella said, smiling at Nicholas, who flushed and nodded.

'Well, I'm no goose-gog so you can count me out. I'm off to see my pals anyway,' Teddy said, waving his hand in farewell.

'Hope you know what you're doing, Merry,' Chester said.

'What do you mean?' she asked.

'Well, that lieutenant's sort, they're ... oh, nothing,' he sighed.

'Come on, there's the tram,' Freckles squealed. Merry watched as her friends sped off on their excursion, then made her way towards the store.

Back in her room, she checked her appearance in the little mirror and wondered where Carey would be taking her today. Her heart gave a leap at the thought of seeing him again. It might only have been a week since they'd last met but she'd really missed him. Remembering he'd said they would be having a special pre-Christmas celebration, she put on her cashmere wrap and ran back down the stairs so as not to keep him waiting.

The hall clock struck twelve and, knowing he was always punctual, she peeped through the window but there was no sign of him. She perched on the chair in the hallway but was so excited she couldn't keep still and began pacing the floor. The clock struck the quarter-hour, then the half-hour but still he didn't appear. He must have been delayed, she thought when the clock chimed a quarter to one. Surely he would have sent a message if he wasn't coming? Perhaps something better had come along, the little gremlin in her mind warned. Had he spent the previous evening at a party? Saphira might be away but hadn't he said Alexandria was a family friend and always visiting? She paced the floor, her treacherous thoughts getting the better of her. By the time the clock chimed the hour she had to acknowledge that he wasn't coming.

Probably never had any intention, that gremlin muttered as she hurried up to her room. Well, she didn't care anyway. Except she did, and it hurt. Heedless of her finery, she threw herself down on the bed and sobbed until she had no tears left. Then anger swept through her. Even if he had changed his mind, he should have had the decency to let her know. Jumping up, she changed into her old skirt and blouse, wrapped her blue shawl around her shoulders and ran out to the yard.

After rinsing her face at the pump, she returned to her room. She was blowed if she'd waste the rest of her day off; it was only a week until Christmas. She'd wrap her presents then prepare her things ready for going home. How pleased she was Mr Fairbright had reminded her to write to her mother and Grozen, and how she missed them.

The next week passed in a blur of clients and wrapping. If there was a stone where her heart used to be then she chose to ignore it. Although Freckles and Prunella had looked askance when they returned on Sunday, for once they'd respected her privacy and hadn't intruded. She was grateful for that, although she suspected it was Prunella who'd kept their inquisitive friend from prying.

Now it was Christmas Eve and, to their surprise, Mr Fairbright closed the store early and they were summoned to his office.

'Well, ladies, first of all I would like to thank you for all your hard work over the past months. Your probationary period is almost at an end and Mr Didcot and I thought it would be opportune to tell you our findings before you depart for the festivities. Mr Didcot is, as we speak, addressing the staff from menswear.'

'That is most considerate of you, Mr Fairbright,' Mrs Smale smiled, patting her bun self-assuredly.

'Not at all, Mrs Smale. However, I shall begin with you, Mrs Winter,' he said, turning to the supervisor. 'You have shown exceptional talent in your dealings with both the staff in the ladies' department and the servants who call to collect their employers' wares. Therefore, when you return after the festivities it will be in the role of manageress.'

'But...' Mrs Smale gasped.

Freckles and Merry exchanged surprised looks.

'Bear with me if you will, Mrs Smale,' Mr Fairbright said, holding up his hand. 'Miss Dyer, you have shown a comprehensive understanding of the stock and a good rapport with our clients so you have passed your probation with flying colours. In future you will shadow Mrs Winter and assist as trainee supervisor.'

Merry gulped. 'Thank you, Mr Fairbright,' she whispered. Trainee supervisor? Well, that would certainly give her something to focus on when she returned after the holiday. Goodness, whatever would her mother say?

'Obviously you have a lot still to learn but Mrs Winter assures me you show great promise.' He smiled at Merry and then addressed them all. 'Mr Didcot and myself feel it will enrich your careers if you each take on a specific responsibility for the running of the department.'

'But what about...' Mrs Smale began.

'All in good time, Mrs Smale. Now, Miss Prim,' he smiled at Pru. 'I am pleased to say you too have passed your probation with flying colours. I am led to believe you have shown a distinct flair for displaying our merchandise. In future, you will take responsibility for seeing the mannequins are seasonally dressed and that our stock is shown to best effect. Mrs Winter, of course, will advise.'

'Goodness, thank you, sir,' Prunella said, flushing with pleasure.

'Miss Brice, I have heard you are particularly good at giving names to, er, well ... everything,' he said, his eyes twinkling.

'Now that is very true, sir,' Mrs Smale smirked.

'Well, when the store reopens it will be receiving new stock and instead of using the usual generic names, we feel it would create interest for our clients if our collections were given individual titles. You, Miss Brice, will have responsibility for this, a job at which I am confident you will excel,' he said, smiling at Freckles.

'Blimey oh rimey, thank you, Mr Fairbright,' Freckles gushed.

'Obviously your pay will be enhanced to reflect these extra duties, and when you return you will find waiting for you the black uniforms and caps denoting your status as fully fledged assistants.'

'But what about me?'

'Ah, Mrs Smale, where would we be without your meticulous writing up of the ledgers? It is clear you have an aptitude for figures, and with business flourishing it is essential to have someone dedicated to keeping the store's accounts. We

317

would deem it an honour if you were to become our bookkeeper.'

'But clearly there is no room for me in the store,' she said, glaring at Mrs Winter.

'We appreciate such a job requires the utmost concentration and have arranged for the office behind this one be prepared for you.'

'You mean I have been elevated to a position upstairs with an office of my own?' Mrs Smale simpered. 'I must agree I am indeed worthy of greater things than being on the shop floor.' She smirked at Mrs Winter, who nodded in a conciliatory manner.

'Right, ladies, all that remains is for me to wish you the compliments of the season and to hand you your Christmas boxes.'

'Goodness, I can hardly believe it,' Merry said, once they were up in their room.

'Did you see old Smelly's face when Fairbright announced Mrs Winter was going to be manageress? For a moment there, I reckon she thought she was out on her ear,' Freckles giggled.

'I can't believe I'm going to be in charge of the mannequins,' Prunella sighed. 'It will give me something to look forward to whilst Mother is wittering on about marriage.'

'Right, let's get our things packed, then we can be off. Chester and I are going for a noggin to celebrate. Do you two want to come with us?'

'And play gooseberry? No, thanks,' Merry said, laughing for the first time in a week. Carey might not value her but it seemed Mr Fairbright did. She would enjoy Christmas with her family and then concentrate on her position here, for hadn't it always been her ambition to make her own way? 'I'll get an early night before Nicco collects me in the morning.'

'Father is already waiting outside in his carriage,' Prunella sighed.

'Well, come along then, girl. I'll walk down to the yard with you. Merry Christmas, Merry,' Freckles chortled. 'And you needn't get any ideas about me kowtowing to you when we get back.'

'And you needn't come up with any rude name for me,' Merry laughed. 'Happy Christmas, Prunella,' she added.

Prunella pulled a face. 'I'd much rather be staying here. Season's greetings, Merry.'

Merry listened to them clattering down the stairs then finished packing her bag ready for the morning. The presents she'd carefully wrapped rustled as she placed her nightdress on top and she smiled, thinking of the skirt she'd made for her mother. Even with her discount it had cost a small fortune, but as soon as she'd seen the warm woollen material she'd known her mother would love it.

She was so looking forward to seeing Mother and Grozen. She thought of the beautiful bed jacket she'd purchased for the older woman. Although her grandmother would say it was too grand and she'd never wear it, Merry knew she would. As a gesture of goodwill, she'd even wrapped a pair of socks for Nicco. He might be possessive and dictatorial but he obviously still wanted her. If he hadn't said he'd collect her tomorrow she'd have had a long walk in the freezing cold.

A knock on the door interrupted her musing and, sighing, she went to answer it.

'Mr Fairbright would like to see you in the parlour,' Joanie said.

'Mr Fairbright?' Merry repeated. 'Why?'

'Don't ask me, dearie, I was just leaving for home when he came bustling in insisting I come and get you straight away.'

Quickly Merry smoothed down her skirts, then followed the woman down the stairs. When they entered the office she noticed that Mr Fairbright was dressed in his greatcoat and muffler, cheeks flushed from the cold and with a dusting of snow on his collar.

'Ah, Miss Dyer, do take a seat, my dear,' her employer greeted her. 'Thank you, Joanie. I'm sorry to have held you up. Compliments of the season to you.'

'And to you, Mr Fairbright,' the housekeeper replied.

'I was on my way home when I bumped into an old colleague who hails from Logh,' Mr Fairbright said, turning to Merry. 'Apparently snow there has blocked the roads. Mindful you were intending to travel to Porthsallos, I enquired if the higher road was passable. Alas, it is not, so I'm afraid you will not be going anyway, my dear.'

'Oh, no,' she murmured, disappointment flooding through her.

'We are off to stay with relatives, otherwise I would have invited you home with me,' he explained, looking so anxious that Merry forced a smile.

'Don't worry, Mr Fairbright, I'll be fine,' she assured him.

'Well, if you are sure?' he said, looking relieved. 'The store is locked, of course, and as Jenkins will be caretaking, Joanie has left plenty of food in the larder so you must help yourself. Season's greetings, my dear,' he added before hurrying away.

Up in her room, Merry lay on her bed and stared up at the moonlight. She'd so been looking forward to going home and seeing her mother and Grozen again. Now she'd be spending Christmas alone.

What a strange day. In the past twenty-four hours she'd gone from despair to excitement at having passed her probation. Now she was back to despair.

Chapter 32

She must have fallen asleep for when she woke the room was flooded with the blinding brightness only snow can bring. It was Christmas, she thought, jumping excitedly from her bed. Then, remembering she'd be spending it alone, she shivered and slid back under the covers.

'Happy Christmas, Mother and Grozen,' she whispered, feeling another pang of disappointment that she couldn't be with them. 'I'll be back to see you soon,' she added. Then she laughed at her foolishness. As if they could hear her. Automatically her mind went to Carey but she firmly pushed thoughts of him away. She'd a good mind to go back to sleep, except her thoughts were ticking like the clock in the store.

Quickly she dressed, then pulling her new blue shawl around her, hurried downstairs and out to the yard. Although it was perishing, everywhere was bright and glistening like a winter wonderland and she could hear the church bells pealing their Christmas message of joy. Having carried out her ablutions, and not relishing the thought of returning to her lonely room, she decided to take a brisk walk.

She soon wished she hadn't, though, for some houses still had their gaslamps lit and, peering in through the open curtains, she could see families gathered around their trees, opening presents and looking happy. Her heart flopped as she felt lonelier than ever. Back home in Porthsallos, her mother would be preparing the food, for no matter how meagre their rations she always managed to make their meal a feast. Grozen would be coaxing the fire into a warming blaze and the very thought made Merry shiver. How she wished she'd packed her knitted hat, she thought, rubbing her cold ears. Sighing as memories of home tugged at her heart, she turned and made her way back to the store. No one could have foreseen the early snow storms they'd been experiencing and it had been kind of Mr Fairbright to return and warn her about the roads being impassable.

Well, she had been the one wanting to leave home in the first place, hadn't she? And she was doing well, for not only had she had passed her probation period, she was to shadow Mrs Winter and be trained as an assistant supervisor. That would certainly increase her future prospects, she thought, her spirits rising. Why, the world was her limpet, as Grozen used to say.

Scurrying back to the store, she made herself a hot drink then prepared a bowl of porridge. It was draughty in the staff-room and she took her meal up to her room and pondered on what she should do. She might have to spend the day alone but that didn't mean she should be idle. At home, her hands had always been busy with her knitting. Remembering her pins and wool were lying neglected in the closet, her spirits lifted. She would make herself a hat to go with her shawl and gloves.

Settling herself down in the little chair, she cast on the stitches and before long the familiar rhythm of her knitting gave her some measure of comfort. She tried not to think what her mother and Grozen would be doing. Of course, had she not spent her days off with Carey she could have gone back to see them before the snow had come.

Carey ... as if thoughts of him had conjured him up, a picture of his aquamarine eyes and gentle smile swam before her. Except it had all been a sham, hadn't it? An act put on to charm the green girl from a fishing village. Hadn't Mrs Smale warned her about men like him wanting only one thing? The thought that he had been using her, playing with her even, hurt but then hadn't he compared her to a bluebell and Alexandria to a hothouse bloom?

Alexandria ... Merry shivered, remembering the malice in the girl's eyes as she'd left the store. Obviously she wanted Carey, and having seen his house overlooking the river Merry had to concede she was probably more his sort. And wasn't she a family friend, in and out of his house all the time? Admittedly he'd said Alexandria was Saphira's friend, but Merry was certain that wouldn't stop the woman calling upon him whilst she was away on her vacation. Hadn't Grozen always said you should stick with your own as you know where you are with them?

With the holiday over, they resumed their familiar routine in the store, except they were all fully fledged assistants now.

'Doesn't that window look bare without the tree?' Freckles moaned as they prepared the store for opening the day after Boxing Day.

'Yes, it does,' Mrs Winter agreed. 'However, doesn't it give us an opportunity to create a stunning new display? The new stock is ready and waiting so, Miss Prim and Miss Brice, you will discuss which lines should be exhibited, bearing in mind the next season will be spring.' As they looked out of the window at the slush-piled pavements, the new manageress laughed. 'Vision, ladies, we need vision. A successful store always demonstrates its new stock to entice the clients.'

'You mean we should con them nobs into parting with their money,' Freckles laughed.

'I prefer the word "persuade", Miss Brice. However, I agree the general idea is to get the public thinking of purchasing new fabrics and accessories.'

'And I guess the store needs to make money in order to keep trading,' Merry mused.

'Exactly, and as long as the store makes a profit we have jobs. Now, as you have grasped the basic principle of trading, Miss Dyer, you will please shadow me today. As well as assisting with clients, I want you to observe exactly how I see to the running of the department.'

'Yes, Mrs Winter,' Merry replied, excitement rising. She would not only observe but prove she had the makings of a supervisor.

'Miss Brice, I want you to go to the stockroom and select those materials and accessories you think will best entice the clients in. Miss Prim meanwhile will prepare the mannequins and shop window for displaying them.'

'Blimey oh rimey,' Freckles said, as she scuttled off to the stockroom. 'She's letting me choose.'

Merry smiled at her friend. Things were certainly going to be different with Mrs Winter in charge.

The week passed in a frenzy of activity. Having engaged her staff's interest, Mrs Winter diligently explained how they should perform their new duties, then left them to it. By the time Sunday came, they were all exhausted yet exhilarated by all they'd achieved. It seemed the boys had also risen to their new challenges and spirits were high as they made their way out of church.

'I think we should go out for a slap-up meal to celebrate,' Freckles declared.

'Well, if you're paying,' Chester replied. 'I'm skint after Christmas.'

'I'm sure you can treat us to a poke of chips,' Freckles cried.

'Actually we thought we might take a walk

around the park,' Prunella ventured, looking coyly at Nicholas.

'I've arrange to see my pals,' Teddy said quickly.

'I really want to finish my knitting,' Merry said. Although she'd enjoyed her busy week as trainee supervisor, she didn't feel up to dealing with the antics of her friends. The only way she could keep her treacherous thoughts at bay was by keeping busy.

Back in her room she changed out of her Sunday clothes, then picked up her pins. She'd just settled into the familiar rhythm when there was a knock on the door.

'Someone to see you, Miss Dyer,' Joanie called. Her heart plummeted. Obviously Nicco had decided to call. She only hoped he'd had the decency to knock on the staff door. Sighing, she ran down the stairs then stopped short.

'Merryn, my dear, how truly lovely it is to see you again.' Merry's heart flipped as she saw Carey smiling at her. 'I have been waiting outside in the brougham for an age and when you didn't appear thought I'd better come and make sure you were all right.'

'But why...? I mean...' She stuttered to a halt. Then her pent-up anger from the past weeks surfaced. 'Tell me why you should expect me to be waiting for you after you left me high and dry on our last date – or should I say "dalliance", for that is what I am to you, isn't it?'

His expression changed from one of delight to astonishment. 'But surely you got my message?'

'Message? Oh, I got the message loud and clear, Lieutenant Meredith.'

'Look, Merryn, there has clearly been some mistake. I apologize for not being able to take you out for our pre-Christmas luncheon. I was that sore when I received orders to return to base, I can tell you. That's why I sent that letter explaining I had to postpone our celebration until today.'

'Letter? I didn't receive any letter,' she murmured, her anger evaporating as she took in his sorrowful expression.

'Oh, Merryn, don't tell me you were waiting for me?' he cried.

'Like a boat when the tide goes out,' she whispered.

'I am so very sorry, Merryn, and I can see by your attire you were not expecting to come out with me today.' She stared down at her patched skirt and old blouse and sighed. Now she did look like a naïve girl fresh from the fishing village. 'That was incredibly rude, Merryn. Forgive me. You look wonderful and I've missed you so much. Would you still consider spending time with me today?'

'Well, I...'

'Please say yes. I feel we need to clear the air and we don't have to go to the Madison.'

'I'm certainly not hungry but...'

'Please, Merryn. At least agree to ride out with me.' As he stood staring at her, his blue eyes clouded, she felt her anger dissipate.

'Give me five minutes to make myself look respectable,' she whispered.

'I'll wait outside,' he said, his expression turning to one of joy.

'Goodness, a woman who keeps to time,' he quipped as exactly five minutes later she appeared beside the brougham. 'I can only apologize again for my message not getting to you, Merryn. Be assured I shan't rest until I find out what happened.' Suddenly feeling shy to be in his company again, she smiled, then settled back in her seat. She was just deciding she'd play it cool when they turned the corner and two dark eyes glared at them through the window.

'Oh...' she gasped.

'Goodness, what a bad-tempered-looking fellow,' Carey remarked as the donkey cart overtook them.

So her hunch about Nicco turning up today had been right after all.

'Still, not to worry, I have been looking forward to this day for so long and, even if we have changed our plans, nothing is going to spoil it.'

Merry nodded, as much to clear the image of Nicco from her mind as anything.

'I'm still horrified that my letter didn't reach you and will question my housekeeper when I next return home.'

'Well, I guess these things happen sometimes,' she said politely.

'Tell me, did you have a good Christmas with your family?' he asked.

'The snow prevented my travelling to Porthsallos.'

'What did you do?' he asked, pale blue eyes clouding again.

'I had a couple of days to myself,' she grinned,

making light of the time she'd spent alone. 'I made myself a warm hat and spent the time reflecting on my promotion.'

'Promotion?'

'Yes, not only have I passed my probation I am to act as trainee supervisor to Mrs Winter, who is now our manageress.'

'That's wonderful. Congratulations, Merryn. A lot seems to have happened since last we met.'

'Yes, it certainly has,' she agreed, endeavouring to keep her voice light.

'Well, a special occasion calls for a special drink,' he said, tapping on the roof. As they drew to a halt, Merry looked out of the window and saw they'd stopped alongside the café beside the water she'd once visited with Nicco. Was this an omen, she wondered, glancing at Carey, but he had jumped down and was holding his hand out to help her.

'Come along, we'll have a glass of their best lemonade and perhaps I can tempt you to a cake?' Her stomach growled in the most unladylike manner in reply, but he didn't appear to notice.

'Now tell me what else has been happening at Didcot and Fairbright,' he invited as soon as they'd been shown to their seats.

'Well, like I said, we all passed our probationary period and are now fully fledged sales assistants.'

'Congratulations again,' he said, raising his glass to hers.

'Prunella is in her element dressing the mannequins. She shows quite a flair for it and only hopes she can stay.' He raised an enquiring eyebrow. 'Her mother has lined up a suitable marriage prospect – suitable in her mother's eyes, that is,' Merry explained. 'She's in love with Nicholas, an assistant in menswear, though. Freckles thinks they should elope.'

'Freckles? That wouldn't be the young redhead who watches us from the upstairs window, perchance?'

'The very same,' Merry laughed. Then remembering their earlier engagement when he didn't show she asked him about his work. He sighed.

'We all had our leave cancelled and were ordered back to base. Lots of briefings followed and we are to be deployed soon.' His eyes clouded. 'That is why I am so grateful you agreed to come out with me today. Tell me, Merryn, have I lost the opportunity to continue walking out with you?'

As she took in his ardent expression, she felt the stone encasing her heart begin to crack.

'No, of course not,' she whispered, her resolve dissipating like the early morning mist.

'In that case, may I give you your Christmas present now?' he asked, delving into the inside pocket of his coat. She glanced around the room but everyone was busy with their food. Curiosity getting the better of her, she tugged at the gold ribbon on the box, then gasped at the silver heart with its filigree edging.

'Oh, it's beautiful. Thank you, Carey.'

'Would you like me to put it on for you?' he asked gently.

Fingering the delicate chain, she shook her head. She wasn't ready for him to come that close yet.

'Thank you, but I will wear it when the

occasion is right,' she whispered. He nodded, then quickly took a sip of his drink.

'I understand,' he said, and she had the feeling that he did. He cleared his throat and looked at her intently. 'I just want you to know you have come to mean a lot to me. When I bought this I intended to ask if you would accept it as a token of my future intent,' he said huskily.

'Oh, you mean...? But surely I am not suitable for...' she began, as a picture of Alexandria and his beautiful house and garden surfaced unbidden. Leaning forward, he placed his hand over hers.

'I can only apologize again for my message not getting through to you, and if I have been insensitive mentioning my feelings too soon after our, er, misunderstanding, then please forgive me. It's just that I had it all planned: a pre-Christmas celebration, nice food, the best lemonade, and well, it all went wrong, didn't it?' As he sat there looking dejected, the last piece of shell around her heart fell away.

'Not quite,' she whispered. 'This is quite the best lemonade I've ever had.'

'Oh Merryn,' he whispered, reaching out and taking her hand. 'I only wish I didn't have to go away for so long. You will wait for me, won't you?'

'I'll think about it, Lieutenant Meredith,' she teased.

Chapter 33

With the weather warming slightly, the store became busy once more. Mrs Winter had turned out to be a good manager and, unlike Mrs Smale, actively encouraged her staff to take the initiative in their dealings with customers. Merry's respect for the woman grew and she was happy to shadow and follow her lead.

One day Merry was returning from the dressing room after showing a client some of the ready-made undergarments when she heard Freckles hiss, 'Blimey oh rimey, cat at twelve o'clock.'

Looking up, Merry saw Alexandria had entered the store with her usual entourage and was smirking at her like the feline who'd cornered her mouse.

'Ah, Miss Dyer. You will no doubt be pleased to hear the staff were delighted with their Christmas presents. Did you enjoy the festivities?' she asked, watching Merry closely.

'Yes, thank you. I trust you did too?' she asked politely.

'Oh indeed, wild parties with good family friends. So wild, in fact, they went on well into this New Year,' she responded.

'How nice,' Merry smiled, refusing to rise to the woman's bait. She fingered the silver necklace beneath her collar and forced her lips wider.

'How may I help you today? Perhaps you would care to see our latest stock?'

'Goodness, as I've previously mentioned, I wouldn't purchase anything here for myself. Only fine couture will do for me, darling. That's how naval officers expect their ladies to dress,' she said, emphasizing the word 'ladies'. 'No, etiquette decreed I come and thank you for your shop assistant's advice.'

'Miss Dyer is renowned for her expert service, Miss Courtland, and you might be interested to know she is now the department's trainee supervisor,' Mrs Winter, who had been watching the exchange, intervened.

'Remarkable,' Alexandria sneered before turning on her heel and marching from the store.

'Thank you, Mrs Winter,' Merry whispered.

'It doesn't do any harm to point these things out sometimes. Remember, Merry, it is manners that make a lady, rather than mere breeding. Now you will be pleased to know it's time for luncheon,' she said, grinning as she turned away. Merry stared after her in surprise, not for the first time amazed at the woman's perception.

'Blimey oh rimey, what was that all about?' Freckles asked as they hurried towards the staffroom. 'That snooty woman's got it in for you and no mistake.'

'She's one of Carey's neighbours,' Merry sighed.

'And a nasty one at that,' Prunella said. 'I reckon she's got her sights firmly set on your lieutenant, Merry.'

'Ah, but will he look in her direction?' Freckles responded, seeing her friend's woeful expression.

'When are you next seeing the dashing lieutenant?'

'Not for another two weeks,' Merry sighed.

'Why don't we sort some material and make you a dress?' Freckles suggested. 'We could make something that'll pop his eyes out.'

Merry laughed. Her friend was better than any tonic from a quack.

'Hey, Joanie, what's the best way to keep a man's attention?' Freckles asked as the housekeeper bustled in with their luncheon.

'Keep him happy, well fed, warm in ... well, you know what I mean,' Joanie chortled. 'Cors that sort of thing's only for when you're wed,' she added.

'Cors, Joanie,' Freckles laughed.

Feeling better after a bowl of Joanie's vegetable broth and her friends' banter, Merry hurried back down the corridor.

'Ah, Miss Dyer,' Mr Fairbright said, leaning over the banister. 'A word, if you please.'

Merry's heart sank. Had Alexandria made a complaint against her?

'Yes, Mr Fairbright?' she asked, looking anxiously at her employer.

'I have just returned from Porthsallos. Your mother seemed anxious about your welfare and although I reassured her you were doing very well, she insisted I give you this.' He handed her a note. 'I understand she would welcome a reply so if you wish to pen one I will take it with me when I return next month. I got the impression it was more than just parental concern about you not being able to get home for Christmas, so if there is anything I can assist with, then please feel free to come and see me.'

'Thank you, Mr Fairbright,' Merry said. Whatever could her mother be worrying about, she wondered, as she hurried back to the shop floor.

'Miss Dyer, perhaps you could tidy the dressing room,' Mrs Winter said as she took her position behind the counter. 'I had occasion to assist a lady during her luncheon break and it needs refreshing.'

'Of course, Mrs Winter,' she replied. As she set about her task, the paper crackling in her pocket reminded her of her mother's note. Quickly, she removed it from its envelope and scanned the contents.

Dearest Merry,

I hope this letter finds you well. We are both well and missed you at Christmas. Nicco has kindly been keeping an eye on you on his regular trips to Plymouth. As you know, it is our express hope that you and he will settle down together. He adores you and does have good prospects. He has, however, expressed his concern about a gentleman who is paying you a lot of attention. I request you bring this man home soonest so that your grandmother and I can satisfy our concerns that his intentions are honourable.

Please send a reply back via Mr Fairbright as to when we can expect you and this gentleman friend to pay us a visit.

Your concerned Mother,
Karenza

Merry screwed up the note and threw it across the room. That Nicco had been keeping an eye on her was bad enough, but reporting her movements back to her mother was unforgivable. She wasn't a child, after all. She was making her own way in the world as she'd always said she would. Should she tell Carey her mother wanted to see him? No, it was too soon. She'd wait and see how their relationship developed before she mentioned it.

When they'd been out a couple of times more and Merry was confident their rapport had been fully restored, she casually mentioned her mother would like to meet him. To her surprise, Carey thought it a good idea.

Now, on a blustery morning, they were making their way to Porthsallos. Merry was dressed in her pink blouse with a blue skirt Prunella had loaned her. It matched the shawl and gloves Grozen and her mother had made for her and she felt smart but not overdressed. As she looked out at the familiar scenery, excitement bubbled inside her. Soon she would be home, although she couldn't help wondering how Carey would react to their tiny fisherman's cottage.

'Do you think I'm dressed smartly enough to meet your family?' he asked, breaking into her thoughts. Merry looked at his sharply tailored coat, trousers and highly polished shoes, and laughed.

'You look good enough to me.'

'I was thinking you look rather fetching, too, in

336

your blue shawl, and I see the pattern matches the band on your hat,' he grinned, pointing to the one she'd knitted. 'They could have been made by the same person, couldn't they?'

Merry laughed. 'That proves how little you know about women and their knitting. Each one can spot their own garments at a thousand paces – well, ten, at least,' she amended.

'Fascinating,' he smiled. 'You mentioned we would need to leave the carriage at the top of the village, and the wind is blowing a hooley so I've brought my naval cap. I mean, I don't want you to be ashamed of me.'

She stared at him in amazement. 'And I've been worrying about the state of our tiny cottage and whether Grozen will be her usual outspoken self,' she admitted.

He chuckled. 'Is that where you get it from? I love a woman who says what she thinks.'

'Which reminds me, your friend Alexandria came into the store recently. She didn't wish to buy anything; in fact, she turned up her nose at our stock. Apparently etiquette decreed she thank me for advising her on what to buy her staff. However, she seemed more interested in telling me about the wild parties you all have.'

He glanced quickly away. 'You don't want to worry about Venus,' he muttered.

'Venus?'

'After the plant the Venus flytrap, only according to my dear sister she ensnares men rather than flies. I understand from Saphira that I was to be her next victim.'

'Saphira has returned from Scotland?'

Carey nodded, his face brightening at once. 'Yes, thank heavens. It was she who discovered why you didn't get the message after I'd been summoned back to base.'

'Alexandria?' she guessed.

'The very same. Apparently she called at the house after I'd left. The housekeeper told her I'd been recalled and that I'd left a note to be delivered to you at Didcot and Fairbright. She said she was going there that very day and offered to take it, only...'

'She didn't,' Merry sighed.

'Saphira was furious when she found out her friend had almost come between us. Told her she was never to call upon us again.'

'Oh goodness, and there was me thinking you hadn't come in to see me because you'd had second thoughts or found someone more in your class,' she sighed.

'Class!' he spat. 'Honestly, Merryn, you're adorable, charming and competent, and really should have more faith in yourself,' he said, smiling at her in the way that made her spine tingle.

Just as they were approaching the turning for the village, they passed another carriage. She caught a fleeting glimpse of Lady Sutherland, who, to Merry's surprise, waved.

'Lady Sutherland lives on the hill opposite our cottage,' Merry began, then saw Carey was waving back.

'Oh, is that where she lives?' he murmured.

'You know her?' Merry asked. He nodded.

'She was a guest at a naval function not long ago. A lovely lady, widowed young, but now

338

betrothed to the Earl of Tavy, I believe.'

'Oh,' she gasped as the carriage pulled to a halt. 'Well, here we are.' She watched as he reached up and carefully pulled a modest yet beautiful tussie-mussie from the rack.

'Some flowers for your mother,' he explained. She looked at the colourful mixture of japonica and rose daphne wrapped in a doily and bound with a pink satin ribbon, and smiled. Then she spotted the single daylily and clapped her hands in delight. Prunella had lent her the book on the language of flowers and she saw his message to be 'sincerity and a desire to please' with the daylily representing the Chinese emblem for 'mother'.

'They're beautiful. She'll love them,' Merry exclaimed, vowing to explain to her mother exactly what they meant.

'Well, if she's half as beautiful as her daughter then it will have been worth bribing Uncle Fergus to pick his best blooms,' he murmured.

'He couldn't pick me, though, 'cos according to you I am a mere wayside flower,' she sighed, recollecting his earlier comparison with that wonderful neighbour of his.

He frowned for a moment. 'But I alikened you to bluebells because of your beautiful eyes and snowdrops because they match the sheen of your hair,' he protested.

'Ah, but I seem to remember you saying Alexandria was a hothouse bloom, though,' she said, wagging her finger at him.

'Yes, because she's temperamental and takes a lot of looking after,' he declared.

'Really?' she said, trying to sound casual, although her spirits had lifted considerably. Now he was gazing at her so warmly her heart flipped and flapped like a fish on a line.

'Come on,' she whispered. 'Mother will be waiting.' Side by side they walked down the hill.

'It's very quiet, isn't it?' Carey commented, staring around the deserted lane.

'The women will be cooking their dinners whilst the men sup their pints in the alehouse.'

'On the Sabbath?' he asked.

Merry smiled at his surprised expression. 'Lavis invites them to drop in so it's not classed as trading. Of course, the men will have to settle their dues tomorrow.' She stared at the fishing boats, breathing in the familiar smells of salt, fish and tar. 'There's nothing like the smell of the sea, is there?' she sighed, pulling her shawl tighter as a gust of wind funnelled up from the harbour.

'Goodness, anyone would think you'd been living far inland these past months,' he teased. She smiled and their eyes locked. Heart racing, she forced herself to look away and pointed up to the imposing granite house that looked down over the harbour.

'That's Lady Sutherland's house,' she said. 'When I was young, I used to dream of living there, wearing elegant clothes and driving in a fancy carriage.'

'Well, you've achieved two out of three so that's not bad, is it?' he said, gazing at her meaningfully until she felt heat searing her cheeks.

'Oh, look, we've reached the warren,' she gabbled, leading the way through the maze of cobbled lanes until they came to the Dyers' cottage. She stood on the step dithering uncertainly. Should she knock or just go in?

Chapter 34

'Come on in, our Merry. Since when did we stand on ceremony?'

As her grandmother's strident voice carried through the open window, Merry laughed. She might have known the old woman would be watching for them. Before she could lift the latch, her mother had opened the door and enfolded her in a tight hug.

'Welcome home, Merry. It's been too long, but my, you're looking good.'

'It must be this lovely shawl you made me, Mother. Thank you so much. I'm thrilled with it. It's really warm, and I made this to match as well,' she said, pointing to her hat.

Her mother smiled, then turned to Carey and gave him an appraising look.

'You must be the friend we've heard about.'

'It's good to meet you, Mrs Dyer. My name is Carey Meredith, but please call me Carey,' he said, holding out the posy.

Karenza paled as she stared down at the flowers.

'It's a tussie-mussie, Mother. Carey chose the flowers especially. They all mean something, you see,' Merry explained.

'Yes, I know,' Karenza whispered, then seemed

to make an effort to pull herself together. 'They are beautiful, thank you, Carey. Welcome to our humble home.' As she stood aside to let them pass, Merry blinked. She'd quite forgotten how gloomy it was inside the tiny cottage.

'That's it; keep our visitor to yourself, why don't you? Haven't I taught you better manners than that, our Karenza?'

Merry smiled at Carey, who had removed his cap and tucked it under his arm.

'Come and meet Grozen,' she whispered, leading him over to where her grandmother was sitting in her customary chair beside the fire. 'This is Carey, Grozen,' she said, bending and kissing the woman's cheek.

'I'm pleased to meet you, Mrs Dyer, and what a welcoming blaze to greet us on this blustery day.'

The older woman looked at Carey for a long moment. 'Like a wood fire, do you?'

'Indeed I do, Mrs Dyer.'

'Better than that dirty coal?' she enquired, staring at him with her birdlike eyes.

He nodded. 'I think the crackling noise and smell of wood makes a place feel homely, and you do have a lovely home here, if you don't mind me saying,' he said, glancing around the room. Merry looked at him in surprise.

'So what improvements would you make, young man?'

'Grozen,' Merry gasped, darting Carey an apologetic look.

He smiled. 'Well, I'm surprised you don't have a picture of yourself adorning the wall. A fine woman such as yourself should be portrayed for all to see.' The room was silent apart from the spit and hiss of the fire. Then, to Merry's amazement, the older woman burst out laughing.

'You'll do. Now, Karenza, where's our tea? I'm right parched and I'm sure these young people are too after their travels. Now, Merryn, come and tell your old grandmother what you've been up to,' she added, patting the stool beside her. 'You can take that chair, young man,' she said, pointing to the one furthest from the fire. Merry stared at the woman, knowing she was testing him.

'Thank you, Mrs Dyer, but first may I help you with the tea?' he asked, turning to Karenza.

'Goodness, whatever next?' the old woman muttered. 'Sit yourself down.'

Not in the least bit put out, Carey smiled at Merry, then did as he'd been told.

'I see you're wearing the shawl your mother made.'

'I love it, and the matching gloves are cosy. Thank you so much, Grozen. I was so sorry not to be able to make it home for Christmas but I've brought your presents with me.'

'It was a right shame about that snow; deepest they've ever had round these parts and that's saying something. Still, couldn't be helped. We'll open our presents later, shall we? I'm starving,' she said, looking pointedly at Karenza, who was pouring their tea. 'Had to look at that all morning, wasn't even allowed a tiny taster,' she moaned, pointing to the jam sponge cake on the table.

'I would have made the traditional hevva cake for you, but with the pilchards not in yet it would

343

have been unlucky,' Karenza said, passing Carey a slice.

'Just as well, or you'd have had that blessed stargazy pie for luncheon. All them eyes staring puts a person off her food,' Grozen grumbled.

Carey frowned a question at Merry.

'It's a fish pie with pilchards' heads peering through the top crust,' she explained.

'Well, sponge cake is my favourite and this is so light,' he added, lifting it from the plate and taking a bite. 'You bake an exceedingly fine cake, Mrs Dyer.'

Karenza smiled and seemed to relax at last.

They spent the next hour happily catching up. Carey seemed content to sit and listen as Merry told her mother and Grozen about her life at the store.

'So now you are a fully fledged sales assistant and trainee supervisor,' Karenza beamed. 'Well done, Merry. I know how hard you must have worked to achieve that in such a short space of time. Mr Fairbright is very good at keeping us informed of your progress but it is lovely to have you sitting here telling us for yourself.'

'Thank you, Mother. And how is life in Porthsallos? Mr Fairbright said he was pleased with the way the knitting sales have taken off in the store, especially with the cold weather we've had.'

'Yes, he's a fair man and the ladies in the village like dealing with him,' her mother agreed.

'Think he's taken a shine to our Karenza, though,' Grozen chuckled. 'Always knocking on the door, needing to consult her for this and that.'

'Now then, Mother, that's rubbish. Besides, I

gave up that kind of thing long ago.'

'More fool you,' the old woman muttered. 'Anyhow, talking of people knocking on the door, Nicco has been very good at keeping us informed of your progress, our Merry. He's the son of the owner of the pilchard-preserving factory at the pallace,' she said, turning to Carey. 'He's a lovely man and a good catch, if Merry would but see it.'

Carey smiled politely then quirked a brow at Merry.

'Grozen, please,' Merry muttered.

'We've invited Nicco for tea this afternoon,' Karenza said, looking meaningfully at Merry. Her heart sank. Would they never give up? 'I hope that is all right with you, Carey,' she added.

'I'll look forward to meeting him,' Carey replied politely

Grozen chuckled. 'Sizing up the competition eh?'

'Meeting it head on, I think.'

At this Grozen burst out laughing.

'I'm sure Carey would prefer to hear about the fishermen and their boats, him being in the Royal Navy.'

'Oh, you're a rating?' Grozen said, turning to Carey.

'Actually...' Merry began, but Karenza got to her feet.

'I think luncheon is cooked,' she said. As she bent to lift the pot from the fire the stone of her necklace reflected in the flames, jogging Merry's memory. Before she could say anything, though, Grozen turned to Carey.

'Good. I'm starving. We only get a decent meal

when we have visitors.'

'Mother, that's a lie and you know it. Now if you'd like to come to the table, I'll dish.'

'It smells delicious, Mrs Dyer,' Carey said, turning his chair to face the table. 'May I assist you in any way?'

'Thank you but no. Do make yourself comfortable, Carey,' she invited.

'Would you think me rude if I removed my jacket?' he asked politely. 'Your wonderful log fire has made me quite warm.'

Grozen smiled as she eased herself into her chair. 'Said wood was best. Go ahead, lad. We don't stand on ceremony here. I suppose being a sailor you'd like a beer, but I'm afraid we've only elderflower cordial.'

'Elderflower would be lovely, thank you. I'm not much of an ale man myself. Mind you, I do hear that it is quite palatable if you sprinkle it with a pinch of ground ginger.'

'Really? I'll have to try that,' she chuckled.

'Merry, perhaps you would pass round the plates,' Karenza said.

Merry stared down at the chicken with its toasted skin, carrots and baked potatoes and grinned. 'My favourite meal. Thank you, Mother.'

'Cors, chicken's always better with them skinny sausages, but the pigs' tails aren't long enough yet,' Grozen said to Carey.

'Nor the ears large enough for silk purses, I suppose,' he replied.

Grozen hooted.

'Really, Mother, I don't know what's got in to you today,' Karenza tutted. 'I'm sure Carey is not interested in your drivel. Would you like gravy?' she asked looking over at him.

'Oh...'

'Is something wrong?' Merry asked, for her mother had gone quite pale and seemed to be staring at Carey's jumper.

'No, of course not,' Karenza replied, absent-mindedly twiddling with her necklace, then tucking it inside her blouse. 'Do begin, Carey,' she muttered, looking quickly down at her plate. The room fell silent apart from the scrape of cutlery as they tucked into their meal.

'This is absolutely delicious, Mrs Dyer,' Carey said a short time later.

When there was no reply, Merry looked at her normally polite mother in surprise. However, she appeared to be making a great study of Carey's jumper again.

'Mother!' she remonstrated. 'Carey was talking to you.'

'Sorry. Tell us a bit about yourself, won't you?' Karenza smiled, but her eyes remained serious. 'I believe Merry said you were in the navy.'

'He's a lieutenant, Mother. Lieutenant Meredith,' Merry said proudly.

'Meredith? That has a certain ring to it, doesn't it, Karenza?' Grozen said, staring meaningfully at her daughter.

'Where do you hail from, Lieutenant Meredith?' Karenza asked.

'Carey, please. My home is just on the other side of the Tamar.'

'His house actually looks out over it,' Merry said excitedly.

Karenza's fork clattered to her plate as she gave up all pretence of eating.

'Now what's wrong?' Merry asked. But her mother ignored her and continued staring at Carey.

'Where did you get that knit frock?' she persisted.

Carey frowned down at his jumper. 'It was my father's. Well, my...'

'Will you raise your arms, please?' Karenza asked.

'Mother, we are eating,' Merry protested.

'No, it's all right,' Carey reassured her, carefully putting down his cutlery and lifting his arms.

'Thank you,' Karenza whispered, and Merry noticed she'd gone as white as the milk in the jug. 'And your father's Christian name was...?'

'Clayton. The thing is, Mrs Dyer...' he began, but Karenza jumped to her feet and began collecting their plates. 'Please, Mrs Dyer, I'd be obliged if you would just listen,' Carey pleaded, but Karenza was noisily stacking the crockery on the side.

Merry glanced at Carey in dismay. He shrugged but was looking uncomfortable.

'If we've all finished, I'll get our pudding, shall I?' Grozen said, breaking the awkward silence as she got to her feet.

Bemused, Merry nodded, then noticed the woman pat Karenza's shoulder as she passed. What was going on?

'Spiced apples with thunder and lightning,' Grozen announced with forced jollity as she placed the dishes on the table.

'Spiced apples, what a treat, though I can't say

I've ever eaten thunder and lightning before,' Carey laughed, trying to match her mood.

'Well, hailing from Devonshire, you wouldn't have. This is our speciality round here. Cream mixed with treacle. Of course, some have it with honey but treacle's our way,' the woman explained with a smile, but Merry noticed it didn't reach her eyes.

'Are you all right, Mrs Dyer? You're looking quite pale,' Carey asked, frowning as Karenza returned to her seat.

'Lieutenant Meredith, what exactly are your intentions towards my daughter?' she asked, her usually soft voice hard as the rocks on the beach. 'It is a game for men of your standing to toy with the affections of lowly shop assistants and house-maids, is it not?'

'Mother,' Merry cried in dismay.

Carey, who had been about to tuck into his pudding, carefully laid down his spoon.

'Believe you me, Mrs Dyer, I am not someone who toys with anyone's affections, least of all someone as wonderful as Merryn. She is a charming, intelligent young lady and my feelings for her are totally sincere. In fact, if she will have me, I would deem it an honour to make her my wife,' Carey replied, staring across the table at Merry. Seeing his ardent expression, her heart flipped. She opened her mouth to reply, but surprise had rendered her speechless.

'That's completely out of the question, Lieutenant. Merry is far too young to be thinking of marriage,' Karenza said in clipped tones.

'That's not what you said to Nicco,' Merry

protested. 'I am eighteen years old and...'

'And far too young to know your own mind,' Karenza snapped.

'Please, Mrs Dyer,' Carey said holding up his hand. 'It wasn't my intention to discuss such a delicate subject at the meal table. However, like Merryn, I believe in speaking the truth. I appreciate she is young in years but I love her and promise to care for her until death us do part, as they say.'

Merry's heart leaped and she held her breath, but her mother merely tightened her lips.

'Perhaps you would agree to our becoming betrothed with the idea of marrying in, say, two or three years' time?' he asked, looking hopefully at Karenza.

'No, Lieutenant. As I said, it is quite out of the question. Now if you'll excuse me, I feel a headache coming on.' They watched in dismay as Karenza rushed up the stairs.

'Grozen?' Merry asked, looking across at her grandmother.

'You heard your mother. There is nothing more to say,' the old woman whispered sadly, hobbling over to her chair beside the fire.

'What's wrong with the pair of you? It's like you've become different people,' Merry cried, jumping up and throwing her shawl around her shoulders. 'Come along, Carey, it seems we are no longer welcome here.'

Chapter 35

How dare they treat her like a child, Merry fumed, stamping her way up the hill. Carey followed, seemingly lost in his own thoughts. As soon as the door to the carriage closed behind them, he reached out and took her hand.

'Don't take on so, Merryn. It was probably the shock. I shouldn't have blurted it out like that. I didn't mean it...'

'So Mother was right, you don't want to marry me,' she whispered, tears welling as anger turned to hurt.

'Oh, Merryn, don't cry, please,' he said, passing her a crisp, white handkerchief. 'Of course I want to marry you. You mean the world to me. I was just saying that I hadn't intended mentioning marriage on my first visit to your family.'

'Oh,' Merry whispered, mollified by his assurance. 'I've never known Mother be so rude. Normally she's mild and understanding, and she's always been a stickler for telling the truth. I guess she's upset because she wants me to marry Nicco and stay in the village.'

'But do you want to marry him?' he asked, staring at her closely.

Merry shook her head. 'It's you I love,' she whispered.

He grinned and gripped her hand tighter. 'That's a relief, for you had me worried there for a moment. We'll come back and see your mother next weekend. By then, she'll have had a chance to think things over and we can discuss them properly.'

Merry smiled at him. 'It might be better leaving it for two or three weeks. Mother doesn't often get riled but when she does it takes her for ever to calm down.'

'My leave will be up by then, I'm afraid. I had planned to spend the time with you so we could really get to know each other before I whisked you off for a romantic candlelit dinner and proposed properly, but your mother pre-empted that,' he said. He stared out of the window, seemingly lost in thought. 'You do want to marry me, I take it?' he asked, turning suddenly.

As he gazed at her intently his eyes bright with emotion, she felt the tightness in her chest begin to ease.

'Of course I do,' she whispered, knowing with absolute certainty he was the man of her dreams. Then a thought struck her. 'By the way, what was it you kept trying to tell Mother?'

'That Meredith is my given name. I was adopted, you see. Obviously I had intended telling you first, but your mother looked so shocked when she heard my name. Then she began firing those questions at me and I wanted to be totally honest. However, she...'

'Never gave you the chance. It doesn't make one jot of difference to anything, though, does it?' she smiled, for he could have been called Mr Mud for all she cared. 'What about Saphira – is she adopted too?'

Carey shook his head. 'Apparently Mother was a delicate child and thought she'd never be able to bear children of her own. Then a few years after they'd given me a home she found she was expecting Saphira. She always treated us equally, though.'

'What about your father?'

'He was away a lot,' he said quickly. 'Ah, here we are at the ferry,' he added, seemingly grateful for the distraction.

As they made their way across the water he pointed towards the dockyard. 'See the black ship with the two funnels and three masts?' When she nodded, he went on, 'That's being victualled for our next trip.'

The thought of his going away again in the near future made Merry feel empty. She was so lost in thought that it seemed no time at all before they were back outside the store.

'I don't suppose there's a chance you could request some time off between now and next Sunday?' he asked.

'Not really. With it being nearly Mothering Sunday, Mr Fairbright is planning to keep the store open longer this Wednesday,' Merry replied. 'He says it will give the servants the opportunity to choose materials and trimmings for themselves when they call to collect their employers' purchases.'

'Will servants be able to afford that kind of thing?' he asked.

'Well, maybe not the part-made garments or services of the dressmaker, but we do have some lovely materials and trimmings at reasonable prices. The girls will want to look their best when they go home, and are used to making their own clothes, after all.'

'Well, you always look lovely and we can take your mother and Grozen some fresh blooms, if you like. Shall I get Fingers to make up another tussie-mussie?'

'Mother really loves violets,' she said.

'Then that is what she shall have. In the meantime, I shall spend all next week thinking of you,' he whispered, leaning forward and kissing her cheek. 'Don't worry, I'll talk your mother round.'

Hearing the sincerity in his voice, she smiled. 'I'm sure you will,' she replied, her spirits lifting.

From the moment the doors were opened the next morning, clients descended on the store requesting to see fabrics and part-made garments of a lighter weight. There was also a demand for new bonnets and trimmings for older ones, so that by the afternoon Merry had lost track of the number of women she'd served. The prospect of spring was definitely in the air, she thought, holding up a swathe of frothy voile to show a woman of middle years.

'Do you think this would be too young for me?' the customer asked.

Merry looked at the fair-haired woman and shook her head. 'I think the butter colour would enhance madam's colouring beautifully,' she assured her. 'And we have ribbon in a deeper yellow if you wish to trim your bonnet to match.'

'Wonderful,' the woman clapped her hands. 'My daughter is getting married this summer and

'I am holding a garden party in order for her betrothed's family to meet ours. He's a wonderful man.'

'You must be very happy,' Merry replied, wishing her mother had showed the same enthusiasm. 'Would you like me to have these wrapped and put these aside for carriage collection?'

'Yes, please, my dear.'

As the woman made her way from the store, Merry couldn't help wondering again about her mother's reaction. She had spent the night mulling over everything that had been said and come to the conclusion it had been because her mother wanted Merry to live in the village. They'd always been so close but she knew ultimately her mother only wanted her happiness.

'I'd like to see some of your part-made garments. Blue is my preferred choice,' a thin-faced woman with a querulous voice demanded.

'Certainly, madam,' Merry said. This woman was harder to please, though, and dithered between three choices.

'I think I'd like to see the first one again.'

'Certainly, madam.' Merry forced a smile as she retrieved the length of pre-cut material in sky blue from behind the counter and held it up. Whilst the woman hesitated, Merry thought back to Carey's surprise proposal. If her mother agreed, would he be happy to marry in her local church? They would have to ensure they had bread or cake for the kimbly. Village tradition decreed that the bride's father walked alone to the church giving a piece of this to the first person he met. Not that she had a father, of course, but perhaps Pucky

Pint or another fisherman could be persuaded to do the honours. It would be such fun to bring her mother here so they could look at material together.

'I think I'll leave it, thank you,' the woman's strident voice broke into her thoughts.

'Of course, madam,' Merry said, suppressing a sigh. Some people were spoiled for choice. Given half a chance she'd happily take any of the lengths.

She began tidying away the materials and couldn't resist running her fingers over the soft voiles. Smiling, she imagined herself dressed in the delicate material.

'Blimey oh rimey, girl, you're looking mighty happy,' Freckles cried as she went past on her way to the dressing room. 'Lover boy give you a good time yesterday, did he?'

Merry nodded, then turned back to her tidying, wanting to keep Carey's proposal to herself a while longer.

'Mr Fairbright wants to see you in his office right away,' Mrs Smale said, appearing by her side.

Merry looked at the woman in surprise. Since she'd removed to the office upstairs she had never ventured back onto the shop floor.

'Is anything wrong?' she asked.

'Just hurry along, I'll explain to Mrs Winter,' Mrs Smale urged, looking at her with such sympathy, she felt a prickle of unease shiver up her spine as she hurried up the stairs.

Mr Fairbright was standing just inside the door, a constable by his side. They were both looking so grave that Merry's heart lurched.

'Miss Dyer, please come and take a seat,' Mr

Fairbright said. 'I'm afraid I have some dreadful news. It would seem that somehow ... that...' Unable to continue, he looked at the constable, who cleared his throat.

'A woman's body was found on the beach just outside Porthsallos this morning. We have reason to believe she was your mother...'

Merry swayed in her seat, unable to take in what he said.

'Drink this,' said Mr Fairbright, holding out a glass. Merry obeyed, then spluttered as the fiery liquid burned her throat. 'Brandy for shock,' he added.

'*Was* my mother?' she croaked, hoping she'd misunderstood.

'I'm afraid your mother's injuries were fatal,' Mr Fairbright said gently.

'But how...? Why?'

'All we know is,' the constable said, opening his notebook and reading, 'a female body was found on the beach at first light by fishermen hauling their long lines. The injuries sustained suggest a fall from the cliff. Dislodged rocks, turf and soil were found scattered on the beach.' He snapped his book shut. 'Until we have the result of the autopsy we won't know for sure what happened, miss, and even then...' He looked at Mr Fairbright and shrugged.

Merry put her head in her hands. Was it her fault? Had her mother been so upset she'd...? No, her mother wouldn't have. Grozen would have... Grozen... She must go home straight away. She jumped to her feet then felt the room

357

sway around her. Mr Fairbright gently helped her down onto the chair again.

'Take it easy, Merry. You've had a terrible shock.'

'I must go home...' she whispered.

'As soon as I heard, I took the liberty of sending a dispatch to Lieutenant Meredith. Mrs Smale is at this moment packing some things for you.'

The door burst open.

'Merryn, my dearest, I'm so very sorry,' Carey whispered, kneeling beside her and pulling her close for a moment. 'I will take her to Porthsallos immediately, sir,' he said, getting to his feet and addressing Mr Fairbright.

Merry remembered nothing of the journey home. The only thing that penetrated her numb mind were the heart-breaking sobs coming from Grozen as they entered the cottage. Delen and Marya were trying to comfort her but stood back when Merry flew across the room and threw her arms around her grandmother.

'Kelys has gone for the doctor, sir,' Delen said to Carey. 'Mrs Dyer's been like this ever since she heard and we think she needs something to calm her.'

'Oh, Grozen,' Merry cried.

'She's dead, Merry. My darling Karenza's gone.'

'What happened?' Merry whispered.

'I don't know for sure. She was that upset after you left. Said she should have listened to what the lieutenant had been trying to say, then explained herself. Insisted she'd go to Plymouth to tell you,' Grozen sobbed.

'Tell me what?' Merry asked, but Grozen shook her head. 'You mean she was on her way to see me when she fell?'

'I don't know, Merry, I really don't know,' she sighed, peering at Merry through red swollen eyes. 'Her bed was empty when I woke.'

'But what did she have to tell me that was so important?' But her grandmother was too upset to speak as her bitter sobs racked the room once more.

Merry turned and stared at Carey in despair, hot tears falling unchecked down her cheeks. She felt consumed by grief but how could she help her grandmother when she knew nothing of the cause of this tragedy?

Chapter 36

Through the long hours of darkness, Merry kept a vigil beside her grandmother's bed. Although the doctor's draught had rendered the woman unconscious, she still cried out from time to time as if the terrible tragedy was invading her sleep. Merry heard Carey moving around downstairs, banking up the fire, tidying crockery away, but remained where she was. Thoughts of that last meeting with her mother went round and round her head. Was it her fault the woman had died? Had her mother been so upset at the thought of her not marrying Nicco and staying in the village that she'd...?

Merry glanced at her grandmother. She seemed calmer now, her sleep deeper. Unable to be still, Merry moved over to the window. A pearly moon was paling against the grey light of dawn. Already she could hear the sounds of activity in the harbour. Everything seemed to be carrying on as usual. How could it when her whole world had changed? Oh, Mother, she sobbed, what were you doing out in the dead of night by yourself? What was so urgent you couldn't wait until my next visit? Turning away from the window, she saw her mother's nightdress neatly folded on her pillow and the tears flowed faster. Impulsively, she snatched it up and held it to her face. As she breathed in the scent that had been her mother, something clattered to the floor. She stared down at the little blue stone on its golden chain and gasped. Her mother had worn her necklace at all times so if she'd taken it off that could only mean one thing, couldn't it?

Hearing her grandmother stir, she hastily stuffed the necklace in her pocket. Grozen was upset enough as it was.

'Karenza, is it morning already?'

'Hush, Grozen, it's only me,' Merry whispered, going over and stroking the woman's arm. 'It's early, go back to sleep.'

To her relief her grandmother closed her eyes again and, leaving her to sleep, Merry slipped downstairs.

Carey was tending the fire but as soon as he saw her he jumped to his feet.

'How are you?' he asked.

Merry shrugged.

'I boiled some water – would you like a drink?' She nodded. Now Carey seemed more like a stranger than the man who'd recently proposed.

Was that really only two days ago?

'Thought I'd go to Logh and see how the aut... how the investigation is proceeding,' he said, pouring hot water into the teapot. 'Can I get you something to eat before I go?'

Merry shook her head. How could he think of food at a time like this?

'You need to eat to keep your strength up,' he added as if reading her thoughts.

'I'll have something when Grozen wakes,' she whispered, holding her cold hands out towards the flame.

'I'll go now then, shall I?'

She nodded again but still couldn't speak.

'I'll be back as soon as I can.'

The morning dragged by. Merry felt an overwhelming need to go to the cliff top but knew she had to stay here with Grozen. Frustrated, she prowled around the tiny room like a caged animal but her thoughts continued to rage. Seeing vegetables on the shelf and realizing Carey was right when he said they needed to eat, she snatched them up and began chopping madly.

It was afternoon before her grandmother came downstairs. She looked as if she'd aged a generation overnight and Merry hurried to help her into her chair, then threw more sticks into the grate. Then she poured tea, cut a thick wedge of bread and handed it to the woman.

'You must eat something, Grozen,' she said.

'And have you? Eaten something, I mean?'

Merry shook her head. 'I've made broth,' she said, pointing to the pot over the fire. 'We'll all have some when Carey returns. He's gone to

Logh.' Grozen nodded and sipped at her tea. They sat listening to the wood spitting and crackling, and after a while Merry was pleased to see some colour return to her grandmother's cheeks.

'Do you think she did it on purpose, Grozen?' she burst out, unable to keep her thoughts to herself any longer.

'What makes you think that?' Her grandmother eyed her sharply.

'This fell out of Mother's nightdress,' she said, retrieving the necklace from her pocket and holding it up. 'She never takes ... took it off and...' Her voice tailed off and they watched as the necklace glittered in the light of the fire. Then her grandmother reached out and took it, letting out a long sigh.

'After you and Carey left on Sunday, I went upstairs to see how your mother was. I was just in time to see her hurl this across the room.'

'But why?' Merry frowned. 'I know she was upset because she wanted me to stay here and marry Nicco, but that didn't have anything to do with it, did it?'

'Oh, Merry, I told Karenza she should have explained. She said she'd go straight away but I begged her to wait until the morning. After all, this has been hanging over her for eighteen years, so another week or so till you returned wouldn't make a halfpenny of difference. But you know your mother,' she sighed. 'Once she decides something she has to do it immediately. Had to, I mean. Oh, it's all my fault she's dead,' the woman sobbed. 'If I hadn't insisted she tell...' her voice trailed away and she stared into the fire.

They were interrupted by a knock on the door. Merry hurried to open it to find the Reverend Mr Mabey on the doorstep.

'I'm so sorry to hear of your sad loss and have come in the hope of being able to offer a small measure of comfort to yourself and Mrs Dyer,' he explained, doffing his hat.

'Please come in, sir,' she invited. 'Can I get you some tea?'

'That is very kind, but thank you, no. Please don't get up, Mrs Dyer,' he said, looking over to where Grozen was struggling to her feet. As if the effort of standing had been too much, the old woman sank back into her chair.

'Karenza was a fine, upstanding woman and I offer my sincere condolences for your loss, Mrs Dyer.'

'Thank you, sir. I'm sure I can count on you to say more wonderful things about her at her funer...' She broke off with a sob.

'Of course. I understand an aut... I mean, when you are in a position to discuss the date let me know. He looked at Merry. 'In the meantime, if there is anything I can do, please say.'

'Thank you, sir,' she replied, seeing him to the door before returning to sit beside her grand-mother.

'You haven't told me what it was Mother needed to explain,' she said, anxious to hear before they were interrupted again.

'My dear Merry, you need to prepare yourself for something of a shock. You already know that your mother left here to go into service?'

'Yes, at a big house this side of the...'

Hearing the sound of the latch lifting, Merry looked up and almost screamed in frustration when she saw Carey standing in the doorway.

'Is it all right to come in? I didn't like to knock in case your grandmother was still asleep.'

'That's all right, lad, you come on in,' Grozen said, the strength returning to her voice. 'Any news from Logh?'

'The investigation has so far proved inconclusive,' he said carefully.

'Come and sit by the fire and tell us what you've learned,' Grozen insisted. Carey looked at Merry, who sighed with impatience.

'But I want to hear what you have to say first, Grozen,' she declared.

'No, Merry, that can keep for a moment longer. First I need to know everything Carey's learned.'

'Like I said, the outcome was inconclusive, Mrs Dyer,' he said, pulling up a seat beside them. 'The injuries are consistent with a fall, but whether she slipped or...'

'Jumped?' Merry sighed. 'If she did, it was my fault for not staying in the village and marrying Ni...'

'Don't torture yourself, Merry,' he cut in. 'Apparently a squall blew up, making visibility that bad she could easily have missed her footing. They're releasing her body tomorrow. I've arranged for it ... her to be transported back here. Oh, and I passed the vicar on the way and he said he can arrange the service for Friday.'

'She were born on a Friday. A true Friday's child, loving and giving,' Grozen muttered. 'Seems apt somehow for her to be buried on Friday.'

'Grozen and I were in the middle of discussing something important, Carey. Do you think you could go up to the rectory and tell Mr Mabey Friday will be convenient?'

'No!' Grozen's voice was so sharp they stared at her in surprise. 'Stay where you are, lad. What I have to say concerns you too.'

Merry frowned. 'But...'

'Hush, child. The sooner this is brought into the open the better I'll feel. Then we can bury my girl with no secrets between us. Pour us all some tea, will you?' Impatient to hear what her grandmother had to tell them, Merry quickly did as she'd been bid.

'Are you sure you're up to this, Mrs Dyer?' Carey asked. 'You've had a terrible shock.'

'Yes, lad, I shan't rest until I get this off my chest.' She waited until they were all seated with their tea, then took a deep breath.

'Karenza left here to go into service...'

'I know that already, Grozen,' Merry snapped.

'But Carey needs to know the story from the beginning,' Grozen remonstrated. 'Now, this is hard enough, so no more interruptions, please. Karenza fell deeply in love with a handsome man who promised her his undying love. As it turned out all he gave her was this trinket,' she said, holding up the necklace. Carey frowned and opened his mouth to say something but Grozen held up her hand. 'In return she made him a knit frock with his initials, C M, under each arm.'

Hearing Carey's intake of breath, Merry turned to her grandmother. 'Go on, Grozen,' she urged as her grandmother took a sip of her tea.

'It was only when Karenza realized she was with child that she also realized she hadn't seen her love for a while. Plucking up courage, she went to see him at his home.' Merry and Carey stared at each other in surprise. 'Yes, it was your father, Captain Clayton Meredith.'

'Actually, Mrs Dyer, he was my adoptive father,' Carey said. The old woman stared at Carey in horror as the full truth began to sink in. 'I was adopted,' he added. 'That was what I was trying to tell you on Sunday but...'

'You didn't get a chance,' Grozen finished. 'Oh lordy, what a mess,' she added, putting her head in her hands and sobbing again.

'So my father wasn't a fisherman like you both said,' Merry gasped.

'To be fair, we never actually said he was. "A man of the sea" was how your mother referred to him.'

'Oh, yes,' Merry whispered. 'But if Captain Meredith was my father why ... what happened?' As Grozen took another sip of her tea, Merry almost cried out in exasperation.

'A well-dressed woman was just entering the house. She was heavily pregnant...'

'You mean Captain Meredith was already married?' Merry gasped.

Grozen nodded.

'Heaven forbid,' Carey groaned, holding his head in his hands.

'So that's why Saphira and I look similar?' Merry cried as the penny dropped.

'I don't know who this Saphira is, but going back to my story, apparently the woman looked radiant and was so pleasant your mother didn't have the heart to upset her. Instead she bought a curtain ring and returned to the village. She told her father and me what had happened but let everyone else assume she'd been widowed and had reverted to using her maiden name.'

'That's why you were both called Dyer then. I always wondered,' Merry said.

'It were easier that way,' Grozen muttered.

'I do think she should have told me.'

'So do I, and that's what I told her in no uncertain terms on Sunday. So you see, Merry, if anyone is to blame for her death, it's me,' the old lady sighed, staring into the fire.

'Not really, Grozen,' Merry whispered. 'If I'd stayed here and married Nicco, as she wanted, she wouldn't have had to make that journey.'

'If I'd insisted she listened to me on Sunday, none of this would have happened. If anyone is to blame it must surely be me,' Carey sighed.

Lost in their own painful thoughts, they each lapsed into silence.

Chapter 37

On the day of the funeral, the sun shone brightly from a clear blue sky yet Merry felt as if she was encased in a blanket of fog. She heard nothing of the service, just stood staring at the simple coffin before her, picturing her mother's body, battered and broken inside. Even Carey's hand on her arm felt cold as he led her outside. The knitting ladies lined the graveside, their pins bare of wool at their belts. Then as the coffin was lowered into the freshly dug hole, they solemnly crossed them over their chests in the time-honoured way of showing respect. However, Merry's eyes were fixed on the casket. All she could think of was her mother's crumpled and lifeless form.

Feeling a hand on her shoulder, she turned to see Nicco staring at her, his dark eyes full of sympathy.

'I'm so sorry, Merry,' he said gently. 'Your mother was a beautiful woman.'

'Thank you,' she whispered.

'You and your father will come back to the cottage?' Grozen invited.

Nicco glanced from Grozen to Carey standing beside her and raised an eyebrow.

'Of course,' Merry muttered, knowing that was what her mother would have wanted.

'I think it's time we were making our way,' Carey said, nodding at Nicco, then placing one arm around Merry and another round her grandmother. With a last look at the grave that was already being filled with the turned soil, Merry let herself be led back to the cottage.

Carey helped her hand out the prepared food and drink to the villagers who'd come back with them for the wake. Despite his solicitous attention, Merry could hardly bring herself to acknowledge him. She felt distant from everything as she moved trancelike around the room, thanking people for coming, forcing herself to nod when they all said what a lovely woman her mother had been. Without exception they commented on Karenza's virtues of honesty and truthfulness, and it took all Merry's willpower not to demur. *If only you knew,* she wanted to scream.

'Whilst Mr Hospitality there is busy charming all the women, may I ask how you are, Merry?' Nicco asked. 'I mean, someone should be looking after you,' he added, glaring at Carey.

'I think what my son means is that we are deeply saddened by your mother's passing and if there's anything we can do, you must say,' Mr Neaple said, squeezing her arm.

Merry nodded, a lump rising in her throat. 'Thank you,' she whispered.

'Are you all right?' Carey asked, appearing at her side and giving Nicco a wary look.

'My son and I are just leaving,' Mr Neaple replied. 'We merely wanted to bestow our condolences and offer our help. Thank you for your hospitality, Lieutenant,' he added, holding out his hand.

'That is good of you, sir,' Carey responded, shaking it.

'Miss Dyer, I just wanted to say how very sorry I am for your loss. Your mother was a truly lovely lady and she will be very much missed, not least by our knitting industry.' Merry looked up to find Mr Fairbright by her side.

Forcing herself to nod politely she said, 'Thank you, Mr Fairbright. She would have appreciated your kind words.'

'Not at all. Praise where praise is due. Now may I offer you a lift back to the store?'

Merry stared at him aghast. 'I can't come back

to Plymouth, Mr Fairbright. I must stay here with Grozen.'

'I see,' he frowned. 'Forgive me if I am being premature. You will be travelling with Lieutenant Meredith then?' he enquired.

'Rest assured, I will see that Miss Dyer is returned to the store when she has had time to recover from her shock,' Carey said. 'It is good of you to come, sir.' Merry watched as he led Mr Fairbright over to the door. Why didn't they all just go away and leave her alone? As if they'd heard her silent wishes, the villagers began leaving.

'Don't worry, Merry, Mr Fairbright will be happy to grant you a month's leave of absence,' Carey said, reappearing by her side. 'It won't be paid, of course, but I know you...'

'You misunderstand,' Merry cried. 'I have no intention of returning to Plymouth, ever. If I hadn't gone there in the first place Mother would still be alive. Besides, I need to care for Grozen,' she said, glancing towards her grandmother, who was staring into the fire.

'Of course,' Carey said quickly. 'Let me help you clear away and then I'm afraid I must return to Plymouth. I hate to leave you today of all days, but regrettably I cannot extend my leave any longer for we sail on the tide tomorrow.'

Just go, she wanted to shout as he stood there staring anxiously at her.

'Then you must leave now, for you must have things to do,' she replied woodenly, ignoring the hurt that sparked in his eyes.

'You've been a great help, lad,' Grozen said, hobbling over and looking at Merry for agreement. Unable to respond, she just stood there fiddling with the necklace around her neck. 'Your mother would have been pleased to see you wearing her precious trinket on this day,' she added.

Grozen's comment seemed to shake Carey from his dejection. 'I've been meaning to speak to you about that,' he said. 'Do you have any idea what that stone is?'

'Meant to resemble a sapphire, I think,' Grozen replied. 'Ironic really, when you think those stones represent sincerity and faithfulness.' She gave a harsh laugh. 'Still, I suppose it's fitting, a fake stone from a fake love.'

'Except it isn't,' Carey said. 'Fake, I mean. I have reason to believe it's the genuine thing.'

'What?' Grozen gasped.

'No?' Merry gasped, snatching the chain from her neck and staring at it.

'Surely you must recognize it? It's identical to Saphira's.'

'Goodness, I noticed how clean it came up when I gave it a polish but I can't believe I didn't spot the resemblance,' Merry frowned.

'Will someone please explain?' Grozen cried.

'Sorry, Mrs Dyer. You see, Grandfather Meredith served on the merchant ships and he purchased these stones from South Africa and had them made into a ring and earrings for his wife. She lost one and turned the remaining one into a pendant. When my father – adoptive father – was going through her things after her death, he found the missing one and put it in his pocket. We'd heard he'd given it away but nobody knew to whom.'

'And you think he gave it to my mother?' Merry whispered.

Carey nodded. 'Of course, nobody realized the stones had any worth until Saphira inherited the pendant and had it valued.'

'You really think this could be the lost one?' Grozen asked.

'I only caught a glimpse of the heart-shaped stone before today, but you wearing it outside your blouse now, Merry, has given me the opportunity to study it. Of course, I'll have to get it verified but if my hunch is correct, far from being a trinket, it is worth a tidy sum.'

'Then you can take it back with you,' Merry whispered, placing it in his hand.

'There's no need...' he began.

'And this,' she added, reaching inside the neck of her blouse and tugging off the silver chain with the heart charm he'd given her for Christmas.

'No, Merry, please don't...' Carey began.

'Thank you for your support today, Carey, but I have no desire to see you again.'

'Merry,' Grozen gasped. 'You don't mean that.'

'You're in shock, sweetheart,' Carey murmured.

'I am not and never will be your sweetheart. Please leave, Lieutenant Meredith,' Merry said, turning away before his anguished look caused her to falter.

He looked at her sadly. 'I regret I have to go anyway, but you can be assured I shall return. Hopefully by then the shock you are experiencing will have eased and you will see things more clearly. Good afternoon, Mrs Dyer,' he added, turning to the older woman.

'Look after yourself, lad,' Grozen muttered, but no sooner had the door shut behind him than she turned to Merry.

'I hope you know what you're doing, girl. That Carey is a good man and...'

'If I hadn't met him, Mother would be alive,' she whispered as once more the swirling fog descended and wrapped itself around her.

Next morning at first light, Merry headed for the cliff top where her mother had met her fate. She hardly noticed the boats bobbing on the water, the fishermen hauling their long lines, as the need to find out what had happened burned away inside her.

'Did you jump, Mother, or was it a terrible accident?' she cried, but only the gulls replied. 'Please, please, let me know,' she screamed. As if in a trance she stared down the cliff face but apart from a few dislodged boulders everything looked as it always had. Even the beach had been washed clean by the tide. 'How can I go on living if I'm to blame? You must tell me what happened, Mother,' she begged. But her words were snatched away on the breeze and the only answer was the roar of the waves, the screech of gulls. 'I'll come back every day until you answer me, Mother,' she cried.

Despite her grandmother's pleas that she stay at home and recover, each day Merry returned to the cliff top. Each time she asked the same questions, hopeful her mother would respond, but there was never any answer and she would return to the cottage more despondent than ever.

Neighbours and friends rallied round, calling

each day with dishes of freshly made broth or casserole, staying to talk about the fine woman
Karenza had been. Whilst her grandmother
seemed to draw comfort from their visits, Merry
resented the intrusion. She didn't want to speak to
anyone. Stealing upstairs, she wrapped herself in
her mother's nightdress then lay on her mattress,
staring up at the ceiling. Twice her grandmother
ventured up the stairs to tell her Nicco wanted to
speak with her but she told her to send him away.

'Nothing can bring her back, Merry. I only wish
it could. You lying here like this won't change
things so why not go out for a walk with Nicco?'
she urged, when he called yet again.

'I don't want to see anyone, Grozen,' she whispered. 'Besides, I walked up to the cliff top
earlier.'

Her grandmother sighed and shook her head.
'You can't carry on like this, girl.'

'Just because you've forgotten her, Grozen,
doesn't mean I can,' Merry snapped.

'Oh, Merry, is that what you really think?' the
woman sighed, sinking herself down on the bed
beside her. 'I may not go around moping but that
doesn't mean I'm not hurting. Your mother was
the best thing that ever happened to me, along
with you and your grandfather, of course. When
he died I wanted to lie down beside him, close
my eyes and never get up again but I soon
learned it was better to keep busy.'

'But I need to know what happened, Grozen,
and until I do I can't rest,' she cried, staring up at
the woman as if she could provide the answer. Her
grandmother shook her head, then took herself

down the stairs. Hearing the door slam moments later, Merry gave a sigh of relief. Seeing Nicco would only compound her feelings of guilt.

Although she continued her daily pilgrimage to the cliff top it didn't bring any comfort or the answer she desperately sought. Life seemed unreal. It was as if she was looking in through a window. After yet another futile journey, she returned heavy hearted to the cottage to find Grozen waiting for her at the door.

'There's someone to see you, Merry.'

'I told you I don't want to see Nicco,' she muttered, instinctively making for the stairs.

''Tis been a long time since I've been mistaken for a handsome, dark-haired follower,' a male voice chuckled.

Merry stared at the snowy-haired old man perched on the stool beside the fire like a little Cornish pisky.

'Cador called in to see how we are doing,' Grozen said quickly, snatching up her basket. 'Now, we've relied upon our neighbours' generosity for long enough so I'm off to get some fish for our luncheon. Will you stay and join us, Cador?'

'Thank you, but no,' he replied.

'Don't get anything for me, I'll not be eating,' Merry muttered. Her grandmother pursed her lips.

'You make sure you get two nice fish,' Cador said firmly. 'Whilst you're out, Merry and I will have a chat.'

Grozen nodded, and as soon as the door had shut behind her Cador smiled gently at Merry.

Again she experienced that strange feeling, as if those piercing jade eyes were seeing into her very soul. 'I'll not ask how you are, my dear, for I can see you are in turmoil. It was a sad thing to have happened to your mother and...'

'But that's it,' Merry cried. 'I don't know what did happen.'

'Would it change anything if you did?' Cador said in his soothing voice.

'Well, yes. You see, if it was an accident that would be bad enough because she was on her way to tell me about my father ... well, who he was. Obviously it was something she should have told me long ago, especially as she always said telling the truth was important even if you knew the consequences would be unfavourable, but she lied...' She stuttered to a halt as Cador reached out and took her hand. Immediately she felt warmth penetrate the cold fog that had surrounded her since she'd heard about her mother, and the tears began to fall.

'That's better,' he said softly. 'Your mother was a fine woman and, as I see it, didn't lie as such, she just didn't tell you who your father was. She was only doing her best to protect you.'

'Maybe, but she should have told me,' she sighed. 'If she did take her own life, then I'm to blame. She wanted me to stay here and marry Nicco, but I insisted on making my own way. It was my dream to leave here and see something of the outside world.'

He gave a gentle smile. 'The yen to travel, yes, I remember.' She frowned for a moment then recalled his parting words on his last visit.

376

'You told me my life and love lay here in Porthsallos. I should have listened, then Mother...'

'Your mother's time here on earth had come to an end, Merry. It's as simple as that. I agree the circumstances were tragic, but I can tell you it was quick and she didn't suffer. That's more than can be said for some. And if you cast your mind back to our last conversation, I never said you had to remain in the village, just that your future lies here.'

Merry frowned. 'But why can't Mother let me know what happened?'

'Because she isn't able to return, at least not as she was,' he said sadly.

Chapter 38

Merry felt as if her heart had been sliced right in two. Never had she experienced such pain, and putting her head in her hands she wept as she never had before. She cried until she had no more tears left. As pent-up misery came gushing out in a storm, Cador sat quietly beside her. Then as her sobs subsided into hiccups, he leaned forward and threw twigs onto the dying fire.

'Remember your sister in blood?'

'Jenna? Of course, but what has she got to do with anything?'

'She asks if you remember the day you went off with Mealy Mouth's box?'

Merry's eyes widened. How did he know the

name they'd given the surly fisherman? But Cador was watching her and waiting.

'We waited until he fell asleep over his fishing rod, then ran off with his maggots,' she admitted. 'After hiding them in our secret hole in the old oak we forgot about them. When we finally returned and lifted the lid they'd turned into bluebottles. As they flew away we cheered because we'd set them free.'

'Freedom,' Cador smiled. 'That's what Jenna wants you to remember, for that is what your mother is experiencing now. Unbeknown to her, she fell in love with a married man and whilst you were her pride and joy, she never got over that, could never move on. She was a prisoner of her past but now she is free and you must be happy for her.'

'But if Jenna can speak to you why can't Mother?'

'She's not ready yet, Merry.'

'But you're a witch – surely you can cast a spell, conjure her up or something?'

He shook his head. 'I am a Cornish Charmer and have certain powers that I use to help and heal. Charms work but not always in the way you might expect, and only when the time is right.'

'But I need to know now,' she cried, tears falling unchecked down her face once again. Cador stared at her with those jade all-seeing eyes. 'Get her to come back and tell me she's all right,' she pleaded.

'That she is all right, I can assure you, and she will send that message,' he promised. 'However, as I said, you will only recognize it when the time

378

is right. Now close your eyes and imagine heaven is the wide open sky and earth a deep pond. Can you picture that?'

'Yes,' she frowned, wondering what on earth this could have to do with her mother.

'Now picture a nymph swimming in the water. One day she sees the shadow of a damselfly soaring free above and yearns to be with her. She can't, of course, for she has yet to grow the wings that will enable this. The damselfly can drink of the water's surface but cannot dive below, for it has evolved and moved on. Such is the way of life.'

Merry frowned, trying to take in what he was telling her. 'So I'll never see her again?' she whispered, tears welling once more.

'Remember damselflies and one day you will understand. Now take hold of my hands,' he instructed.

Hesitantly she reached out and placed her hands in his. Immediately a feeling of peace spread through her body. She gazed at him in surprise but his eyes were closed, his lips moving silently. After a few moments, she felt the intensity of his gaze boring into her.

'Take comfort from the fact your mother is free from the guilt that plagued her throughout her time on earth. Rejoice that she is happy and know that one day, when you are healed, you will be too.' He stared at her for a long moment, his jade eyes seeming to peer into her very soul. Then, as if satisfied, he got to his feet and left.

As Merry sat mulling over his words, Grozen came bustling in, her basket laden.

'That wind's blowing like blazes so no fish for us today. We'll have to make do with bread and cheese. Still, Pucky Pint says the pilchards should be coming in soon. There's been sighting of a shoal further round the point.'

'Bread's fine, I'm not very hungry anyway,' Merry sighed.

'But you need to eat and do some work,' her grandmother said firmly. 'The money from our knitting has seen us through the winter but we've not done any since...' her voice trailed away. Sighing, she set the rest of her things on the table. 'Anyway, we need to get back to it or Mr Fairbright won't be happy when he returns. Once we've eaten we'll settle by the fire and pick up our pins.'

'Oh, I don't think...'Merry began.

'Well, it's time you did. This food didn't just jump into my basket, it needed paying for,' Grozen said as she cut into a fresh loaf. 'If you're not going back to Plymouth then you'd better carry on with Kar ... Karenza's ... knit frock.' Grozen swallowed, her eyes suspiciously bright. 'There'll soon be work at the pallace as well. I can't do everything by myself, Merry.'

As her grandmother stood there wagging her finger at her as if she was a child, Merry felt a wave of shame wash over her. Rushing over, she threw her arms around her grandmother.

'Oh, Grozen, I'm sorry I haven't been much help but I feel as if I'm in some kind of cold, miserable fog.'

'I know that feeling only too well but, like I said, you need to keep busy and you can start by making us some tea to go with luncheon. I'm fair parched.'

Merry gave a tremulous smile and did as she'd been asked.

'So how did you get on with Cador?' Grozen asked when they'd finished their meal.

Merry shrugged. 'He mumbled on about nymphs and damselflies. It was a load of rubbish, really. Said when I saw them it would be the sign I was looking for. I mean, what on earth could that have to do with Mother?'

'He works in mysterious ways, does Cador. But I've never known him be wrong,' Grozen said, going over to the fire and jabbing it with the poker. 'Come and sit down, Merry, the clearing up can wait.'

Merry nodded but no sooner had she sat down than her grandmother fell asleep.

As she sat listening to her gentle snores, Merry felt guilt sweep over her again. How could she have left everything for Grozen to do? It really was time she contributed towards their upkeep. And as for that Cador, he was an oddball and she'd take his gibbering with the proverbial pinch of salt.

It seemed the pilchards would be reappearing soon and she would have to work at the pallace. That would mean seeing Nicco. The alternative was to return to her job in Plymouth, but that seemed a world away now. Her grandmother grunted in her sleep and Merry shook her head, knowing she wouldn't feel comfortable leaving her alone. She wondered how Freckles and Pru were and then, seemingly out of nowhere, a picture of

Carey appeared in her mind. She smiled, re-membering his tender looks, the fun they'd had. Then, like a blanket, the fog descended. If she hadn't met him her mother would still be alive, wouldn't she? She frowned into the fire, lost in contemplation once more.

'Right, girl, I need to get on with my knitting,' Grozen's voice penetrated her thoughts, making her jump. 'Honestly, girl, you're a bundle of nerves. Why don't you do some with me? It will take your mind off things and you might find the rhythmic motion soothes your nerves.'

As Grozen stared at her sagely, Merry couldn't help smiling, for hadn't she said the very same thing to her grandmother after Ma Somers had died?

Over the next few days, Merry made a supreme effort to pull herself together. Despite her best intentions to help her grandmother, however, she only succeeded in annoying her.

'You're getting under my feet and on my nerves with all this fussing. I'm quite capable of preparing a simple meal,' the woman snapped as Merry picked up the carrots she was about to scrape. 'Why not go out for a walk or something?'

'I went to see Mother earlier,' Merry sighed, for there'd still been no sign and, despite her reserv-ations about Cador, she had secretly been hoping for one.

Slowly they picked up the threads of their old life. Mr Fairbright, whilst disappointed Merry wasn't returning to her old job, agreed she could go back to knitting her frocks with the shell pattern. She didn't feel up to joining the others in the shelter of the pig house. Their giggling and gossiping seemed infantile and frivolous now. Instead she spent her time sitting beside the fire with her grandmother. Occasionally the woman would mention her mother but mostly they would knit in companionable silence, lost in their own thoughts and memories. When pictures of a handsome man in naval uniform invaded her mind, she pushed them firmly away.

One day, she was on her way back from visiting the cliff top when Nicco fell into step beside her.

'How are you, Merry?' he asked, his dark eyes serious for once.

'All right, I guess. How about you?' she asked politely.

'Missing you,' he muttered. 'We begin salting the pilchards up at the pallace tomorrow. Your grandmother says you're not returning to Plymouth so will you come and join us?'

Her heart sank, but knowing they needed to make up for the weeks after her mother had gone when they'd not earned anything, she nodded.

His eyes lit up. 'We could go for a drive in the trap at the weekend, if you like?' When she remained silent he continued. 'A trip out of the village would do you good, Merry,' he cajoled in the voice he used when wanting his own way.

'I'm not ready for that, Nicco, but I will see you at the pallace tomorrow evening.'

'It's good to have you back in the village, Merry. I would have visited more often but Father said you needed time to grieve.' Swallowing down the lump in her throat, she nodded. 'Well, the boats are in, I see, so I'll see you tomorrow.'

Merry watched him go, then stared around the bustling harbour as if noticing it for the first time. Some men were busy unloading their catch, others sat on the wall overhauling their nets. The weigh machine was being prepared and children ran happily around. She looked up at the imposing house on the hill and shook her head. Everything was the same and yet her life had changed so much. She remembered the times she'd stood here dreaming of her future, planning how she'd escape from the village and make her way in the world. For a while she'd succeeded, yet here she was back again. As painful memories surfaced, the blanket of fog descended, engulfing her once again in its cold, dismal mantle.

Grozen was pleased when Merry told her she'd be returning to the fish factory. She felt strangely nervous as she made her way there but was joined by Ailla and Marya. Their friendly chatter helped her relax and, as if by tacit consent, no mentioned was made of Karenza.

'We're going to be busy tonight for they are saying this is the largest haul they've ever had,' Ailla said.

'They'd better be careful how many they net or one day there'll be no pilchards left in the sea,' Marya joked. Then her expression changed. 'We've missed you, Merry. How are you?'

'Surviving,' she said, trying to keep her voice light. 'Everyone's been very kind. Oh, look, we're here already.'

The other women were already inside and

spirits were high at the thought of the money to be earned. They greeted Merry warmly, then set about the salting process. She had forgotten how hard it was building up the bank to the required depth and before long her back was aching from the unaccustomed stooping. Nicco made a point of smiling every time he passed and even if she hadn't seen the nudges the other women were giving each other, it would have been hard not to hear their teasing comments.

'Do you think they'll be walking out again soon?' Tressa asked.

'Not if I have anything to do with it,' Wyllow muttered. 'She can't just strut back in here as if nothing's changed.'

'Don't know why you're worrying; Nicco made a point of ignoring your little invitations,' Kelys pointed out. 'Quite right too. It's unseemly the way you've been throwing yourself at him.'

'Things have changed since your day, old woman,' Wyllow pouted.

Merry shook her head. Nothing had changed around here – apart from her mother being gone, of course.

By the end of the evening her hands were red and sore, and she grimaced, remembering how Prunella had lent her the wonderful cream that had made them smooth again. With a pang she realized just how much she missed her life at the store and the new friends she'd made. Still, she'd promised she wouldn't leave Grozen and now she'd just have to adjust to her life here. Perhaps she could make her own salve, she mused.

'Walk you home?' Nicco asked, appearing by

385

her side. Without waiting for an answer he fell into step beside her.

'You did well tonight. It's almost as if you've never been away, but then this is your home.'

The memory of linking arms with her mother as they returned to the cottage popped into her mind and Merry swallowed down a lump in her throat.

'Yes, and I must go and make sure Grozen is all right,' she said, quickening her pace.

'I've really missed you, Merry,' he began. 'Whilst I'm sorry about ... well, you know, it's good to have you back. Now that you've got that travelling thing out of the way, I want you to know my offer of marriage still stands. I'm sure that you will see what a good opportunity I'm offering you.'

Merry frowned. He really was as pompous as ever.

'Nicco...' she began but, as ever, he ignored her.

'I understand that Lieutenant Meredith's disappeared back to sea. Good riddance, too, for they say a sailor has a girl to comfort him in every port and that must be hard on his betrothed, don't you think?' He turned to Merry and quirked his brow but she turned away. Carey had told her about his father's dalliances and the thought he could be like that too hurt her more than she could ever have imagined.

'See you tomorrow,' she muttered, throwing open the door to the cottage and hurrying inside.

'Was that young Nicco?' Grozen asked, looking up from her knitting. Merry nodded. 'It wouldn't have hurt to invite him in for a hot drink.'

'Sorry, Grozen, but I'm worn out. I'll see you in the morning,' she replied, bending and kissing the woman's cheek.

'You do look pale. I hope you haven't overdone it?'

Merry shook her head and, wanting to be alone with her thoughts, ran up the stairs.

Lying in the darkness, she heard Nicco's words going round and round in her mind. Carey's adoptive father had hurt her mother so much her life had been blighted. Surely his son, even an adopted one, could have the same traits. Then there was Nicco's preposterous assumption she'd be grateful he still wanted to marry her. Why should she even want to tie herself to any man? She'd stay single and be in charge of her own destiny, she resolved. But a picture of Carey and his gentle smile sprang unbidden into her mind and no matter how much she tried to ignore it, refused to go away.

Chapter 39

Spring turned to early summer and apart from the addition of her daily pilgrimage, life settled back into its familiar routine. Where once she'd found it boring, now Merry welcomed the repetitive pattern that kept her too busy to think. Her greatest challenge was trying to avoid Nicco. He'd seen her crying one day when she returned from the cliff top and offered his shoulder to cry on. Now, it seemed he had taken it upon himself to wait at the bottom of the path each morning and escort her back to the cottage. Although on the surface he seemed considerate and caring, Merry couldn't help feeling he had an ulterior motive and was biding his time.

One morning, she was leaving the cottage at first light, when he fell into step beside her.

'Morning, Merry.'

'Nicco, what are you doing here this early?' she asked, staring at him in surprise.

'It's going to be a beautiful day so I thought I'd walk up to the cliff with you.'

'Shouldn't you be down on the quay?'

He shrugged. 'I want to speak to you whilst no one's around.'

She stared at him, her heart sinking when she saw the determined look in his eyes.

'Look, Merry, it's been a while since Karenza died and I think I've been patient enough.' At the sound of her mother's name she felt the familiar stab in her chest. 'I feel it is high time we got married.'

'But...' she began.

'Think of the fun you'll have setting up our home. You'll have a good life here in the village,' he continued regardless.

She shook her head. 'I don't think...' she began.

'It has always been my intention to marry you and it's what your mother wanted,' he reminded her.

Knowing it was true, she sighed. 'So much has changed since then,' she replied.

'Like what?' he demanded.

'I've changed, Nicco. As I've already told you, I

have no intention of marrying anyone ever.'

'That's rubbish and you know it. All women want a ring on their finger, the respectability of marriage...'

'I need to go to Mother,' she said quickly. 'I'll see you up at the pallace this evening.' She turned towards the path.

'You might not. Father's given me the task of dealing with the shipping out of the barrels, so I shall have to spend more time supervising things down on the quay,' he said, puffing out his chest importantly. Her heart lifted. Praise be to Mr Neaple. 'Of course, I'll insist he pays me more for the responsibility,' he added, looking at her meaningfully. 'In fact, I'll go and see him now. Tell him I need the money to set up a home for us.'

Merry groaned in exasperation. Feeling like a fish in a net that was closing around her neck, she hurried up the path. How mean he was mentioning her mother like that. It was tantamount to blackmail. Yet as she climbed higher, she couldn't help wondering if he was right, after all. Her mother had wanted her to marry him. A shudder ran through her at the thought. She'd bide her time and keep out of his way until she'd thought everything through. With any luck, he'd be occupied overseeing the barrels onto the boats when she went to work that evening and she wouldn't have to see him.

Reaching the spot where her mother had gone over the edge, she threw herself down on the rough grass. If only you could tell me what to do, Mother, she thought, idly plucking at the wild campion and thrift. Staring down at the pink and white flowers in her hands, she couldn't help recalling how her mother had loved their bright colours. Deftly she fashioned them into a little posy then tossed it down to the beach below. It spiralled its way down the cliff side and she watched as it landed on the spot her mother had.

'Oh, Mother, will life ever get better?' she cried, but as ever it was the gulls that screeched in reply.

How she wished she could stay here away from everyone and everything. Then reason returned and, knowing she had a busy morning ahead, she turned and hurried back down the path. Both she and Grozen had knit frocks to complete before Mr Fairbright made his regular visit to the village. Although the pattern came naturally to her, her heart wasn't in it and she knew she needed to make more effort. Grozen kept urging her to join in with the knitting ladies again, saying the company would do her good. So far she'd managed to resist.

Hearing voices coming from inside the cottage, she paused on the doorstep. Then she heard a familiar chuckle that set her pulses racing. Surely that was Carey? Then the door was thrown open and there he was, resplendent in his uniform, standing before her.

'Merryn, it's lovely to see you again. How are you?' he asked. As he stared at her in the way that made her feel she was the only woman in the world, her heart gave another jolt. Hardly daring to believe he was here, she beamed in delight, and as he grinned back, her heart leaped. Then in a snap, memories of their last meeting came flooding back and like the early morning mist, her euphoria evaporated.

'I'm well, thank you, but extremely busy,' she added briskly, indicating her pins and wool on the table. He frowned at the abrupt change in her manner.

'Mr Fairbright told me you've returned to your knitting. As soon as my ship docked I went to the store but, of course, you weren't there.'

'Nor will I ever be. My place is here with Grozen. She needs looking after.'

'Piffle,' the woman scoffed. 'And where are your manners, Merryn Dyer? The good lieutenant's come all this way to see you, yet you leave him standing in the middle of the room. The least you can do is offer him a seat and refreshment.'

'I don't wish to impose, Mrs Dyer,' Carey said.

'Friends never do. Now sit yourself down, young man. You'll have to excuse me, though, for I was just off out when you called.'

Merry stared at her grandmother in surprise. 'You never said you were going anywhere.' But she was talking to fresh air for Grozen had already shut the door firmly behind her. For a long moment Merry and Carey stood facing each other awkwardly across the room.

'I won't stay long, Merryn. I just need to satisfy myself you are all right,' he said, looking at her enquiringly.

She shrugged, for a lump had risen in her throat and she couldn't speak.

'I have spent the time at sea thinking of you, dreaming of you, even. Dare I hope you might have given me a passing thought?' When she shook her head, he sighed. 'I was hoping time might have healed the gap between us.'

'Time the big healer?' She gave a hollow laugh. 'Well, it hasn't eased the pain of Mother's death and the fact still remains she wouldn't have died if we hadn't met.'

He flinched at her words. 'Believe you me, I have done nothing but blame myself. If I'd persisted in telling her I was adopted...'

'But you didn't,' she replied. 'And if I'd not insisted on going to work in Plymouth in the first place then none of this would have happened.'

'Mr Fairbright said you have a promising future and has promised to keep your job open for you for when you are ready to return,' he said, staring at her hopefully.

'He already knows I have decided to stay with Grozen and he has permitted me to return to my knitting. Grozen needs the money I bring in to help pay the rent, and now the pilchards are here I'm salting up at the pallace as well.'

'There isn't any need for that now, Merryn,' he said, fishing in the pocket of his jacket and drawing out a silk kerchief. Carefully unfolding it, he drew out her mother's necklace and held it up. She flinched as the memories of her mother wearing it came flooding back. 'As I suspected, this is one of the Old Meredith sapphires and worth a considerable amount,' he said, holding it out to her.

'And you think money will make up for Mother's death? Or is it some sop to salve your conscience for your father's deception?' she asked, keeping her hands firmly by her sides.

'No, of course it's not,' he cried. 'It was given to your mother by Father and now by rights it's yours,' he said, holding it before her.

'He ruined my mother's life,' she whispered, making no move to take it.

'Yes, I know, and others besides. That is why you must believe me when I say I would never do anything to hurt you, Merryn. Now please...' he coaxed moving closer.

She shook her head and took a step backwards.

'You obviously need more time to come to terms with things but I am a patient man.' He paused, a glimmer of amusement in his eyes. When she didn't respond, it vanished in an instant. 'Oh, Merryn, you are the most important person in my life and it is my dearest wish that one day you will become my wife. I shall go now but I beg you, please think over what I've said.' He paused again and she forced herself to nod but still couldn't say anything. He sighed.

'In the meantime, please take what is rightfully yours,' he begged, once again holding out the necklace. Merry stared at the blue stone twinkling in the shaft of sunlight that filtered through the window.

'Mother would never have accepted that if she'd known it was valuable.'

'Perhaps that was his way of showing he cared,' Carey murmured, taking a step towards her, then sighing as she backed away.

'Look, had my father married your mother...'

'But he didn't. He didn't even have the decency to tell Mother he was married,' she snapped, glaring at him. A heavy silence descended until finally he shook his head.

'I will keep it for now,' he said, tucking it

carefully into his kerchief and placing it back in his pocket. 'I have made arrangements to stay here in Porthsallos and will return when you are calmer. In the meantime, Merryn dearest, please take the greatest care of yourself.' He paused, hoping for an answer, but she turned away.

Holding herself rigid, she stared into the fire until she heard the door click behind him. Then, with a sob, she ran upstairs, threw herself down on the bed and cried until she had no tears left. She didn't hear the bedroom door open and was only aware of her grandmother sitting beside her when she patted her shoulder.

'Come along, Merry, your mother wouldn't want you to take on so. I saw Carey on my way home. He looked that unhappy I had to ask what was wrong. He told me about your mother's necklace. Who'd have thought it, eh?'

'I'll not take it,' she whispered.

Grozen let out a sigh. 'What about his desire to marry you? He's a good man and...'

'You've changed your tune,' she muttered. 'You and Mother spent months badgering me to marry Nicco.'

'We did, and happen we were wrong. Of course, you hadn't met young Carey then and when true love strikes...'

'Love,' she spat. 'A fat lot of good it did Mother.'

'I agree. Regrettably she gave her heart to the wrong man. Once she found out he was married, it was like a lump of ice encased her. She was unable to move on, frozen in time. If it wasn't for you, Merry ... well...' The woman sighed. 'Your mother would want you to be happy, you must

394

remember that.' Her grandmother crept from the room and Merry gave herself up to the comforting blanket of fog that numbed her emotions, preventing her from feeling or thinking.

Having fallen into an exhausted sleep, it was late when Merry dragged herself downstairs the next morning. Her grandmother had left her a plate of sandwiches on the table with a note propped up against the milk jug, saying she'd taken their knit frocks to Mr Fairbright for payment. Guilt swept over her. How could she have left the older woman to make the trek to the dealer's office at the top of the village? Sighing, she made herself a pot of tea and vowed to get a grip on her emotions. She'd thought she was getting herself together, but seeing Carey again had brought the events of the past weeks flooding back.

She was half-heartedly nibbling at the bread when there was a knock on the door. Thinking it was Carey, she ducked down in her chair. She really wasn't up to seeing him again.

Chapter 40

'Merry, are you there? Please open the door.'

Hearing her friend, Merry felt her heart lifting and she flew across the room.

'Saphira?' she whispered, staring at the elegant woman in surprise. 'What are you doing here?'

'I came to see you, you dolt. Well, can I come in?'

'Yes, of course,' she said, standing back as the stylish young woman swept into the room. Merry couldn't help noticing how well Saphira was looking with her fine clothes and new hairstyle, and she knew she must look washed out by comparison. The woman's cheeks were flushed as well. Then aware she was staring, she asked, 'Did you enjoy your vacation?'

'Yes, thank you, but I didn't come to talk about that. I'm here to offer my condolences on the sad loss of your mother. I would have come before but Carey said you needed time,' Saphira said, taking Merry's hands in hers. 'You must be devastated. I know I was when we lost our mother last year.' Seeing the genuine empathy in her eyes, Merry felt the bond between them strengthen and, for the first time since her mother's death, felt less alone.

'Thank you,' she whispered, then stood there not knowing what else to say.

'I'm parched, is there any tea left in that pot?' Saphira asked, settling herself on a chair by the table.

'Oh, yes, sorry,' Merry said, hurrying to fetch her mother's best cup and saucer from the dresser. 'What are you doing here in Porthsallos?' she asked, finding her tongue at last.

'I'm staying here with Carey. Oh, Merry, he is so unhappy. I thought you and he were ... that is, I had high hopes you and he would ... well, I've always wanted a sister, especially one who can make a decent cup of tea,' she added, grinning impishly.

'Since Mother...' Merry couldn't continue.

'Carey told me about the accident,' Saphira

said. 'It is tragic, I agree, and heaven knows you must miss her, but you mustn't blame yourself.'

'How can I not, when I don't know what happened?'

'Even if you were to find out, it wouldn't change anything, would it?' Saphira echoed Cador's words, staring at Merry with her bright blue eyes.

'I guess not,' Merry sighed.

'Look, Merry, I'll be frank. I hate seeing Carey so unhappy and fail to see why your mother dying should prevent you from getting betrothed. Or is it, as Alexandria insisted on telling us, that you don't really love my big brother?'

'Alexandria?'

Saphira shook her head. 'Don't worry about it. She still refuses to believe Carey should prefer your charms to hers. Anyway, that's irrelevant now. Do you or do you not love my brother?'

'Yes, I do,' Merry admitted, realizing with a start that it was true.

'Well, what is it then? Come on, pretend we are sisters. They share confidences, don't they?' she asked, giving Merry such a wide smile, she couldn't help returning it. As she did, she felt something stir inside her.

'Everything's muddled in my mind. Carey goes away to sea and Nicco says sailors have a girl in every port willing to offer them comfort.'

Saphira arched an immaculate brow. 'And this Nicco is a paragon of virtue, I suppose?'

'He looks at other women, but he wouldn't cheat on me,' Merry declared.

'And that's good enough for you? As you know, my father had an eye for the ladies and he certainly didn't think twice about deceiving them, as you are now only too well aware. He cheated on my mother from the beginning and hurt her terribly, but Carey is different, Merry. He saw what Father did to Mother and hated him for it. His conscience would never permit him to deceive you. Besides, he is too sensitive to intentionally hurt anyone.'

'But Nicco said...'

'Ah, the wonderful Nicco again,' Saphira cut in. 'I understand he also wants to marry you?' She jumped to her feet and went over to the window.

Merry frowned. 'Well, yes, and my mother thought he would be a good catch. That was before I met Carey, of course, but... What are you looking at?' Merry asked as Saphira stood on tiptoe and pressed her nose against the glass.

'You'll see. Come on,' she instructed, pulling Merry to her feet.

'But I need to change,' she protested, grimacing down at her frayed old skirt.

'There's no time for that,' Saphira murmured, hurrying her out of the cottage.

'Where are we going?'

'Down to the quay, oh, do hurry,' Saphira urged, quickening her step. Blinking as the bright sunshine hit her eyes, Merry followed after her.

As ever, the harbour was bustling with activity, but Saphira let nobody get in their way as she pushed her way through the groups of fishermen waiting to have their catches weighed. Many turned to look at them, exclaiming in surprise, but whether it was because of their haste or similar looks, Merry couldn't tell. Then Saphira stopped abruptly, smiled up at Merry and linked arms with her.

'Isn't it a glorious day, Merry?' she said in a loud voice. 'Oh, hello again, Nicco,' she added, drawing to a halt in front of the open-mouthed Nicco. He stood gaping from Merry to Saphira, then went bright red and scuttled away.

'Oh,' Merry said, staring after him. 'I guess he must have been surprised to see us.'

'Indeed he was,' Saphira said, narrowing her eyes.

'Hold on a minute. How did you know his name or even what he looked like?' she asked. Saphira frowned around the busy quay, then linked her arm through Merry's once more and drew her away from the crowds.

'Right, let's sit here,' Saphira said, finally stopping by the point.

'So what was all that about?' Merry asked as soon as they'd settled themselves on the wall.

'I met your Nicco earlier today when I was taking a stroll. At first he thought I was you, then he realized his mistake and...' She looked down at the ground.

'And?' Merry prompted.

'Well, there's no easy way to tell you this,' Saphira said, looking at Merry with her clear blue eyes. 'He turned on the charm. Honestly, the compliments dripped from his tongue like butter off a hot spoon. He offered to take me for a ride in his pony and trap, saying we could make a day of it. Apparently, he knows some charming little place where we could get to know each other over supper. Honestly, Merry, that man made me go hot for all the wrong reasons,' she said, wrinkling her nose.

Incredulous, Merry could only stare in disbelief. Then she remembered Saphira's flushed appearance when she'd arrived at the cottage. That Nicco could have behaved in such a despicable way only hours after declaring his undying love and proposing marriage was inconceivable. Yet hadn't she had doubts about his loyalty?

'He only ever took me out in his donkey cart,' she muttered, then laughed at her banal statement.

Saphira patted her hand. 'It's not Carey's integrity you should be questioning, is it?'

As her friend echoed her own thoughts, Merry stared unseeing over the water. Saphira was right and she needed to go to see Carey.

'Where are you staying?' she asked as the shock receded.

'Over there,' Saphira said, pointing to the granite house on the hill. 'Carey's rented it for the summer whilst Lady Sutherland is away on honeymoon, though, of course, she's no longer Lady Sutherland...' she began, but Merry didn't let her finish.

'I must go to see him right away,' she cried, jumping to her feet.

Saphira stared at her for a long moment. 'I'm afraid he's left,' she said eventually.

'Left?' Merry gasped.

'He said he couldn't stay without...' Saphira stuttered to a halt.

'Without?' Merry prompted.

'You, I guess.' Saphira looked at her sadly.

Merry swallowed down the lump in her throat. Why hadn't she listened to what he had to say? He must have taken her words literally, then changed his mind about staying in the village.

'I think you should go home, Merry,' Saphira said, breaking into her thoughts. 'You've had a frightful shock and are quite ashen.' She stood up and smoothed her skirts. 'I don't like to leave you like this but I'm expected back for high tea. Look, why don't you come and visit when you have recovered? I can tell you about my vacation, show you my sketches.'

Merry nodded, then watched Saphira walk elegantly away.

Sighing she stared at the granite house. To think Carey had been staying there. But now he had gone. *Too late, too late,* the gulls seemed to cry as they circled overhead. Unable to sit still any longer, she jumped to her feet and hurried up the cliff path.

As she climbed, her shock turned to anger. How dare Nicco try to sweet-talk Saphira, she fumed. Thank goodness her friend had told her. And how many other women had he tried to win over? To think he'd told her only recently how much he loved her. She stopped in her tracks. Had he ever actually uttered those words? She racked her brains but could only remember him telling her he wanted to marry her, intended to marry her. He'd said he wanted her as his wife but she couldn't remember him ever saying he loved her. It had always been about what Nicco wanted. While Carey had gone out of his way to make her feel cherished, wanted and loved. It had taken her all this time to realize it. What a fool she had been.

By the time Merry reached the place where her mother had fallen, she had worked herself up into a right state. Throwing herself down on the grass near the cliff edge she stared out to sea.

'If only you knew what Nicco was really like, Mother,' she cried. As ever, only the roar of the waves and screech of the gulls replied. 'I think I love Carey. No, I *know* I love him,' she whispered, for the fog that had engulfed her since her mother's death was lifting and she could see things clearly at last. 'I don't know if you can hear me, Mother, but I want you to know it is all right for us to marry because he was adopted. That was what he was trying to tell you,' she added. 'Except it's too late, for he's gone away. Oh, Mother, how I wish you were still here.'

Feeling totally spent, she continued sitting on the warm ground and idly watched as a beautiful sapphire-blue damselfly hovered above the pink campion in front of her. Then it landed and spread out its translucent lacy wings to dry.

'It's my own fault. I didn't listen to him,' Merry sighed. The damselfly fluttered its wings and settled on her arm as if consoling her, trying to look deep into her soul with its large twinkling eyes. Then it took to the air, soaring and dipping, then soaring again. It looked so carefree.

Something stirred in the recesses of her mind. What had that funny little man Cador said? Jenna wanted her to remember the word freedom, yes, that was it. And that was because ... she groaned in frustration as the elusive memory hovered on the brink. The damselfly fluttered close again, soaring and dipping, soaring and dipping. Cador had mentioned nymphs and damselflies, too, hadn't he? He'd explained, about nymphs below the water evolving and turning into damselflies then soaring free above. When you see a damselfly you will understand what I mean, he'd said. And suddenly she did. Her mother was no longer a sad prisoner of her past. She had been released from her earthly cares.

'Oh, Mother, if that is you, let me know you are really happy and free,' Merry pleaded. The damselfly fluttered its wings faster and as it flew in a circle right around her she was filled with a warm sense of contentment that spread through her entire body. She shook her head in wonderment. 'You really have evolved and moved on, just like Cador said,' she laughed, feeling truly alive for the first time since that tragic day. 'I thought he was mad, gabbling on about nymphs and damselflies. I'm so pleased to know you are happy, and Grozen will be when I tell her. Not that she'll believe you're a damselfly, of course.' She giggled, knowing her grandmother would say she should be locked up for having such absurd notions.

Of course, now she understood what everyone had been saying. Whether or not it had been a tragic accident didn't really make any difference. Nothing could change things. If only she'd listened when Carey had tried to tell her that, she might have saved herself a lot of anguish. A picture of her handsome lieutenant flashed vividly before her.

'Oh, Mother, if only I could be happy too. Now

I know Carey is the man I want to marry, do you think it would be too forward of me to go to Plymouth and tell him?'

The damselfly settled on her arm once more and she could see two eyes boring into her, just as Carey's had.

'I know you were intent on me settling down with Nicco, but now you know the truth about everything, please can you show me you agree I should marry Carey?' she cried, for suddenly it mattered she had her mother's approval. The damselfly soared and dipped, soared and dipped, then hovered above the cliff before disappearing over it.

Merry jumped to her feet and ran to the edge. Leaning over, she strained to see where it had gone and was just in time to see it land exactly on the spot her mother's body had. Suddenly, she heard a shout.

'Merryn! Wait. I'm coming, Merryn.' Turning she saw Carey hurrying up the path towards her and her heart flipped.

'Thank you, Mother,' she whispered, then ran towards him as fast as she could. His arms closed around her and, as she leaned against his trembling chest, her heart swelled with love for him.

'Oh, Merryn, I thought you were going to jump,' he murmured into her hair.

'And I thought you'd gone back to Plymouth,' she cried.

'I did, but only because I needed to collect this,' he said, reaching into his waistcoat pocket and drawing out his kerchief. Then to her surprise, he fell to one knee and stared up at her beseechingly. 'Dearest Merryn, please say you'll marry me.'

As she stared at the ring with its heart-shaped sapphire, she thought she'd burst with happiness.

'Yes, Carey, I will,' she cried.

Overhead a damselfly soared and dipped, then completely encircled them.

Chapter 41

Twelve Months Later

Merry stared out of the mullioned window as she waited impatiently for Carey's return. Down below, the boats were being overhauled as they were made ready for the next evening's fishing. Men sat mending their nets; the women were knitting and chatting, whilst the children ran around playing. Then she spotted dark-haired Nicco scuttling along the quay. How quickly he'd succumbed to the obvious charms and close attentions of Wyllow. After all the angst he'd caused Merry with his overbearing ways, it made her heart sing to see him dancing like a puppet to his new wife's bidding.

Smiling, she twisted the gold band around her finger. So much had happened in a comparatively short space of time. Of course, if it hadn't been for Saphira, she and Carey might never have married. Overjoyed when Carey told her the news of their betrothal, she'd taken Merry aside.

'Merry, my conscience is plaguing me and I really must confess to using a little subterfuge that day we sat at the point.'

'What do you mean?' she'd replied, although she already had her suspicions.

'When I told you Carey said he couldn't live without you, I might have put those words into his mouth, so to speak. I knew you were right for each other and guessed the only way to make you see that was to demonstrate what Nicco was really like. Then when you said you had to go to see Carey, I let you think he had returned home for good, although I knew all along he'd gone to collect that,' she said, pointing to the sapphire ring Merry was wearing. 'He inherited the ring when Mother died. Anyway, he said he wouldn't be able to live with himself if he hadn't at least asked you to marry him. Believe me, I only had your best interests at heart, so am I forgiven?'

As clear blue eyes stared into hers, Merry smiled. 'Only if you're sure you don't mind me having the Meredith ring?'

'Goodness me, no. When I marry I shall expect a brand-new one. How else will I be able to judge the man's worth? Besides, we both have our sapphire necklaces, don't we?'

'I can't believe Mother wore it all those years without realizing its value. Mind you, I was none the wiser until Carey explained. I have to confess I'm happier wearing this one, though,' Merry said, stroking the silver chain with its heart charm.

It had been ten months since she'd married Carey, at their Walking Wedding, so named because of the long walk to the nearest church. Mr Fairbright had given her away, taking his role as the bride's proxy father very seriously. Dressed

406

in white duck trousers, blue coat, a high hat and white gloves, as tradition decreed, he'd walked alone to the church, handing out a piece of cake as the kimbly gift to the first person he met on the way to ensure good fortune. Carey's uncle had acted as best man as well as providing their beautiful flowers, whilst Saphira, Freckles and Prunella had been bridesmaids. Prunella had been radiant, confiding that she and Nicholas were to be betrothed. Apparently, she'd satisfied her mother by agreeing to be called Prim-Smith after the ceremony.

As ever, Freckles had been full of mischief and when, on leaving the church, Merry had put up her parasol and been showered with rice, she'd convulsed into hysterics. Chester, meanwhile, had tied tin cans to the back of Carey's carriage. She shook her head, remembering the clattering that had followed them all the way from the village.

She'd shared her bridal spray of red roses between her mother and Jenna's graves, and had been ecstatic when not one but two damselflies had fluttered overhead. As expected, Grozen had pooh-poohed her notion that they were her mother and friend flying free, yet Merry had seen the woman's joyful smile as she watched them soaring and dipping their way overhead.

She stared around the bright airy room, with its comfortable furnishings, still marvelling that she should have ended up living in the home of her dreams. Carey had been surprised when she'd tentatively voiced her preference to reside here in the granite house perched high on the cliff over-looking the village.

'But wouldn't you rather live in Plymouth?' he'd asked. 'Perhaps return to your job until we are wed? It would be such a shame to waste your skills.'

She'd smiled. 'I'd be more comfortable here. Mr Fairbright has already asked if I would continue knitting my shell-patterned jumpers for him to sell from his outlet here. He even hinted that I might oversee this operation in the future. So you see, this would be the perfect place to raise a family, and I'd be able to keep an eye on Grozen too.'

'Well, your wish is my command, wonderful wife of mine,' he teased. 'As it happens, Lady Sutherland has agreed to my having a long-term tenancy on this place. I'll remove the housekeeper and cook from Plymouth to look after us. Why not ask Grozen if she'd like to come and live here? It's plenty big enough and will be much warmer for her too.'

'Oh, I don't think she'll want to leave her cottage. Still, I can ask.'

Now, clattering from the kitchen roused her from her reverie. She could hear Grozen explaining to the cook how stargazy pie should be made. To Merry's surprise, the older woman had jumped at the chance to move in with them.

'Why would I want to stay in that draughty old place when I can live in comfort here with splendid coal fires to warm my bones?' she'd muttered, conveniently forgetting her previous predilection for wood. 'Of course, I'll have to make sure the cook produces nourishing meals for you, especially now.'

Merry winced and ran her hand over her swollen stomach. 'Not long now, little one,' she sighed, easing herself into her chair and taking up her pins. Whilst the wool she was knitting with was much softer than that she used for her knit frocks, she had incorporated some of the traditional patterns into the cot cover. Sighing, she remembered the day she'd met Cador in the village. Having only just found she was expecting, she wasn't even showing but the wizened man had stared at her with those jade eyes and told her he could see a cot blanket would be needed before long.

'Pink will be the perfect colour, and the baby's name won't pose you any problem now, will it? Although, of course, if she developes a passion for rock pools, like her mother, she might also be known as the Sea Shell Girl,' he'd grinned.

Smiling at the memory, Merry cast off the final stitch, then smoothed out the blanket on the table before her. The seeds and bars provided the perfect border for the shells she'd worked into each corner, but it was the damselfly in the middle she was really proud of. It had taken a lot of work but at last it was ready for when Karenza Jenna decided to make her appearance. And as if she knew, her baby gave another kick.

Then the door opened and her heart flipped as Carey, resplendent in his uniform, stood there grinning. Her love was home from the sea, and just in time, it would seem.

Acknowledgements

With grateful thanks to the wonderful team at Penguin. Teresa Chris for her continued support. My friends at BWC for their encouragement. The staff at Polperro Harbour Heritage Museum for answering my numerous questions and showing me their splendid Guernsey sweaters, known as knit frocks.

This Large Print Book for the partially sighted, who cannot read normal print, is published under the auspices of

THE ULVERSCROFT FOUNDATION